365
SHORT-SHORT
STORIES

Robert V Kesling (signature)

BY

ROBERT KESLING

HATS
OFF™

Published by Hats Off Books™
610 East Delano Street, Suite 104
Tucson, Arizona 85705

ISBN: 1-58736-2215-5
LCCN: 2003093527

A story is not a story until someone reads it. Only then is it imbued with life. Until such time, it remains inert, inanimate, a jumble of symbols composed of ink impressed onto a thin processed wafer of some unrecorded dead tree.

ACKNOWLEDGMENTS

My everlasting thanks to Amelia, my wife of over sixty years, who offered many helpful suggestions, and who patiently put up with the piles of typescript cluttering my study. Appreciation also goes to my three children and eight grandchildren, who became astute critics. I add my gratitude to the late Cathleen Jordan, editor of *Alfred Hitchcock's Mystery Magazine*, whose advice stressed accuracy and clarity in writing.

TABLE OF CONTENTS

iv

vi

INTRODUCTION

My adventure with short stories began years ago with my grandchildren. Whenever the family gathered, the little ones crowded onto my lap. "Papa," they begged (I have always been "Papa" to them), "please tell us a story." No indulgent grandfather could refuse. So, I'd spin a yarn that I'd more or less prepared.

As they grew older, I typed up a batch of new stories for them to read on each of their visits. They were my first short story critics, quick to point out any discrepancies in the plots.

Later, my attempts to write short-short stories for *Alfred Hitchcock Mystery Magazine* became an obsession. Condensing plot, setting, and character development into a 250-word limit became the ultimate challenge. Every word needed to be significant, each verb adding to the action, each adjective precisely describing the characters or coloring the plot. Some genius may be able to type out a perfect short-short story offhand, but I need revision after revision.

There are rewards. For the reader: the whole story can be grasped in minutes; no need to wait for the denouement in the final chapter. And for the author: a degree of satisfaction.

Now that my years have exceeded four score and five, the time seems appropriate to put some of my favorites in print, so that some day my great-grandchildren may have an inkling of what "Papa" was like. The story does reveal the writer.

These selections from my short-short stories will, I trust, bring you laughs, shivers, and perhaps a few pauses for reflection.

Happy reading!

Robert Kesling

BRIDGIT

We had traveled far, the hour was late, and the sturdy little donkey was tired. The old man stopped the cart atop a hill and pointed to grayish thatched cottages below, ghost-like in the dusk.

"Yon lies Comleagh, t' village ye seek."

"Are you certain?" I asked, showing him the faded photograph of my late grandmother dancing with villagers on the green.

"Aye, that were Comleagh," he said wistfully. "But deserted it's bin these forty year."

"Sir," I ventured, "was Bridgit Shaunnesy really a witch?"

He hesitated. "Some thought so. It begun when beautiful Bridgit went walkin' o' nights wit' young men, one after t'other—meself included. 'Twere perfectly 'armless. But t' village priest, Father Fogarty, went to Bridgit. ''Tis sinful,' 'e says. 'Ye must marry at once!' Bridgit laughed, 'I keep meself pure.'

"Father Fogarty thundered in Church: 'BRIDGIT IS BEWITCHED!' 'Er own father disowned 'er." He. paused.

"And then?" I prompted.

"One night a heart-piercin' shriek roused us from bed. 'Twas full moon and on this selfsame spot stood Bridgit. 'Er long gown—thin as cobweb—and 'er red hair streamed behind in t' wind. Raisin' 'er arms, she cried out, 'I be innocent! God's curse upon Comleagh, and may t' priest become a *real* jackass!'

"A cloud passed o'er t' moon and she were gone. Nor was Father Fogarty seen agin. Dire troubles come to Comleagh. Within t' year, all families moved away."

He stopped speaking. From somewhere below came the disconsolate braying of a jackass.

GHOSTS AND THE HEARTBROKEN CHEF

Late one night during my annual vacation at Edelweiss Inn, I sat with my old friend Heinrich Baum, the owner, reminiscing before the still-glowing fireplace. I mentioned the Ghost of the Heartbroken Chef.

"As I recall," I said, "it was quite melodramatic. You gathered your guests on the upper balcony on nights of full moon and recited the eerie tale: how long ago the daughter of this inn's owner fell in love with the young chef at Inglehof Hotel across the mountains. They met here secretly until her father discovered them together and forbid her to see her lover ever again. In despair, she committed suicide, as did the young chef when he learned of it. But every night of full moon thereafter, his ghost skied back to hers.

"When we were totally enthralled, a figure in a chef's white apron and hat did ski over the mountain and disappear somewhere below us! We gasped, dumfounded. How did you stage it?"

Reluctantly Heinrich admitted, "I hired Fritz Hochenspiel from Inglehof. He'd ski over and disappear by hiding in the kitchen below."

"It was thrilling!" I declared. "Why did you stop it?"

"One evening—February 15th, 1978—Fritz gave his finest performance. As I went downstairs to pay him, the phone rang. It was Fritz's wife Helga. He'd died *that afternoon!*"

Heinrich added uneasily, "Tonight Helga phoned again, saying Fritz was on his way."

"Why would she do that?" I asked.

"God knows...old Helga herself died *yesterday.*"

THE PRICE OF HONESTY

"Yes, Inspector Farragut," I testified, "I was Sir Humphrey Matthew Sykes's chauffeur. Last Tuesday I drove him from the mansion to Chelmsford railway station. He was going to his London law office as usual, and I left him on the platform... How was he dressed? Quite properly, bowler hat, umbrella, briefcase, morning attire—No, sir, I've not seen him since."

The disappearance of England's most famous barrister caused quite a sensation. Known as the "Dauntless Defender of the Destitute," he never charged his impoverished clients. His sole income, I knew, came from his wife Heloise, heiress of the Blankenship fortune. Sir Humphrey was scrupulously honest.

Just yesterday I chanced upon him. He was shabbily dressed, selling pennywhistles on a London street corner. "My lord!" I gasped.

"Steady, Chumley," he responded. "I'm making a fresh start after Heloise ejected me from her mansion."

"Whatever for?" I inquired.

"I won the case of the impecunious renters against Dinglehurst Corporation—exorbitant rentals charged for cramped, unsafe, squalid tenements."

"But, sir, you were honest, surely cause for celebration."

He winced. "Honest? Yes, but unwise. I'd forgot that Heloise owns Dinglehurst Corporation."

"I sincerely wish you well," I declared sympathetically.

His championing of the underdog led to Sir Humphrey Matthew Sykes's downfall. Basically it was his *honesty* in all things. His honesty would always be his handicap.

As I walked sadly away, I heard him intoning: "Cheap pennywhistles, anyone? Poorly tuned . . . manufactured under sweatshop conditions . . . known to contain mercury . . . Pennywhistles, anyone?"

CHRISTMAS EVE AT GALEN SANATARIUM

The woman's voice on the phone declared, "Doctor Gertruda Schlambach calling from Galen Sanitarium. A patient is missing."

I relayed the message to my deputy, Sam Osborne, who grunted, "Another nut loose—on Christmas Eve yet!"

We sped out to the sanitarium. The gateman waved us through and we hurried inside. The psychiatrist offered us seats, saying, "Most unfortunate, gentlemen. We were progressing marvelously with Eileen Klinger, but the human psyche runs deep, often unfathomable—"

"Please," I interrupted, "just her description."

"Here is her dossier, complete with photograph."

I glanced at the photo and passed it to Sam, who gasped, "Good lord! This is *you*, doc!"

At that moment another white-jacketed lady rushed in, shouting, "Come along quietly, Klinger!"

As orderlies led the pseudo-psychiatrist away, her replacement stated, "I am Doctor Gertruda Schlambach. Unfortunately, Ms. Klinger sometimes imagines she is I and I am she. It won't happen again."

"You sure?" asked Sam dubiously.

"Absolutely!" The woman drew herself up indignantly. "We aliens from the planet Krypton are infallible!" Giggling wildly, she dashed outside across the floodlighted grounds. We located her clinging to the exercise maze and screaming, "Quick, dammit, beam me up, X-32!"

"Sam," I sighed, "it looks like a lo-o-ong night."

Toward morning we discovered the *real* Dr. Gertruda Schlambach, bound and gagged in the shrubbery. At least we *think* she's the real one. Anyhow, Sam and I went home to celebrate Christmas with an old friend—Jack Daniels. We had no doubts about *him*.

ANTICIPATING YOUR VISIT

Dear George and Emmaline—

Naturally we were surprised to receive your unexpected letter saying you will be free to visit us with your five darling children, your Uncle Amos, and your Newfoundland dog. Anne and I haven't been well this spring, and your visit will cheer up our little two-bedroom cottage.

All the flowers hereabout were killed by the blight, which also destroyed grass on local golf courses. No need to bring your camera or golf clubs.

Authorities have tried to keep secret the horrible outbreak of bubonic plague here. They claim it's transmitted by fleas carried by the giant rats, which seem to be everywhere. Some rats also have rabies; their bites are frequently fatal. You folks should also avoid the poisonous spiders, very prevalent this season. Undertakers are offering family rates.

You asked about fishing, George. The only fish anyone has seen this year are dead ones littering the beach.

Neighborhood septic tanks overflowed during recent storms, so Anne is boiling extra drinking water in anticipation of your visit. Despite swarms of malarial mosquitoes, we'll have a wonderful time!

As always,
Ralph

P.S.: Please bring your sleeping bags. Mildew ruined all our extra mattresses.

P.P.S.: Perhaps I should warn you that Anne's Cousin Cedric now lives with us, spending his days sitting atop a tall ladder in the shrubbery, poised to attack strangers with his pitchfork. Otherwise, he's usually harmless and—with any luck—we'll convince him you're friendly before it's too late.

TRUE CHARACTER

Our Friday night group had gathered as usual in Duggan's Bar. The hour was getting late. Suddenly old Charley Baylor declared, "Christmas brings out a person's true character."

We groaned, for whenever Charley utters a philosophical statement, he invariably follows it with a protracted and ofttimes pointless example. This was no exception.

"Okay," grumbled Tom Withers, "get it over with."

"Well, if you insist," said Charley stiffly. "This happened years ago here in this town. Two poor, struggling young people—call 'em Jim and Kathy—fell in love. He owned a little garage, and she had a tiny beauty shop.

"One evening as they sat smooching in her parents' living room, Jim said, 'I think I'm getting rheumatism, crawling under all them cars. I wish I had a hoist—but it costs $5,000.'

"'My job's bad, too,' Kathy complained. 'Smelling shampoo and hair spray all day gives me headaches. I wish I had air-conditioning—but that also costs $5,000.'

"Christmas was approaching. Jim sold his garage for $5,000 and bought the finest air-conditioner for Kathy. Then—"

"We know," interrupted Tom. 'It's that old O. Henry story, *Gift of the Magi*. She sold her beauty parlor and ordered him a hoist."

"She did not!" snapped Charley. "That Christmas showed her true character. Kathy figured anybody who sold his only means of livelihood without planning for the future was a poor marriage risk. She married someone else—after Jim installed the air-conditioning in her beauty shop."

HIGH-RISE VICTIM OF LOVE

Theodosius Wilhelm Vanderschotten, widely acclaimed for his high-rise buildings, met a tragic end. He was, I believe, the only trillionaire to die from love without experiencing it. This requires explanation and, as his personal valet, I can attest to the gruesome details.

Theodosius began life as an ambitious but penniless architect. In desperation he married Henrietta, heiress of the Astorfeller fortune. She was unbelievably unattractive—porcine features and hulking figure. Theodosius, however, didn't mind. He ecstatically began planning countless high-rises.

Henrietta was, unfortunately, addicted to the color purple: purple walls, purple rugs, purple furnishings—purple everything. The crisis arose when she painted his billiard table purple.

Naturally enraged, Theodosius roared, "I'm leaving!"

There ensued acrimonious exchanges involving marital inadequacies (which I forbear repeating). Then he turned to me, "Come, Eversham, we'll take refuge in my latest high-rise being built!"

His construction crew obediently hoisted us up to the fifty-ninth level. Around noon, using his cellular phone, Theodosius ordered a sumptuous repast delivered there. Money accomplishes wonders. Waiters bearing food were soon borne upward. We started dining on an I-beam. Our meal was interrupted by approach of a small purple plane. It was Henrietta, towing a long banner reading: PLEASE COME HOME TEDDY DARLING PURPLE BILLIARD TABLE REPLACED I LOVE YOU VERY MUCH!

"She really loves me!" exclaimed Theodosius, leaping upright. Those, alas, were his final words. Whiplash of the extremely long banner caught him. Theodosius Wilhelm Vanderschotten was, quite literally, catapulted to his doom by unfulfilled love of his wife.

"PERSON OR PERSONS UNKNOWN"

At the depot awaiting the five-oh-eight
Stands Sir Edmund Thigby, unyielding as stone.
He's been to court on behalf of young Kate,
Whose husband met death at recent date
By hand of "Person or Persons Unknown."

Sir Edmund's well known by his bowler hat,
Umbrella furled, and briefcase much-used.
Even crusty Judge Ingalls admitted out flat
Sir Edmund's the finest barrister that
Ever defended young widows accused.

By his wits he exonerated, all told:
Miriam, Helene, Florette, and now Kate,
Despite the Crown's contention bold
And the presence of four bodies cold,
Each having met unnatural fate.

In each of the boudoirs were fingerprints
Which police determined were *not* the wife's own.
They added them to their evidence,
But after searching thither and thence
Never found "Person or Persons Unknown."

Oh, they apprehended the usual suspects,
But none of their prints the murderer's matched.
The Superintendent is highly vexed
Having no clue as to where to turn next
For the killer who neatly four husbands dispatched

Sir Edmund has not lost a case to date;
In legal circles his fame has grown.
As for Miriam, Helene, Florette, and now Kate,
Each prefers Sir Edmund to her recent mate.
You see—*HE* was that "Person or Persons Unknown"!

THE TALKING OSTRICH

Life at isolated Wadi-el-Bateeh oasis became extremely dull. Young Kareem longed to see the sights and experience the sinful delights of city life he had heard about from passing cameleers. He devised a plan.

"Father," he said one night, "from a passing caravan master himself I learned of a special school in Cairo that teaches small birds to speak. Imagine how miraculous if they teach Ozzi-jee-Ahn, my pet ostrich, to talk. Passing caravans would pay handsomely to hear him. We would become rich!"

Kareem was very persuasive. At last his father agreed and gave him all the family savings. Leading Ozzi-jee-Ahn by a rope, Kareem happily joined the next caravan heading for Cairo.

From the cafes of the big city, Kareem sent back glowing reports. "Ozzi-jee-Ahn now says 'Good morning' very plainly." "Ozzi-jee-Ahn has learned evening prayers." "Ozzi-jee-Ahn can recite the Koran!"

Finally the impatient father ordered Kareem to return with the marvelous talking ostrich. He could not refuse. But one problem remained: he had sold Ozzi-jee-Ahn in the Cairo marketplace.

When Kareem came back alone, his father demanded, "Where is our talking ostrich?"

"It is a long story, father. During our return, Ozzi-jee-Ahn said to me, 'I can hardly wait to tell what your father did that night your mother was asleep and the caravan transporting beautiful slave girls encamped at the oasis. Ooooh!'

"Well, hearing such terrible lies, father, I buried Ozzi-jee-Ahn to his neck in desert sand as punishment."

"Leave him there, my son!"

11

IN MY ABSENCE

It had been a long and tiring business trip, but at last I was home. I paid the taxi driver and turned to see Jared Abernathy, my taciturn old gardener, his pruning shears in hand.

"Afraid it's bad news, sir," he announced. "Yon rose bush got crushed."

"How?" I inquired, curious.

"Yore wife backed the car over it. She was in a terrible hurry. Happened 'round sundown Thursday."

"Emergency?"

"Depends how you look at it, sir. She was runnin' off with Ed Brooks, the bachelor next door."

"Surely not!" I was shocked.

"Yep," the old man declared positively.

"Well, the police can get my car back."

"'Fraid not. She was so excited-like, she run over the mayor's wife."

"Kill her?"

"Nope. Put 'er on crutches. Mayor got the license number as yore missus sped off. Says he'll file all kindsa charges."

This was dreadful. "Did they locate my car?" I asked.

"Yep. She was drivin' so fast it turned over out at Stonyface Mountain. Complete wreck."

"Quick, man! Was she killed?"

"Not quite, sir. She's in Mercy Hospital. Doctors say she'll need *very* expensive operations."

"What about Brooks?" I asked, fearing the worst.

"Not hurt bad. No insurance, though. He tole police yore wife was drivin' so it's yore responsibility. He's got hisself a lawyer."

"Good lord, Jared!" I exclaimed. "Haven't you *any* good news?"

"Wel-l-ll," he drawled and pointed, "I jest might save yore rose bush. A leetle careful prunin' here and there, y'know...."

12

THE HUMANITARIAN

Winter is the real disadvantage of living in the country. I was only ten miles from home when my car skidded on the icy road, landing in a deep ditch. Freezing drizzle was still falling, making footing treacherous. I'd never make it back until the weather improved or some good Samaritan came along to offer a lift. The latter seemed highly unlikely.

A floodlight glowed faintly from the Boy Scouts' summer camp nearby. The winter caretaker, Amos Pilcher, was reputedly the meanest man in the county. I hesitated to ask shelter there, but had little choice. I approached gingerly, easing across the ice-glazed outdoor basketball court, and knocked.

A strange raucous cacophony arose inside. Finally Amos opened the door. "Whatcha want?" he asked gruffly.

I explained my situation.

He relented somewhat. "Reckon you kin come inside and git warmed." I glanced around the room in astonishment. Wild animals everywhere! Rabbits scooted underfoot; pheasants roosted on chair backs. "I rescued these poor devils from the storm," Amos explained. "Sorry I couldn' save all the wild critters hereabouts."

My opinion of him changed immediately. "That was a very humanitarian act!" I declared.

"Aw, 'twarn't nothin'," he scoffed. "Wanta stay fer supper?"

"Why, that's very generous, Mr. Pilcher," I said. "I'd really appreciate it."

"Have somethin' fixed in a jiffy," he said cheerfully, adding wood to the cast-iron stove. "What suits yer fancy, friend—fried rabbit or stewed pheasant?"

STRAIGHT FROM HELL

On Monday, the Assistant Editor of *Macabre Magazine* said, "Chief, this one's well written."

The Editor glanced at the transmittal letter:

Dear Sir:

The enclosed manuscript, entitled Hell—I Like It, *submitted for publication.*

Sincerely yours,

Roger Rampart,

General Delivery, Devil's Hole, Wyoming

Quickly scanning the manuscript, the Editor declared, "Just another 'I'm-here-in-hell' story. Send our usual rejection."

On Wednesday, the Assistant Editor reported, "Chief, that Rampart fellow sent two more manuscripts: *Hell is What You Make It* and *It's Hell Here Without You.*"

"Persistent devil," snorted the Editor. "'Reject—make it plain!'"

On Friday, the Assistant Editor called attention to four more submissions from Roger Rampart: *Pleasures of Hades, Lucifer's Cozy Hideaway, Exciting Excursions Through Hell,* and *Hell Can Be Beautiful.*

"Dammit," swore the Editor, "can't that jerk understand we don't want his confounded stories? Write him to go to hell! I'll sign it."

The following Friday, the Assistant Editor, trembling, laid the following letter on his chief's desk:

Editor, Macabre Magazine:

Your recent communication advising me where to go was quite superfluous. Did you not wonder why my manuscripts were typed on asbestos paper? As P.R. man for Lucifer, I have offered you ample opportunity to give us favorable publicity. Upon reading your letter, His Satanic Majesty declared vehemently, "We have places for editors, but for this one—who will join us soon—I have special plans!"

Looking forward to your visit,

Roger Rampart

P.S.: Your appointment is 05:47 next Tuesday.

THE *REAL* ROSITA

As her manager, I oughta know. Rosita was billed as Queen of Burlesque, not only because of her beautiful face and full figure: her act was perfect. As saxophones wailed "Sweet man, I love him so..." she would slowly, tantalizingly, strip off one garment after another. Flickering her long lashes, she'd toss a garter to her slavering fans. When she whisked off the rhinestone G-string, lights would go out and the audience erupt.

One night, the King of Monastein attended her performance. That same night he proposed. Thus, the *real* Rosita emerged as Queen of Monastein.

To everyone's astonishment, Rosita became a most honored and beloved monarch. She introduced reforms, raised standards of living, and turned Monastein into a model country. Nobody went hungry, medical attention was free, taxes were low. Queen Rosita was showered with medals for her diplomacy. Her subjects adored her. She was truly miraculous.

Then came her golden wedding anniversary. Rosita hadn't forgotten me. I packed my tux and, invitation in hand, headed for Monastein.

All crowned heads and nobles of Europe gathered in the royal palace. Champagne flowed freely. The evening was warm. From the street below, the music of an organ grinder floated upward through the opened window: "Sweet man, I love him so. . . ."

Queen Rosita stood hypnotized. Slowly, tantalizingly, she unzipped her gown and shimmied it off. As the stunned court gasped, she flickered her eyelashes and coyly flipped a garter to the King of Braganza. Then things got worse . . . .

15

A SIMPLE BUSINESS TRANSACTION

Eavesdropping was completely out of character for old Peter Schiller. He had served City Bank & Trust for thirty-seven years, ever since it was founded by Frank J. Anson, its autocratic (some said heartless) president. However, when Schiller heard his own name mentioned, he stopped outside the door of Philip Anson. Recently, President Anson had installed his son Philip as vice president, the position to which Schiller had looked forward for years.

Young Philip Anson was conversing with Nancy Davis, officially the executive secretary but rumored among the other employees to be more than a business associate of Philip—*much* more.

"You have to understand, darling," Philip was saying, "it's our whole future. I hate to think what Father would do if he discovered I owe Angelo Marino 50,000 dollars—or what Marino would do if I don't pay."

"But Peter is such a nice old gentleman," she objected.

"So what if Schiller spends a few years in prison? He hasn't much life left anyhow. I took the cash from his investment accounts and hid it in safety deposit box 371 . . . . Don't worry, Nancy, we're safe."

Schiller withdrew silently. Obtaining the key to 371, he slipped into the vault. After all, the money *was* his responsibility. He retrieved it.

Later that morning, he looked up from his desk to recognize Angelo Marino, the loan shark. The man's scowl fitted his reputation. Smiling, elderly Peter Schiller rapped on the office door before announcing, "Mr. Marino to see the vice president."

16

GIFT OF THE MAGICIAN

Late December of the Year 1002 was particularly bitter throughout the realm of King Kargon the Cruel. As the Magician rode toward the castle, the moon illuminated cloudlets from his snorting steed and from the pack mules behind. It also shone upon a figure bound to a stake—a young maiden, naked in the frigid air.

Questioned, she explained, her teeth chattering, "The K-K-King hath bet I cannot s-s-survive the n-night."

He cut her bonds with a curiously curved knife, then wrapped her warmly in furs to await his return.

Crossing the drawbridge, he passed his flask among the guards, lingering until they fell senseless. Presenting himself at the banquet, the Magician amazed King and nobles alike with feats of legerdemain.

"And now, Magnificent One," he announced, "my finale!" Barrel after barrel he rolled into the great hall, removing the oaken tops.

"Wine?" questioned King Kargon eagerly.

"Nay, sire, a *far* more precious gift, one which can be presented only by an Angel. I take her this small one as gift for her services. Wait! She will magically appear!"

He removed the bung from the keg, which, as he carried it toward the gate, spilled strange black crystals. Mounting his steed and leading his pack mules across the unmanned drawbridge, he flung back his torch to the trail of gunpowder.

The explosion, first known in northern Europe, ended the kingdom of Kargon the Cruel.

Swinging the maiden behind him, the Magician rode steadily eastward through the frosty night, his mission accomplished.

BATHTUB FATALITY

Lecherous old playboy-millionaire Simon Toklar was drowned, his head leaning over the edge of his elegant Louis XIV tub and immersed in scented bathwater. Nobody mourned his demise. At least a dozen husbands in southern California were secretly elated.

Fortunately for Detective Barker, they could be ruled out; each was outside the high, electrified iron fence surrounding the estate. The only persons inside were his wife, lawyer, butler-cook, chauffeur, and maid.

"Did you kill him?" he quizzed each of the assembled suspects. Each denied it.

Archibald Pierce, the elderly lawyer, stated: "I was invited for the weekend. Mr. Toklar said he had legal problems, but didn't explain."

George, the chauffeur: "I was outside tuning up the Rolls."

Luigi, the butler-cook: "*Si*, as I prepare breakfast in my kitchen, I hear the motor revved up."

Fiona, the shapely, almond-eyed fourth wife, declared: "Why would I kill Simon? He gave me whatever I wanted."

The detective turned to Mirabelle, the plump, round-faced maid now into her thirties. "You reported the death. Exactly what happened?"

Her matter-of-fact voice replied, "As I bent over to test the water, I heard Toklar rushing up behind me. I sidestepped, he struck his head, he drowned."

"Didn't you attempt to revive him?"

Mirabelle shrugged. "Not my assigned duty."

"Why would he attack you from behind?"

"The alimony, I suspect. I figured I needn't serve as maid to collect it. Simon insisted."

"Then you were—"

"Yes, before I put on weight, I was the first Mrs. Toklar."

TWO TRAVELING SALESMEN

With completion of the Dubuque & Hannibal Railroad in 1902, we traveling salesmen expanded our territories. That's how Phil Jabbers (Ladies' Beautifying Cosmetics) and I (General Hardware) both fell in love with beautiful Sandralee Hopkins, the belle of Mayburg.

She played us fairly, dating him one visit, me the next. Then Phil and I talked it over.

"This competition is gettin' us nowhere, Fred," he declared. "It's just makin' us enemies."

To that I readily agreed.

"So," he continued, "I'm lookin' elsewhere. But I'll tell you this as a friend: like you, Sandralee loves mysteries. Just whisper, *'I've got a new way of murder for you,'* then tell her the plot. She will melt."

I could hardly wait. As she came down Main Street that evening, I drew her aside and whispered the magic words.

Sandralee screamed, hoisted her skirts, and ran as fast as her shapely legs could churn.

On my next call at Mayburg, I learned that Sandralee had become Mrs. Phil Jabbers. They had moved west to Nebraska. I asked the local hardware dealer, "What went wrong between her and me?"

He looked at me strangely. "I reckon it was your bein' in prison for murderin' your first four wives."

"I've never been married!" I practically shouted.

"That's all right," he tried to calm me. "Phil told everyone in town all about it. We understand."

So did I—*then.*

Now I enjoy particularly gruesome murder mysteries, always imagining that the victim is that lying, double-dealing Phil Jabbers!

THE TRAVELER

The southbound local chugged out of the Paris terminal. Ten minutes later, the pale, handsome young man with whom I shared the compartment was fast asleep. He mumbled something which, because of the clicking of the rails, I couldn't quite discern. A very pleasant dream, I decided, inasmuch as he unconsciously smiled from time to time.

At some little station, the train stopped with a jolt and the young man awoke. He must have noticed my unpardonable stare, for with a lop-sided grin he inquired, "I was talking in my sleep again?"

I nodded, then offered a weak excuse for my impertinence.

He accepted it in good humor and we began a friendly conversation. He introduced himself as Jacques Cambray. He had been a traveling salesman—quite successful he claimed, without seeming to brag. Now he was headed for an interview in Bordeau. Somehow we led into the subject of crime.

"In Paris alone," he declared, "tens of thousands flaunt one law daily."

"To which do you refer?" I asked.

"The law concerning relations outside wedlock... And yet, in obeying the matrimonial law, one may break another."

"Surely not!" I challenged.

"I should know. It led to my imprisonment."

I was shocked. This well-mannered young man a common criminal?

He laughed at my astonishment. "My unbreakable habit of sleeptalking led to my conviction. My wife Isabelle testified that I described vividly intimacies with Jeanine, Maria, Arabella, and Nanette.

"'Twas true. My crime had been in *marrying* all of them."

THE TRAVELER'S CHOICE

By chance I found myself once again sharing a train compartment with Jacques Cambray, the personable young man who had served a prison term for bigamy. To resume conversation, I said, "I trust, M'sieur Cambray, your life is returning to normal?"

"Yes, indeed," he assured me, "although prison was not wholly unpleasant. My jailer, Eduard Foucheau, was extremely kind. Every night, anxious to escape the acid tongue of his wife Margit, he brought wine and cigars and we played chess. Now I'm employed and married again."

"Which wife did you choose?" I inquired.

"All my former wives were special. Isabelle was a *cordon bleu* cook—ah, such delicious dinners. Jeanine was the most beautiful—unforgettable face and perfect figure. Maria was the most intellectual—we often discussed literature together. Arabella was the ideal housekeeper—everything spotlessly clean and in its place. And Nanette—ah, Nanette! She had talents every lover dreams about; every night with her was memorable."

"So, tell me please, which did you re-marry?"

"Oh, none of them, actually. By agreement with my former jailer, M'sieur Foucheau, he divorced his shrewish wife Margit and I married her."

I was astounded. "But *why?*" I blurted.

"He was such a kind and deserving man, so considerate of my every need. It was the very least I could do for him."

"Perhaps," I told him, "you were over-generous."

Jacques Cambray laughed and winked. "My present employment involves travel between cities where live Isabelle, Jeanine, Maria, Arabella, and Nanette."

SCARY MESSAGE

Thelma Graham was determined to succeed in Chicago. She had landed her secretarial job with surprising ease. But now, strange happenings were frightening her. She almost wished she were back on her father's farm in Minnesota.

The message was first scrawled across one wall of her room when she returned late from work: *Hello Dear.* Later that night, a masked man pushed up her window. Thelma screamed, and the intruder scurried down the fire escape. The police asked questions; they went away.

Next morning in the basement garage, the same crude lettering had been sprayed on her windshield. While she was wiping it off, a masked man grabbed her from behind. Yelling, she dug an elbow into his midsection. As he backed off, she jumped into her car and burned rubber out onto the street.

Thomas Edwards, her handsome young boss at Allied Shipping, was sympathetic. "Why not move in with me for a few days?" he suggested. Thelma blushed and declined.

Her car wouldn't start one morning. Thelma started walking to work through a run-down district. Then she saw it, spray-painted on an abandoned warehouse: *Hello Dear.* Same words, same lettering, same twice-circled "o". It had not been there yesterday, of that she was certain.

Thelma Graham paled under her makeup, and a chill crept up her spine. But she was prepared.

Suddenly the man, masked, stepped out from between buildings. Without hesitation, Thelma felled him with a baseball bat.

The mask slipped aside.

"Why, Mr. Edwards!" she gasped.

HONESTY

In front of the Spokane police headquarters, a white-whiskered gent wearing ragged clothes approached a television crew. "Is this the place," he asked timidly, "where a person turns in lost money?" In his hand he held a sheaf of bills held together by a unique silver clip initialed Y.J.Q.

Reporters followed him inside. There the elderly man identified himself as Oliver Franklin, unemployed, living at the city's homeless shelter. The captain counted, "Exactly $143. If unclaimed within thirty days, the money's yours."

Television played up the human-interest angle: "Honest man turns in needed money." The widespread publicity resulted in numerous offers of employment.

Oliver Franklin reported to the suburban mansion of wealthy manufacturer Lewis Merkel, who suitably outfitted him. Oliver proved to be the ideal butler/servant/handyman. He quickly learned his duties.

Within the month, Mrs. Merkel was allowing Oliver to arrange details of her lavish dinner parties. To her guests, she confided, "Honest servants like our Oliver are rare indeed!"

While the Merkels were away, Oliver discovered his employer's "second set" of business records and copies of his tax returns. He photographed them.

On his afternoon off, Oliver Franklin visited the local Internal Revenue office, presenting his findings.

"Yes," agreed the agent, "your employer still owes $575,000 in taxes. You are due ten percent for reporting him."

"I know, sir."

In front of the Fresno police headquarters, a white-whiskered gent wearing ragged clothes approached a television crew. "Is this the place," he inquired timidly, "where a person turns in lost money?"

23

THE GREAT TOILET TRAUMA

The head of the F.B.I. addressed his top agents, "It's a national emergency!"

Agent Sally Fawcett interrupted, "Chief, you mean the Great Toilet Trauma?"

"I do. I'll speak quickly because I'm also affected. As you all well know, all across America people have the urge. Supermarkets have sold out all toilet paper. Restaurants, bars, hotels, and airports have long waiting lines at the johns—even the men's. Leading doctors are mystified; this outbreak is more than simple diarrhea. That can be medically cured, but the urge persists."

"Maybe the Iraqis have started germ warfare," someone suggested.

"Food & Drug Administration experts have tested all sorts of foods and pronounce them safe," responded the chief. "Oops! Gotta go!"

"Strange," said Sally to her partner Dan Travers. "Surveys show only remote rural areas remain unaffected. The rest of us suffer this constant urge. It's unreal—like everybody's been hypnotized."

"Hypnotized?" repeated Dan thoughtfully. "Perhaps that's the answer!"

"A conspiracy of hypnotists?" she scoffed. "There aren't enough to afflict the whole *nation.*"

"Millions are afflicted by what? *Television!*"

"Oh, come, Dan," Sally objected. "It's not that bad."

"See you later!" He dashed for the men's room.

"Right!" She rushed to the ladies' room.

"Chief," reported Dan excitedly, "I've solved it! It was done by subliminal suggestion. Some bright P.R. man for a toilet tissue company inserted suggestive frames in their television spot commercials. Here are some examples—"

"Please," declared the chief, raising his hand, "I'd rather *not* see them."

WAITING FOR KAPPADOULIS

The fat man in the blue stocking cap glanced nervously at his launch, which was beached in the little cove nearby. He turned to his companion, a lanky blond with a snake tattooed on his left arm. "Slick, are you sure this is the place?"

"It's gotta be, Bull. He told me specifically, 'By the abandoned village with the old ruins.'"

A cloud drifted across the face of the moon, and a chill breeze swept down from the mountains.

"Not like old Kappadoulis to be late," remarked the man called Bull.

"He'll show," predicted Slick. "All that talk by the parents about cleaning the island of drugs—that won't scare old Kappy."

"He's a pusher's pusher, that old man," acknowledged Bull. "Hard to figure how an island this small can have so many users."

"Or where the young ones get the money," added Slick.

"Hope he comes soon," said the fat man, pacing anxiously. "I've got two hundred thousand drachmas worth of cocaine in my boat."

Neither man spoke. Minutes passed. The moon emerged once more.

The tall blond pointed, "Look, Bull! I didn't notice that old marble head before—that one on the wall."

"Looks *exactly* like old Kappadoulis."

"It sure does!"

Both laughed. They strolled over, and Bull picked up the head. "Awfully light," he announced, "and—hey!—the thing's wet!"

It was then the two men became aware of the dark pool beneath it, and the drip, drip of blood from the freshly severed neck.

FLAME OF THE KLONDIKE

The most courteous man in the Klondike,
To ladies quite genteel and mild,
Though men fear his name, is the man they call Flame,
Who would harm neither woman nor child.

The Moosehead saloon became quiet
As Flame strode up to the bar,
Where, with mud on their boots, stood five mean-eyed galoots,
And the meanest was Big Jacques Le Mar.

Then a pretty young gal came in begging.
Kat-ze-tu was her Indian name.
"Have pity," she cried, "for my father just died,
When these bad men drove us from our claim.

"The worst was their leader, who knifed him."
She pointed at Jacques, "'It was you!"
Big Jacques lunged with his sticker, but Flame was much quicker
And his derringer's aim was true.

As the rest of the gang stared at the body,
Flame spoke in a voice icy cold,
"If you boys do not mind, I'd regard it most kind,
If you give this young lady your gold."

"Come, madam," he said, bowing low,
"I will see you home safe on my sled.
"My huskies await, there's no time for debate!"
And into the darkness they fled.

What became of the two? No one knows.
But somewhere out there in the wild,
Where men fear his name, is the man they call Flame,
Who would harm neither woman nor child.

ACTING EXPERIENCE

Peter "Shark" Lamar controlled casting for spot commercials. Before my test was complete, he interrupted, "Jason Jaggers, you need acting experience."

Acting experience! At twenty-five, I had played summer theater for twelve years.

Next day I was back at his office under the name "Anglebert Hollingsworth." My stooped shoulders, gray wig, and the uncomfortable appliance inside my cheeks aged me fifty years.

I startled his secretary. Peering from beneath my bushy white eyebrows, I rapped sharply on her desk with my cane, gasping loudly, "IF MISTER LAMAR...DOESN'T WANT...A TWO-MILLION CONTRACT...HE COULD AT LEAST...SAY SO HIMSELF!"

Lamar erupted from his inner office, a money-hungry smile dripping from his jowls. Gently assisting my progress, he steered me inside to an upholstered chair. "Sorry to keep you waiting."

"Sir," I panted, "I represent a new conglomerate...very hush-hush. Need casting director for numerous products.... If interested...meet me tomorrow...ten sharp! My room, 213 Hilton." I struggled upright and abruptly left.

He came as expected. I introduced my wife as "Doctor Pheelum."

"Now, sir," I began, "if you'll kindly disrobe—"

"What?!" Lamar demanded angrily.

"My superiors *insist* on healthy casting directors.... Last one suffered illnesses...costly delays."

Greed overcame modesty. He obeyed.

"Face the video camera," ordered my wife. Straight-faced, she asked embarrassing questions while prodding, probing, pinching.

Next day I showed Lamar my results.

"You'd send copies to *Variety* and other publications?" he fumed. "That's blackmail!"

"No," I retorted, "just acting experience." Smiling, I pocketed my lucrative contract.

THE SLEEPWALKER

I hardly recognized Bill when I saw him on the street. He was walking with crutches, his arm in a sling and his head bandaged.

"Great heavens, Bill!" I exclaimed. "An accident?"

"Not exactly an accident," he said evasively.

"No?" I was confused. "Then what happened?"

"I was walking in my sleep."

"Oh, so you bumped into some furniture?"

"If you must know," Bill grumbled, "I fell downstairs."

"But your apartment is on the first floor," I objected. "How could you fall downstairs there?"

"I didn't," he replied. "I fell down two flights of stairs from the third floor."

"I see. You stumbled in your sleep."

"I didn't stumble. My wife Consuela hit me, then shoved me down the stairs."

"That doesn't sound like Consuela. I thought you two were an ideal couple," I told him. "Why would she hit you?"

"She woke up, found me gone, and started searching the apartment house. She spotted me coming out of the apartment of Viola Lefleur, the voluptuous young divorcee in apartment 3-B."

"How did you get there?"

"Sleepwalking. As Viola tried to explain to Consuela afterwards, I'd been visiting her a few hours every night for weeks."

"Let me get this straight, Bill," I said. "You got up without waking your wife, opened the door, climbed two flights of stairs, and spent hours with an attractive young women—all in your *sleep*? I find that hard to believe."

"So did Consuela."

THAT'S MY DADDY

When Big John Ottwell spoke, his employees listened. Ottwell was owner, manager, and editorial commentator of radio station KNBY. He looked up from his paperwork at Tom Alton, the youngest reporter on his staff.

"Alton, our listeners are fed up with news about the current wave of bank robberies. Get something fresh for tonight."

"What, sir?"

"Use your ingenuity!" snapped the big man irritably. "Street interview some kids. Get going."

Tom Alton thought the idea dumb, but Ottwell paid his salary. Shouldering his equipment, he left the station.

"This is Thomas Alton, your roving reporter. Today I am standing in front of the Toys-N-Joys store. Here comes a little fellow who looks happy with his purchase."

Actually, it had been the shapely short-skirted mama who attracted his attention. Microphone in hand, Alton squatted down. "What is your name, little man?"

"Freddie."

"Freddie Jenkins," supplied the smiling mother.

"That's a nice name. How old are you?"

"Three."

"What did you buy, Freddie?"

Hesitantly, "Superman."

"Superman! I'll bet he's strong, isn't he?"

"Not as strong as my daddy."

In a low-voiced commentary, Alton said, "In these times of stress and violence, folks, isn't it heart-warming to encounter the love, the honest adoration of a little boy for his father?"

To the youngster: "Now, Freddie, why do you think your daddy is stronger then Superman?" He thrust the microphone forward expectantly.

"'Cause yesterday he knocked over the Savings & Loan buildin'—alone. Today he's holdin' up the National Bank, *all by himself!*"

LOCAL COLOR

Residents of Buck Creek never suspected that their own Rose Shaffer was actually Doralynne Lemoine, popular author of romantic novels set in the hypothetical town of "Deer River." Local persons, however, could hardly fail to recognize that "Deer River" was *precisely* like Buck Creek, and every steamy episode in Lemoine's novels had its *exact* counterpart in their small town.

Miss Edwina Culpepper, the local librarian, first noticed the amazing coincidences. She read the entire series. "You know," she confided to everyone she met, "Rose Shaffer is the only person in town who makes frequent trips to New York. Obviously, she's the one providing Miss Lemoine with information about everybody, shamelessly blabbing about our indiscretions, exposing them to the world!"

A sober little delegation called upon Rose one night. Old Johnathan Fulton, the banker, spoke first, "Exceptional coincidence that in *Banker's Choice* the leading character has an affair with his head teller."

Rose stammered, "Th-th-that's fiction."

"Well," added Widow Turner, "how about the motel manager's wife stabbing her husband when she finds him bedded down with the chambermaid?"

"B-but you were acquitted at the trial," protested Rose.

"Furthermore," declared Tom Killins, owner of Buck Creek Hardware, "the whole plot in *Backwoods Love* involves the daughter of the hardware dealer getting an illegal abortion."

Relentlessly the delegation closed in upon Rose . . . .

Buck Creek residents are absolutely convinced that Doralynne Lemoine got the unsavory background for her "fictional" characters from Rose Shaffer. After all, when Rose disappeared, didn't Lemoine's series abruptly cease publication?

THE ADOPTED SON

Jack Allstair was such a naive young man he needed an older woman to give him some down-to-earth advice, to mother him when he needed it most. I sort of filled that role. When my husband Albert died, he left me the corporation. I'd rather he'd left me children, but that's how it was.

Jack had graduated with degrees in English and history—not outstanding assets in the business world. But he possessed a certain charm (yes, I admit it, even at my age) and he had drive. I hired him in on the ground floor, nursing him along to a higher position. Now Jack was upset. His foster parents were both killed in an airplane disaster and he was determined to find his natural parents. He'd had no success. I called him into my office.

"Jack," I told him, "even with the new freedom-of-information laws, it's hopeless. A young unwed mother is frightened, desperate, and ashamed. Immediately after giving birth, she'd report a fictitious name for the father. Later she'd change her own name. If you really need a mother," I said flippantly, "I'll adopt you."

That restored his pleasant grin. "Thanks for the advice, Mrs. Bancroft. I guess I was dreaming the impossible dream."

I was tempted right then to tell him it wasn't impossible, that I had been that scared teen-age mother who'd given him up for adoption.

I didn't, though. Who knows what his reaction would have been? He might have rejected me. That's frightening.

THE PLANTING OF ELVIRA

From upstairs came her shrill voice, "Christo-PHER, I see weeds in the dahlias! What were you doing all morning? Come up here! Let me smell your breath."

"Damned cantank'rous woman," he muttered to himself. Prob'ly Elvira had bin young and luscious oncet, but danged if'n he could remember them days. Now she was jest a harpin' old shrew who made his life miser'ble. Elvira and her flower beds! 'Twasn't as if she did any of the spadin' and hoein' in the hot sun. No. She only give orders, Christopher do this, Christopher do thet. He'd put up with it 'bout long enough.

"I'm a-comin'," he growled. Dragging his spade, he climbed the stairs.

No neighbors lived close enough to hear what transpired that Friday afternoon.

As usual, Christopher cooked his own supper. As he munched on bread, ham, and beans, he thought: "Anybody ast me, I'll tell'm Elvira went to Washington to a meetin' of the Flower Sassiety." Washington sounded far away.

He leaned back and decided on the large petunia bed. When darkness settled, Christopher spread the canvas on the lawn and meticulously troweled out each plant. Three feet should be deep enough.

He shoveled soil atop Elvira and carefully replanted each petunia. Christopher slept soundly. Next morning he stared out the bedroom window. The wilted plants precisely covered a two-by-six foot plot.

Elvira hadn't been around to warn him, "Christopher, *always* water petunias after re-setting."

The pounding on the front door was Officer Clanahan, also an avid gardener.

JUNGLE TALE

For an old man living in the Amazon jungle, Pedro Mandillo was nobody's fool. He was hiding out after his last scam in Rio backfired. He needed one big score to escape the country. When he spied the young couple camping nearby, Pedro began craftily planning.

He'd previously located an isolated mesa, a high, sheer-sided island of rock accessible only by a bridge of vines constructed long ago by natives. Lure the woman there, destroy the bridge, and demand ransom from the husband for revealing her whereabouts—nobody hurt, and he, Pedro, would be away free! With money!

Maria and Franco Tomasi had reasons of their own for camping so far from civilization. With bank guards only minutes behind, they had stolen the motorboat and sped upriver. Mosquitoes were certainly preferable to Rio jails.

Coquettish Maria quickly made friends with the ragged, mudsmeared old man who unexpectedly appeared in the clearing. He might be useful. When he promised to show her where Indian treasure was concealed, Maria was ecstatic.

Warily, the two inched across the swaying bridge. "Where?" she asked eagerly.

Pedro pointed. "There!"

When Maria rushed forward, Pedro slashed the vines and watched the bridge fall. Running back to camp, he twisted his ankle. The pain was intense! Pedro cried desperately, "Help!"

The camp was deserted.

Franco Tomasi was far upstream, taking loot and all supplies. The motor sputtered—quit—out of gas. Franco shuddered as crocodiles began circling . . . relentless. . . waiting . . . .

Somewhere a jaguar screamed, breaking the jungle stillness.

RECLAMATION

Armand Schantz called his business Reclamation, Inc., although all that he reclaimed was the metal from old cars. Armand had a flair for efficiency and high-volume operation. The scrap cars, driven or towed into position, were picked up by a giant electromagnet running along an overhead track to the furnace. There the metal was melted down, while the rubber, cushions, and other combustibles went up the tall stacks in smoke.

It was the stifling, irritating black smoke to which area residents objected. They wrote letters—some pleading, some threatening. Now they had enlisted Roger Turnbull in their cause. He was the crusading TV filmmaker from station KWFH.

Schantz hired the best lawyers and established contacts in Washington. He was not worried about any expose on television. That was trivial, as long as his affair with Jeanette Turnbull remained a secret from her husband.

The owner of Reclamation planned carefully. He invited Roger Turnbull to witness the operations on Saturday, when employees were away. He also positioned the "Visitor Parking" sign directly under the huge electromagnet. Turnbull himself would become part of the objectionable smoke. Quite fitting!

From inside the warehouse, Schantz heard the car pull up and park. Immediately he threw the switch, starting the machinery, then ran outside to enjoy the spectacle.

Instead he saw the familiar red Chevette, suspended, on its final trip, with Jeanette frantically clawing and screaming.

"My God!" Schantz groaned.

At that moment, Roget Turnbull drove up. Smiling, he alighted, his camera rolling.

34

DAYLILIES

Abner Scully (his present name) was an unusual individual. Not many men are both mass murderers and keen gardeners. From experience, he selected his brides meticulously: elderly, no relatives, a substantial home on the outskirts of a mid-size city, and, of course, money. He planned retirement after his present double-header: Sarah in Toledo and Mary in Dayton.

An advertisement in one of his numerous horticultural catalogues proved irresistible: *Revelation daylilies,* newly developed in Austria, deep magenta with white throats . . . . Abner planted beds of them at both his Toledo and Dayton "homes."

He told each wife he was gathering background for his great Midwestern novel. That explained his absences, and both Sarah and Mary accepted it.

Sarah was away, so he'd visit Mary. Light-hearted, he drove south to Dayton. Abner entered the front door as usual, then saw *Sarah* emerge from the kitchen.

"What?!" he gasped. That was his last word. Mary clobbered him from behind.

Having permanently established Abner beneath the bed of Revelation daylilies, the two old ladies sat down in the living room to tea.

"Odd," confided Sarah. "On my way back from visiting an old college roommate in Cincinnati, I just happened to notice your daylilies—*exactly* like those Abner planted for me. I wanted to ask, what fertilizer do you use?"

"I think," tittered Mary, "Abner himself will suffice."

The other Widow Scully rose to go. "Do come visit me in Toledo."

"And you come back, darling."

"This," laughed Sarah, "has been a real 'Revelation'!"

THE BUTLER'S STORY

Kindly step inside, inspector. My master, Lord Eversham, regrets, I am certain, that he is unable to welcome you personally.

Yes, sir, it was I who requested your presence, taking the liberty of using the mansion's telephone ... My name? George Wofford, his lordship's butler, as you doubtless gathered....

The matter? Certain irregularities seem to have arisen in the normal routine of the household which, in my humble opinion, definitely require your attention...

Their nature? Inasmuch as both my master and his lady are unable to respond, it falls my lot to explain. With your permission, I shall begin with...

But, inspector, I am "getting on with it," as you phrase it. I am presenting a synopsis of the situation, as his lordship would have wanted...

Where is Lord Eversham? Somewhere at the foot of the cliff forming the northern boundary of the estate, I should judge...

Accident? Oh, definitely not. He drove over the edge at considerable speed, thoughtfully taking the runabout rather than the limousine. He was at the wheel himself, the chauffer being unavailable...

Of sound mind? Naturally Lord Eversham was of sound mind! You have but to ask fellow members of his exclusive clubs...

When did it occur? Soon after the shots, sir...

You misunderstand, inspector. No one shot at the master. Quite the reverse, in fact. In point of time, it was only minutes after he discovered Lady Eversham and the chauffer in her boudoir—in intimate association, one might say—and shot both.

CASABLANCA REVISITED

As we patiently maintained surveillance on Camelback Street, I explained to Sergeant Malik: "It began years ago, back during the War. This city of Casablanca was a beehive of intrigue, spies everywhere. The Allies' intelligence centered around five of the best, code-named the Black Knight, Bishop, King, Rook, and Queen.

"The Bishop was Father Ledoux, the French priest, the King, Mayor Ben Hassan; and the Rook, Ali al Abdul Rabaq, the rich merchant who lived in the castle-fortress to the east."

My sergeant's eyes widened. "Ledoux, Hassan, and Rabaq! All murdered within the past week! But who were the Black Knight and the Queen?"

"The Queen was Fatima, the most beautiful young woman in all Casablanca. And the Black Knight was Baron Wulf, then a traitorous Nazi oberlieutenant. He now calls himself Hermann Braun—the man we've been shadowing."

"Here he comes now," whispered Malik. "Seems harmless."

As the old German lumbered up the cobblestone steps of Camelback Street, I almost felt sorry for him. Years of Nazi imprisonment and torture had taken their toll. Nevertheless, he was behind the murders of his former colleagues, undoubtedly suspecting betrayal.

At the crest of the street, he waved his forefinger in the air, signaling the letter Q to his hired assassin—just as he had previously signaled B, K, and R.

Regretfully I centered my rifle sights on the heart of the Black Knight.

Please understand my dilemma. Although he was my father, Fatima—the Queen—is my mother.

Evil international conspirators threw him into this deep pit, assuming he'd meet his end. But he—Alfie, world's greatest secret agent—outwits them. He builds a pyramid, boulders at the base, smaller rocks above. Soon he'll reach the top and freedom...

"Alfie!" It's the store manager. "I'll explain once more. Stack canned pineapple here, canned peaches over there. Never together. Keep your mind on track."

"Yes, sir."

Track...the train thunders down the track. From afar he sees the convertible stalled on the crossing, its lovely blonde driver frantic, helpless. He floors the gas pedal. His sleek sports car hurtles forward, accelerating, faster. The train's almost there! But he—Alfie, winner of the Indy 500—will yet save the beautiful maiden.

"Alfie!" the manager yells. "Stop racing shopping carts down the aisles and bumping into customers. Remember, the store is crowded today with ladies taking advantage of our Two-for-One sale. Now, stoop down here and rearrange those frozen foods on the bottom shelf. And don't let me spy you goofing off!"

"Yes, sir."

Spy...reliable informants report that Lilibelle Latour, his best spy, will be kidnapped by Sinister Forces. But he—Colonel Alfie of Counterintelligence—will spirit her safely away to his secret ice cave. Among hundreds of passing women, he spots her shapely legs and trademark white high-heeled open-toed shoes. He must act quickly!

"ALFIE!" The store manager is livid. "Release that lady immediately! And for God's sake, close that freezer door before everything thaws out!"

HAZARDS OF GENETIC WARFARE

After having his ID and Top Secret clearance checked a third time, Professor Stanley Majkowski was admitted to the CIA office of Andrew Carbeck. The latter got right to business. Handing a photograph and magnifying glass to Majkowski, he asked, "As the world's leading botanist, what's your opinion?"

The professor scanned the picture and pronounced, "Unquestionably *Amaranthus graecizans*, the common tumbleweed."

"Our conclusion exactly. Does it have natural enemies?"

"Well, there is a tiny beetle—*Chompopterus vulgaris*—which feeds upon its foliage and roots—"

"Everything fits! That tumbleweed *must be destroyed!*"

The professor grinned. "Then pull it out."

"Sir, that photo was taken thirty thousand feet above the Iraqi desert. Our photo interpreters calculate that tumbleweed is fifty meters tall, and the concentric furrows around it are tracks of heavy tank trucks delivering fertilizer and water. The enemy has genetically developed a giant strain. What if its seeds were introduced into our United States? Grasslands destroyed, airports shut down, cities choked with tumbling tumbleweeds! Chaos!"

Prof. Majkowski examined the photograph more closely. "Wait! There's a little desert jumping mouse in the shade of that tumbleweed. The plant must be normal size."

Carbeck snatched the picture. "Damn!" he groaned. "You're right. That stupid reconnaissance photographer forgot to remove the close-up lens. Disastrous!"

"How so?"

"Our scientists already genetically engineered colossal *Chompopterus* specimens, planning to drop their eggs over that Iraqi desert to eradicate the giant tumbleweed.... Professor, what the hell can I do with beetles *two meters long?*"

TWO CONFESSIONS

Gabriella Czerny and Josef Tarlov owned large estates, situated side by side, the richest on the Polish plains. As they approached middle age, neighbors speculated wildly upon the reasons why neither had married, for he was still handsome and she beautiful.

The two were devoted friends, however. One afternoon Josef again called upon Gabriella. Over tea he impulsively asked, "Why, my dear, have you remained single these years?"

"My true love never returned from the war," she confided. "Although sick with fever, I traveled to a village near the front, there to wed in the local chapel when he got leave. It was not to be. And you, sir?"

"I have been married these twenty years," he confessed.

Gabriella was shocked. "To whom?"

"Alas, I know not."

"How can that be?" she inquired.

"It is a strange story, one I have never revealed to anyone. During a ferocious battle, I became separated from my command. Wounded and weary, I stumbled into a chapel somewhere to ask my way.

"The priest rushed forward. 'No time to lose,' he urged. 'The bride is ill, overcome with anxiety. If you would save her, come forward now.'

"The white-clad bride awaited at the dimly lit altar. If I could alleviate her suffering, why not? Spontaneously I agreed. The priest hastily pronounced us man and wife. Then the bride revived and looked up. 'You are not Franz!' she exclaimed, and fainted.

"I quickly departed to locate my regiment. That's my story."

"My God," breathed Gabriella. "*It was you!*"

Sobbing, they fell into each other's arms.

40

THE JEB WARFEL CORRESPONDENCE

To Andrew Oakley, president, Shur-Gro Company, Pleasant Grove, Iowa

Dere Mr. Oakley,

As this pitchur plainly shows, that cottonwood tree I bought from you ain't doin so good.
Jeb Warfel
Buzzards Arroyo, Arizona

Dear Mr. Warfel:

Cottonwoods do not thrive in deserts. We suggest you transplant your tree near a stream.
Andrew Oakley, president, Shur-Gro Company

Dere Mr. Oakley,

My little spread ain't got no stream. But I jest hafta save this cottonwood! It's a memorial to the great Coswell Gotch.
Jeb Warfel

Dear Mr. Warfel:

Water those roots daily! Incidentally, who was Coswell Gotch?
Andrew Oakley

Dere Mr. Oakley,

I'm plumb dumfoundered you ain't heerd of Coswell Gotch. You folks in Pleasant Grove must not git around much. Coswell was my cousin, Mama's side of the family, and the best cattle rustler in the West. Wiped out seventeen herds before the posse strung him up from a cottonwood! I chopped down that tree to make sooveneers. Every rancher in Rattlesnake County bought one. But them sooveneers will likely git burnt for firewood durin a blizzard, and Coswell be forgot. So, when my cottonwood gits big enuff I'll nail a sign on it: "In Memory of famous COSWELL GOTCH, Rustled cattle for Years, Only got hung Once." It does seem a mite better today.
Jeb Warfel

41

HE WHO LAUGHS LAST

By the time old Barney Finch died, all he had left were 220 acres bordering on Mink Creek. His only surviving relatives were grandsons John, who farmed nearby, and Roy, who worked in the Oklahoma oil fields. The two first cousins conferred after the funeral.

"Don't wanta cheat ya," declared John. "I'll take jest them hundred acres alongside the creek—floods a lot in spring, y'know. Yew kin hev *all* the high ground."

"Sounds fair," agreed Roy. They shook hands.

As Roy came down to check-out of the hotel, he overheard John boasting to the desk clerk, "Yeah, I got the good fields—gave Cousin Roy thet rocky hill." They laughed.

Roy left town quietly.

Two weeks later, John went to inspect his prize acreage. A drill was chugging away on the stone-strewn hilltop. Curious, he went to investigate. It was his cousin.

"Hi!" he hailed him. "Drillin' a water well? Gonna build a home here?"

Roy looked up, surprised. "Careful!" he warned. "Don't slip into that pool of oil!"

"Oil?" queried John, then shouted "OIL!"

"Yeah. Worth millions. But I might sell for less—cash." Mortgaging everything he owned, John raised $500,000. "It's all I got," he declared.

"Wel-l-l...seems fair enough," stated Roy, pocketing the money. Next morning the hilltop was deserted.

Roy was driving merrily back to Oklahoma, now-empty crude oil drums bouncing in back of his pickup. Behind he towed the portable drilling rig he had rented.

Half a million! Seemed almost too easy.

A POISONOUS TRANSACTION

The long black Mercedes purred smoothly along the country road. In the rear seat, sandwiched between two dark-suited, darkbrowed unsmiling young men, Alfred Barker again whined, "You're kidnapping me! That's a federal offense."

The driver chuckled, "Kidnapping? No, Mister Barker, we go to inspect the lake front property you sold to our papa."

He slowed, braked, and pointed. "There it is. 'Fresh water from the spigot, wild birds to watch, a rippling lake at your doorstep,' that's what you tell him." His voice hardened, "Only guess what we find, Mister Barker? That spigot connects to a big bottle of spring water up the hill, them birds is all dead an' stuffed, an' the lake is polluted by your mill aroun' the bend. Poison killed alla fish."

The silence grew lead-heavy. Finally Alfred Barker spoke, his voice quavering, "Okay, so I conned old Vittorio Manzone. But you know the saying: 'Let the buyer beware.'"

"Drag him outta the car," ordered the driver, Marco Manzone.

"Please," begged Barker, "I'll give him his money back." Then he saw the Luger in Marco's hand. "Oh God," he moaned, "You're gonna shoot me."

"Shoot you?" Marco laughed derisively: "No! No, that would give our Manzone Family the bad name. Instead, my brothers an' me, we gonna watch you take a *b-e-e-e-g drinka water* from your 'oh-so-beautiful' lake!"

THAT OLD GANG OF MINE

Friday night. My old gang; gathered as usual in the back room of O'Dell's Bar. Little Bill was the first to speak. "There musta been some good in old Eddie."

Walt snickered, "You'd never get his ex-wife Sally to agree. He beat her up every weekend. When he started on their kid, she left for good."

"Eddie was a daredevil," declared Ikeyo. "He'd do things others of us wouldn't try. Remember when the high school principal expelled him? That night Eddie sneaked into his garage, slashed all his tires, and poured sugar in the gas tank. Ruined the motor. Principal couldn't afford a new car—had to walk to school."

"Have the police found out who shot Eddie?" asked Lou.

"Naw," answered Walt. "You ask me, they ain't lookin' too hard. Not after all the trouble Eddie caused 'em."

At that point, Little Bill went out front to fetch five more beers. As he returned he said, "That Eddie was a handsome sonofabitch. Always got his way with women. Recall when he bet he could make out with the beauty queen? Within a week he got both her and her kid sister pregnant."

"Yeah," said Pete, "he was always into some kinda devilment. Still, I sorta miss Eddie, always laughin', jokin' with us guys. He's probably lookin' down at us right now, cool as an icicle."

Pete's wrong. I ain't lookin' down and I ain't cool. Frankly, I'm peerin' *up*. And talk about *hot*—it's really hell down here....

A GLOWING INSULT EVERY NIGHT

Our town of Stoney Glen, Arkansas—population 305—got national publicity. It made every evening telecast for weeks, with *pictures*. The place still swarms with reporters.

I suspected something big was about to happen when Hal Kinkaid poured a trail of tar from an old coffee pot and Egbert Macartle followed along behind covering it up. A crowd gathered.

"What's that stuff, Egbert?" someone asked.

He glanced up, grinning. "Sand—with our special ingredient.... A BIG surprise for Mayor Fritsch!" The pair zigzagged down Main Street, extending their string of tar-and-whatever.

Now, it's no secret that Mayor Fritsch hates Hal and Egbert. They own Nite-Glo, the company employing half the town to make light switches and watch faces that shine in the dark. Their factory sits on the best property in the valley—property the mayor wants to expand his Fritsch Screw Manufacturing Plant. He repeatedly hassles Hal and Egbert by requesting the Environmental Protection Agency to check safety at Nite-Glo. So far, Nite-Glo has passed every inspection.

After streetlights were turned off that night, somebody deciphered the secret. The news quickly spread over the Internet. Mayor Fritsch is furious, threatening to sue for defamation of character. Ha! No jury hereabouts will ever convict Hal and Egbert.

Meanwhile, tabloids are having a field day. Airlines detour their regularly scheduled night flights to pass over Stoney Glen, giving all their passengers a laugh.

Below, spelled out in eerie greenish-yellow light, are the words:

MAYOR FRITSCH IS A HORSE'S BEHIND!

THE MIRACLE

Don Miguel José Garcia-Fernandez was a proud man. He was also short-tempered, so it was not surprising that he railed out at Camilla, his bride, soon after the honeymoon. It was a trivial matter, really, but she had fled to live with her cousin. Two years later he learned that she had given birth to a son.

A son that could—nay, *should* have been his! Anger gnawed at his heart. Whatever love he had once borne for Camilla vanished, replaced by hate.

Don Miguel José Garcia-Fernandez had a vengeful streak in his soul, doubtless inherited from his father, who reportedly killed seven men in duels.

Hence, when rumors reached him that Camilla was returning to the little local chapel, he armed himself, vowing to kill both her and her lover-cousin.

Sunday morning found him sitting in the rear of the chapel, his pistols cocked.

Camilla came forward, bearing the inert body of her son. "I have sinned in leaving my husband," she wailed, "and now God is punishing me. My son is dying of the fever, which has already claimed his father."

Father Ignatius intoned solemnly, "God's mercy is strong and everlasting." He waved his crucifix over the boy, who opened his eyes and smiled.

After the service, someone exclaimed, "A miracle!"

The priest looked toward the doorway. Don Miguel was departing, the child held tenderly in his arms and Camilla by his side, her hand clinging to his.

"A miracle?" murmured Father Ignatius. "Nay, at least *two* miracles."

WARTIME LETTER HOME

August 23, 1943

Dear Mother and Father:

Last week we landed on this island, but I'm not allowed to tell where. Unfortunately, Sergeant Wolansky came along. I wrote you how in boot camp he made me do fifty pushups because my boots weren't polished, then run ten laps around the base because my bed wasn't made—all the while using the most *vile* profanity.

Must close for now. Wolansky is sending me on night patrol.

August 24, 1943

Dear Mother and Father:

Last night was horrible beyond words. Don't worry, I'm not seriously wounded. While on patrol I became hopelessly lost. Sometime after midnight I stumbled, falling onto a huge pile of five-gallon cans. Being thirsty, I opened one. Nothing but gasoline. I lit a match to see if someone left a canteen around. BWOOM!! Next thing I knew a friendly native was carrying me back to camp.

Sergeant Wolansky was waiting. He yelled, "You blankety-blank goof-off! And burned holes in your camouflage outfit. You're on KP 'til hell freezes over!"

"HOLD IT, SERGEANT!" roared Colonel Hazlett, our commander. "My native spies informed me that this man, single-handedly and at great personal risk, destroyed General Yokoyama's supply cache. *You* are demoted to private, effective immediately. Dismissed!"

The colonel put his arm around me, gave me a pretty medal, and promoted *me* to sergeant.

Your loving son,
Harold

P.S.: Now that I'm a sergeant and that stupid-ass Wolansky is a goddamn private, I may make this frigging Army my career.

47

OBSERVATION AND DEDUCTION

As they stepped from the hotel elevator, the Great Inspector explained to his understudy, "You understand, Sydney, I've already arrested the killer. This is merely an exercise to improve your observation and deduction."

"Oh, thank you, sir," responded Sydney gratefully.

The older man led the way into room 1109, nodding to the patrolman on guard as they passed.

"The chalk outline marks where the body of my late friend, Jerome 'Kid' Pardee, was discovered. Great welterweight in his day, followed boxing all his life. He was scheduled to referee a bout tonight. Yesterday he confided to me that something was amiss. Note, if you will, his right hand pointed toward the window."

"Amazing," murmured the understudy.

"The suspects included the fight judge, Kenneth Ord, and the two contestants, Terence Scott and Billy Van Dyne. Now, what see you out yon open window?"

Sydney leaned far out. "The hotel dining terrace. I get it: *Terence* Scott was guilty. *Terrace—Terence.*"

"Wrong. Try again," urged the inspector patiently.

"Well, there's tables where people dine. Aha! So Van *Dyne* did it."

The Great Inspector sighed, "You do need help. How many tables? What shape?"

"Sir, I count thirteen and they're round."

"Now you're learning. A thirteen-round bout means what?"

"A knockout—K.O. It had to be Kenneth Ord! But, inspector, that's pretty thin evidence. Think you can make it stick?"

"Absolutely!" declared the Great One. "Oh, I neglected to mention: Ord was apprehended while dashing through the lobby waving the gun."

MURDER IN THE MANGROVES

The knock on the door of his shack startled old Manny. He quickly hid the pages he was reading before venturing to open the door.

The stranger introduced himself as Andrew Palmer, a private investigator. "Sorry to bother you so late at night," he apologized, "but I'm searching for a man named Jeffery Allston."

"Oh," said the old man, "you mean the guy who wrote *Corpse in the Canyon?*"

"You know him?" asked Palmer eagerly.

"I read a lotta mysteries. What happened?"

"He's disappeared. Missing. In his last letter to Zell Publishers he said he was down this way to get local color for his new novel to be called *Murder in the Mangroves.*"

Manny grew thoughtful. "I got it!" he exclaimed suddenly. "Jeffery Allston was murdered for a manuscript he was writin'. Knowin' he was doomed, about to be killed by a man named Groves, he somehow sneaked out that letter to name his slayer. Mangroves—*man Groves!* Get it?"

"Sorry, old timer," said Palmer, concealing a grin, "you've been reading too many Ellery Queen stories with their dying victim clues. That only happens in fiction.... Well, if you should meet Allston, notify the county sheriff."

Old Manny watched the private investigator disappear into the nighttime mist swirling up from the mangrove swamp. Locking his door, he finished reading the manuscript. Of course, he'd have to type up a new title page for Allston's novel.

Burial in the Bog by Manfred Groves—yes, that had a nice sound.

THE GRAVESTONE SLAB

My Sicilian host, Gino Marcellino, appeared truly drunk. Still, not wishing to invoke his anger and risk his dagger, I guarded my answer carefully when he asked, his speech somewhat slurred, "Tell me, *camariere*, you notice anything unusual in my gardens today? Anything?"

"Sire," I said, "only two of your workmen resetting a great marble slab. One poured hot tar or asphaltum along the edge, dashing back and forth to the fire to keep it molten. The other covered it with finely crushed stone—almost as if to conceal it."

"*Verita*! You observe well. That slab is a gravestone."

"You jest," I remarked uneasily.

"I do not! Beneath it lies my old enemy, Nicolo Satano. With my own dagger I kill him. *Quattordicesimo* times I stab him—one for every insult! I believe not the stupid peasants who say he is the Devil himself. I have bury him where nobody ever find him."

Marcellino drowsed off and I slipped away to bed, but sleep was impossible. *Pericolo!* Danger all around me!

In the morning, the servants were alarmed. Their master could not be found anywhere. It seemed a good time to leave.

I had to pass the gravestone slab of Nicolo Satano. To my amazement, it had been thrust aside. From the empty cavity below arose the acrid odor of brimstone. But what sent chills racing up my spine: *the asphaltum seal had been melted from below!*

Gino Marcellino was never seen again.

THE GHOST OF OLD HAVILAND

"Speaking of the macabre," said Wilberforce unexpectedly, stirring in his chair, "did I ever tell about the ghost of old Haviland?"

All the other club members, myself included, were instantly alert. All except Murgatroyd, who, as usual, snorted, "Rubbish!"

Ignoring him, Wilberforce went on, "You remember Caleb Haviland? A member here for years untold? Died a few years back? Of course you do! Hulking fellow, sloppy dresser, deep-set eyes, and a peculiar manner of tilting his head forward. Unforgettable chap. Anyhow, I was touring Morocco last month. In Casablanca I saw him. The subtropical sun at midday was glaringly brilliant, so there was no mistake. He was shuffling up one of those unlikely little cobblestone alleys from the Casbah. My mouth dropped open.

"'Haviland!' I gasped.

"'Yes,' he answered, his voice unnaturally deep.

"'You're *dead*,' I declared. 'I attended your funeral myself.'

"With that, the figure turned and, without another word, ambled on its way. In a moment I started to follow, but it had disappeared! Gave me quite a turn."

Breaking the ensuing silence, someone muttered, "Remarkable."

Old Murgatroyd cleared his throat. "Nothing so ruddy remarkable," he declared in his customary deprecating way. "How well did you know the Haviland family?"

"Just Caleb," admitted Wilberforce, "and he was always quite reserved."

"Thought so," snapped Murgatroyd. "That was his twin brother Aaron, black sheep the family sent off to Casablanca."

Old Murgatroyd always was one to ruin a good story.

51

THE MIRACULOUS CURES

Improbable as it seems, Marco began attending the Church of Our Lady of Truth. But that experienced con man was never one to do the expected. Actually, he was already planning his next caper.

Marco sized up Father Dominic as sufficiently gullible. After mass he approached him and asked, "How do you do it, Father?"

"Do what, my son?"

"Instantly recognize people's ills. What is it? ESP?"

Flattered, the simple priest replied, "A God-given gift; I suppose."

"Our meeting was foreordained," declared Marco, "for I possess great curative powers. With your diagnoses and my healing, you could become famous! Make bishop—maybe cardinal—then, who knows?"

Father Dominic was easily persuaded. When Mrs. Agnostino came to confession, he pronounced, "It is revealed to me that you have an ulcer. Fortunately, I know someone who can cure you."

"Yes, I do have occasional stomach upsets," admitted the suggestible woman.

A meeting was arranged. After Marco's mumbo-jumbo, the priest declared, "You are now cured."

"How marvelous!" tittered Mrs. Agnostino.

The reputation of the Dominic-Marco "miracles" spread. There followed "cures" of lumbago, cataracts, appendicitis, and fallen arches among female parishioners—each offering Marco a generous "contribution."

Then the priest summoned Marco once again. "This lady," he said solemnly, "suffers from high blood pressure."

Looking up from her prayers, the woman exclaimed, "Marco! Who deserted me with four hungry kids! Father, he couldn't cure a hangnail!"

Marco departed the village hurriedly. Father Dominic, alas, never made bishop.

THE ACCUSATION

Few acquaintances knew that his real name was Roger Carstairs. Everyone called him "Buck." He was one of those rare individuals with perfect physique, uncanny coordination, and a devil-may-care attitude. Buck accepted any challenge—and invariably won.

I hadn't seen Buck since graduation, but he'd been on my mind lately. Billionaire Norman Cardeau had been murdered at his mountain retreat, stabbed in his sleep. His fabulous 15-carat diamond ring was missing from his finger. Trusted bodyguards had been posted along all roadway approaches to the lodge. Nevertheless, someone obviously scaled the near-vertical cliff that night—an almost impossible feat that only Buck could accomplish.

By chance I spotted Buck in a restaurant, sitting at a corner table. He sat stiffly erect, not getting up when I approached. "Why did you do it?" I asked.

"What are you talking about?" he inquired innocently.

"You know damned well—the murder of Norman Cardeau last week."

"Last week," Buck declared, "I was in Saravejo, fighting for the Bosnians. I just got back."

"Most unlikely story," I sneered. "Why didn't you stay there?"

"Oh, my usefulness there ended."

"That's the weakest alibi I ever heard, Buck."

"Sheriff, I don't give a damn what you believe," he snapped. He reached his hand under the table, and I prepared to draw my revolver. Buck fumbled with the controls, and his wheel chair rolled back. Buck Carstairs was a double amputee.

FRED, ME, AND THE MAD DOG CAPER

"Absolutely nothing can go wrong, Ernie," Fred assures me. "I've researched old Cynthia Deveaux's habits thoroughly. Every night she leaves her mansion at precisely 10:05 to walk her yappy little Pekinese—"

"Hold it," I interrupt. "No kidnappin'!"

"Just listen," he tells me. "We also walk a dog just then—"

"We ain't got no dog," I remind him.

"We'll obtain one. Anyhow, the minute she comes out I squirt foamy shave cream over my dog's face and yell, 'Mad dog! I'll save you, madam!' I kick the mutt, which runs off. Being extremely grateful, she invites me into her mansion. Five minutes later, you ring her doorbell. She answers it. You say, 'I saw *everything*, Miss Deveaux! Entertaining a strange man at night!' Greatly embarrassed, she offers you a fortune to keep quiet."

Fred's very persuasive. We visit the dog pound. "That one's real cute," I say. "I'll name him 'Rocky.'"

"The name don't matter. It's not like we're *keeping* him." We get Rocky for $25 and a lecture.

Things don't work out. Fred squirts poor Rocky, who runs yelpin' to me. Miss Deveaux screams, "I saw that, you unspeakable wretch!" and beats Fred with her umbrella until police come to rescue and arrest him. "Is that your unfortunate dog, sir?" she asks me.

"Yes, ma'am," I answer. "His name is Rocky."

"I need a kind-hearted man to oversee my kennels. I'll pay $500 a week."

I visit Fred in jail. He's black-and-blue and somehow don't want to hear my good news.

DEATH OF A SHERIFF

One after another the "mourners" extended their "sympathy" to Emma Hinkle. The last was Ezra Boggs. "He wuz good at providin' fer yew," he said (which was undoubtedly the only virtue Sheriff Joe Hinkle ever had). Ezra considerately did not elaborate that much of the aforementioned "providin'" came from half-starving inmates and confiscating just about anything Joe wanted as "evidence" in false accusations.

The Widow Hinkle had been crying—not because she grieved over the mean old so-and-so, but because now she'd either have to go to work or catch a new man. With her looks, the latter seemed highly unlikely.

"At least my son Jake will now take over as sheriff," she remarked.

"Yew might warn Jake that bein' sheriff has become downright hazardous here in Cold Creek County."

"I reckon he knows *that* much." Emma Hinkle's eyes narrowed. "What actually killed Joe?"

"Hard to say, Miz Hinkle."

"You're the coroner," she stated accusingly. "You *must* know."

"Coulda been one o' them fifteen .30-.30 slugs, ma'am. Or it mighta been one o' them thirty-odd .22 bullets. Or even one o' the nine stab wounds. I honestly doan know."

"Well," snorted the widow, "I'll have Jake take those bullets to the crime lab in Asheville. *They'll* find out whose guns they fit."

"I hate to inform yew, Miz Hinkle," drawled Coroner Boggs, "but somebody broke inta my office last night. Stole every last piece of evidence I had. There's lotsa crim'nals loose hereabouts."

THE JEWEL THEFT

Lady Ffinch-Rolff hated to accuse Nanette. Beautiful and efficient maids like her were rare indeed, but it had to be done. Her diamond brooch, emerald pendant, sapphire earrings, large ruby ring—all missing. Reluctantly, she rang the bell.

"Nanette," the lady began, "your service for these two months has been outstanding." Her tone changed. "But now my jewels are gone. Only you could have taken them. What have you to say?"

Expecting her maid to be repentant, Lady Ffinch-Rolff was shocked when Nanette boldly asserted "Sure, I took them."

"You must return them at once! I'm quite willing to forgive this little, shall we say, lapse."

"No deal," said the defiant maid.

The older woman's face grew livid. "You leave me no choice, you insolent girl. I'm phoning the police!"

"As you wish," declared Nanette, "but you might first consider the insurance company."

"Wh-what do you mean?"

"Suppose I tell police that on June 17th you sold the *real* jewels to Lemoyne's Jewelers. The owner, Jacques Lemoyne himself, handled the sale and made paste replicas. You still kept the insurance on the original jewels. The penalty for fraud is—"

Lady Ffinch-Rolff paled. "Wh-wh-what do you want?"

"Five thousand pounds. Rather cheap, considering your social position and all."

Seething, the lady flounced down at her antique desk. The check she wrote was good.

That evening Nanette and Jacques Lemoyne met in an expensive little restaurant. "You know, father," she smiled, "I think we have a remarkable business relationship."

DIABOLICAL PACT

That Sunday morning two witches, convincingly disguised as shapely young women in shorts, occupied adjacent poolside chairs at the exclusive Palmetto Country Club.

"He's really putty in our hands," giggled blonde Hepzibah, glancing up at the young athlete suspended in midair above their heads.

"Yeah," agreed Sabrina, "Terry wants to win the Olympic diving competition above everything else. We've convinced him that if he gives up his faith he'll be able to float like a feather, fly like a bird, and perform all sorts of acrobatics before hitting the water."

"His Satanic Majesty should give us a big bonus for sealing the fate of this simple boob."

"Levitate him up another, ten feet, Hepzibah. That should *really* erase all his doubts."

"Okay." The blonde witch pointed her finger upward, and Terry Atwater suddenly found himself floating high above the two very desirable young women.

"We've got him now!" chortled Hepzibah. "He's agreed!"

Unfortunately for their plan, the bells of the nearby cathedral chimed out the call to early mass, instantly breaking the witches' insidious spell. The young athlete fell down heavily....

The Monday edition of *The Palmetto Tribune* featured a front page story:

UNFORTUNATE ACCIDENT

While practicing diving at the Country Club yesterday morning, Terry Atwater, our local Olympic hopeful, tripped and accidentally fell upon two unidentified elderly ladies, fatally injuring both. Coroner Jason Chatham reports both victims, wearing identical long black dresses and blood-red cloaks, were "extremely old" and bore curious forehead protuberances.

SING "MISTY" AGAIN

Bryan's Bistro, New Orleans. August 20, 1983, ten-thirty at night. Bryan, the owner, and his wife Eileen confer at a dimly-lit corner table.

EILEEN: I'm no longer young.

BRYAN: I'll never ask you again, babe. But this is our big score. This billionaire Harley is absolutely nuts about jewels. I've convinced him to buy rubies for five million—cash! You charm the old guy, find out where he's stashing the dough. Hush, here he comes... (loudly) Sit down, Harley! Drink?...No? Then let's finalize plans. The rajah will land by helicopter nearby around midnight tomorrow. Very hush-hush. He insists on cash—hundred-dollar bills.

HARLEY: Agreed. What about last-minute hitches?

BRYAN: I've thought of everything. Come back here tomorrow night, same time. If the deal's still on, Eileen will sing "Misty" onstage.

Eileen leaves with Harley.

Same place. The following night, ten o'clock.

EILEEN (whispering): The dough's in the trunk of his Lexus outside. Here comes Harley.

BRYAN: Good girl. Get up there and sing "Misty." Then meet me at the airport. Our plane for Rio leaves in one hour.

Harley's Hideaway, Rio. August 23, 2001, eleven at night. The elderly proprietress, still retaining traces of beauty, circulates regally among her patrons.

YOUTHFUL ADMIRER: Please, Eileen, sing "Misty" one more time.

EILEEN (reluctantly): My voice...it's aging, too.

ANOTHER YOUTH: You'll never be old. Nobody sings "Misty" like you!

EILEEN (teary-eyed): It's just that "Misty" always reminds me of my two late husbands.

The piano player riffs a soft intro. Eileen begins.

GENTLEMAN GERALD MEETS HIS MATCH

Despite continued publicity surrounding the Ruby Crucifix, Mother Felicia continued to wear it openly around the cathedral. To the bishop, who expressed concern, she replied, "Our Lord will protect it."

The crucifix had been presented to her by her older brother, Emile Ledoux, the noted explorer, when she took her first vows. In its back was embedded the faultless 16-carat ruby.

Gentleman Gerald, the Rhyming Robber, knew all about the fabulous gem. To himself, he said:

"I'll have that ruby, that I swear,
"It's just a matter of when and where."

Disguising himself as a nun (no problem for that great impersonator) Gerald presented himself to Mother Felicia as a novitiate. On his third day in the cathedral, he addressed her:

"A miracle has been revealed to me,
"Join me tomorrow and you will see."

She agreed and the following day accompanied him high up to the cathedral top.

Always a gentleman, Gerald knelt and said,

"Gimme that ruby and maintain silence,
"I'd rather not resort to violence."

In answer, good Mother Felicia pulled a whistle from her robe and blew it. Gendarmes materialized from behind every pillar.

As he was being handcuffed, Gentleman Gerald asked:

"Tell me, lady, if you can,
"What made you certain I'm a man?"

Mother Felicia, herself a bit of a wit, answered:

"One thing I noticed in the chapel
"Was your bobbing Adam's apple.
"Then I was sure, sir, 'twas quite simple:
"It made a ripple in your wimple."

THE BAD LUCK BLACK CATS

The hour grew late. Conversation in the pub turned to superstitions. "Fer a fact," declared Stevens, the elderly retired patrolman, "black cats bring bad luck."

"Any proof?" challenged the stout man at the end of the bar.

"Take the case of Emil Collingsworth," replied Stevens. "Afore yore time, I dare say. Anyways I'm pullin' desk dooty that mornin' at the station 'ouse. The phone rings. 'You've *got* to do something about those two black cats!' the man yells.

"'Wot cats? And who's this?' I ask.

"Turns out the bloke is Emil Collingsworth, residin' at 702-D Rose Terrace. 'Those cats are ruining my law practice at number twenty-one Temple Court!' 'e raves. 'Get rid of them! Immediately!'

"So, at noon I'm off dooty. I nips 'round ter 21 Temple Court. Sure enough, two black cats are paradin' back and forth in front of 'is law office. I squats down and they rush ter me and purr."

"Wot's the bad luck?" someone asked.

Stevens frowned at the interruption. "Cute buggers they are, so I takes 'em 'round ter 702-D Rose Terrace that evenin' ter ask wot ter do with 'em.

"I knock. No answer, I knock louder. The apartment buildin' super 'ears me and comes up, 'Oh,' 'e says, 'you found Missus Collingsworth's cats. She'll be glad ter see 'em agin.' 'E unlocks the door.

"But Missus Collingsworth ain't glad. She's lyin' stone-cold on the floor, a knife in 'er 'eart and blood everywheres.

"And *that's* when Emil Collingsworth's bad luck begins."

THE COMPETITIVE EDGE

Captain Rodriguez tried to calm elderly Eileen Graham, owner of the Elegante Restaurant. "You still claim your competitor next door is killing your employees?"

Miss Graham sniffed, "That man would do *anything* to get ahead of me—including murder."

For decades, old Caleb Andrews, owner of the adjacent Royale Restaurant, had been Eileen's bitter rival. She ran specials, he ran specials; she started al fresco service, the next day he bought sidewalk tables and chairs.

"Think about it," continued the old lady. "Edwin McConnell, my head waiter for forty-three years—struck by a car in front of the Royale. Then Patricia Clarke, my cashier for years and years—stabbed in the alley behind the Royale."

Rodriguez raised his hand. "Hit-and-run and assault-and-robbery, by persons unknown. Nothing connecting Mr. Andrews to either death."

"But now," declared Eileen, "my faithful old cook, Randolphe Pierson, hasn't shown up."

"Please be patient, ma'am. We're investigating."

At that moment a patrolman burst in. "We found Pierson, sir. Bludgeoned. His body was concealed among the sidewalk chairs piled next door."

"What did I tell you!" exclaimed the elderly woman triumphantly. "Caleb's done it to me again!"

Both men rushed out.

Left alone, Eileen Graham smiled maliciously. Who would suspect a frail little old lady like herself could drag aged Randolphe next door at midnight and stack Caleb's chairs upon him?

Or suspect her motive in killing her three employees?

Now she'd never have to pay their retirement benefits! That alone gave her a competitive edge.

RETURN TO LIFE

Upon opening the door, Joanne Kimberly screamed, "*JIM!* Good God! We thought you died when your plane crashed in Africa."

"Sorry to disappoint you by surviving, dear wife. Natives treated my broken bones, nursed me to recovery. Now, may I enter my own house?"

"Damned awkward. You see, I invited your brother Earl—"

"To share your bed? Earl always was a fast worker—behind my back. We'll sort things out later. I'll check with mother."

I could murder you, she thought.

"My darling Jim!" exclaimed his mother. "But your return complicates matters. I-I-I spent your insurance money on a round-the-world cruise and—"

"Forget it, sweet mother," Jim declared bitterly. "I'll repay the insurance company from the family corporation's assets."

Why couldn't he have remained dead? she wondered

"So, you did survive, big brother," said Earl, scowling. "Just when I got the corporation running my way. Dammit, you're always lucky—"

"We'll make other arrangements now."

I could kill him, thought Earl. *Only the family knows he's alive....*

The Kimberly family gathered in the ancestral home. "I can't understand it," said the old matriarch. "Jim promised to meet us here."

"Amnesia, perhaps," suggested Joanne. "He seemed rather confused."

"Why did he return?" complained Earl.

They waited. And waited. Each eyed the other two suspiciously, speculating, *Who killed Jim?*

All during the trans-Atlantic flight back to his wealthy girlfriend in Cairo, Jim Kimberly smiled. Let his family forever worry that he might return again.

SHINING KNIGHT TO THE RESCUE

As a freelance writer I look for human interest in run-down places. Barney's Place certainly qualified. I went in, ordered a beer. The only other customers were three leather-jacketed toughs and a lovely girl in a pristine white dress. She obviously didn't belong in such a sleazy bar.

"Gonna be trouble," hoarsely whispered the bartender, as a gentleman in top hat hesitantly entered.

Suddenly one young tough grabbed the girl roughly. "Okay," he snarled, "gimme the key. We seen ya ride up on that new white scooter."

"P-p-please," she begged.. "You're hurting me. I need that scooter to get to my job."

The gentleman strode forward. "Release that lady immediately!" he demanded.

The three hooligans laughed. In moments they lay sprawled helpless on the barroom floor. The gentleman had easily overpowered them. "Come, miss," he said gallantly, "I'll see you safely home." Together they rode off on her scooter. Minutes later the three toughs roared away on their motorcycles.

"Wonderful story!" I exclaimed. "Shining Knight Rescues Fair Maiden!"

"She ain't no maiden," rasped the bartender. "And you gotta feel kinda sorry for that poor boob."

"Why?" I asked, puzzled. "He did a very noble deed."

"You really didn' get it, mister. She's Molly McGuire. She and her brothers pull that scene whenever a swell comes in."

"You mean that attack on her was *faked*?"

"Of course!" snorted the bartender. "Her brothers will be waitin' at the waterfront when she delivers the gent there. They'll probably hold him for ransom."

THE SOUL OF THE BANKER

The darkening overcast threatened still more rain. The swollen, muddied river roiled noisily under the bridge in Memorial Park. I spotted my old friend George and, leaning my cane against the park bench, sat down beside him.

"A depressing day," he remarked, nodding toward a passing woman. I looked. She was shabbily dressed, bareheaded, without any umbrella. As she mounted the bridge, she dropped her purse as though it no longer mattered. She leaned over the rail, staring at the ominous brown swirling water. I sensed her desperation.

"My God, George!" I cried. "She's going to jump!"

"Possibly," he said. "But any alarm would surely decide her. Besides, at our age we couldn't save her."

Just then Jason Bartlett, our town's banker, strolled past. "What that wretched woman *doesn't* need," I whispered, "old 'Flint-heart' himself, who probably drove her to these straits by foreclosing on her little home."

Bartlett saw the woman. Picking up her abandoned purse, he opened it, inspected the contents, then replaced it on the bridge.

"Heartless beast!" I declared. "Looking to see if she has a dime left!"

"Ah," said George, "but didn't you notice? While the lady's attention focused down on the turbulent muddy river, old Bartlett emptied his billfold and slipped the money into her purse."

Approaching the woman, Bartlett spoke softly. All I heard was: "...there is always hope, madam. Believe me, I know."

Slowly she turned, studying his face for a full minute. Then, retrieving her purse, she walked calmly, resolutely, away.

THE WIFE WHO DID EVERYTHING BETTER

Marrying Gertrude had been a mistake, Henry now realized. She had become a tyrant. Romance was beyond salvage. Whatever he tried to do, she took over. Worse yet, he had to admit she did it better.

Like the time he started mowing the lawn. Gertrude burst from the house. "Hen-RY!" she screeched. "You set the blade too low. You're positively scalping the grass. Here, let me do it." She proceeded to trim it perfectly.

That afternoon the kitchen sink became clogged. Henry carefully laid out his tools, crawled under, and started loosening the pipe. "Stop!" yelled Gertrude. Startled, Henry straightened up, striking his head painfully. "Pipes unscrew *clockwise*," his wife snorted. "You'll strip the threads. Crawl outta there! Let me fix that—right."

That was the last straw. Nursing the bump on his head, Henry decided to end it all. As a final show of defiance, he'd commit suicide in front of her. As he entered her bedroom, Gertrude glared at him. "Henry! What on earth are you doing here? And what's in that glass you're carrying?"

"You drove me to this," he declared dramatically. "This water contains twenty dissolved sleeping tablets. This is farewell!" He swigged it down.

"Oh, Henry!" she wailed. "Wait here! I'll fetch something."

"She really *does* love me," muttered Henry, hope suddenly kindled. Gertrude returned. "Drink this, Henry." He quickly obeyed.

"What is this, dear?"

"Strychnine. Any idiot knows sleeping tablets take forever. You never could do *anything* right!"

TOOLS FOR A LADY'S GARDEN

"Let's face it," Bill sighed. "We ain't much good at this private eye business."

"Something will turn up," I predicted.

Amazingly, something did—beautiful, curvaceous, in her twenties. "I'm Beatrice Spade," she confided demurely. "I want to hire you to find three missing persons: Ho Chan, our cook; Ron Raker, our butler; and Harry Sprinkle, our gardener."

"We do good work," I assured her.

We accompanied Beatrice out to the mansion and met her elderly husband, Algernon Spade.

"Spare no expense," he declared. "Find 'em!"

Bill and I strolled in the garden. "Beautiful chrysanthemums," I commented.

"Oh, thank you!" gushed Beatrice. "I recently planted them myself."

Late that afternoon, I opened a tool shed. "Look!" I exclaimed. "A hoe, a rake, and a sprinkler!"

"So what?" muttered Bill.

"Don't you get it? It's the killer's scorecard: *Ho* Chan, Ron *Raker*, and Harry *Sprinkle*. Mr. *Spade* is undoubtedly next."

Next morning I explained my theory to Captain Hennesey. "Nonsense!" he snorted. "Last night Beatrice Spade informed on her husband. He murdered all three. Buried 'em under some chrysanthemums. Naturally, he denies everything, but we got him dead to rights."

Bill and I returned to the Spade mansion. There in the tool shed hung a hoe, rake, sprinkler—and a *spade!*

Beatrice approached. "Oh!" she exclaimed. "You startled me. I must write you a generous check for your wonderful services. You were amazing!"

Of course, Bill and I offered to help her re-plant those chrysanthemums, hoping she would recommend us to her friends.

HIS LAST RIDE

The passing scene seemed unfamiliar. In fact, the whole situation had become bizarre. Why was he—the Honourable Percival R. Hardlestone—riding on back of a white motor scooter driven by a lady in pristine white? He leaned forward. "Miss—I say, miss, where are we going?"

She glanced back briefly. She was nominally attractive. "My orders are to deliver you to Final Judgment. Where you go from there depends."

"Final Judgment?" he queried. "Never heard of the place. Anyhow, I'm due at Parliament. Take me there. Immediately!"

"Sorry, sir, but you won't be returning to Parliament. Your proposal to exempt slum landlords from taxes will *never* be heard."

"*What?* Is this some dastardly plot of the opposition to kidnap me?"

The lady laughed lightly, "You really don't remember?"

"Remember what, madam?"

"Daydreaming, contemplating fabulous payoffs from big corporations, you stepped from the kerb smack in front of a lorry."

"Bloody hell!" exclaimed Hardlestone. "You mean I'm—"

"Exactly. Quite dead."

"Oh. Then you must be an angel?"

"No—at least, not yet. Old Peter assigned me to Delivery duty for a year to atone for my past—shall we say—indiscretions."

"I'd rather hoped—"

"They all do," she declared, gunning the motor. The scooter abruptly left the pavement, soaring aloft. "Got a busy day ahead: fatal shooting in Soho, a suicide in Mayfair, and—"

"W-w-what will happen?" he interrupted, suddenly fearful.

The driver shrugged. "There's Final Judgment just ahead. You get off there. Good luck, sir. *You'll need it!*"

THE CORRUGATED TIN WEB

Villagers crowded the school auditorium, their attention riveted on the speaker. After all, Wyburg was a poor community and opportunities for extra money were scarce.

The dapper speaker waved a letter aloft. "This government contract guarantees my proposed factory. Production can begin as soon as machinery arrives. Of course, I'll employ some fifty men—and women—to meet quotas."

Murmured approval swept the room.

Sylvester P. Roland continued, "You folks of Wyburg have been very kind. Mayor Kimball and Constable Hawkins even granted me free use of the abandoned sawmill. In all fairness, you should partake of this good fortune. I therefore offer you shares in this enterprise—one hundred dollars each. I'll be at the sawmill tomorrow. Thank you."

The audience applauded. Sylvester P. Roland (his current name) smiled broadly. It always worked: he'd show up in some village, his truck loaded with showy office furniture, and spin his enticing, irresistible web.

Early the following morning, all the villagers gathered at the old corrugated tin sawmill, cash in hand. Right into his web! Kimball and Hawkins greeted him. "May we be first?"

"Of course, gentlemen!"

The mayor closed the door behind them, "'T won't work, Whatever-your-name-is. I phoned Washington; there ain't no 'Roland Enterprises.' Three people tried that scam here before. *All three disappeared.*"

Before the astonished con artist could react, Constable Hawkins shot him.

Mayor Kimball stepped outside. "Time to start the auction, folks! Here's this fine Mack truck of the late Mr. Roland. What'm I bid?"

"Stop that motor scooter!'" yelled the frantic little man from the doorway of the Royal Bank.

Immediately a London bobby ordered HALT! holding forth his white-gloved hand.

The attractive lady braked the white scooter. The gentleman in top hat riding behind her asked, "Anything wrong, officer? I am the Honourable Percy Arbuthnott. I always travel this way to Parliament. Keeps up the common touch with my constituents."

"Sorry, sir. Let's go inside and straighten this out."

"Oh, very well. My secretary Jeanette can remain outside."

The bank manager and head teller were waiting. "That's he!" cried the latter. "Mr. Arbuthnott requested a private consultation in our conference room. There he threatened me with a pistol, again accusing me of failing to credit his account with twenty pounds for an alleged deposit. My books *always* balance."

"Naturally they do!" stormed Arbuthnott. "You *pocketed* my twenty!"

"Why didn't you sound the alarm?" inquired the manager. "That's proper procedure."

"Well," admitted the teller, "I-I rather thought *I'd—*"

"I'm afraid," interrupted Percy Arbuthnott, "your head teller suffers delusions. I have no pistol. I *insist* on being searched!"

The officer obliged. "No weapon on 'im," he reported.

"I'll personally credit your account with twenty pounds, Mr. Arbuthnott," said the manager. "Please leave with my apology."

As the two rode away on the motor scooter, the secretary whispered, "Er...sir...."

"Something wrong, Jeanette?"

"Well, actually, riding with your toy pistol is becoming *dreadfully* uncomfortable in the place where I concealed it."

WHY MRS. BIGGERS SITS THERE

"I can't understand why Ernie doesn't leave her," said my father.

"Or why he married her in the first place," added my mother.

"The woman's absolutely balmy. No wonder Alfred took off and never came back. She just sits there all day, staring at the water."

"She needs professional help...."

My parents didn't know I was listening from upstairs. They were talking about Mrs. Biggers again. Grownups tell a joke around town: the 'END' sign and stop reflectors at the foot of Noonan Street aren't necessary—one look at Marlene Biggers' big fat bottom just ahead would stop *anybody*.

Rain or shine, she sits in her folding lawn chair at that same spot on the beach. Around noon, she sends her present husband, Ernie, over to McDonald's for carry outs.

Everybody feels sorry for Ernie—he's allergic to sand fleas—but then they also felt sorry for her first husband, Alfred Moore, who simply disappeared. Marlene sold his flower shop soon afterward.

I know why she sits there. But I don't dare tell. Two years ago (back when I was only nine), I promised to ride my bike straight home from Billy Hunter's birthday party. I disobeyed. I took a roundabout way, along the beach.

That's when I spotted the lantern. I braked my bike and sneaked closer. Maybe pirates were burying treasure right there beyond the end of Noonan Street!

But it wasn't pirates and it wasn't treasure. Marlene and Ernie were burying her husband Alfred.

KEEPING UP APPEARANCES

Over breakfast Lord Ainsley-Smythe remarked, "Rather sticky wicket, m'love."

"What, Chauncey?" asked his wife Rosalind.

"The bank refuses further credit. Deucedly afraid we must economize. Perhaps we could dispense with old Percy?"

"What!? And let our friends know we can't afford a butler? Impossible! And our cook needs some fresh veggies."

"Then we really must go *personally* shopping, dearie. The Rolls is quite low on petrol. You can drive your motor scooter."

Lady Ainsley-Smythe donned her helmet and Chauncey mounted behind her, their carton strapped on the rear. She maneuvered expertly to the open market and they began filling the cook's list. They had quite finished and started back to the mansion when a greengrocer yelled, "Stop that bloody scooter!"

An officer stepped forward, blocking the way. "I say," said Chauncey innocently, "is something the matter?"

"Hi'll say somefin's th' matter!" sputtered the grocer. "That bloke nicked some o' me produce!"

"Utter rubbish!" protested Chauncey. "Search me, officer."

The officer patted him down. "Nothin' on 'im," he reported.

The grocer's attractive daughter spoke, "Hi knowed a gen'lman like 'im wooden do nuffin' like that."

"Why, thank you, miss," said Chauncey gallantly, doffing his voluminous top hat and bowing. Thereupon the cantaloupe he'd hidden under his hat rolled off his head, smashing at his feet.

This so alarmed his wife Rosalind she quaked violently, dislodging from beneath her skirt the small plastic bags of tomatoes, lettuce, oranges, and turnips that she'd managed to secretly hook onto her garter belt.

MR. HARDLESTONE'S FINAL 1040

The gold-lettered sign on the door still reads: Edgar Hardlestone, Investigator. But the founder of the detective agency is nowhere to be found. The April 16th headlines declare: Noted Tracer of Lost Persons Missing/Foul Play Suspected.

I'd only worked at the agency one week, trying to arrange Mr. Hardlestone's records for his annual 1040 to the IRS. What a mess! His secretary, Alice Thebold, and his assistants, Bill Stedman and John Paulson, frantically helped.

We finally finished. Alice was typing the last page. In burst Hardlestone yelling, "Hold it! I forgot to deduct expenses in the Carruther's case."

Alice whited out the original and typed in the correction.

Hardlestone frowned when he read it. "This doesn't mention my expenses in preparing Social Security forms."

"What expenses?" I asked.

"Well, I had Bill run over to the Federal Building to clarify procedures. Ask him about it."

Bill couldn't recall what it cost in gasoline and company time. I made a guess.

"And, while you're revising," added old Hardlestone, "there's the matter of John's travel. Seems I've misplaced his vouchers."

Scowling, John made an estimate.

Alice was beside herself. One hour before the midnight deadline, she pounded out the final draft. John and Bill anxiously awaited to dash to the post office.

Old Hardlestone rushed in. "I just thought of something else..."

Edgar Hardlestone disappeared without a trace that very night. I know *why*. I just can't figure out *how* they did it.

THE DEVIL OUTWITTED IN EDINBURGH

In Hell's hottest section, Satan lolled on his throne. "So," he inquired, "how did you handle the case of Brian Mcleod?"

"Sire," replied Maggotty, Devil Third Class, "I tempted him with Margaret McDuff, the luscious young wife of the elderly banker on Princes Street. He was putty in my hands."

"Excellent. And then?"

"I made her husband aware of their affair."

"Absolutely fiendish!" chuckled Satan gleefully. "Continue."

"Her angry husband accused her in his office. She staggered outside, fearful, distraught—ready for harvesting."

"Marvelous."

"She muttered, 'I'd gie *anything* to be just a black cat.' I stepped forward, 'Your soul, perhaps?'

"'Aye, aye,' she agreed eagerly.

"'It's a deal, my sweet,' I declared, and transformed her instantly.

"'That were easy,' she mewed. 'But ye could nae do t' same wi' Brian Macleod a-coomin' yonder.'

"I accepted her challenge, quickly turning him likewise into a black cat. 'Now,' I demanded triumphantly, 'give me your soul!'

"'Ye failed!' she spat at me. 'Were I a *real* cat, I'd nae care wha' happened to Brian. I still ha' my soul—and ye can gae to hell!'

"Sire, I need your advice."

"Fool!" thundered Satan. "She outwitted you. You should have seized her soul *first*. Now, you can't restore her to human form without reneging on your bargain. Meanwhile, the two lovers cavort all over Edinburgh, without her husband's knowledge—and with eight more lives. *Imbecile!*"

Satan leveled his finger. A bolt of lightning, a puff of acrid smoke, and Maggotty disappeared forever.

THE WHITE RAT

"While you're out golfing this Saturday morning, Peter," said Miriam Harker, "your partner John has offered to go jogging with me."

Her husband responded absently, "That's fine. But tell me, dear, isn't that a white rat sitting in your chair?"

"Just my napkin that fell off the table. Maybe you need a long vacation. Your imagination is acting up again."

Peter Harker was certain it was a white rat. He'd glimpsed it yesterday in their bedroom. He said no more, shouldered his golf bag, and drove to the links. Maybe Miriam was right.

An hour later, John Albritt pulled into the Harkers' driveway. Miriam was still in her negligee. They embraced passionately. "It's working!" she announced gleefully. "Soon Peter will be seeing a psychiatrist. Then I'll have him committed and *we* will own Harker & Albritt Investments!" They never got around to jogging that morning.

Miriam awoke Sunday morning to find her husband gone. She tottered into the bathroom. There was a note taped to the mirror: "Darling—Gone golfing again. About that white rat I've been imagining, I saw Mikael Vrascu, the psychiatrist, yesterday afternoon. He suggested I prove to myself that it doesn't exist. So, I got my old classmate Brad Johnson, the herpetologist at Reptile Gardens, to loan me a large rattlesnake. You'll probably notice it around the house. If it doesn't show a considerable bulge after a day or two, it proves there was no white rat. Love, Peter."

Immediately behind her Miriam heard an ominous, heart-chilling rattle-rattle-rattle.

JUSTICE IS *NOT* BLIND

Flamboyant Harvey Heppelwhite was a highly successful defender. He now turned sharply to the elderly lady in the witness box. "You claim, Miss Springsteen, you saw my client, Miss Ardell, strike the blind accuser—Mr. Jameson—with her motor scooter?"

"Yes. She was driving erratically. Irresponsibly."

"When?"

"Late Friday night."

"How late?"

"Nearly midnight, I suppose."

"Hardly a time for *respectable* ladies to be on *dark* streets." Hepplewhite winked at the jurors. "But, regardless, you maintain you saw her clearly?"

"I did. While walking home from the concert—"

"Miss Springsteen, let's be honest. Your last eye examination was three years ago. You lost your editing job because of poor vision. Perhaps you came here hoping Mr. Jameson would reward your false testimony?"

"No...NO!" Bewildered, the old lady began sobbing.

"Not guilty!" declared the jury foreman.

Miss Ardell whispered archly to her attorney, "Want to ride to my apartment on my scooter and collect your fee? I'm not drunk *this* time."

"Gladly, my dear!"

Miss Springsteen walked out despondent, her spirit broken. Then she saw them coming down the street, weaving through heavy traffic. "They've ruined the rest of my life," she muttered. "They might as well end it." Deliberately she stepped in front of the scooter.

At the last second the girl swerved—directly in front of a bus—with fatal results.

"Didn't you see the traffic light?" asked the officer.

"Young man," replied Miss Springsteen resolutely, "it was just proven in court that my eyesight is completely unreliable."

THE ULTIMATE RIDE

Of course I'm only the Braithwaite's butler-chauffeur, but I considered Sir Reginald Allingham rather a prig. He was obviously visiting the mansion that week to get up nerve to propose to Hortense, the older Braithwaite daughter, the goal being his title and her wealth. Hortense was snobbish as her mother. Her younger sister Florence inherited her father's common sense.

"Baxter!" called out Hortense. "Sir Reginald must get to Number 10 Downing Street to deliver his new economic plan!" He stood stupidly clutching a box of documents.

"Sorry, ma'am," I informed her, "the Rolls won't start."

"Drat," she muttered, "I'll phone a cab." Moments later she yelped, "Now the damned phone's gone dead!"

"I'll get him there on my motor scooter," offered Florence. "Well," snapped her sister, "I suppose that will have to suffice."

So, they set off, Florence driving, Sir Reggie stiffly erect behind her, and his precious papers strapped on the rear.

Night came. Still no sign of them. Around midnight Florence put-putted up the driveway. Sir Reggie, minus his top hat, was grinning. "We were quite concerned about you two," declared the master. "What happened?"

"Oh," replied Florence lightly, "we motored hither and yon. Incidentally, we're engaged." Her sister Hortense fled weeping up the staircase.

Next day I encountered Florence in the garage repairing the Rolls. Somehow she'd mysteriously "discovered" the missing distributor. "You must have taken Sir Reggie for quite a ride," I ventured.

She smiled and winked. "Yes, Baxter, one might truthfully say that."

THE DROWNING OF OSWALD

"My brother-in-law drowned," stated the rotund little man calmly. "I came to explain how it happened."

The desk sergeant at the precinct station dutifully noted the time—23:42. "Your name, sir?"

"Henri Armitage. I own the fine little restaurant on Childers Street."

"Go on."

"It started when my wife Arabella said, 'You need a vacation, Henri. I'll get my brother Oswald to manage the restaurant while we're away.'

"I should have known better. All the time we were at the beach I worried. When we returned this evening, my maitre d'hotel, Adolphe Legare, met me at the airport. He seemed dejected.

"'Anything wrong?' I asked anxiously.

"'We've had problems, sir,' he answered sadly.

"'What sort?'

"'Late Tuesday evening some tourists stumbled over the sidewalk chairs Mr. Oswald left outside. They've hired lawyers. Then on Thursday several patrons became ill on the chicken cordon bleu, I suspect because Mr. Oswald accidentally disconnected refrigeration the day before—'

"'But surely,' I interrupted, 'my chef Pierre detected the tainted meat?'

"'Unfortunately, sir, Mr. Oswald fired him earlier.'

"'Whatever for?' I gasped.

"'Pierre objected when Mr. Oswald added cayenne pepper to the soup. Mr. Oswald then took over the cooking. And on Friday—'

"I could bear no more. I had Adolphe drive me directly to my restaurant."

"But, Mr. Armitage," said the confused desk sergeant, "you were saying your brother-in-law *drowned*. Exactly how?"

"Oh, Oswald drowned, all right. I plunged his stupid head into a huge vat of his abominable bouillabaisse."

A MOST DEVOTED COUPLE

To everyone in Bamsford, Sam and Sadie Morrison were a most devoted couple, looking forward to their twenty-fifth wedding anniversary. Sam had started remodeling their antique shop just as Sadie wanted, shifting walls, raising the ceiling.

Not even nosy old Mrs. Pringle next door suspected Sam had started a torrid affair with young Arletta Griggs. But Sadie found out. She couldn't bear sharing Sam with another woman. She decided on murder and suicide: sleeping pills in coffee. She set the two cups aside to cool. He husband came home. She rushed to meet him.

"Why the tears?" he asked.

"Oh, Sam," she sobbed, "I know...everything."

Sadie stood right under a loose rafter. Sam's golden opportunity. Reaching up, he pulled the heavy beam down onto her head. Before he phoned Arletta and then dialed 911, Sam decided that delicious smelling coffee might settle his nerves. He drained both cups, then, overcome with drowsiness, collapsed on the floor.

Police established the sequence. Sadie died from the blow of a falling insecure rafter; then Sam expired from overdose of sleeping tablets in coffee. Chief Rawlins questioned neighbors.

"Such a devoted couple," old Mrs. Pringle told him. "Sam, poor dear man, was doing his best to make Sadie happy, remodeling their shop and all. As I see it," she declared confidently, "he discovered the accident and, overcome with sorrow and unable to continue living without his beloved wife, mixed them pills into his coffee and drank it."

"Sure looks that way," agreed Chief Rawlins.

FRED & ERNIE, ROOFERS

Fred proudly handed his partner a stack of printed cards:

FRED & ERNIE, ROOFERS
Inexpensive—SATISFACTION GUARANTEED!

Ernie read one slowly, then declared, "We don't know nothin' about roofin'."

"Beside the point," snapped Fred. "We delight some old rich dame with our astounding offer. She signs a contract and makes a substantial down payment."

"Then we skip?"

"No, Ernie. Think big. When we don't start for weeks, what does she do?"

"Slams us in the pokey?"

"Definitely not! She sues us—that's what rich people do. We show the judge our contract specifying we have one year to complete. Case dismissed. We immediately file counter suit for defamation of character—that's legal talk, Ernie. Rich people hate appearin' before judges. She settles generously out of court. We hire a reliable roofer to do the job, and split the profits! Come along, Ernie. I've already lined up a wealthy old pigeon."

In an exclusive neighborhood, Fred rang the doorbell. Mrs. Tabitha Armbruster herself opened the door. "Come right in," she invited. "Your prices are so reasonable, I've signed the contract."

"You won't regret it, lady," Fred assured her.

"You do have a license?" she asked sweetly.

"Er—not yet."

Just then a policeman emerged from the kitchen. "Wanta press charges, ma'am?"

"Not if they'll rent ladders, purchase supplies, and start *immediately.*"

As they nailed shingles in the rain, with Tabitha Armbruster shouting up instructions from under her umbrella, Ernie said, "This is fun!"

"Oh, shut up!" snarled Fred.

CHRISTMAS IN GOTCH'S BAR

There'll never be another Christmas in Gotch's Bar like the last one. Hairless Harry Howard is due outta the hospital Tuesday. Trouble starts when Gus Gotch, genial bartender and owner, suffers a severe attack of Christmas spirit. Just after Thanksgiving he installs this lopsided Christmas tree in one corner.

Comes Christmas Eve, Cauliflower O'Toole, the retired welterweight, is standin' at the bar. Gus says, "Let's do this right, Cauliflower. Go into the back room and put on the Santa outfit I hung there. At midnight I'll light the candles on yonder tree, and you drag in a big bag fulla Bud Lights, which you distribute free to customers." Cauliflower likes the idea.

Gus lights the candles. In waddles Santa Claus, ho-ho-ho-in', stoppin' in front of the candle-lit tree. Shoutin' "MER-R-R-RY CHR-R-ISTMAS!" he bends over his bag.

Smoke rises from his butt, then flames. Yelpin', "Holy Christopher!" Cauliflower disappears into the alley, trailin' fire and sparks.

The day after Christmas, Cauliflower again enters Gotch's Bar, walkin' gingerly.

Everybody's mum except Hairless Harry Howard, whose mouth is bigger than his brain. Harry laughs like a hyena and yells, "Don't just stand there, Santa Claus! Sit down with us!"

Cauliflower's got a short fuse. Grabbin' a bottle of Bud Light by the neck, he strides over to the table and growls, "How'd you like a present, bucko?"

Without waitin' for an answer, Santa Claus (alias Cauliflower O'Toole) delivers his belated Christmas present—thunk!—right on top of Harry's bald head.

THE ICING ON THE CAKE

Soon as I got out of jail, I rushed back to my little bakery. My wife Sally was hanging a new sign on the wall: "THE CUSTOMER IS ALWAYS RIGHT!"

"Keep that in mind," she said pointedly.

I'd always tried to accommodate customers. That was before my neighbor Joe Palosky came in.

"We're running a special today, Joe," I said. "Any name in pink icing—free—on any birthday cake."

After looking over the display for fifteen minutes—while other customers waited—he pointed, "That one."

I took it from the case. "Nice choice, Joe."

"I want purple icing instead of pink."

I hesitated. "That's rather unusual—but for a neighbor I'll do it. Now, how do you spell your name?"

"Instead of my name, I want a purple layer on top of the white."

"No dice," I told him. "That's not what I advertised."

"But you'll do 'Happy Birthday' and my old Polish name?"

"Of course," I replied, relieved. "What is it?"

"My first name is Stanaslowski—spelled S-T-A-N-A-S-L-O-W-S-K-I." I wrote it down carefully.

"And my middle name is Ostrowski-Kaharskovich. That's O-S-T-R-O-W-S-K-I-hyphen-K-A-H-A-R-S-K-O-V-I-C-H. Got that? Now my last name is much longer. It's—"

"Hold it, Joe!" I yelled, boiling mad. "Rather than mess up this beautiful cake with purple, you can have it free!"

His eyes lighted up. "I hoped you'd say that."

Despite other customers watching, I leaned over the counter and shoved it into his smirking face. I was still shouting, "Happy birthday, you bastard!" when police arrived.

81

HIS GREATEST DISAPPEARING ACT

Lieutenant Bixby and I later agreed that it was Marvello the Magician's greatest trick. It was based on distraction, and we fell for it.

Everyone knew that Harvey Wentworth (professionally known as Marvello the Magician) had unwisely become chummy with Babette Lefleur, girlfriend of Giuseppe Scanio, local mob boss. She was now Marvello's stage assistant. Reliable sources said that Scanio had given a contract on Marvello to Julius Niccolo, his favorite hit man.

Lieutenant Bixby and I tailed Niccolo everywhere, hoping to nail him—preferably before the hit. When he bought a ticket to Marvello's performance at the Rialto, Bixby and I found seats nearby.

"And now, ladies and gentlemen," announced Marvello, "before your very eyes a man will *change into a tiger!* I need a volunteer. You, sir, will you kindly mount the stage?"

He pointed to Niccolo! Anything could happen any second. Our attention riveted on the dark-browed hit man.

Assisted by scantily clad Babette, Niccolo entered a glass cage. She draped a black curtain around it. Marvello pronounced some mumbo-jumbo, and a cloud of pinkish smoke arose.

The audience involuntarily shuddered as blood-curdling shrieks came from the stage. Something was wrong! The lieutenant and I were there in moments, ripping aside the black curtain.

Inside the glass cage, a tiger was mauling the blood-spattered remains of Julius Niccolo. Harvey Wentworth (AKA Marvello the Magician) and Babette Lefleur had both disappeared—through a trap door, we discovered.

We're still looking for them, but not too hard.

THE THANKSGIVING WINDOW DISPLAY

The window displays at La Femme Department Store were the talk of the city, each more exciting and dramatic than the last. That was because Harold Freiheit, who designed and created the displays, took great pride in his work. The man was a genius—an unappreciated genius.

Rosamund Halliday, the store manager, was forever criticizing his productions. The situation reached a climax just before Thanksgiving.

Harold had re-created Norman Rockwell's familiar painting of the family happily gathered around the festive table. He considered it his masterpiece.

"Harold," said Rosamund sharply, "that mannequin heading the table won't help sales at all. Dress her in our new late fall line,"

"But, Miss Halliday," he protested, "that dress fits in with the spirit of the whole display. She's supposed to be the grandmother proudly serving her assembled family to celebrate. She's not some skinny debutante who's never cooked a turkey."

"Don't argue with me!" Rosamund retorted. "And for God's sake remove that stuffing from her front. Customers would think La Femme is catering to stout women. I'll give you half an hour to change it."

Seething and grumbling, Harold complied.

"Ah, that's *much* better," declared the manager.

Late that night the display was restored to its original form. Harold Freiheit went outside the store to check its appearance. "Almost perfect," he said to himself. "Rockwell would be proud of it. I really must change that floor-length tablecloth tomorrow. But for tonight, it conceals Miss Halliday's body quite well."

A SORDID DOMESTIC AFFAIR

Jake Bland shot his wife Sallie. Of that there was no question. Neighbors heard the loud arguing, then six shots. They immediately dialed 911. When I arrived he was standing over her body, sobbing and pulling the trigger on empty chambers...click...click...click. He was slightly drunk.

Bland offered no resistance when I disarmed him. I steered him into a chair and began questioning, "Why? Why did you do it? Why did you shoot your wife?"

His only response, mumbled over and over, was, "I trusted her. I trusted her."

I tried again. "Is this your revolver?"

Bland became aware he wasn't alone. "No. Not mine. Belongs to Alex."

Just then a tall man came into the room. "Who are you?" I asked.

"Alex Crenshaw. I'm a boarder here."

"Do you know what motive Mr. Bland had to murder his wife?"

"I suppose it's because I told him she was having an affair."

"Is that true?"

"Why would I lie, officer?"

"Tell me exactly what happened," I ordered.

"Well, Jake came home tipsy—not unusual for him on Friday night. I looked up from oilin' my revolver—you're holdin' it now—and told him, 'Sallie is runnin' around on you, Jake.' Then I went out."

"Leaving your revolver where?"

"On the table."

"Why, man? Didn't you suspect what he might do?"

Alex Crenshaw shrugged. "Frankly, I was gettin' tired of makin' love to Sallie...every day...every day...."

GHOST TO GHOST

As the train rumbled through the darkness, I read again the strange letter from my old classmate Gary Brandon: "David, old friend, if at all possible, come visit me on the night of Wednesday the 23rd. I've had a fearful experience I *must* share with you. Gary."

The train slowed, then, with a screeching protest of brakes, stopped at Chilham station. I alighted and set off on foot to the old Brandon home nearby. Parkinson, the elderly family butler, answered the door, looking ages older than when I last saw him.

"Come in, sir," he said in a strangely subdued voice. He took my valise and retired.

Gary suddenly appeared and we embraced. "So glad you came," he said, motioning toward chairs.

"What's this mystery?" I asked.

"Ghosts."

"Ghosts?"

"Yes, the ghosts of my mother Jessica and my late wife Daphne."

"That would be unsettling," I admitted.

"Unnerving, actually. My mother disclosed that my father Marvin murdered her."

"What did the—er—ghost of Daphne say?"

"She said she now understood that murder was inherited in males of the Brandon family, an uncontrollable trait. She forgave me for killing her."

I was shocked!

Parkinson re-entered the room. "Would you care to join the others, sir?" he whispered.

"Others?" I queried, turning to Gary for explanation, but he had vanished.

"Yes, sir, at the wake."

"Wake? Whose wake?"

Parkinson registered rare surprise, "Why, Mister Gary's, sir. He died Sunday, you know. Suicide. His funeral is tomorrow."

THE PERIL OF CIGARETTE SMOKING

I whispered to the nurse, "Is Mr. Kalinsky...you know?"

She whispered back, "Off the critical list. But make your visit brief. He's had a great shock." She pushed the door open gently.

The great movie director lay flat on the sterile-sheeted hospital bed, bandaged head to toe.

"Dmitri," I broke the silence, "'tis I, Cyril Montague, star of your *Passion in Paducah*. Remember?"

He stirred, mumbling somewhat through bandage, "Ah, Cyril. Never made the box-office history, that film. But my new production—*Duel in Dubuque*—now there is successful! I must be returning to direct it. With my genius...." He ended with a moan, but whether from pain or realization of necessary re-shooting, I could not determine.

Finally he resumed, "We approach the climax. Great scene! Specatacular in grade-B way. The heroine Wilma with two—*two* yet!—lovers can't making up the mind between Percy and Orville. They fight the duel. Gigantic suspense! Naturally I load pistols with black powder—not bullets, since they have two-year contracts. For instant retakes I have more black powder in open keg."

"Excuse me, Dmitri," I said. "I can't stay long. What happened?"

"Friend Cyril, former star of silver screen, it was cigarettes. Sonja, my third wife—maybe my fourth—she is warning me of danger smoking. But do I listen? No, I do not listen.

"During big duel scene—already I'm telling about it—I light up cigarette. Toss match, which lands in powder keg. BOOM! Colossal!"

BLACKMAIL, ETERNAL BLACKMAIL

When the mousy little man answered his knocking, Arlo Bruckner, the famous mystery writer, said "You're certain your wife's away?"

"Oh, yes," replied Nathan Sobell, "Justine's gone to another damned computer exhibit. She keeps me broke buying latest model computers, hardware, software—you name it. Look at all this junk! The house is overflowing. You did bring the payment?"

"Yes. But this continuing blackmail keeps me poor."

"Not really, Mr. Bruckner. Your latest book made bestseller lists. And we wouldn't want your adoring public to learn you plagarized your first novel from an obscure work, would we?" The little man laughed nastily. "But I'll forget everything if you'll find a safe way to murder my wife."

"Now, just a minute, Mr. Sobell—"

"Just hear me out. You've seen Justine?"

"Only from a distance."

"Fat, repulsive, chain smoker. I only married her for money to start my business. Well?"

Arlo Bruckner suggested a poison he'd read about. "Good luck, Mr. Sobell," he said in parting.

The next day Justine Sobell waddled into Bruckner's home unannounced.

"Get out! Immediately!" he demanded.

"Calm yourself, dearie. Tape recorders are useful, despite what my late husband thought."

"*L-l-late* husband?"

"Yes, Nathan died from the very poison you suggested. Incidentally, copies of your recorded conversation are deposited with trustworthy friends—just insurance, y'know."

"Wh-wh-what do you want?"

"I'm a *very* lonely widow. Now, by moving your word processor, sweetie, we'll have room for my new computer setup...."

THE MYSTERIOUS VISITOR IN THE NIGHTTIME

Melissa stared at the white ceiling. "The man is tall—about as tall as my husband—and simply stands there in my bedroom. I know it's impossible, doctor. That's why I'm seeing you."

"This—er—experience, Mrs. Arden," said Dr. Ballinger cautiously, "you say only occurs when Mr. Arden is away?"

"That's right. Peter doesn't understand it either. He installed locks on my bedroom door and put alarms on the windows. Nobody, he assures me, could possibly get in. Yet, whenever he's away, the stranger returns."

"Any special feature about your visitor?"

"Nothing. His face is somehow veiled. That's the frightening part."

"I'll be perfectly frank, Mrs. Arden. You suffer from deep anxieties, ingrained fears. This will take time."

Melissa made an appointment for the following Tuesday and departed.

As Peter left, he said, "Sorry about this important trip, sweetheart. Keep calm...relax."

Melissa purchased a revolver and kept it loaded under her pillow. *No,* she assured herself, *I'm* not *imagining. I'm* not *insane.*

That night she awoke. The figure was standing there again. She drew the revolver and fired. As it collapsed, she switched on the light. Leaping from bed, she yanked off the silk mask.

"Peter!" she screamed. "WHY?"

"Needed your money...love another woman...." he mumbled. Melissa fired again.

"Doctor," Melissa confided, "like I told police, that stranger returned. In the darkness and confusion, Peter was shot with my gun. The stranger fled, leaving behind his mask. I'm *certain* he's gone...forever."

ESCAPE FROM HADES ISLAND

No one ever escaped from Hades Island. Even if an escapee made it across the crocodile-infested river and into the jungle, natives would return him for trinkets. Sentence to "exile" was sentence to death—a slow, agonizing death.

Barefoot in dungarees, under blistering sun or torrential downpour, we prisoners labored to build the road that led nowhere. It was the brainchild of Commandant Lemoine. Breaking rocks in the quarry, toting baskets of rubble on bare backs, and pounding the road level, always under watchful eyes of armed guards—it broke men's spirits as well as bodies. And when the road reached the perimeter of the compound, it was dismantled, stone by stone, and another road started.

Men died each day, their numbers dutifully recorded; replacements arrived on the next ship.

Commandant Lemoine delighted in tormenting me, probably because I was better educated. He came to my cell that night. "Tomorrow, Henri D'Estang, I leave this beautiful island to you," he taunted. "I am being promoted home."

In desperation I throttled him, cleaned up, and donned his spotless uniform, Fortunately, he was also slender, and we looked much alike. I recorded the death of "Henri D'Estang," then fed Lemoine's body to the crocodiles.

The ship docked. An official greeted me, "Congratulations, M. Lemoine, on your promotion! One trifling detail: we need to verify your fingerprints."

"Sir," I said quickly, "with regret I decline the promotion, I desire to improve administration here on Hades Island."

So, here I remain. Forever.

FRED AND ERNIE, PRIVATE EYES

"This here's a purty posh neighborhood, Fred. I ain't up to no second-story job."

"Quiet, Ernie. I'm on a case."

"You mean a six-pack?"

"No, no, a criminal case. I've been reading detective stories. They always involve prominent folks—dukes and stuff."

"Who?"

"In this instance, very rich people—that's what counts. See this newspaper?" Fred moved under a streetlamp. "That fat dame who's *reportedly* vacationing in Paris is Daphne, wife of Doctor Cecil Widmore, world-famous plastic surgeon."

"What kinda plastic, Fred?"

"That just means he changes people's faces."

"So why are we standin' here past midnight?"

"I've been observing their mansion with keen insight. You noticed Daphne Widmore when she got outta the taxi and went inside?"

"Yeah, some babe!"

"Now you're catching on, Ernie. She's no longer fat and she's much better looking. *He's changed her appearance completely!* We wonder why."

"We do?"

"Exactly. They are doubtless hatching some nefarious plot. Peek in yonder window, Ernie."

"Gee, Fred, whatever 'nefarious' means, they're sure doin' it."

"Aha! 'Tis time to unmask their insidious machinations."

Fred rang the doorbell insistently. The man who finally answered, clutching his bathrobe, growled, "What is it?"

"Your little ruse didn't succeed, doctor. We know *everything!*"

"I see. Step inside. Perhaps we can reach an understanding."

Later, as Fred handed Ernie half the $500, he said, "Remember our solemn oath not to reveal the good doctor's surgical miracle. He's restoring Mrs. Widmore to her original form next week."

THE HONOURABLE SHAKESPEAREAN GHOST

My old friends George and Mildred Oakshott invited me for the weekend to their pre-Victorian thatched cottage near Stratford-on-Avon. After dinner my hostess remarked, "Our home is haunted, you know."

"Indeed!" I said, "I'd like to meet your ghost."

"You undoubtedly will," laughed Mildred. "You two should have much in common. He was also a Shakespearean actor. He claims he was William Shakespeare's closest friend. His name is Cyril Hartsworth. Unfortunately, the only portrait of him was painted after his tragedy. George, show our guest the portrait."

He arose and drew aside the black velvet curtain, revealing the most horrifying, grotesque face ever seen.

"Poor devil!" I involuntarily gasped. "What happened to him?"

"During a performance of *Hamlet*, the theater caught fire. Poor Cyril was terribly burned. A friend secretly painted him during his convalescence. Upon recovery, Cyril saw his reflection and called for a mask. 'Nevermore let mortal man see my face,' he declared."

I retired highly excited. At midnight, a shrouded figure appeared. In a hollow, resonant voice it began, "To be or not to be—"

"—that is the question," I continued. Together the ghost and I recited the rest of the soliloquy.

"Excellent!" he laughed, and tossed back his cowl. *It was the ghastly, scarred face of the portrait!*

Recovering my speech, I said, "Cyril, old boy, you were undoubtedly a great actor, but you lied about not revealing your face to mortal man."

My eerie visitor recoiled. "Sire," he declared, "I am an honourable gentleman. Did you not realize you died one minute erenow?"

GENEROSITY

As I travel across this great nation, I gather background for my new book: *America—Land of Eternal Opportunity.* It is in the small towns, I've discovered, where the pioneer spirit still flourishes in neighborliness and generosity.

One Saturday morning, I found myself in Turnip Center, Michigan, population 1,834. A horde of children—possibly a hundred—flocked into Churchman's Chocolate Shop. The gilt sign in the window advertised "Gold Flake."

On a wrought-iron bench in the park opposite sat a white-bearded old gentleman. I remarked to him, "Mr. Churchman's Gold Flake candy bars seem very popular."

"Yep," he responded. "Lots of sugar in 'em."

"Those kiddies must save their little earnings all week for this special treat."

"Nope. It's all free today."

"How generous of Mr. Churchman," I declared, "sharing his bounty with the future generation."

The old man eyed me quizzically. "You must be a stranger hereabouts. Old Churchman never gave nothin' away. Every Sattiday all those sugary Gold Flake candy bars is paid for by Harley Fillmore."

"Oh? Then Mr. Fillmore is the benefactor. He must love children."

"Doan' rightly know about thet, mister," my informant drawled. "I'd reckon it's a matter o' plannin' fer the future."

"*Now* I understand! Mr. Fillmore is building good will throughout the community. An admirable American tradition! I hope his generosity will ultimately yield well deserved rewards."

"I'm purty shore it will."

"Incidentally, what business is he in?" I inquired.

"Don' you know? He's the town dentist."

JOURNALISM IN COYOTE CROSSING

Even with my degree in journalism, jobs were scarce that year. I was thankful to land a position on the Coyote Crossing *Chronicle*. The crusty old editor, Martin Dingley, pointed to a newspaper: "This here's a editorial in the *Coyote Bugle*, our rival newspaper. Write our reply."

I read: "The demented editor of that worthless blab, the *Chronicle*, suggests stupid civic improvements which anybody with sense of an idiot prairie dog knows is hogwash..."

I inquired all around town, "Who is this Ebenezer Klinger who edits the *Bugle*?"

Nobody knew. "Must be some dingbat furriner," people suggested. Nevertheless, I discovered that every household in Coyote Crossing subscribed to both newspapers.

I drafted an editorial response: "The editor of the *Bugle* has nothing to gain by his slanderous statements against Mr. Dingley. Has anyone actually seen Mr. Klinger? He hides behind anonymity..."

Old Martin Dingley read my editorial and snorted. "Too blasted tame!" he declared. "Start out: 'That polluted polecat Klinger has gone too danged far. When I catch that disease-ridden galoot, I'll publicly horsewhip him—after slicing off his ears...' There, thet oughta git attention."

"Shall I actually print *that*?" I was aghast.

"Of course! Knock down thet type I set up to print the *Bugle* and git started."

Suddenly, it dawned on me. "You—you're also Ebenezer Klinger!"

"Right, sonny."

"Why the two identities, sir?"

"Young feller, nobody kin make a livin' in Coyote Crossin' publishin' jest *one* newspaper. But with *two*, we stand a chance—long as we give our readers the news."

"WE CAN MAKE A DEAL"

Edward Higgins declared to the FBI agent, "Actually, sir, I'm glad you caught me."

"Well," said Agent Ball, "when Mr. Simpson at Federal Savings Bank reported the $50,000 shortage and linked it to you, I had no choice. Where's the money?"

"All gone."

"Where? You haven't spent it on anything here—cheap room, junk furniture, no car—what happened to $50,000?"

"It's been this way all my life. Years ago I embezzled $2,000 from the Farmers' Loan. The manager said, 'Higgins, we can make a deal—$150 a month and I'll give you an excellent recommendation to the Co-op Trust.'

"So, I started at Co-op. Soon I needed money to keep paying the Farmers' Loan manager. I took $10,000 from Co-op. The president found out. 'Higgins,' he said, 'we can make a deal—$500 a month and a good recommendation to Lake Trust.'

"Same story there. Paying off both the Farmers' manager and the Co-op president, my money ran out. I embezzled $20,000 from Lake Trust. I was found out, of course, and the manager said, 'Higgins, we can make a deal—$1,000 a month and I'll recommend you to the Federal Savings Bank.'

"Now, Mr. Ball, I'm ready for the handcuffs. Prison will be a relief from all my worries."

"Funny you should mention prison, Mr. Higgins. I discussed your case with Mr. Simpson. I think we three can make a deal—"

At that point, Edward Higgins attacked the FBI agent with his bare hands.

THAT TROUBLE ON BALDWIN STREET

Our neighborhood may never be the same. It began that overcast windy afternoon when old Miss Perkins let her kitten out and Jonathan Carruthers was walking his huge hound. The hound broke away to chase the kitten, which found refuge by clawing its way up onto the head of Sam Wilson, who was smoking a fresh cigar while accompanying Mrs. Wilson on her way downtown. The kitten dislodged Sam's hat and glasses. His hat blew down the street and Mrs. Wilson gave chase.

Meanwhile, Wilson, near-sighted without his glasses, retrieved what he thought was his cigar—only to discover it *definitely* was not a cigar. In disgust, he flung it away. It sailed through the open window of Will Jameson's car as he drove by, landing smack in his face. Enraged, Jameson braked his car and jumped out, just as Mrs. Wilson returned breathless with her husband's crushed hat.

"I'll fix you!" shouted Jameson, advancing menacingly. Thinking he meant to attack her, Elvira Wilson yelped, "Help! Rape!"

From down the street Dave Hawkins heard Mrs. Wilson's agitated screams. Rushing to her aid, he floored Jameson. Shaking his head groggily, Jameson staggered to his feet to retaliate.

Sam Wilson, confused by all the activity, got down on all fours, groping for his lost glasses. Elderly Miss Perkins, out searching for her kitten, spotted Sam down below.

"Pervert!" she screeched. "Trying to peek under my dress!" She drubbed him with her umbrella.

Then police arrived....

THE SUICIDE ON PEACH STREET

The Atlanta chief of police thrust his head in the office door of officer Montague Guinard. "Quick," he said, "I just got a report of a man threatening to kill himself in the 800 block of Peach Street! You've had special training in suicide prevention. Take a squad car and get there as fast as possible!"

No question where the potential suicide was: a crowd had gathered on the sidewalk in front of the Southern Life & Casualty Company, their necks craned upward. Guinard braked the patrol car and jumped out. There above, teetering uncertainly on the tenth floor ledge, was a middle aged man in shirt sleeves.

Guinard ordered the crowd back, and they grudgingly complied. Then he raced inside to the elevator, punched "10," and hoped he wasn't too late. Flinging upon the door of the nearest office, he dashed to the open window and leaned out.

"Ah'm just heah to help," he drawled soothingly.

"Don't need no help," the man snapped.

"Befo' y'all do somethin' drastic, think of yo' deah ol' mothah."

"I'm an orphan."

"Then considah yo' lovely wife."

"Ain't married."

"Yo' girlfriend then. She'd cry her lil' heart out. Might nevah recovah."

"I hate women!"

Nearing his wits' end, Guinard said, "At least considah yo' great heritage from Robert E. Lee an' Jeffahson Davis."

"Who are they?" the man asked.

As a true Southerner, Montague Guinard was aghast. "Okay!" he yelled. "Go ahaid an' jump, ya damned Yankee!"

THE VAMPIRE LEGEND

An aura of mystery surrounded Vladimir D'Aracule. He was uncommonly handsome, except for his elongated canine teeth. He frequented my favorite restaurant, so inevitably we struck up a friendship.

I was surprised to see him dining there with Michelle Delaney, the rich heiress. She'd be beautiful as her press photographs, were it not for two pink blemishes on her neck.

Later I mentioned it to Vladimir. "Yes," he said, "she's giving me $2,000,000 for my research into legends."

"Like myths?" I jested.

"No, legends always have some basis. Take my family back in Transylvania. Every male develops long pointed canines. Hence, the vampire legend."

"You could consult a dentist," I suggested.

"Deny my heritage? No, thanks. Incidentally, if you're not busy this week, let's fly up to my cabin for some fishing."

"Sounds great!" I agreed.

Vladimir piloted his own pontoon plane, setting it down on a remote lake. Fishing was great, and the cabin comfortable.

Next morning I awoke to delicious smells of bacon and coffee. "Sleep well?" Vladimir inquired.

"Quite well. I didn't even wake when apparently two mosquitoes bit my neck. Very generous of you to invite me. Actually, I suddenly feel we're brothers under the skin."

He laughed, "An excellent simile. Indeed we are—now. Next, I'll teach you flying."

"But," I protested, "I've never handled a plane."

"That doesn't matter," Vladimir declared solemnly. "By the time we return, you'll be able to fly like a bat out of hell."

A CHRISTMAS BLESSING

In Travelers' Rest, somewhat less than a two-star hotel, old Ernest Grogan was janitor-repairman-bellhop. Unexpectedly, his boss, hotel manager Harry Fiegel, said, "Here's twenty-five bucks for Christmas, Ernie. Gonna get drunk?"

"No, sirree. I'm gonna buy toys!" Ernest blurted, immediately regretting his confession.

"*Toys?*" Fiegel laughed uncertainly. "For *yourself?*"

Embarrassed, Ernest replied, "Naw, fer my sister's grandkids." Why had he lied? he wondered. He had no living relatives. Actually, he'd become fascinated by the window display at nearby Second-Hand Toys, Inc. With Christmas approaching, he wanted to give somebody *something.* Toys he could afford.

"Okay," said Fiegel, "take the afternoon off. No guests comin' in this gawdawful snowstorm."

Tossing on his overcoat and galoshes, Ernest hurried to the toy store. He purchased a rag doll, nearly complete Lego set, a battered fire engine, and a dozen other items.

He stopped a couple with children. "A doll for your little girl?"

"Stolen merchandise, no doubt," the woman declared. "Get lost!"

The next mother screeched, "Don't touch it, Marylou! Probably loaded with germs!"

On Ernest trudged. Encountering a young mother with two small children, all shabbily dressed, he inquired hopefully, "Would you like some Christmas toys?"

"Bless you!" the woman exclaimed. "You *are* Christmas!"

"Take 'em all, ma'am."

His heart exhilarated. Through cold and slush Ernest headed home. He didn't make it.

Paramedics arrived. One tried reviving the old man. His buddy asked, "What's he mumbling?"

"Sounds like, 'She actually *blessed* me!' . . . It won't matter. The guy just died."

THE HERO OF THE PURPLE PALACE DISASTER

With a family name like Thigwhiff, you'd expect tracing your genealogy to be easy. Actually, I found it quite the opposite. Then I came across a reference to the "Thigwhiffs of Talladaga County, Alabama." I headed south.

In Whippoorwill Junction, I discovered a statue in the village park identified as that of "Jefferson Thigwhiff, 1898-1931, Hero of the Purple Palace Disaster." I was ecstatic!

Asking around, I located his younger sister Amybelle, now a dignified old lady, who said he was my great-grandfather's brother. "Please, ma'am," I pleaded, "what was his role in this 'Purple Palace Disaster'?"

"Jeffahson was an enterprisin' young blade," she reminisced. "He owned a paddlewheel boat on the Coosa Rivah, the Purple Palace, an elegant little restaurant caterin' to aristocratic gentlemen and their ladies. Fyah broke out, but Jeffahson bravely stayed aboa'd 'til every customah was safely off. Cost him his life, po' boy."

Later I interviewed elderly Carolina Bufont, whose version was somewhat different. "Jeff Thigwhiff? Remembah him *quite* well. Ah was one of the gals servin' drinks on his floatin' casino in the Coosa Rivah. Handsome devil—but snaky! Jeff fleeced every yokel within miles. He stahted thet fyah fo' the insurance, and quickly sold twenty seats in the only life boat at $10,000 each. Trouble was, the leaky lifeboat held only six. Lucky people jumped ovahboa'd.

"Yes, honeychile, Jeff died in thet fyah—tryin' to salvage illegal whiskey stowed below decks...."

Suddenly I realized why my family had never mentioned Uncle Jefferson.

THE GREAT GIOVANNI BELLACCIO

Only the presence of uniformed Nazionale Carabinieri kept the infuriated villagers from attacking the man.

The local priest stepped forward. "Why, pray, do you desecrate the bust of the great Giovanni Bellaccio?" he asked angrily.

"*Per favore*, Father," said the man holding the hammer and chisel, "I am Guiseppe Farazoni, Curator of Sicilian National Treasures. You believe Giovanni Bellaccio was great?"

"*Certamente!*" replied the priest. "With his own hands he sculpted the cherubs in our humble cathedral. Facing death, he created this likeness of himself, fired and glazed it with his last bit of strength, and presented it to our village of Carrubamonte. How can you have the audacity to destroy the image of such a man?"

"Begging your pardon, good Father," replied Farazoni, "but I must disillusion you—"

"Beware! It is sinful to speak ill of the dead!"

"Let me explain. *Dite la verita*, Giovanni Bellaccio did have a little artistic talent, not much. He was an art thief. His plan was to steal a statue, coat it with clay, and sculpt in a different facial expression. Then he fired and glazed it, passing it off as his totally original work.

"This bust of himself, we had excellent reason to suspect actually enclosed the fragmentary ancient Greek statue known as the Nymph of Cefalu, which was stolen from the Palermo Art Museum.

"As plainly evident, the parts of the nymph I have already exposed definitely did *not* belong to Giovanni Bellaccio."

JOURNALISM IN WOLFBRIDGE

The Depression gripped the nation the year I graduated in journalism from State College. I'd started looking for a job with high hopes, but I was becoming desperate. Finally one editor said, "No jobs here—but you might try the *Journal* over in Wolfbridge. Old Jethro Trumbull can teach you real journalism."

I caught the next train to Wolfbridge. I found Mr. Trumbull with muddy boots propped on his desk, meticulously oiling his six-gun. "I really need a job," I told him.

He looked up. "Read and write purty good?"

"Why, yes, sir," I answered.

"Fine! Git acquainted with everybody hereabouts. Come back tomorrow."

When I returned next morning, Trumbull growled, "Read this tripe, writ by thet no-account polecat Abner Garson, editor of the Wolfbridge *Chronicle*, our rival newspaper."

The article began, "The editor of the Wolfbridge *Journal*, that worthless rumor-mongering rag, proposes our fair city should install expensive and unnecessary gaslights. Naturally our intelligent readers know what an inveterate hypocrite that scoundrel has become since he developed diseases of mind as well as body...."

"Why, sir, that's grounds for libel!" I declared. "Aren't you going to sue?"

"Nope. Now, proofread the headlines fer our evenin' edition."

I read:

EDITOR OF CHRONICLE SLAIN!

BULLET-RIDDEN BODY DISCOVERED IN OFFICE

Sheriff Seeks Killer

"But, sir," I protested, "Mr. Garson just walked past the window. That headline can't be right."

"Don' fret, sonny," he said. "By the time we git it printed, I'll make sartin the story's correct—every dang-blasted detail!"

THE DOWNFALL OF SIR HENRY

The butler coughed discreetly. "That person is back, m'lord. Shall I send her away?"

Sir Henry Farthingale grew livid. "Bertha! That damned persistent sister-in-law of mine! I'll go to the door, Jefferson."

The heavyset woman on the mansion's doorstep was flanked by a dark-complected girl and the constable. "Well, Henry," she said loudly, "are you going to let us search for my sister's body?"

"I've already told you," he bellowed, "she left me! Who's that gypsy waif?"

Bertha protectively drew the large-eyed girl to her. "Madina is clairvoyant. She *knows* Alice is buried nearby."

"Hah!" declared Sir Henry triumphantly. "My friend, Judge Wilberforce, will *never* issue a warrant for you to invade my home."

Meek little Constable Clives spoke. "Oh no, Sir Henry, we wouldn't do that. No. But could we dig a mite down by your lily pond?"

Farthingale snorted. "As much as you like. Dig to China, for all I care!" He slammed the heavy oak door.

Jefferson returned. "M'lord," he said deferentially, "knowing how anxious you've become, I took the liberty of moving our little, ah, *secret* from the basement—"

"Where, dammit, where?" shouted Sir Henry.

But he knew the answer. Dashing out onto the sloping lawn, he gazed down at the circle of lantern-light. He heard the ominous thunk of spade in soil and the clink of metal upon metal.

The soft voice of Constable Clives floated uphill. "There's Sir Henry's rook rifle...and I do believe there's a long wooden box below it...."

ACT ONE OF "REVELATIONS"

Like other summer visitors, I'd come to Julie's Cove to relax. I was dozing under a beach umbrella on the veranda of the Lobster Inn when voices awoke me. Two others had taken seats under nearby umbrellas.

"Daddy," said the young woman crossly, "I don't care if you've rented rooms for the week. I'm returning to New York *now!*"

"Why?" her father asked. "I thought you and young Ronald Worthington were having a fine time dating."

"It was that play—Revelations—in the old Shipwreck Theater. Soon as Ron and I were seated, I excused myself to visit the ladies' room. Too much lemonade at lunch. That old building is a labyrinth, its twisty hallways crammed with discarded theater props."

"Then what, precious?"

"I finally found it. The stalls had no doors! I spoke to the maid mopping, 'Damn, doesn't this dump offer any privacy?' She fled in confusion. I used the facility, adjusted my makeup in the cracked mirror, and returned."

"So why are you so upset?"

"I finally groped my way back and asked Ron, 'What's the plot so far?'

"He just sat there grinning! 'Oh,' he said, 'the scene was the ladies' room in a rundown hotel. A maid was mopping when some young woman wearing a dress *exactly like yours* barged in and complained about privacy in the stalls. The maid left. After using the facility, the young woman fixed her makeup in the mirror and walked offstage.'

"Damn Ron! He could've yelled to warn me!"

THE TRIALS AND TRIBULATIONS OF SANTA CLAUS

If you've never been the Santa Claus in a department store, take my advice: don't even consider it. It could ruin your Christmases yet to come.

It wasn't that I needed the money; I just wanted an opportunity to spread happiness among little children. Thus, I became Santa in Dalton's department store. Oh, joy.

The wooly red outfit over my regular clothes was steamy hot. Somehow, between the pillow stuffed inside and the squirming of youngsters on my lap, my zipper slid down. When nobody was looking, I bent over to correct the situation.

Unfortunately, my beard got caught in the zipper. I straightened up without it. "Look, Daddy," exclaimed one observant little tyke, "Santa lost his face!"

I leaned over again, untangled my beard, and was adjusting that confounded zipper, when O'Leary, the store detective, barged up, bellowing, "I don't care if you are Santa Claus, you can't do *that* in public!"

Finally, I placated O'Leary, who walked away still suspicious. Then a small boy rushed up and viciously kicked my shins, shouting, "See, momma, he *is* real!"

"Lady," I yelled, "control your damned brat!"

His momma declared, "I'm summoning the manager!"

She didn't have to. Hearing the commotion, he came running. "Apologize! IMMEDIATELY!"

"Go to hell," I retorted. "I quit!" Shocked parents covered their offsprings' ears.

Storming out of the store, I shucked off the Santa outfit, tossing it into the gutter. Whereupon a nearby patrolman gave me a $25 ticket for littering.

Scrooge was right. Humbug!

SANTA GETS HIS HEART'S DESIRE (?)

Soon as his eyes adjusted to the very dim light inside Jo-Jo's restaurant, Freddie spotted her. A lady with class! She sat in a far corner, dark eyes, shoulder-length black hair, low-cut blue silk dress. He strolled over. "Mind if I join you?"

"Oh, please do," her throaty voice replied. They fell into conversation.

Every night they met there, Annetta and Freddie. She shyly held his hand.

Christmas was approaching. Freddie wanted to impress this lady. His salary as a clerk wasn't nearly enough.

Wearing a rented Santa outfit, he roamed the streets. A bright neon sign—Nicky's Place—beckoned. Freddie entered the crowded bar waving a toy pistol. "Gimme your money! Nobody gets hurt!"

The bartender, a hulking gorilla, knocked the pistol flying.

He dragged Freddie, beard askew, into the back room. A woman counting cash there glanced up.

"Freddie!" she gasped. "You're Santa Claus!" He looked closer. It was Annetta!

She spoke to the bartender, "He's the guy I told you about, daddy. The Organization could use a smooth-talking dude like him."

"Great! The boys'll arrange the weddin'. Frankly, Annie, I never thought at your age you'd land another husband. Let's hope he don't end up like the last one."

"Last one?" Freddie gulped.

"Yeah, tried to run out on her. Didn't get far."

"Oh, I'm so happy!" exclaimed Annetta, advancing, arms extended. In the harsh light Freddie noticed, for the first time, her facial wrinkles, her sagging neck, her smeared mascara, the gray roots of her dyed hair....

TAKE TWO ASPIRIN

It was not a good neighborhood to be walking a beat at night, thought Patrolman Tim O'Connell, even though he knew most of the residents. At the corner, the Salvation Army man disconsolately rang his bell now and then, warily guarding the few coins in his kettle. It was almost Christmas.

A disturbance in Klepstein's Drugs caught O'Connell's attention. Behind the faded "SALE ENDS TOMORROW" sign, Otto Klepstein held a small crying boy by the ear.

"What's goin' on here?" demanded the patrolman

"What's goin' on?" repeated Klepstein. "I'll tell you what! This little thief came in with a few pennies askin' to buy two aspirin. *Two!* Naturally I said no. Then when my back was turned, he swipes a bottle, opens it, and takes out two tablets. Here's the bottle for proof!"

O'Connell looked down at the boy. "Jimmy Viachi, ain't it? Why did you want two aspirin, Jimmy?"

The boy stopped sniveling. "The social worker, she tole my mama, 'Take two aspirin,' I didn' have enuff money (sniff) fer a whole bottle."

O'Connell turned to Klepstein. "Missus Viachi *is* sick. I think we can let him go. I'll pay fer the bottle meself."

"NO!" argued the druggist. "He's got to be made an example. I insist! Arrest this boy!"

"I see you're puttin' the bottle back on the shelf," observed O'Connell.

"Of course," snorted the store owner. "In this neighborhood, who can count?"

"Then I'm arrestin' you, Otto Klepstein, for violatin' laws regardin' fraud-u-lent merchandise. You have the right...."

ATWATER'S LITTLE CHERUB

My current partner and I were sitting at our usual park bench. "Look at this, Iggy," I said, pointing to my opened newspaper.

"Hey," snorted Iggy, "that's just a pitcher of some stone statchoo of a nekkid kid."

"Ah, but you haven't read what it says," I retorted. "This particular miniature statue is owned by millionaire collector Cyrus P. Atwater. It was sculpted by Bernini and thought to have been one of a pair. Anyhow, Atwater offers $1,000,000 for discovery of the missing mate to his cherub."

"We ain't got no missin' cherub," declared Iggy, "so fergit it." For all his lock-picking wizardry, my partner lacks ingenuity.

"Who knows but what that long-lost marble cherub presently resides right here in New York?"

"Fat chance," snickered Iggy.

"Enough of our penny-ante midnight capers," I told him, "We're going big time." I explained my plan....

Two days later we loitered outside the Waldorf, where Atwater dined daily. He emerged finally and we approached him. Stealthily, I unwrapped the statue.

His eyes popped. "Amazing!" he exclaimed. "Wherever did you find it?"

"Our secret," I whispered. "We already have an offer—"

"I'll pay $1,000,000—immediately!" he shouted.

Together we went to his bank. Iggy and I departed with the money in cash. Atwater waltzed away, overjoyed with the marble cherub.

Iggy and I immediately caught a taxi to the airport. That wasn't the mate to Atwater's cherub; we'd stolen the original from his mansion the night before.

THE UNIQUE GIFT FROM EGYPT

My husband and I were returning from our vacation. Suddenly he dropped the suitcases and groaned. "Oh no! It's that brother-in-law of mine again. What other damned screwball would stack sharp-edged boulders around my new lily-and-goldfish pond?"

"Calm down, Philip," I told him. "Sure, Randy's eccentric and unpredictable, but he has a heart of gold. You embarrassed him so much about his painting your pool table purple that he promised to bring you something unique from Egypt."

Philip was boiling mad. "To hell with Egypt *and* your stupid brother. That moron! I'm going right out there and move every blasted boulder if it kills me."

In a way it did. I never saw Philip again—not ever.

Randy came around the next day, bubbling over, oblivious to my anxiety. "Did Philip like my present?" he asked. "I took great care so it would be here to greet him."

"Randy," I said gently, "Philip's disappeared. The p-police are searching everywhere. He'd just gone outside and moved a couple of those boulders from around his p-p-pond and—vanished." I started crying again.

"Oh no!" my brother exclaimed.

"What is it?"

"My present. Now it's probably wandered off, and Philip won't ever get to enjoy it. I'm sure he'd get real close to it."

"What present are you talking about, Randy?"

"The biggest crocodile ever captured from the Nile! Over twenty feet long! Oh, we'll find it somehow. Philip will simply *love* it."

A MEMORABLE CHRISTMAS PAGEANT

'Twas a Christmas pageant the congregation of Bethel Church won't *never* forgit. It started traditional-like: candles lit, Xeroxed programs rustlin', a few babies frettin'. The primary choir filed in, one trippin' on his robe, and launched a quavery "Oh Litt-tull Town of Bethl—"

Just then four white-sheeted figgers rose up in the loft. They wasn't angels. The one wavin' the gun yelled down, "NOBODY GONNA GIT HURT! HEV YORE MONEY READY!" They scrambled down the stairs to start their Christmas collection.

Pan-dee-*monium* broke out! Some people milled in the aisle, others clumb over pews. One robber fired his gun inta the ceiling fer attention. But the shot and fallin' plaster only made the women-folk scream louder. Children wailed.

"'Tain't gonna work," another robber muttered, makin' fer the door. A lotta people barred his way.

Nothin' is quite clear after that. They say the first was K.O.ed by a Wise Man (Heinrich Koch, our butcher)—one blow. The second accidental' knocked over a candle, settin' his sheet afire; those nearby stomped out the blaze and him, too. As fer the third, Mother Mary grabbed the Baby Jesus doll and clobbered him. The last one *almost* got away—but a Shepherd tripped him with his trusty crook.

After police come and hauled the bad guys away, we revived old Mrs. Jenkins, who said, "They oughta use the King James version."

By that time, 'twas *so* late we postponed the pageant, blowed out the candles, and wished one another "Merry Christmas!"

A DAY IN THE LIFE OF AN ARSONIST

"This is your last chance, Fireball," growls Big Man Manusco. "Don't flub this one, like when you burned down the wrong warehouse."

"Oh, I'll pay close attention," I promise. "What's the job?"

"Harry Milburn wants his plants blasted and torched. It's gotta be tonight, 'cause his insurance runs out tomorrow."

"Harry Milburn. Got it, boss."

"Okay. Take my car. The dynamite's in the trunk."

"I'm on my way!"

I drive Big Man's new Cadillac real careful, fill the gasoline cans, and ease 'em beside the back seat. Then I look up Harry Milburn in the telephone directory. 942 Melrose Place. I drive over to case it. Lotsa people goin' in and out.

I ask somebody, "What's happenin'?"

"Oh," the guy says, "Mrs. Milburn is holding open house to show off the exotic plants in her garden shed,"

Milburn—plants—everything fits.

That night I'm back. One sticka dynamite's plenty. I douse the shed, light the fuse, and scram.

BLOOEY! The whole wall blows out along with Mrs. Milburn's exotic whatevers.

Suddenly I wonder, why all that extra dynamite? Then it hits me. Big Man musta meant the *Milburn Manufacturing Plants* down by the waterfront. Still plentya time—if there's enough gasoline left. I open the Cadillac's rear door and light a match to see.

WHOOSH! I land thirty feet away and the car's a ragin' inferno. Then it explodes—KABOOM!! Cadillac pieces everywhere!

Quick! Know any opening for an arsonist in Mexico? Morocco? Manchuria?

THE NEWS FROM BEECHBURG

The Beechburg news center isn't a building; it's the low board fence separating the back yards of Elvira Perkins and Minnie Huddle, over which these two intrepid investigators verbally record latest village news.

Monday, 09:20. (Both reporters have hung out their weekly wash.)

ELVIRA: I noticed Maria Simpson tearing down her OPEN HOUSE signs yesterday.

MINNIE: Yes, she cancelled it. The state offered to buy her property for the new highway.

ELVIRA: That woman's absolutely naive. *Things* go on right behind her back.

MINNIE: She shoulda suspected *why* her husband Harold installed that expensive sofa in their garden shed. He wasn't planting petunias!

ELVIRA: Harold left town last Thursday. Probably lining up another you-know-what.

MINNIE: No doubt!

Tuesday, 11:15. (Both reporters have completed ironing.)

ELVIRA: Maria loaded most of her furniture into a big U-Haul and headed east.

MINNIE: State workmen stored dynamite in all her buildings. They must plan to level the place.

Wednesday, 20:30. (Reporters have finished dinner dishes.)

MINNIE: Harold's home. Just parked his car in the garage.

ELVIRA: Didn't he notice the wiring for the demolition?

MINNIE: He wasn't seeing anything but that sexy blonde he brought back.

Thursday, 04:45. Special Communiqué.

ELVIRA: It was horrible! The explosion blew Harold and his girlfriend over the fence!

MINNIE: I ran right over. Both lay there stunned—naked as jaybirds! Maria must feel terrible, returning home in the dark and accidentally connecting all those wires.

ELVIRA: The poor dear is devastated! Let's bake her some cookies.

111

TIMES CHANGE

A heavy downpour drenched all Rome. Nevertheless, Maria waited patiently under her umbrella at the old meeting place, halfway up the stone steps to the Trinita di Monti. Today was the day Giuseppe would be released from prison, and she dared not be late.

He approached slowly under a large umbrella he'd stolen somewhere that morning. His hair, she noted, had turned white and his face was now wrinkled. "How was it?" she asked sympathetically.

"Real hell without newspapers or radio," he growled. "But I had fifty years to plan our big heist."

"What, exactly?"

"Rob Rome's biggest bank! Get a million lire!"

"Lire are no good. Italian money is now euro dollars."

"Oh? Well, whatever. We start by swiping a couple fast horses off the street—"

"Wait! All fast horses are now at racetracks, well guarded. Everybody has an automobile nowadays."

"Okay, so we swipe an automobile."

"A couple problems, Giuseppe. First, people guard their automobiles with unbreakable steering wheel locks and burglar alarms—"

"But *someone* must get careless. What's the second problem?"

"Neither you nor I know how to drive."

"Maybe we could catch a taxi?" Giuseppe suggested hopefully.

"With all the *turistas* visiting the city, we'd be lucky to get one in an hour."

"*Madre di Dios!*" Giuseppe swore in exasperation. "A man might as well get an honest job. Is there no way a clever criminal can rob a bank in Rome these days?"

"Of course. But now it's all done by computers."

"What's a computer?"

ABSENT-MINDED COUSIN MELISSA

Elmo Eggers wasn't universally popular in our Friday night poker group. Some wanted to tell him outright we were sick and tired of his drawn-out, pointless yarns, every one ending predictably.

Ralph openly declared, "Elmo's a damn bore. Anything mentioned reminds him of some asinine tale."

Actually, I think we'd all miss Elmo if he didn't show up. Wearing his perpetual grin, Elmo arrived an hour late. "You're late," snapped Peter. "Forget it was Friday?"

"That reminds me of my cousin Melissa," Elmo said. "She was the most forgetful person ever."

We groaned in anticipation. If Elmo noticed, he continued anyhow. "Melissa did gardening in her younger years, had a little potting shed in back. She'd forget where she left her trowel—couldn't find it for days. Her husband Christopher Huggins, a rotten bounder, played around with a barmaid named Jessica Griffith; one weekend they both disappeared.

"Anyhow, Melissa finally needed to go to a retirement home. She held an open house for prospective buyers. Bought signs and promptly lost 'em. As expected, she couldn't find the deed. Searched everywhere. Got Sally Adams, her cleaning woman, to help.

"Rheumatism had made Melissa give up gardening. Her potting shed was falling apart—one wall completely gone. Poking around there, she and Sally noticed loose floor boards. They pried them up and—"

"We know," we exclaimed in unison, "the deed!"

Elmo looked surprised, "No. Cousin Melissa was *very* forgetful. It was the bodies of her husband Chris and Jessica Griffith."

BLABBERMOUTH

Want me to do a quick dye job on that white strand of your forelock? ... No? Just as well, since I'm in a real hurry. Police just phoned. They picked up a couple guys matching the descriptions I gave of the robbers who held up Community Savings yesterday. They want me to come down to the station and identify 'em. A girl don't get such a chance often. Maybe you saw my picture in the morning newspapers? *Only witness to spectacular robbery,* the reporter wrote. It musta been Fate. Can you believe it? I live out south of town—1763 Walnut Road—and I was late driving to work 'cause I overslept. You ever oversleep? No, I don't suppose you do. I can tell such things; it's sorta a gift. Anyhow, as I went past Community Savings Bank, two thugs dashed out carrying big sacks of money. Leastwise, I figured it was money. They yanked off their masks and I got real good looks at both. There must be a big reward, I thought, so I U-turned my yellow Toyota and gunned it back to the police station. That good-looking reporter was there... Y'know, I just happened to remember something: the gal driving the getaway car had a white streak in her forelock exactly like yours! Now, I ask you, what are the odds of that happening? Why, it's astronomical! ...That permanent is twenty bucks. If that's all, dearie, I'll close my little shop and be on my way to fame and glory!

THE MACTAVISH BAGPIPERS STRIKE AGAIN

The Mactavish brothers formed a circle around the exit of the newly opened car wash. The strident skirl of their bagpipes could be heard all over that section of Edinburgh.

Brian Mactavish stopped playing to remark, "'Twon't work. Tom McGill owns th' place an' he's a true Scotsman. He'll ne'er pay us a shillin' to gae away."

"Aye, but we'll colleck all th' same," declared Angus, the oldest of the brothers, confidently.

"Hoo?" Brian remained doubtful.

"Ye recall th' time we played in th' new department store an' we all fell doon th' escalator?"

"Aye."

"T' judge gie us 20,000 pounds damages. An' whin we played in th' new McDonald's doon th' street? Tobin spilled hot coffee o'er hissel' an' we got 10,000 pounds."

"True," admitted Brian, "but we canna fall doon here an' we got no coffee."

"Patience, laddie. Any minute a car will coom barrelin' oot o' yon car wash right inta Robby's backside. F'r 'is sufferin' we mought e'en git 50,000 pounds. Keep playin'!"

TALLYHO!—ER, ALMOST

Lieutenant Farthingale carefully parked his shiny new BMW convertible, then strode confidently over to the stables. Flicking his riding crop against his polished boots, he said stiffly, "Saddle my mare, Jenkins—and be quick. As I've told you time and again: Ambition pays off!"

"Must be a 'undred 'orses in yonder park, guv'nor," remarked the stable boy. "Parade?"

"Actually, we're going to capture that dastardly little robber who's causing the mischief in Locksley Park. The fellow makes his victims disrobe."

Jenkins grinned. "The telly calls 'im the Locksley Fox. They say 'e leaves 'em stark nekkid."

"Well, *I* shall outwit him. Superior intellect always wins, my good man. I've deputized all members of my hunt club. Before sundown we shall flush him out and have him handcuffed."

"Oh? Well, 'ave a good ride, guv'nor."

The dapper officer swung into the saddle and galloped off to join his deputies, His plan was brilliant: Riders would encircle Locksley Park, then gradually close ranks toward the center.

They flushed hedgehogs; they alarmed flocks of rooks. But by sunset they still had no trace of the Locksley Fox. Discouraged, Lieutenant Farthingale headed back to the stables. His new convertible was gone!

A scrawled note was tacked to the stable door:

Yer wuz absolutely right, lootenant—ambition does pay off. I now got enuff joggin soots and runnin shoes to start me own bizness. They fitted jest right in back of yer BMW. Thanks fer the advice.

—Jeremy Jenkins
(the retired *Locksley Fox)*

BITTERSWEET VERDICT

Old Charley Morris joined the group gossiping in my law office. The long-retired D.A. asserted, "Even losing can bring success." When someone vociferously disagreed, Charley declared, "Take the case of Jimmy Nagel, a small-time yegg, back in 1932. I'd just joined the firm of Smithers, Waller, & Claiborne. We strode to the courthouse single file, with me as junior man in the rear. The senior partners were there to observe my first prosecution...."

Nagel (Charley continued) was accused of attempted safe-cracking at Faber's Jewelers. The defense lawyer put Gloria Tillett, Nagel's girlfriend, on the stand. "Where was the accused on the night of August 10th?"

"Sleeping with me."

The lawyer smirked at me, "Your witness."

"Miss Tillett," I began, "a hardware dealer swears you purchased this drill and bit found at the scene of the aborted robbery. Are they yours?"

She ran an experienced fingertip over the bit's end. "He's ruined it!" she shrieked.

"Who?"

"Ernie Mathers, the guy I rented it to."

"How?" I asked, puzzled.

"Didn't lubricate it properly—not like Jimmy woulda done."

"You're certain?"

"Absolutely! I've watched Jimmy drill safes at Jenkins' hardware, Kirk's market, Flagg's clothing—" She caught herself too late.

After Nagel's acquittal, I sadly faced my partners. "I botched it."

"Nonsense!" boomed old Smithers, "We'll defend Gloria Tillett—claim entrapment. Then we'll represent Nagel's wife, who'll certainly sue for divorce. You'll prosecute Nagel on new charges. And Ernie Mathers presents opportunities for both defense and prosecution.

"You did fine, my boy!"

THE CASE OF JONES VS. BROOKSIDE HUNT CLUB

The trial reached its second day. Justice Eustace Granville proceeded deliberately, convinced this would become a landmark decision. Jones vs. Brookside Hunt Club—he liked the sound of it.

He rapped his gavel, quieting the crowded courtroom. "Continue your testimony, Sir Farnsworth."

"Your Honour, as I declared yesterday, club members have been recently harassed by animal rights activists—"

"Such as the plaintiff?" asked the justice.

"He was most vociferous, Your Honour."

"Continue."

"We were gathering to start the hunt in Quimby Wood when Mr. Jones dashed through the pack—"

"Disconcerted the hounds, did he?"

"Very much, sir. He then shouted, 'You cowards! Attacking a defenseless, innocent fox! Any human could outwit you—bare and with no weapon whatever.'"

Justice Granville leaned forward. "Precisely what ensued?"

"We members of Brookside Hunt are honourable gentlemen, as Your Highness well knows. We accepted Mr. Jones' challenge. We disrobed him at once and started the hunt—"

"Giving him a sporting lead?"

"Quite. At least six furlongs before releasing the pack. We ran him to ground—within the hour—in Abernathy's sheep cote."

Rick Jones leaped to his feet. "I protest this whole farce—"

"American, aren't you?" interrupted His Honour.

"Yes, but—"

Justice Granville grew livid. "You," he sputtered, "have attempted seditious overthrow of a national British institution: the fox hunt. You have maliciously maligned upright citizens. In addition, you have committed indecent exposure, running unclothed about the English countryside. Ours, Mr. Jones, is a *civilized* nation.

"Guilty! Thirty days in gaol!"

THE PROPHECY

The brownstone houses lining E Street seemed far removed from the anxiety and turmoil that had gripped the city in recent years. Scattered shrubbery, now budding into leaf, added slight cheer to the neighborhood. Number 13 differed from other houses only by the small sign in the window corner: Madame Seraphina, Clairvoyant.

On the sidewalk stood a handsome young man, a familiar figure in the city. He wore a top hat and longcoat, and carried an umbrella against the threat of the drear overcast April sky. He strode forward resolutely.

Even as he reached the weather-beaten door, it was opened to him. Adjusting his sight to the interior gloom, he made out the form of the woman. She wore a long gray robe; her only color in dress was a blood-red turban. Her coal-black eyes were unfathomable, her age indeterminable.

"Enter, kind sir," she said. "You are expected."

"I've heard," he stated guardedly, "that your remarkable power foresees the future."

"Be seated, please." She bent over a huge crystal sphere that seemed illuminated from within.

The man hesitated, then asked, "What will happen tonight?"

Her answer seemed contradictory. "You will leap to fame—and thereby break your leg."

He sniffed. "Will people remember me?"

"You will be forever remembered."

"Remembered favorably?"

"The crystal dims. I can say no more."

"Ah! Then I need take no more of your time, madam."

Satisfied, the young man cavalierly tossed a $20 gold coin onto the table. With that, John Wilkes Booth departed to his destiny.

THE IMBALANCE

I'd been clerking at Judson's Leather Goods exactly one month when it happened. At closing time the doorway was blocked by Mr. Judson himself and two policepersons, one male and one female.

"I'm sorry," old Judson announced, "but there seems to be an imbalance between cash intake and inventory. Therefore, I must ask each of you clerks to submit to a personal search."

It was embarrassing! We girls were taken into the ladies' room and searched skin-deep by the policewoman. She even delved into my large leather handbag, discovering the uneaten portion of my lunch, along with lipstick and certain feminine items.

Police evidently had no better luck with the other clerks. "Sorry about the inconvenience," old Judson apologized. Yeah, I thought, I'll bet you are.

"Mr. Judson," I declared angrily, "this is harassment! I've half a mind to sue you. Anyhow, I'm quitting!"

He turned several shades of gray. "Pl-pl-please," he stammered.

"No, that's final!" I stormed out of the store.

The old fool was right: there was an imbalance. Fortunately for me, he'd never caught on that I arrived each morning with my lunch and accessories in a paper bag—and left with them in a fine new leather handbag.

I think I'll apply for clerking at Harrison's Jewelry next. After all, who notices whether a clerk arrives with or without earrings? Also, earrings should be easier to pawn than those twenty handbags I filched from Judson's Leather Goods.

I'll have to remember to remove the price tags first.

THE CHRISTMAS SANTA CLAUS GOT BURNED

Christmas Eve was very special at our little country church. Ralph was then six and I was five. We stood awestruck upon first glimpsing the little fir tree beside the altar, shimmering with tin-foil icicles.

As mother seated herself between us boys, Ralph asked, "Where's dad?"

"Hush," she whispered. "He'll join us later."

After old Mr. Rehnquist read the Bible story, we sang hymns...more hymns...and carols. Then we gasped in amazement as Ollie, the church janitor, lit the candles on the Christmas tree.

"Ho-ho-HO!" boomed from the doorway.

Everyone swiveled and the children shouted gleefully, "Santa Claus! He's here!"

He stomped snow from his boots, brushed snowflakes from his red suit, and, fingering his bushy white beard, waddled up the aisle to stand right in front of the candle-lit tree.

"Ho-ho-ho! Have I got surprises for good boys and girls!" he exclaimed, bending over to open his huge gunnysack.

Smoke arose from Santa's behind, then flames. "Holy Jesus!" he yelped and dashed back down the aisle, his pants blazing. Trailing sparks he disappeared into the night.

Miss Olson, our Sunday School teacher, took charge distributing the presents.

Somehow the magic had gone.

On Christmas morning Ralph asked, "Dad, why are you eating breakfast standing up?"

"Boys," mother quickly interjected, "your father *can't* sit. He's suffering acute gluteus maximus inflammation." She suddenly buried her face in her apron and her shoulders shook.

I put a sympathetic arm around her. "Don't cry, Mama. He's getting better. He just tried to smile."

THE MEMORIAL PARK BENCH

As claims adjustor for Allied Fire & Casualty, I travel a lot. Seems like my whole life has been a series of short-term stopovers from the time I ran away and joined the circus at eleven. So when I came to Conover to assess damages from a tornado, the town seemed familiar.

What is now Conover's city park is a natural bowl surrounded by low hills, the place where Hallerby-Flotz circus used to pitch its big top during its summer tour.

What memories that park brings back! I was Bo-bo, the littlest clown, and others in the troupe practically adopted me.

A lot went on that a young boy shouldn't know—not that it was any worse than television today. Atlas, our strong man was having an affair with Nanette, the wife of Pierre Lafontaine, our ringmaster. Everyone knew it but her husband.

I remember vividly our final tour. Roustabouts had pulled stakes and folded the big top when Lafontaine unexpectedly announced, "We're going to leave a memorial to the circus right here in Conover: a bench set in concrete!"

He personally supervised a local mason in laying the slab. In the confusion, Atlas and Nanette had disappeared. Speculation was they'd run away together. The troupe sympathized with the ringmaster.

"Hard to believe she'd do this to me," declared Lafontaine, wiping his eyes.

Pierre Lafontaine's memorial bench still stands, now weather-beaten. I'm pretty sure what's under that concrete slab. But I don't plan to check my suspicion.

MEETING IN THE PARK

The park is deserted. A thin blanket of snow covers the fallen leaves, and the air bears a wintry chill. I really should be on my way south, but—sentimental fool that I am—I stand here gazing at yonder bench.

It was there we met last spring. After a profitable morning, I was resting on that bench.

"May I join you?" she asked shyly.

"But of course, madam!" I replied.

She wasn't beautiful, but she possessed a certain wistfulness. She'd been crying.

For something to say, I inquired, "Come here often?"

"This park reminds me of my late husband. He adored it."

"Dreadfully sorry," I murmured.

"Don't be, sir. You are so kind to care." She reached into her large handbag for another Kleenex, neglecting to close it. I couldn't help noticing her shabby wallet.

"Madam," I declared, "hope springs eternal. See those children flying their kites—so carefree—so innocent."

She turned, smiling. While she was distracted, I deftly lifted her wallet.

"Oh, you do understand!" Impulsively she drew me close, kissed me, and whispered, "You've made all my troubles vanish." She stood quickly and tripped blithely from view.

I opened the wallet. No name, no address, only two dollars. Still, every dollar counts. I started to transfer them to my billfold. *It was gone!* So was my savings bundle—all $4,586, gone....

So, I daydream about what a marvelous team we'd have made. Where is that wonderful woman now? If only I knew her name!

THE WOMAN WHO WAITED...AND WAITED...

By chance I returned on business to my old hometown. As I passed the park, it seemed strange not to see Miss Rebecca Crowder sitting on the bench, vainly waiting for her lover to come down the broad steps from what we called the "Plateau."

I recalled the details vaguely. Around 1918 (older people said) Rebecca was quite beautiful and madly in love with Ronald Simpson, a young infantry captain. His regiment was called up, and on that park bench they said their tearful goodbyes.

"No, darling, don't come," he had said. "Let me remember you there, where we spent so many happy hours." He waved a sad farewell from the top step and was gone. Ronald went off to fight in World War I and was never heard from again.

Rebecca became a tragic figure, sitting on that bench every day—rain or shine, winter and summer—waiting, hoping, waiting....

I asked old Doctor Yardley about her.

"No, Rebecca isn't dead," he told me. "She's in the asylum."

"She seemed harmless," I ventured.

"Well, she and young Ronald agreed that if either stopped writing, the other was released from the engagement. She received no letters, and the postmaster, Gerald Tibbals, tried courting her. She'd have none of him.

"Then on his deathbed, Tibbals confessed that he'd intercepted all their letters. Rebecca choked him to death—the hospital nurse needed help to pry her fingers loose."

124

QUIMBY PARK—AN AMERICAN STORY

I spend my vacations traveling. Like that fellow Charles Kuralt, I discover stories revealing the heart of America. One November evening I pulled into Brandon, Iowa. Supper in Dave's Diner was country-fried chicken. Afterward I wandered about in the twilight, coming across the town park, which lay dusted with new-fallen snow. A white-haired old gent was leaning on his cane and staring at the stained bronze plaque identifying it as "Quimby Park."

"Beautiful park," I commented.

He spat, quite accurately dotting the "i" in Quimby. "By rights," he rasped, "it oughta be named 'Carstairs Park,' after me, Jim Carstairs."

Sensing a story, I prompted him, "Why so?"

"Happened back in '12," he said, turning watery blue eyes toward me. "Me and Eddie Quimby was travelin' salesmen, me in Hankins' Hardware and him in Lawson's Ladies' Accouterments. We both fell in love with May-ellen Jenkins, the belle of Brandon. 'Twas a draw.

"Finally Eddie says, 'Here's the deal: Zeke Barlowe, the barber, has hidden a ring; whichever finds it marries May-ellen—the other leaves town.'

"Immediately I started turnin' over rocks, pokin' inta corners everywheres. I was still searchin' frantically when Eddie and May-ellen eloped to Dubuque. I left Brandon brokenhearted.

"Eddie and May-ellen settled here. He got elected mayor and named this park for hisself.

"Years later I returned and, still curious, asked Zeke Barlowe, 'Where in tarnation did you hide thet ring?'

"My question completely flummoxed old Zeke. 'Ring?' he said. 'I never hid no ring!'"

THE DWINDLING POPULATION OF
COYOTE, WYOMING

On May 10th the population of Coyote, Wyoming, was exactly 310, not counting local ranchers. I'd recently moved there from Chicago (for reasons I'd prefer not to mention) to set up a law practice.

On May 11th the population was 309. Jedd Coldwell, the banker, had been shot by a robber just as he was closing his safe at sundown. $25,000 was missing.

My telephone rang. "Mr. Jaynes, you gotta help me," pleaded the voice. It was Curly Noonan, the local bartender, calling—from the jail. I hurried over.

"Wasting yore time, Jaynes," snorted Sheriff Parker. "Mayellen Yager, the teller, got a good look at the robber. It was Noonan. He owed everybody hereabouts."

I consoled Curly in his cell. "Be brave. All is not lost."

"I'll pay *anything.* Just git me outta here."

"I'll try," I promised.

The following day Mayellen Yager disappeared. I said to Sheriff Parker, "It would seem, sir, she was an accomplice of the actual robber and fled with him."

"I thoughta thet. But Charley Yager, her husband, says she got a call from me to meet behind the livery. I didn' phone her."

Next night Charley Yager also dropped from sight. The sheriff deputized half the county and searched everywhere.

"It was worse than I imagined," I told him. "The Yagers were in cahoots. Probably in California by now."

"Reckon y'all're right," he conceded. He released my client. Curly Noonan paid me $20,000 without protest.

Shortly thereafter I left Coyote, population 307.

THE FINAL CONTEST OF THE UMBOLTS

The Astor Hotel ballroom. Winning couples in the World-Wide Puzzles contest, including Otis and Maybelle Umbolt of Nevada, have been wined and dined. Excitement mounts as stage curtains part.

SCENE 1

EMCEE: Welcome and congratulations. *(Applause.)* As the highlight of our gala evening, we will award the grand prize! *(Cheers.)* My lovely assistants will, on signal, hand each couple a special puzzle. Whoever has the first correct solution wins a brand new cherry red convertible Lexus! *(Gasps.)* Ready?

(Rustling of papers as puzzles are distributed.)

SCENE 2

Five minutes later.

OTIS: I got it! That convertible is ours!

MAYBELLE (*grabbing puzzle from him*): Not so fast. Lemme check it. We gotta be sure.

OTIS: Give it back! I already checked it. It's correct!

MAYBELLE (*pondering his solution*): Won't take a sec.

OTIS: No! (*He pulls on the puzzle, which tears in half.*) Oh my God!

EMCEE (*loudly*): We have a winner, folks! Mr. and Mrs. Tutweiler of New Jersey! If they will kindly step forward, I will hand them the keys to their *new Lexus convertible!*

SCENE 3

Police have been summoned. The captain questions witnesses.

CAPTAIN: Go over it again.

EMCEE: I'd just announced the winner of the grand prize when Mr. Umbolt strangled his wife.

CAPTAIN: Is that true, Mr. Umbolt?

OTIS (*mumbling, his eyes glazed*): I had it right...had it right...had it right....

CAPTAIN: Okay, you'd best come quietly, sir. You have the right....

CURTAIN

WHY JOE-JOE WON'T BE BACK

Around midmorning I struggled up the beach of Resurrection Bay, a tired old fisherman. The three big coho salmon I'd just landed flapped lustily against my boots, adding to my difficulty over slippery, seaweed-covered rocks.

Some Aleuts I'd met that week were sitting solemn-faced under a blue tarp, unusually silent, watching my progress. Knowing that they'd already caught, filleted, and iced down several chests of salmon, I hadn't expected any of them to stay around, but three remained.

As I approached, Dolphin shoved forward a campstool. "Coffee?" he invited.

"Great!" I said, accepting a steaming mug. "Where's Joe-Joe?"

"Joe-Joe no be back," declared Dolphin morosely.

"Why not?"

"Him too smart."

"Oh?" I said inquisitively, hoping he'd continue.

"Joe-Joe got his salmon the too-easy way."

"How's that?"

"Him pirate State trap-net. Oh, Joe-Joe plenty brains. Him swim out and fill 'im's big net there. Pull 'em ashore in nighttime."

"So," I ventured, "the game warden spotted him swimming out there?"

"Not Joe-Joe. Him paint white spots on 'im's black wetsuit—look just like killer whale."

"Did they catch him pulling his net ashore?" I asked.

"Not Joe-Joe. Him wait 'til he see warden drive off home at night."

My curiosity boiled over. "Dolphin," I pleaded, "please tell me *what happened to Joe-Joe.*"

"I tell you straight. Him too damn smart—but not smart enough. Oh, Joe-Joe fool warden plenty okay. But him no fool *real* killer whales swimmin' up-bay after salmon."

DEJA VU

The TV flickers. Bo and me have seen this thousands of times. Always it ends with that *same* stop sign stuck in that *same* cane thicket alongside that *same* back country road.

"It was yore fault," growls Bo, punchin' my sore arm.

The sizzlin' heat keeps us both antsy. Sweat makes my bra cling, my skin itchy.

"Whatta ya mean, *my* fault?" I retort. "If you'd had any brains we'd a ditched that stolen getaway car an' melted inta the crowd at the fair."

"Yeah? Strollin' around totin' bags fulla money with 'First National' printed all over 'em? Git real!"

"You was the macho guy, breakneckin' at 90 mile an hour through the boondocks."

"I *hadda* drive fast—because you didn' spot the alarm system when casin' that bank." Bo is hell to live with these days.

"Anyhow," I add, "you shouldna speeded up when that deputy sheriff waved his stop sign."

"Let him arrest us? Go back to prison? No way, stupid!"

"What I mean is, you jerk, hittin' him threw the car outta control. That's why we're here."

"He shore did fly, didn' he?"

"Right on up. But thanks to *you*, we went the opposite direction."

"Damn, it's hot."

"You got *that* right." Finally we agree.

Suddenly the picture's all blur and static. It don't matter. Nothin' matters. Hell, we'll see it all again tomorrow.

With all the clout Satan claims, you'd think he'd get a better TV set—and maybe *one* new cassette. *Anything* different.

THE RAJAH'S LOST DIAMOND MINE

I suppose we'll never know whether Clayton Wallis was a misguided practical joker or a sadistic devil. One thing is certain: he and his wife Marjorie were completely unsuited.

Say what you will about Clayton, he was daring. The fellow feared nothing.

It began one night in the British Club in Mandalay. Clayton turned to his wife, "Dear, how would you like diamonds—diamonds galore, big as pigeon eggs?"

"You're drunk or kidding," she replied. "Maybe both."

"No, I just learned that somewhere back in the jungle is the fabulous Rajah's lost diamond mine. *We* are going to find it."

She showed interest. "Where?"

"It's through swamps and. dense undergrowth, but we'll persevere."

"There'll be snakes." She shuddered. "Leeches. And crocodiles. I-I couldn't do it."

"Of course you can!" he laughed, and winked to the rest of us.

Well, he practically forced Marjorie to accompany him. They spent the whole weekend floundering through swamps. Marjorie came back trembling with the recollection.

"We'll try again," grinned Clayton.

Despite Marjorie's pleading, they went again—and again. Marjorie was becoming a nervous wreck.

Some of us called Clayton aside. "This had gone far enough, dragging your wife through muck and quicksand for your imaginary diamond mine."

"Nonsense!" he boomed.

They set forth again the following weekend. Marjorie returned alone, muddy and exhausted.

"Clayton slogged on ahead," she said, "and somehow we got separated. I suspect he's finally found his damned diamonds. Let's hope so."

Nobody ever saw Clayton Wallis again.

OLD RACHEL'S ANTIQUES

Dr. Nathaniel Flowers returned late to his Seattle mansion. His wife Elena greeted him at the door.

"Hard day at the hospital?" she asked.

"House call kept me late. Elderly widow named Rachel Sanders—charity case."

"If she's that old, why are you grinning?"

"You wouldn't believe the valuable antiques she has crammed into her ramshackle old house—pine press cupboard, walnut chest-on-frame, highboy, piecrust tip-top—"

"I thought you said she was a charity case?"

"Absolutely destitute, totally unaware what they're worst. She told me her ancestor brought all those priceless antiques from New England in his sailing ship. I spotted an early 18th Century secretary easily worth $40,000—just sitting back in her dilapidated old shed."

Elena's eyes danced. "Just what I've always wanted! Oh, Nate, let's buy it!"

"Darling, I'll get them all—for a song. But I'll have to act fast. She's starting an open house tomorrow."

Early next morning Doctor Flowers called again on Rachel. "Madam," he said solemnly, "I sincerely want to help. Throw away that OPEN HOUSE sign! Here's a purchase agreement: $50,000 for your property and all contents as of closing date. Come to my office Friday."

Old Rachel showed up on schedule, gratefully accepted his check, and surrendered her key. Elated, Doctor Flowers drove directly to his new acquisitions.

On a cheap Formica table top was a note:

Dear doctor,

Knowing you young folks like everything new, I traded my old furniture for these lovely items at Sam's Discount.

Rachel Sanders

THE BUTCHER'S WIFE AND THE STORK

Residents of Grossthal were not alarmed when loud, blasphemous curses emanated from above the shop of Hans Wiedemeyer the butcher. It was late Saturday, night and Hans was drunk as usual. Neighbors couldn't understand how his wife Katrina put up with him.

"I seen ya," Hans bellowed, "feedin' per-fect-ally good meat to that filthy bird agin."

"Please, Hans," Katrina whimpered, "it was just scraps. Besides, the poor stork has three in her nest to feed."

"Reckon they'll sh-sh-shtarve after I lops off th' momma's head with m' cleaver."

"Oh, Hans! You wouldn't!"

"Yeah?" he snarled. "Doan' know why I married a scrawny, bird-lovin' ol' cow."

"Because," Katrina retorted, "I was the only girl stupid enough—"

"Hahhrr! I got lotsa women—loverly young things—ever'wheres...ever'wheres...."

There came the welcome sound of a falling body. The listening neighbors relaxed; old Hans had at last passed out and now they could sleep.

Katrina missed Church next day. But she opened the butcher shop promptly on Monday morning. Her left eye had swollen shut.

"Where's Hans?" customers asked.

Katrina simply shrugged. That week she remodeled the place, scrubbing everywhere, even cementing the basement floor herself. She became an efficient butcher.

Villagers couldn't help noticing that the stork and her brood grew exceptionally fat that summer.

Nearly everybody has forgotten Hans. But if anyone does inquire, Katrina gives a peculiar little smile, "Hans sort of flew away with the birds—south, I think."

ISOLATION

Every clap of thunder overhead resounded inside Jim's head with explosive force. The fever was inconvenient—made him shake uncontrollably at intervals—but the opportunity might never come again.

Obviously Fred, his diabetic business partner, suspected nothing or he wouldn't have agreed to this hunting trip. That morning he had driven blithely back to the city for more supplies.

Jim struggled down the mountainside and planted the explosives under the bridge spanning the chasm. Nearly exhausted, he ran the wires back to the cabin. The storm would erase all traces. They would be isolated for a week, maybe longer. When the insulin gave out, Fred would slip into a coma and...the business would be all his!

The walls of the cabin seemed to spin. Probably the excitement. Jim absently wiped perspiration from his forehead. Then over the beating of the rain he heard it: the rattle of the Jeep crossing the bridge. Jim counted to ten and connected the wires. BRROOM! Not unlike another clap of thunder.

Outside, Fred cut the motor. He came through the door, his poncho dripping and his arms, laden with wet bags of groceries. "God, what a storm, Jim!" he exclaimed, dumping his load onto the rustic table. "Trip took forever."

Fred rambled on, "Dropped in on Doc Sutherland. Got some more insulin and mentioned your symptoms. He suspects it's a virulent spotted fever going around up this way. Anyhow, he's driving up to check you later tonight...."

The throbbing in Jim's head increased.

133

DR. WATSON REPORTS HIS FINAL CASE

The fog, which I encountered upon leaving Scotland Yard, clung heavy along Baker Street. Dismissing the hansom cab, I groped my way until I came to 221-B. Sad-faced, Mrs. Hudson met me at the door.

"How is he?" I asked, keeping my voice down. "Low," she replied. "Terrible thing, Inspector."

I followed her up the stairs. Dr. Watson lay motionless. I approached the bed. "Sir," I said quietly, "you sent for me?"

The old eyelids fluttered. "Harrumph. Is that you, Lestrade?"

"Yes, Dr. Watson."

"Come closer." His breathing became labored. "I...killed...Sherlock Holmes."

"No," I humored him, "he's right here in this room."

The tall man standing beside me spoke. "I'm Mycroft, Sherlock's brother. It's true, Inspector. Watson murdered Sherlock—years ago. I've known for some time."

I was incensed. "You should have reported it!"

"What? And ruined my brother's international reputation? He was, unfortunately, retarded. Nevertheless, I wanted to grant him his wish: to be remembered as the most famous detective of all time. I solved the cases made public."

I was shocked. Taking out my notebook, I turned to the confessed killer near death. "Is this possibly true, doctor?"

"Yes, I...strangled him..." the haggard man replied, "...had to inform you...might spare some innocent man."

"But *why?*"

"I could stand damned violin...tobacco in slippers...even his cocaine habit (gasp)...but when he said—hundredth time—'Elementary, my dear'...."

Dr. Watson was dead.

Mrs. Hudson entered timidly, bearing a tray with tea and freshly baked scones.

THE MISSING LADY PENGELLY

The hostility was mutual. Pauline stood at the doorway, glaring. "You've murdered my sister!" she screamed.

"As I said before, she's away," Lord Pengelly responded heatedly. "Anyhow, no judge is going to issue a warrant to tear up my home on your stupid suspicion."

He wondered why he'd ever romanced shrill-voiced Pauline—but that was before he met her much younger sister Alice.

Pauline continued unabated, "You'll not get by with it! I've got all her friends watching you. And your smug butler Jefferson, too. We'll dog your every move!" She stormed down the marble steps, jumped into her red sports car, and took off, leaving black streaks of burned rubber on the driveway.

Pauline was true to her threat. When Lord Pengelly left for his club, some woman amateurishly tailed his limousine. Then the midnight telephone calls began: "May I speak to Lady Pengelly?" The connection would suddenly be broken. Next day the postman delivered numerous perfumed letters addressed to Alice, each marked "Urgent."

"What shall I do with them, m'lord?" inquired Jefferson.

"Put them aside," answered Pengelly absently. Dammit, wouldn't that sister-in-law ever let up?

The long-awaited call from Switzerland came through. "Darling," came the excited female voice, "I won the downhill ski championship!"

"Congratulations!" said Lord Pengelly enthusiastically.

"You've kept our secret?"

"Very discreetly, my love."

"Excellent! I've always wanted to surprise my nosy sister Pauline."

"Oh, I have no doubt she will be surprised. Please hurry home, Alice. We can tell her together."

135

WHEN THE CHIPS ARE DOWN

"It's simple, really," declared Jim Garrels smugly, "and worth millions in the wrong hands." The young electronics expert paused.

"If ya don't mind, Garrels," said the unsmiling man at the head of the conference table, "let's hear it once more."

"Certainly, Mr. Mitelli. My company manufactures the best computer chips. The circuitry in our various models performs perfectly, from simple video games to highly sophisticated—"

"Just skip the technical crap," ordered Big Man Mitelli.

"Very well. But I must explain that chips can be programmed to malfunction on a certain signal—"

"Okay!" Mitelli was an impatient man. "Give us an example."

"Say, you deposit $500 in a bank in which I have installed the system. Later, you ask to have *exactly* $491.76 transferred to your account in another bank. The teller will do it electronically. But when those exact figures, 4-9-1-7-6, are entered, the transfer will be $491,760. The teller will not be aware of the actual amount, nor will anyone else," stated Garrels confidently. "My system is foolproof."

"Why come to us?" the big man demanded, his eyes narrowing shrewdly.

"Because your organization is the only one is a position to afford my fee—twenty million. I hardly need point out the possibilities in laundering illegal money."

Mitelli nodded to the man beside him. The silencer muffled the shot and Garrels slumped dead.

"Dangerous men, these damned computer experts," growled the big man. "Why, one like Garrels could destroy the Mafia's whole computer network."

THE LOST MATCHES

Frank Groves sat at the kitchen table, sighting along his freshly oiled Winchester. "I think," he ventured cautiously, "I'll go hunting up at the cabin this weekend."

His wife Ellen gave a bitter little laugh. "I shouldn't think you'd need a rifle to entertain Martha Nichols. And you wouldn't have to hunt too hard for what you're after."

His mouth dropped open in astonishment. "How—"

"A wife knows such things," she interrupted grimly. "Her husband Raymond's away again. Go ahead! But don't expect an easy divorce."

Nervously, Frank shouldered his backpack and started up the steep mountain trail. Snow was falling. Soon he spotted Martha, waiting, shivering, stamping her feet.

"This storm seems to be getting worse," she said timidly. "Maybe we should go back, Frank."

"No," he insisted stubbornly. "Another ten miles and I'll build a cozy fire in the cabin."

She trudged along behind him. Frigid winds drove snowflakes in stinging, blinding gusts. At last they sighted the cabin. The door lay shattered.

"Oh, no!" Frank gasped. "Evidently a bear searching for food—"

"And look," wailed Martha, "he's torn our sleeping bags to shreds!"

Minutes later, Frank asked anxiously, "Dear, do you have any matches?"

"You know I don't smoke, Frank."

"Oh, God! I've lost my matches."

For five days, blizzard conditions delayed searchers. Then they found Frank and Martha, huddled in one corner of the cabin, both frozen stiff.

At the church, Ellen smiled. Using one of Frank's "lost" matches, she lit a candle in his memory.

It began two years ago. Emily Dawson listened as her companion-housekeeper read her the morning mail.

"Here's an invitation to your college reunion, with a list of members the committee's located."

"Read it, please, Dora."

The names brought old memories flooding back. Charles Eberly!

She couldn't remember why they had quarreled. Now, forty years later, it seemed so stupid.

That Saturday noon, Dora had prepared to leave for the weekend. "Anything I can do before I go?"

"No, thank you."

As soon as Dora's footsteps died away, Emily had reached for the phone. "Operator? Charles Eberly's number in Versailles, Indiana...714-6203?...Thank you."

Trembling, Emily phoned. Years dropped away. Both had so much to talk about. Yes, he had served in the war. No, he wasn't married. She had retired from teaching.

Every Saturday afternoon. thereafter, alone, Emily groped for the telephone, positioned her fingers, and punched the now-familiar little muted tinkly tune.

"Charles, old love, how was your week?"

"Emily, dear, tell me...."

On and on. Heart-warming, tender, endearing conversation.

Another Monday morning. Dora announced excitedly, "You have a visitor, Miss Dawson."

"Emily!"

She recognized his voice. "Oh, Charles! I have a confession. I should have told you—"

"Please," he interrupted, "I had to come, darling. I simply *had* to come."

Then she experienced the fingers softly touching her cheeks, her nose...caressing her forehead...exploring her lips, her chin.... The revelation came as a brilliant illumination, and Emily *knew!*

Charles was also blind.

RISKY IMPERSONATION

Once more Alfred Ingersoll studied the picture in the newspaper and compared it with his own reflection. He trimmed the false beard just a fraction. There! A perfect likeness to the mysterious actor, Bertil Wycoff.

Ingersoll glanced again at the headlines: "HOLLY-WOOD LINKED TO MAFIA? Noted Actor to Testify!"

His plan would get national attention, possibly land him an acting role. He had memorized everything ever written about Wycoff, who two years ago had gone into seclusion. He imagined the look on the face of Charles Sawyer, the famous director, when he revealed his true identity. A host of motion picture celebrities would be at the party tonight.

Alfred Ingersoll strode confidently up the marble stairs, to the door. "Good evening, Harry," he said to the butler. "Long time no see."

The man faltered. "Why—why, it's Mr. Wycoff!"

"Thought I'd surprise my old friends. How's Fiona?"

"Mrs. Sawyer? Quite well. I must inform her you're here." The butler hurried inside.

Ingersoll elbowed through the effervescent throng. "Hell-LO," he greeted his host. "Hope you don't mind my crashing your little affair, Chuck?"

"Bertil!" exclaimed the director. "Good timing! I have a new script in my study."

As the door closed, two muscular men seized Ingersoll. "What's this about?" he inquired nervously.

"You're testifying, old boy," answered Sawyer. "And after we paid you to keep silent."

"B-b-but I'm not Wycoff," protested Ingersoll. "I'm—"

His explanation was cut short as the silenced gun made a sound very like the cork leaving a champagne bottle.

THE SIGN

Two cars were parked on solid rock but disturbingly close to the cliff edge. As the girl got out of one, she frowned. She had hoped to be alone. A young man sat cross-legged at the perilous edge, the boundary between life and death. The girl shrugged and approached him. She would have been beautiful had she smiled, but she wasn't smiling.

Upon hearing footsteps, the man turned. The girl gave a start. "Paul! I haven't seen you in—"

"In months? No, Myra, I couldn't face you again, a failure in everything." His voice was bitter.

"Not in everything, dear," she said consolingly. "I think your paintings are quite good."

"You're the only person who does. I haven't sold *one.* How's the theater?"

"No roles for a might-be. Every producer sympathizes but—'Sorry, no parts to fit your personality.'" Myra shivered. "Not much point in going on."

It started snowing. Paul stared out into the turmoil of gray beyond the edge. "You're right, old dear. Damned little point."

An electrifying mutual understanding gripped them both. "So, that's why you came here," she breathed. It was not a question.

"And you, too," he said knowingly.

"I think of this place as the End of All."

"I still have a coin," Paul said harshly. "Heads I'll go first." He flipped it.

An unexpected gust sent the coin spinning into the gray void. They listened...only the sighing wind.

"It's a sign!" exclaimed Myra, laughing unsteadily, crazily. They fell into each other's arms, kissed, and turned back.

CUSTER'S LAST, ABSOLUTELY FINAL STAND

The wind had died but the air was still bitterly cold. On a barren, snow-covered rise, two men in heavy sheepskin jackets stood looking down. The corpse at their feet was stiff under its coating of frost. He had been shot once—through the heart. Ranger Rob Rankin spoke. "Know who he is, Ted?"

"Yeah," his assistant replied. "He was in a Deadwood saloon yesterday. Claimed he was Tiny Bull, great-great-grandson of Sitting Bull."

"What else did he say?"

"He said old Sitting Bull buried Custer's rifle wrapped in oilskin. Then he showed everybody this metal detector, see, sayin' he knew just where to look."

"You were supposed to patrol yesterday," snapped Rankin. "Why didn't you stop him?"

Ted Tompkins answered lamely, avoiding his superior's eyes. "I figured he was drunk, just spoutin' off. Anyhow, I didn't think *anybody* would venture out in that blizzard."

Ranger Rankin squatted down to investigate. "There's the metal detector," he announced, brushing the snow from it. "And here's the rifle. He found it all right. Looks like he accidentally hit the hammer with his spade."

"Probably blinded by the snow," offered Tompkins, trying to ingratiate himself.

"Seems that way," grunted the ranger.

He stood and turned toward Tompkins. "You're sure gonna catch hell from Washington," he declared.

His assistant gave him a quizzical look. "For what?"

Rankin snorted. "You don't understand Washington. They'll hold you indirectly responsible for the final casualty in the Battle of the Little Big Horn."

141

"*Arrête!* Wh-who ever you may b-be!"

The quavering voice startled me and I turned around. I hadn't expected the old *abbé* to climb up here to the top of the cathedral.

"'Tis only I, Father," I answered. "François Chabbois."

"Ah, you return again, my son. But why come you each year to inspect and repair these grotesque gargoyles?"

"You will keep my secret?"

The old *abbé* bristled. "*Certainement!*"

"*Très bien.* It is my sworn duty to my family."

"Explain, my son."

"It is *mystérieux*, unfathomable—yet I must believe. Back in 1165 when this cathedral was being completed, four demons—Pride, Greed, Envy, and Lust—seized villagers hereabout. These demons then pursued the first *abbé* and cornered him here atop the cathedral. In desperation he held forth his crucifix and they were instantly encased in bronze. He had workmen set them at the corners of this spire. Before his death, the *abbé* told his brother, my ancestor, the first François Chabbois. Every generation afterward, someone in the family ensures that the casing remains intact."

"Fool!" The voice suddenly became harsh. "You cannot confine evil forever. A fifth demon was sent from Hell to find and release his brothers. And I am he!"

He threw back his cowl. *It was not the old abbé who confronted me!*

Just in time I flashed my crucifix. I'm still shaking.

Want to buy a bronze gargoyle, *m'sieur?* I'm offering a devil of a bargain. Certain restrictions apply.

DIFFERENT PERSPECTIVES

Construction sites fascinate me. Unreasonable, perhaps, but I feel I'm personally participating—excavating giant craters, erecting actual buildings soaring up to take their place on the city's skyline. Contractors provide peep windows in the barricades to accommodate us "sidewalk engineers." Anyhow, my friends and I are back again today.

Eddie, on my left, declares, "That crane operator knows his stuff! Balanced that load perfectly."

"I noticed," I agree. "That riveter up there is one brave guy."

Phil, on my right, says, "In that apartment house overlooking the excavation, a man and his wife are having a real battle on the third floor."

"Never mind that," snaps Eddie. "Keep your eye on the guy riding up on that I-beam!"

"She threw an iron at him," continues Phil. "Missed. Broke a window."

A worker strides casually along a high girder. While I'm praying fearfully for his safety, my friends chatter on.

Phil says, "He caught her. Seems to be choking her—"

"They're starting a *sixth* story," remarks Eddie.

"She broke loose. He heaves a chair. She ducks, making the man madder yet—"

"I wonder whether they'll finish it in brick, concrete, or stainless steel."

"He's rushing at her," reports Phil. "She sidesteps. Oh-oh, there he goes, right through the broken window! Down...down...all the way. She's leaning out, laughing hysterically—"

"What's the matter with you, Phil?" demands Eddie. "Aren't you interested in keeping up with what's happening in our city?"

143

"Gee, officer," said Archy Scully, "I'm sorry I got you excited. It's all settled now,"

"But," objected Detective Trimble, "you reported your aunt Florabelle blackmailed you for $50,000. What was that about?"

"You swear everything I say is confidential?"

"Well," the detective hesitated, "okay, I promise."

"There's this burlesque queen in town my wife don't know about. But I paid off Aunt Florabelle."

"Where'd you get the money."

"Simple, sir. I blackmailed Cousin Bernie for violatin' his parole."

"And how did this ex-con raise $50,000?"

"From Uncle Cecil—by threatening to expose his counterfeiting. But Cousin Bernie made sure he was paid off in real money."

"Cecil Scully, eh? He parted with that kinda money?"

"Oh, he made it up easy enough, officer. He blackmailed my sister Della."

"What for?"

"She drove the getaway car in the recent epidemic of bank robberies. She spent most of her share of the loot, unfortunately."

"Then where did she get $50,000 to pay off your uncle Cecil?"

"Oh, that. By threatening to inform the cops about Cousin Elmo's numbers racket."

'I see. So, it was gamblers' money that started this chain of payoffs?"

"Gee, officer, I never thought about that. All I know is Cousin Elmo got his $50,000 by blackmailing Aunt Florabelle."

"For what?" inquired Detective Trimble.

"Well, Aunt Florabelle sings in the church choir and doesn't want the minister to know she controls prostitution in the city."

"So, the $50,000 circulated from Florabelle to Elmo to Della to Cecil to Bernie to you and back to Florabelle."

"Right, officer! All in the family."

TWO HALLOWEENS

On October 31st, 1996, Jason Adler rapped his gavel and declared, "This weekly meeting of the Slen-Dor-Rite Corporation will come to order." The old CEO was a stickler for formality, even though only officers of the diet pill company were present around the polished oak table.

"Any new business?" he asked.

Martin Westerman, the advertising manager, spoke up, "Those six asinine skeletons on display outside give the public an adverse impression of our product. They imply death could result."

Vice-president Sam Tyler added, "Whoever dreamed up laughing skeletons with big red hearts? They're absolutely ridiculous!"

Adler grew livid. "I'll have you know Miss Rossby, my private secretary, made those figures—didn't you, dear?"

Eileen Rossby began sobbing, "J-j-just as you instructed, Mr. Adler."

The old CEO rapped his gavel furiously. "This meeting's adjourned! Westerman and Tyler, I'd like to see you privately."

On November 1st, 1996, it was announced that Martin Westerman and Sam Tyler had gone to establish branches of Slen-Dor-Rite in Ethiopia and Bangladesh. They sent back no reports. Later it was rumored they'd found other employment.

On Halloween of 1997, Jason Adler and his new bride, the former Eileen Rossby, themselves put up *eight* skeletal figures in front of the Slen-Dor-Rite Corporation. Strangely, the fourth and eighth figures faced away from the public gaze. That was perhaps just as well, for neither had a laughing face or a big red heart.

THE GRAVE IN THE BASEMENT

"Come down to the basement, dear," invited Walter Twitchell.

"I'm watching Lawrence Welk," snapped his wife Sybil. "Besides, I've seen your piddlin' little grave down there."

"Oh, drat! I wanted to surprise you. I'm going to bury you there so I can marry Trudy Lipscombe, my voluptuous secretary."

"Sure you're up to it, Walter? The police questioning? Another honeymoon?"

"I'll manage," he replied petulantly.

"Exactly what's this love-starved secretary got, anyhow?"

"*She* lets *me* decide things. *You* always advise me."

"Oh, very well. Don't dilly-dally! Come along. And don't forget your shovel."

Walter followed her meekly down the stairs. "Too shallow!" declared Sybil. "You want Trudy to notice what an inadequate grave you've provided me? Dig deeper!"

Walter began digging, meanwhile protesting, "You're making it awful hard."

"And square those corners, too! It's my grave." Three hours later. Sybil announced, "Your bedtime, Walter! We'll continue tomorrow night." On Friday night, Walter's excavation reached ten feet deep. "Steady that ladder and climb outta there!" ordered Sybil. "More tomorrow."

After drying off from the shower, Walter flopped exhausted onto the bed. Sybil massaged him all over with Ache-Away. "Gotta keep you in shape to finish the job," she said.

"Sybil," he said, "I've changed my mind. I can't live without you."

"What about my grave down there?"

"Could we maybe fill it in?"

"Don't be wasteful, Walter!" commanded Sybil. "Invite Trudy to dinner tomorrow night. If you can't think of something to put into your basement hole, I will!"

LESSON TEN

It was too early for the regulars at Gorsky's Bar, and we were the only customers. The slender gent in the checkered vest at the other end of the bar seemed friendly. Somehow we started talking.

His name was Nathan Monroe. "Call me Nate," he said, buying another round.

Unexpectedly, Nate asked, a twinkle in his eye, "Where's your wallet?"

"Right here in my trousers." I felt, then exclaimed, "Good lord! It's gone!"

"No," he laughed, "it's now in your coat pocket."

"Hey, Nate," I said, "that was pretty clever."

"Just trying out Lesson Two of the *Crime Guide*—Successful Pickpocketing. I just pull that for kicks."

"You mean there's really a *Crime Guide?*" I asked.

"Rather secret, $100 a lesson."

"Could I join?"

"I have the address—local post office box 129. Cash only."

I joined, sending in my first $100. I received Lesson One: Successful Shoplifting. Intrigued, I kept on. I was up to Lesson Nine: Successful Bank Robbery. Then I started wondering: Who wrote this stuff?

Donning my Successful Disguise (Lesson Five), I watched P.O. Box 129. Nate Monroe himself collected several envelopes from it!

The guy had a really good thing going. Such a scam was too good to pass up.

Nate vanished completely—right after *I* wrote Lesson Ten: Successful Murder.

I introduced myself to a friendly patron of Gorsky's Bar. "I'm Nathan Monroe—just call me Nate." After some casual conversation, I inquired, "Incidentally, sir, where's your wallet?"

HOW-TO IN A MARRIAGE

Stella had had enough. More than enough, actually. No matter what she did trying to help, her husband belittled her efforts, saying, "That's *man's* work. You're liftin' that heavy sofa all wrong. Bend down first, put your back into it—like this. *You'd* never learn how."

Yes, Boris would have to go.

No use asking for a divorce. Boris would find it laughable, heaping more scorn on her. Perhaps poison was the solution, she mused, sitting on the porch and watching him mow the lawn. All at once she realized how many chores would be left to her during widowhood. She'd better delay Boris' demise for a while.

"How did you start the mower?" she asked.

"Turned on the ignition, pressed this suction to prime gas into the cylinder—hey, you're not gonna try runnin' my mower, are you? You'd probably cut off your toes, maybe ruin the shrubbery."

"Just wondering, dear."

During ensuing weeks, Stella observed how Boris hung storm windows, replaced furnace filters, and changed oil in the car, always asking questions and always getting curt, demeaning answers. She read half the How-to books in the local library.

One evening at supper, she announced, "The compression cylinder on our garbage compactor went dead."

"I'll phone a repairman tomorrow," Boris said.

"I already replaced it."

"Gee, you did?" he asked in amazement. "Soon as I help clear the table, would you show me how?"

"It's pretty complicated, darling," she replied, smiling.

THE RECLAMATION OF TIM O'RYAN

"Father Mulcahey," I told 'im, "'tis desperate I am."

"My son," he said, "your sins can be forgiven."

"No, no, Father. 'Tis about me best friend Tim O'Ryan."

"Ah, you've come about Timothy's unfortunate drinking problem. I'm afraid neither I nor his wife Noreen have been able to overcome his temptation by Demon Rum."

"'Tis straight *rye* he's drinkin'. We must act quick, afore he starts seein' pink panthers."

"Pink elephants, Michael."

"Them, too. Here's my plan." I explained it.

"Deceitful—but I'm sure we'll be forgiven in view of the cause. What time do you suggest?"

"Friday night, after Tim's had a snootful at Clancy's."

"May the Lord guide us."

Approachin' Noreen, I said, "Next Friday night, ten o'clock, drag Tim from the pub to Church—elsewise, Father Mulcahey will 'communicate 'im."

The priest was waitin', whilst I hid behind a pew. In me red longjohns and Halloween mask, I really *did* look like the Devil.

Noreen led Tim inside. Father Mulcahey served 'em communion. Thin he said, his eyes blazin', "Timothy O'Ryan! Satan himself tempts you with liquor! He stands behind you now!"

Up I stood.

Noreen screamed, yanked 'er pistol from 'er purse, and started shootin'. BANG!

"Lord, please make her miss!" the priest prayed. BANG-BANG-BANG-BANG-BANG!

I ducked, but Saint Bartholomew's statue got chipped bad. "Saints presarve us!" yelped Tim. "I'm *really* quittin', Father! One dram o' communion wine and me wife shoots at the Devil—and misses six times."

SCORECARD

Alongside the driveway of Happy Howie's Tavern, eight garish skeletons twisted in the chill November wind. In the back room, the co-owners were arguing again.

"You're deliberately sabotaging my business!" accused Howie Carter. "Halloween's been over for weeks, and still you leave those ridiculous skeletons outside. They're driving customers away!"

"I'll take 'em down when you sign your half of the tavern over to me," declared his wife Lizzie. "After all, my daddy left it to me."

"It was a wreck!" retorted her husband. "My hard work made it into Happy Howie's Tavern."

"Somethin' else botherin' you?" demanded Lizzie.

"Yeah! I want a divorce. I finally met an understanding woman—Rachel Eisenberg, who delivers our beer."

"Hah!" snorted Lizzie. "Face it, buster, you ain't the lover-boy you think. As I recall, there was Trudy, Maxine, Wendy, Erica—"

"Stop it!"

She continued, "—Hayley, Celia, Josephine, and Angela. *Every one left town suddenly!* Now, I gotta get back to tend bar. You want them skeletons down, do it yourself!"

After Howie's fatal accident, Pete Jurgens testified, "I was havin' a beer when Howie rushed in yellin', 'Ohmigod! They're *real!* That's her *scorecard!*'"

"What did he mean?" asked the D.A.

Jurgens shrugged, "Who knows? Howie grabbed his keys, jumped into his pickup, and zoomed off doin' ninety. Hit a tree just down the highway."

The verdict was accidental death while of unsound mind. Everything's back to normal at the tavern. Lizzie disposed of the skeletons, but nobody really noticed.

Sergeant O'Toole stood ill at ease on the doorstep. Finally, gathering his courage, he knocked. Minutes later the door opened. "Mrs. Murphy," he began, "we've known each other for a long time."

"'Tis true, Timothy, since ye were a wee babe in y'r mither's arms. An' a cute little tyke ye were."

"Er—that's why the captain thought I should be the one to bring you the sad news."

"Saints presarve us! What sad news?"

"Robbers drilled the safe at National Bank of Ireland last night."

"Did they git me seven pounds six shillin's?" she asked, anxious.

"Oh, the bank will make it good."

"Thank hiven!" exclaimed old Bridget Murphy. Then she frowned, "Ye mentioned sad news?"

"Yes, I must tell you that investigators found a footprint of your son Patrick, a button from the shirt of your son Mike, and lint matching the trousers of your son Eamon beside the safe."

"The nerve o' thim scalawags! Not only do they rob me bank, they stole Patrick's shoes, Mike's shirt, an' Eamon's trousers!

"Sure, an' I'm wishin' ye th' luck o' th' Irish in catchin' thim. A body can't feel safe with th' likes o' sich divils runnin' loose in th' village."

MY MOST RECENT BRIEF CAREER

Mr. Coddington of Federal Manufacturing frowned as he scanned my resume. "Hmmmm," he murmured, an ominous sign, as I knew from experience. "I see," he continued, "you've had seventeen jobs and never held one more than six weeks."

"I'll go now, sir," I said.

"No, wait! I believe in always helping the underdog—looks good in my annual report. Therefore, I'm willing to take a chance on you, Tibbals."

"Oh, thank you, sir! My lucky day!"

"However—" (Oh-oh, I told myself, here comes the cockroach in the ointment) "However," he went on, "you must be enterprising, my boy. Never let an opportunity pass to bring favorable publicity to the corporation."

"You mean I'm hired?" I asked, amazed.

"As of this moment. Now, take this letter to the president of Amalgamated Industries, our rival."

Hoping to help Mr. Coddington, I opened the letter en route. It began, "Dear Bernice—" Aha, I thought, what wonderful publicity—heads of two big corporations in love! I detoured to the *Tribune* and several tabloids.

Returning, I completed my first day sweeping offices.

Next morning, Mr. Coddington summoned me to his office, boiling mad. "Did you see the *Tribune's* morning headlines: 'Rumors of Merger Plunge Stocks of Federal and Amalgamated/Secret Deal Hinted'? And this tabloid: 'Wedding Bells for Business Rivals'? Well?"

"I was trying—" I began.

"Bernice Randolph is suing me! My wife threatens divorce! The board is replacing me!"

"You mean I'm fired again?" I inquired.

"OUT!"

THE KITTY IN THE SEWER

As Patrolman Muldoon stepped around the corner of Liberty Street and Broadway, a man carrying a black satchel came running full speed toward him. The fellow was short, around five-feet-five, with crew-cut red hair and a scar on his left cheek; he was wearing a pea-green jacket.

"What's yer hurry, me bucko?" demanded Muldoon.

"Oh ! Er—ah—it's my cat, officer," the man replied nervously.

"Cat? I don't see no cat."

"Of course not. Y' see, it fell down an open manhole in the 200 block north. It's lost somewhere in the sewer system. I spotted it down a storm drain in the 700 block south and I'm coaxin' it back to where it fell in."

"Can I help?"

"Indeed you can!" The man pointed to a nearby drain. "Just call 'kitty-kitty-kitty' down that while I try the next block!" He dashed northward clutching his satchel.

Muldoon was on all fours yelling, "Here, kitty-kitty-kitty!" when a patrol car screeched to a stop. The Chief leaped out, exclaiming, "Muldoon! What the hell are you doing down there?"

"'Tis a long story, Chief—"

"Never mind. A thief just robbed Quality Jewelers. Watch for a little chap, around five-five, crew-cut red hair, scar on left cheek, wearing a bright pea-green jacket."

"I'll be doin' just that, sir. Meanwhile, I'll help this citizen recover his cat."

"What citizen? What cat?"

"Little guy, mebbe five-feet-five. Crew-cut red hair, scar on his—Holy Christopher! *'Twas HIM himself!* An' probably somebody else's cat!"

SURVIVAL DURING OCCUPATION

I firmly believe in cooperation. It is the key to survival, even in times when one's country is overrun by invaders. Hence, when three more men in uniform, rather dirty and sloppily clad, beat on my door with the butts of their automatic weapons, I hastened to answer. "Welcome! Come in! Would you like tea? Coffee, perhaps?"

The three poured through the doorway, somewhat confused by my hospitality. The bearded captain, the leader, stated gruffly, "We're searching for Abdul ben Ghajji."

I declared in a loud voice, "He's not here!" But I beckoned the captain aside and nodded toward one of two large chests standing in the atrium. He winked his understanding and, weapon ready, moved noiselessly toward it. His two soldiers slouched nearby, waiting for orders.

Now, the pit viper is a nervous snake, especially once it's been handled. The captain flung open the lid. In a flash the viper inside the trunk struck.

"Help!" I yelled, pointing. The soldiers quickly dispatched the viper.

"Quick," I said, "get the injured captain outside!" They complied, but he was already dead. Behind me I heard a scurrying, as Abdul darted from the other chest into the one vacated by the snake.

"Come back," I invited the two soldiers. "You haven't searched that other chest." Reluctantly, they opened the lid.

The chest was empty, of course. They went away, mumbling thanks for my "generous cooperation."

It will be difficult to find a replacement. Pit vipers are getting scarce in the local area.

THE FRENCHMAN MUGGED IN DUBLIN

The well-dressed man lay stunned and moaning in a Dublin alley. Patrolmen Michael O'Dwyer and Patrick Moynihan came upon him while making their round through the unsavory district.

"Sure, and who might he be?" asked O'Dwyer. "Don't recolleck seein' 'im before."

"Passport in 'is pocket says he's Pierre Lamont from France," reported Moynihan.

"Why's he lyin' there, Patrick?"

"Mayhap a mite too much ale at yon pub. Frenchmen drink only wine regular, I've heerd."

The mugging victim stirred, holding his throbbing head. "*Mon ami, secour!*" he mumbled.

"And did ye hear that, Patrick?" said O'Dwyer. "We'd best hunt f'r the woman. She's somehow mixed up in this."

"Who?"

"Weren't ye listenin'? Some woman named Mona Meesecoor."

Pierre Lamont pleaded, "*S'il vous plait!*"

"Patrick, me boy, she stole 'is silver plate! So, start lookin' f'r a suspicious female named Mona Meesecoor runnin' off wit' Mr. Lamont's silver plate."

"Crime's sure increasin' lately," remarked Moynihan.

"That it be," agreed O'Dwyer.

The man on the cobblestones muttered, "*Mon Dieu! Pourquoi moi?*"

"What'd he say?" asked Moynihan.

"'Tis worse than we thought, Patrick. Monday she robbed poor Kwam-wah—probably a visitin' Chinese."

"Faith, and what do we do now?"

O'Dwyer leaned over the stricken man. "Don't fret, Mr. Lamont. Wit' a bit o' luck, by the time ye sober up, Patrick an' me will have arrested the thief—Mona What's-'er-name—an' have y'r silver plate back safe as Killarney shamrocks.

"No, don't thank us. Captain's orders: 'Give special help to all furrin tourists.'"

THE OSTRICH DISASTER

My cousin Yussef—may his soul suffer eternal torment—returned from America with strange ideas. Sad fool that I am, I listened to him. Which explains, sahib, why I started my Rent-a-Camel agency here at Dhar-el-Dammitt Oasis. "You'll be a millionaire!" declared Yussef. I still wait for my first customer and meanwhile feed ten ever-hungry camels.

About the Ostrich Disaster I mentioned, sahib? The tale is best told from the back of a rented camel while touring the oasis. Ah, you wish to rent one, then! I offer this unexcelled racing female for only ten U.S. dollars a day. She will do? Let me assist you to mount, most gracious sahib!

Comfortable, no? Let me begin. Yussef came again, saying, "Good fortune awaits, cousin! I have a hot ostrich."

"Of course it's hot," I said. "It's the desert sun."

"No, no, I mean it's illegal. Ostriches are protected. I have captured one, and buried it to its neck out there. Ostriches produce meat, feathers, and fine leather. You can sell it for much money to the next butcher, hat decorator, or shoemaker who calls at your Rent-a-Camel agency."

I should have known better, sahib. We rode two of my camels to the spot. I dug out the wretched ostrich. Once free, it kicked me viciously—see the scars?—then trotted away at great speed.

Frightened by that bedeviled bird, the camel bearing Yussef galloped off across the desert. It was never seen again. I really miss that camel—but not Yussef.

FORTUNE IN THE LABYRINTH

Always one for the grand entrance, Timothy O'Rorke strode into the Friendly Irishman Pub, announcing loudly, "I'm back!" He was dressed to the nines and held his coat back to display a huge diamond stickpin.

"Haven't seen ye aroun' lately," someone remarked. "Looks like ye found the leprechaun's gold."

"In a manner o' speakin'," responded Tim, "I have. 'Tis all a matter o' showmanship and business sense. What sets all Englishmen daft?"

"The sweepstakes?" suggested Benny the bartender.

"Nyah," scoffed Tim. "It's Shakespeare!"

"*Shakespeare?*" questioned Benny. "That don't explain your sudden wealth, lad."

"Actually, I leased the auld Farrington estate, the one with the labyrinth in back."

"You're jokin'! Old Sir Farrington has been losin' money on it."

"That's because he lacks showmanship. I advertise that Shakespeare is buried in the center o' the labyrinth. Fer a shillin' ye can enter and seek his tombstone."

"Hold on!" someone objected. "Shakespeare's buried in Holy Trinity Church, as everybody knows."

"So they *say*," declared Tim. "But stubborn Englishmen have to check everything fer thimselves. Customers line up dawn to dark, arguin' amongst themselves—and each payin' me a shillin' to go inta the labyrinth. Besides, that tombstone only cost me fifty quid."

"But," protested the bartender, "at that price nobody can get rich."

"Ah, my good man, that's where business sense comes in. 'Tis only a shillin' to *enter*, but I charge ten pounds to lead 'em *out* after they git lost in there. I'm makin' a fortune."

A TIGHT FIT

The well-dressed man was sitting in a folding beach chair, letting the waves wash over his shoes. I recognized him from the description given by Max Schuster in the hospital. Without question, he was Bugsy Galiotti.

I approached quietly. "Mr. Galiotti," I said, "you're under arrest for assault and battery against Max Schuster, the shoemaker. No funny moves! I've got you covered."

"That rat!" he exploded. "It was justifiable whatever."

"What do you mean?" I asked.

"Just lemme sit here while I explain." He shifted in the chair. "I do a lotta sailin' in my yacht—the *Bloody Belinda*. So, I go to Schuster askin' for a pair of black oxfords, size 9 1/2-AA, that won't shrink in seawater. Three C-notes the robber charges me!"

"I understand. But why assault him yesterday if you're just testing the shoes now?"

"You don't unnerstand nothin'!" Galiotti growled. "I tested 'em yesterday. The damned shoes shrunk so tight I couldn' get 'em off. I hobbled back to Schuster demandin' my money back. He laughed! *Laughed!* He tells me, 'The guarantee—right on the receipt in fine print—states that if dissatisfied the product will be replaced with one of equal value.' Then I socked him."

"Go on, Mr. Galiotti."

"I'm not testin' these blasted shoes. I'm soakin' 'em in seawater *again,* hopin' to *get 'em off.* My feet are killin' me."

I let him go. I bought my shoes from Max Schuster's store and my feet were also killing me.

LILY OF THE HEARTLAND

Superintendent Neumann declared, "This fellow Tomaso Vitello was shot in his hotel room around midnight, one .25-calibre bullet in his forehead. Nobody heard anything. Maid discovered the body. Yet you found a million American dollars in a valise in the closet? Obviously not robbery."

"Right," confirmed Inspector Sfalzi. "The only clues are a fresh matchbook from the Purple Whale Club and this." He tossed a memo pad across the desk. Written below the hotel name, in ballpoint, was:

OhIO LIL

Neumann frowned. "Any connection between matchbook and message?"

"Undoubtedly. I went to the Purple Whale. Their star stripper is billed as 'Lily of the American Heartland.'"

"She's from Ohio?"

"Cincinnati, actually. She said, 'Everybody knows Tommy. Big-spending playboy.' But she was doing her act until well past midnight. She couldn't possibly have shot Vitello."

"Well, somebody did," retorted the superintendent grimly. "You didn't arrest her?"

"On what charge?" asked Sfalzi. "No, it's a professional hit. From the money involved, I'd say drug-related. Vitello probably ratted on somebody in the past—or the killer thought he had."

Inspector Sfalzi reached for the memo pad. A moment later he exclaimed, "My God, we're looking at it all wrong!" Before Neumann could react, Sfalzi dashed from the office.

He did not return until late afternoon, exhausted, He reported, "We captured the killer—ballistics match—and also a million in cocaine."

"What?! So, Lily told you where he was?"

"No, the phone company did. Turn that message upside down." Puzzled, Superintendent Neumann obeyed. He read:

7/7 0/4O

CHRISTMAS AT THE CABIN

Big fat Sally Mosely was a 240-pound embarrassment to her husband Henry. The winter turned bitter cold. Stranded in their unheated mountain cabin, she'd quickly become frozen blubber. Afterward, he'd tell investigators: Her doctor predicted Sally would suffer this heart attack if she didn't diet.

Sally eagerly agreed to go. "I'll pack a big picnic hamper. We'll spend Christmas there!"

She squeezed into the back seat of the car. After stopping for gas, Henry sped on his way. The car skidded on the ice-glazed mountain road...over the edge...down...down....

Regaining consciousness, Henry tried to crawl from the wreckage. "For God's sake help me, Sally!" he screamed.

All was silent.

At the inquest, Sheriff Barker testified, "Mrs. Mosely phoned me Christmas Eve, saying her husband Henry hadn't returned from their cabin out on Goat Mountain and she was worried about him. Avalanches blocked the road for three days. When the way was finally cleared, we discovered his car had skidded and plunged fifty feet down an embankment. Henry Mosely's body was frozen stiff."

Sally insisted on making a statement. "We'd planned to celebrate Christmas at our mountain cabin. When Henry stopped for gas, I trotted across the street for more choco-lates—it being Christmas. When I came out, Henry'd driven off. When he didn't come back for me, I just *knew* something dreadful happened to him.

"Henry was s-s-so romantic," she sobbed, "w-w-wanting to share Christmas in the cabin wh-where we'd s-s-spent our honeymoon."

CAPTURING SLICK MALVASI

"Remember," cautioned Superintendent Robinson, "he's called 'Slick' Malvasi with good reason. He's eluded every trap set for him. But this time we have the advantage. My reliable informant reports that Slick will spend the day at Surfside Beach, relaxing after his successful robbery of Grant Brothers Clothing Store. He's five-ten, 175 pounds, dark hair. Watch him at all times! His first illegal move—*nab him!*"

My partner Bill Norton and I arrived at Surfside at 14:23. As we surveyed the crowd, Bill asked, "Anybody know Slick Malvasi?"

"Sure," replied a dark-haired stranger in Bermuda shorts, around five-ten, 175 pounds, "that's him sitting in that beach chair—the gent wearing the gray pinstripe and black fedora, reading a newspaper."

"Thanks," Bill said, as the stranger strolled away smiling.

We took turns watching Slick. He was evidently asleep, for he didn't move a muscle. At sundown Bill went out for sandwiches and Cokes. Still Slick hadn't stirred.

The tide was rolling in. The water reached Malvasi's shoes. He seemed unaware. Soon it reached his knees. He didn't move.

"Good lord, Bill," I told my partner, "he's dead!"

We waded out to investigate. Sitting in the chair was a *store mannequin!* Its label read: "Property of Grant Brothers Clothing."

"Remember that guy who pointed out 'Slick Malvasi' to us?" asked Billy, thoroughly dejected.

"Unfortunately, I do," I replied.

We tossed that blasted mannequin into the ocean, watching it drift away, finally disappearing...like our promotions.

"It's not every day," observed Superintendent Neumann dryly, "that an envoy from Villamancha is blown to bits at Angenehm See. Where is Villamancha, anyhow?"

"In a little Central American republic," answered Inspector Franz Sfalzi. "Esteban Velasquez was a middle-aged bachelor sent here to Austria to promote a trade agreement involving bananas for machinery. He was killed in a rented villa."

Neumann sighed. "Find out what you can."

Which villa was obvious: windows shattered, the door hanging by one hinge. Inside, furniture was blasted against the walls. Curiously, remnants of a table held pieces of a jigsaw puzzle *glued in place.* The explosive device had been magnetically detonated.

Sfalzi questioned neighbors. One elderly couple cooperated eagerly. "Carried on like honeymooners," volunteered the hisband. "Never bothered pulling the blinds."

His wife added, "She was Helga Braun from Amstetten. She dropped a letter once, which I returned. I supposed he was Herr Braun, but nowadays who knows?" She shook her head.

Located in Amstetten, Johann and Helga Braun had perfect alibis, reliably confirmed.

Later, Inspector Sfalzi reported to Neumann, "Braun did it."

"Why?"

"The usual—unfaithful wife."

"You're certain he's guilty?"

"Absolutely. Johann Braun wiped away all *fingerprints—except* some in the glue under the puzzle pieces."

"But," objected the superintendent, "if Braun was in Amstetten, who set off the magnetic bomb?"

"Esteban Velasquez himself. A *loose* piece contained a metallic strip. After all, who can resist putting in the last piece of a jigsaw puzzle?"

I GIVE YOU THREE WITCHES

Gilbert Samuelson was drunk. Unquestionably. He'd been fired as a teller at Citizens' Bank that morning. As he staggered along the beach, he spotted a bottle. Still sealed! His luck was changing.

Eagerly he extracted the cork. Out oozed bluish-gray smoke, slowly materializing into a turbaned genie, who intoned, "I give you three wishes, master."

"Three w-w-witches?" stammered Gilbert.

"Granted!" *Poof!* In the genie's stead stood three ugly, stooped, black-gowned witches.

"I'm Marella," rasped the one with bony fingers. "I'm Saffina," droned the one with fiery eyes, "And I'm Hepzibah," cackled the one with the warty nose. "What's troubling you, sweetie?"

"That Henry Tuttle at the bank. I wish I had *his* money."

"You got it!" the witches giggled, pointing to a satchel. Trembling, Gilbert opened it. Twenties, hundreds—nearly a million, he estimated.

"Anything else?" queried Marella.

"I wish he was dead!"

"You'll see it on the newscast, dearie. He's just been fatally stabbed."

"Great!" declared Gilbert. "Now I wish I was in Tahiti."

"Whoa!" exclaimed Saffina. "Tahiti's outta our range. But here's an airline ticket for tonight's flight."

"Haw-haw-haw!" Gilbert laughed uncontrollably. "You gals have been just great! Hee-hee-hee! And to think I never believed in witchcraft. Maybe we'll get together sometime."

"Too bad police arrested Gilbert at the airport," lamented Marella. "I sure miss the little guy."

"Me, too," added Saffina. "He seemed so greedy and vindictive—just like one of us."

"Perhaps, sisters," said Hepzibah thoughtfully, "we shouldn't have stabbed old Henry Tuttle with Gilbert's knife."

PETER POMEROY'S PERFECTLY PRESERVED PUMPKINS

The glare of the overhead light awakened old Peter Pomeroy. He bolted upright in his bed and stared at the masked intruder holding the pistol.

"Is this s-some kind of Halloween prank?" he queried.

"I'm deadly serious, Mr. Pomeroy. They call me the Patent Pirate. I've followed your career with interest since you retired from the munitions industry and took up horticulture."

"Wh-what do you want?" asked Pomeroy, trembling.

"First, I must bind you to a chair. I know your handyman Paul Peckham won't return before morning. We have all night." The Pirate produced a rope and proceeded to tie the old man securely.

"Now," he declared, "my spies report that you genetically alter pumpkin seeds to produce pumpkins that never decay. You even hire guards to patrol and protect your precious pumpkin patch. The commercial possibilities are limitless. *I want those plans and I'll stop at nothing!*"

"Please, no violence," pleaded Pomeroy. "My old heart couldn't stand the strain. The plans are hidden on the porch—"

"Exactly where?" demanded the insidious invader impatiently. "And no trickery!"

"Where else?" answered the oldster, "Inside the jack-o'-lantern there."

"You'd better be telling the truth!"

"Just lift off the top," said the old man.

The Patent Pirate departed. As Peter Pomeroy patiently awaited his handyman Paul Peckham's arrival the following morning, he chuckled softly to himself, anticipating what would happen next. His prognosis proved positively correct.

The explosion plastered the porch with perfectly preserved pumpkin—along with pulverized pieces of the pernicious Patent Pirate.

WE REMEMBER SALLY

Our class of '79 at Prairie High held its tenth reunion in the rented VFW Club. A group of us gathered at one side, nursing our watery drinks along. We spotted Joe Fenwall, who was already far along on the hard stuff. "Come, join us!"

"You know," I began, "I had the strangest dream about Sally Jones last night. I suppose it was this upcoming reunion."

"Poor Sally," sighed Mary Osborn (now Mrs. Garver). "I've never told anyone before, but just days before she hung herself on the night of graduation, she confided to me that she was pregnant."

"Shocking!" exclaimed Tom Egan. "I'd never have suspected Sally played around. She was the most straight-laced, sincere girl in our class."

"In my dream," I continued, "Sally kept repeating, 'Please, it wasn't my fault!' She was crying."

"My father was the town physician," stated Jack Garver. "He asked me point-blank if I'd got Sally in a family way. I hadn't. I never told anybody, not wanting to soil Sally's reputation."

"That skunk who got her pregnant," declared Mary, "must have raped her. What else did you dream, Rob?"

Joe Fenwall suddenly paled and dropped his drink. He staggered out into the parking lot, took the revolver from his glove compartment, and shot himself.

Our remarks that night had all been contrived speculation. And our invitation to Joe to join our group had been carefully planned. We all loved Sally. It seemed the least we could do in her memory.

MURDER IN THE WHITBY'S SHED

Bein' sheriff wouldn't be so darned hectic if it wasn't for women. I'd just got home, tired from chasin' skinny-dippers outta the creek, when my wife Sally declared, "You must investigate immediately, Henry! The most awful thing happened!"

"What?" I asked.

"I got it straight from Jenny Powlis, who learned all about it from Becky Loomis—"

"Exactly *what?*" I interrupted.

"Eleanor Whitby's husband George murdered her lover in that dark little potting shed back of their house!"

To sort it out, I started with Mrs. Powlis. "Jenny, what's all this about the Whitbys?"

"Oh, sheriff," she replied, "Becky Loomis saw it all! Eleanor and some stranger went into her *so-called* 'potting' shed. Stayed for an hour! Then her husband discovered them. It was horrible!"

Maybe this was serious. I checked with Mrs. Loomis. "You'd better act quickly, sheriff," she said. "The way Eleanor behaved, this man was *no stranger to her.* They disappeared together into that mysterious shed she keeps. Later George went inside. *Only the Whitbys came out!*"

George Whitby was at home. When I told him about the rumors circulatin', he laughed, "Come meet Eleanor's cousin Jeff." He opened the shed door and introduced Jeff Armbruster.

"Danged gophers are ruining the foundation," George explained. "Jeff's setting traps."

I told everybody concerned about the situation.

Next day Fred Wythe, the lawyer, approached me. "We'll plead insanity, Henry."

"*Insanity?*" I gasped. "For what?"

"Collusion with the Whitbys to hide this notorious Chicago gangster. Mrs. Loomis told me everything...."

THE REPO JOB

In the woods twenty-seven miles west of Turberville stands a dark little house only sixteen feet square. It arouses such painful memories I plan to leave Turberville for just about anywhere else. But I'm getting ahead of my story.

Upon graduating from high school, I avidly read the Chicago *Tribune* want ads. One intrigued me: "Repo man wanted. Must be alert. Apply Box 103, Turberville, IL." I assumed they wanted an alert *reporter*. Was I wrong!

After considerable correspondence, I learned the Turberville Collection Agency wanted somebody to *repossess* unpaid-for items. They hired me. My first assignment was a sofa bed in that accursed little house. My boss, Joel Snyder, informed me that Hector Farthingdale had missed several payments. Driving the company Ford, I finally located the house and knocked.

"Go away or I'll shoot!" shouted Mr. Farthingdale from inside.

"Sir," I shouted back, "I've come to repossess your sofa bed!"

"Just a minute!" he yelled. I heard pounding and ripping sounds. The door opened and various pieces of wood, upholstery, and stuffing were flung out. I loaded them into the Ford's rear seat and returned.

Mr. Snyder wasn't pleased. "Show initiative, boy! Go back and get something of equal value. Here, take my pistol."

In the gunfire exchange I lost two toes and the bill of my Chicago Cubs baseball cap; my jacket ended beyond repair. But finally Mr. Farthingdale surrendered all his possessions: his rusty old rifle, a battered kettle, a dull hatchet, and two cans of beans.

A CURSE OF ANOTHER COLOR

Over afternoon tea beside an isolated, windswept graveyard, four witches compared their latest victories. All were jubilant as Wartella chortled, "I really ruined that latest Middle East peace conference. The delegates left angrier than when they arrived."

"And I," cackled Sabrina, "spread armed warfare in central Africa. Villages burned, thousands maimed!"

"My contribution to evil," rasped Badilla, "was introducing drugs to more teenagers."

"Good work, sisters," declared Flamella. "But we're not perfect yet. Remember Antonio Scabrini, head of the Sicilian Mafia?"

"Dear little Tony," said Wartella dreamily. "So wicked, immoral, and vicious—just like a son."

"Thoroughly vile," added Sabrina. "One couldn't help loving the fellow. What became of him?"

"Sadly," answered Flamella, "I must report he's having a bad time again."

The gaiety stopped abruptly. "That's hard to believe," said Sabrina. "The last time he appealed to us a rival threatened his organization. As I recall, we prepared two bags: a red one and a green one. The first was for him to offer as a gift to his enemy; whoever opened it would be cursed with ten years of misfortune. The green bag contained enough jewels and bonds to make the owner the richest man on earth. Didn't you deliver them with instructions, Wartella?"

Suddenly Wartella wailed, "Oh, that poor guy! And it's all *your* fault, sisters."

"What do you mean?" they demanded.

Salty tears coursed down Wartella's wizened face. "You girls *know* I'm color blind!" she sobbed.

MCNABB'S PUMPKIN RAIDERS

Deputy Dan Coggins stood stock still in the center of the moonlit pumpkin field, mentally reviewing Sheriff Dawkins's instructions: "Dan, boy, we'll forget last year's disaster—can't remedy that now. But if you let one pumpkin get stolen outta Mayor Jarvis's patch this October, you're fired!"

"That you, Mr. Coggins?" The voice startled him. Dan gripped his pistol as a dark figure arose from behind a huge pumpkin. "Wh-wh-who's there?" he asked fearfully.

"Just Billy McNabb, sir. The gang thought you was a scarecrow but I told 'em no, that's fearless Deppity Coggins stationed here to protect these lovely pumpkins—"

"Don't you dare touch one, Billy!" interrupted Coggins.

"Oh, I wouldn't think of it, sir, not after you saved me from a lifetime of crime. Know how we did it? Keep watching those bushes along the south border of the patch, that's where we usta sneak through, matter of fact, that's where I heard some naughty boys will try again tonight..."

Two hours later Billy was still explaining, "...we started out swiping just one apiece for jack-o'-lanterns, sir, next we got bolder and took enough for our friends, then stole enough to sell commercially, but I'm glad you're here to keep me honest. Well, goodnight, deppity. *Keep watching those bushes at the south end!*"

"Thanks, Billy."

Deputy Coggins stared intently southward all night. At sunrise he turned to see that McNabb's gang had stolen *every pumpkin from the north half of the field.*

TESTING WITH ELEPHANT

Elephants have always fascinated me. That's why I suddenly braked my car while driving along a particularly barren stretch of old US 66. A well-dressed man was coaxing a baby elephant from an old airplane hangar out into the desert. What further intrigued me was the huge billboard sign: TESTING GROUNDS. I strolled over to a bronzed gentleman holding a clipboard.

"Sir," I inquired, "are you testing elephant intelligence?"

"No, mister," he replied. "Elephants all have about the same IQ—highly intelligent animals."

"Then why conduct this experiment?" I persisted.

He looked at me disdainfully. "If you must know, that man is the subject. I'm testing him for an executive position."

"Oh, now I understand. He must demonstrate patience, perseverance, and persuasion in getting that baby elephant across yonder line. Very ingenious way to examine leadership ability."

"Yeah, that's part of it," he informed me.

"There's more?"

"Of course," he declared impatiently. "See that culvert over there? The subject could take refuge there. Or he could try hiding behind the billboard. Or he might attempt dashing back into the hangar for safety."

"But why would he want to do any of those things?"

"We're really testing the subject's ability to make quick decisions during crises. You see, mister, as soon as he coaxes the baby elephant across the line, my assistant in the hangar whips the blindfold off the mother elephant. Then comes the *crucial* part of the test—survival in a hostile environment."

GOSSIP

Changes were bound to occur when Tompkins Manufacturing was taken over by Allied Products. Edgar Tompkins remained temporary head of his company, nearing retirement anyhow.

Tompkins welcomed Jim Banner from Allied, even loaning him and his wife Marie use of his lake cottage until they could find housing. Jim and Marie also met George and Roberta Wilson and Bill and Helen Snyder; George and Bill were holdovers from Tompkins Manufacturing. Unexpectedly, someone sent Jim two matinee theater tickets—unsigned.

Returning from the theater performance, the Banners delayed going indoors. Instead, they sat in the porch swing, savoring the glorious sunset over the lake.

"I still can't figure out who sent you those tickets," said Marie. "Somebody knew your birthdate—your new boss, perhaps?"

Jim laughed, "That old has-been? No chance! His young wife maybe."

"Stella isn't likely to send *you* theater tickets. Whenever her husband's out of town, she has another torrid affair with George Wilson. But Roberta Wilson shouldn't mind; she flirts with every man around. Her latest conquest is Bill Snyder."

"I'm surprised Bill can spare the time from fudging Tompkins's books."

"Sun's down, darling. Let's go inside."

As soon as Jim opened the door, he was greeted by a perfunctory "Happy Birthday" by Edgar and Stella Tompkins, George and Roberta Wilson, and Bill and Helen Snyder. None seemed overjoyed that Jim had reached another birthday. In fact, they seemed to resent it. Yes, corporate changes were inevitable.

BETWEEN TWO WORLDS

It was a desperate, forlorn feeling I shared with Sean O'Connell. We were hundreds of miles up the Amazon, our supply boat long overdue, batteries in our radio run down, our medicines exhausted, and we both had jungle fever. Natives might survive there, but we belonged in a different culture.

Sean, my colleague in archaeology, was from the University of Dublin. Together we were investigating rumors of a "Great City of Beautiful Things," but so far we had seen no artifacts. Natives declared the place possessed "Big Magic," some sort of taboo. We two lay on our cots, our clothing sweat-drenched, occasionally waving away mosquitoes.

"Mother can move into the house of her dreams," Sean was muttering, "now that Father is rich."

I paid little attention because my head throbbed agonizingly. "And soon, old friend," Sean rambled on, "I'll know all about the 'Great City'." With an effort Sean arose. "Now I must meet the boat to take me home." He stumbled out the door.

Another delusion, I decided. When he didn't return, however, I wobbled toward the landing. The supply boat *had* arrived. The captain was bending over a body.

Sean was dead.

Somehow the captain got me to a hospital and arranged to ship Sean's body home. Later I learned Sean's father *had* become rich, winning the sweepstakes.

Did Sean dream it? Or was he somehow midway between this life and the next, knowing both? Maybe I was delirious and only imagined what he said. Regardless, it mystifies me.

AN ARTISTIC DEATH

In central Tuscany, the ancestral castle of the Buonarrotis towered defiantly above the village of Caprese. Impregnable, it had through the centuries withstood innumerable sieges because of the deep well in its basement, attainable from above by a ladder. However, by 1475, that well had gone dry.

In that year, twins were born to the Buonarroti family. Almost from the moment of birth, it was obvious that the older, Primoangelo, was abnormal. Ashamed, his parents kept him hidden. By age ten, however, he became so vicious that he was secretly spirited away to the care of discreet peasants.

At age twenty-five, his younger twin, Michelangelo, was already famous as a sculptor and painter. He had secluded himself in the castle to complete several paintings commissioned by Pope Julius II.

At this inopportune time, a rider arrived in the night, breathless, bearing news that Primoangelo had escaped. Michelangelo began preparations against his brother's certain vengeful return.

From his basement refuge, Michelangelo heard his brother above, shuffling, searching. His torch illuminated his form in the opening. He started descending.

Before Primoangelo realized the ladder was only a painting, he broke through the thin canvas and flailed down...past the basement floor...down...until he crashed at the bottom of the well.

The artist waited several minutes for further sounds ... There were none. After dragging the heavy oak cover over the mouth of the ancient well, Michelangelo retrieved the real ladder and climbed slowly past his ruined masterpiece.

THE JOKER

We all miss Eddie Jelk. But I suppose we'd also miss arthritis, poison ivy, and ulcers if we had endured them for years. Eddie was a practical joker, although the "practical" description baffles me.

Take the time he sent out invitations in the name of his friend Dan Frye, inviting fifty people to a banquet. It was bad enough when we showed up only to discover it was a hoax, but Eddie had arranged by phone with the restaurant for an expensive menu and wines—all in Dan's name. No question who did it; but Eddie, straight-faced, denied everything. Poor Dan ended up in a lawsuit.

Why his wife Mary put up with Eddie nobody understood. His favorite target was her plump older sister Joanne, who claimed to have a heart condition. If she didn't before, she did after her dinner chair broke (Eddie sawed the legs nearly through) and her dessert exploded in her face (Eddie constructed the mouse-trap device).

He never understood our resentments. "Take a joke," he'd chuckle. One afternoon Eddie had an enormous old safe delivered to his home.

"You can help," he grinned. "At tonight's party, I'll hide somewhere. You yell, 'Help! Eddie's locked himself in!' They'll worry for hours!"

"It's too small," I objected. "Nobody'd believe—"

"No, I'll show you." He opened the door and crouched inside. I slammed it shut, spinning the dial, remembering how his poison-pen letters destroyed my marriage.

Then, I yelled, "Help...!"

POWER OF THE PRESS

"Never underestimate the power of the press." Whoever said that first was the smartest man who ever lived. I have only a small press—an outdated linotype machine—and just five subscribers, yet I make a yearly fortune. I could retire anytime.

I'm only thirty, a high-school dropout who managed to buy a second-hand sloop. Plying the South Seas, I discovered uncharted islands, scarcely more than isolated specks in the vast ocean.

Then in a Sydney bar, I made friends with a New York gangster who was on the lam. For merely $20,000 a year, I would "rent" him one of "my" islands and deliver monthly supplies at "actual" cost. Within weeks I lined up four others, same deal.

The thatched-roofed shacks I constructed are invisible from the air, and I made certain none of the five took a radio ashore.

There are two worlds: the real world and the one rolling off my press. In the latter, during just the last twelve months, inflation increased five-fold, Wall Street collapsed, and China declared war on Australia.

World conditions steadily deteriorate.

All five are extremely grateful to me for providing them such safe havens. They've begged me to manage their financial affairs. When they're broke, I'll still deliver their necessities.

I'm not heartless.

RETURN TO THE STAGE

The audience is hushed. My host of admirers out there breathlessly await my entrance upon the stage. Tonight they shall witness my finest performance! I step from the wings into the spotlight...

The quality of mercy is not strain'd,
It droppeth as the gentle rain from heaven
Upon the place beneath...

I exit dramatically. "Bravo!" erupteth the audience. "Bravo!" A curtain call. And yet another.

But hearken! Doctor Stevenson and his servant Arthur approacheth. I hear them conversing yonder. Arthur is saying, "You were right, doc. There she is, standing by that pillar. Does she always come here to this deserted old theater?"

The doctor replies, "Invariably. She was a great Shakespearean actress in her time. I remember, as a boy, my parents brought me here to see her perform. Don't worry, she'll come quietly." Stepping forward, he addresseth me, "Miss Langley, it is time to return to the home."

Laughing, I inform him, "Tonight I am Portia in *Merchant of Venice.*"

"Of course. And a marvelous one! But—"

"Was I really that great, kind sir?"

"At the peak of your career!" he assures me. "But we sorely miss you. Come."

I take my final bow. "Farewell, gracious ladies and gentlemen!"

Doctor Stevenson offers me his arm. "Hurry, dear Miss Langley. Let us make our triumphal exit."

Arthur comments, "That sure was easy, doc."

Poor Arthur. Reality escapeth his grasp. He seemeth oblivious of the throng of happy theatergoers, homeward bound with memories they will cherish forever.

WEB OF THE SPIDER

Our Chief of Intelligence, Balkan Division, closed the door before announcing, "Agent X has delivered precise locations of Iraqi germ warfare laboratories."

"Quite a coup," commented Agent John Garver. "You have it secured?"

"Absolutely!" said the Chief. "It's in my safe yonder. Not even Rumanian Secret Police suspect we are anything but an import business. This office is on the twenty-fourth floor of the only skyscraper in Cladescu, floodlighted at night . I've installed high voltage devices at all doors, and my men guard elevators and rooftop."

"Wise precautions, sir,'" I said.

"Yes," declared the Chief, "only Spider Man himself could get in here tonight."

After Garver left to check our warehouse inventory, the Chief turned to me. "Such information is a tempting target, worth billions! Meet me tonight behind the old cathedral."

We huddled in the chill mist rolling up from the Guvonic River. "What's that you're carrying?" I inquired.

"A newly developed holographic projector," he replied.

As we watched, a figure scaled the building. When it reached the twentieth floor, the Chief flicked on the projector. Unbelievably, a giant three-dimensional spider began descending the sheer face!

The climber spotted it, screamed in terror, and fell...down...down...

I dashed forward. "My God, sir!" I gasped. "It's John Garver!"

"Yes," said the Chief, "I suspected he was a traitor."

I shuddered. "A horrible death. But your report from Agent X is safe."

As he turned away, the Chief declared unemotionally, "There was no report. 'Agent X' never existed."

DINNER AT L'ELEGANTE

Their dinner at L'Elégante had lasted two hours and forty-three minutes. Elaine knew exactly, for she had sneaked glances at her diamond-studded wristwatch—another ostentatious gift of Niccolo Rossini—hoping he wouldn't notice. She knew better than to complain, remembering when she'd tried to break their engagement.

"*Nobody* refuses Niccolo Rossini!" he'd hissed, twisting her arm painfully.

This evening had been pure agony, starting with the menu.

"I want good Italian food!" demanded Niccolo. "Not this puny French garbage!"

His loud outbursts continued over the wine: "Ain't you got anything fit to drink?" And the entree: "What kinda dump you run without no pasta?"

Elaine had little appetite left.

Finally the bill was presented. "Robbers!" shouted Niccolo. "For this wretched little snack you want $275?"

The waiter said quietly, "I must consult M'sieur Pierre—"

"I'll consult the bastard myself! Lead the way!"

A half hour passed. The waiter returned and bowed. "Our sincere regrets, mademoiselle. Your escort will not be returning. *Le docteur* has been summoned."

"Doctor?" queried Elaine, confused.

"*Oui, mademoiselle.*"

"But Niccolo's in perfect health," she objected. "Exercises regularly, so it can't be his heart. Perhaps a little indigestion—he does overeat, you know."

"Far worse, I fear, *mademoiselle*. M'sieur Rossini seems to have, ah, over-extended himself. He will *not* recover."

Elaine felt exhilarating relief. "You're certain?"

"*Oui.* M'sieur Pierre offers condolences—and there will be no charge for the dinner. He trusts that you will find future happiness by dining at L'Elégante as his guest."

PRINZ-DUNNE COLLEGE

Prinz-Dunne College is not widely known. It was founded in 1674 by Horatio Prinz and Ebenezer Dunne, two enterprising traders whose non-discriminatory policy included slaves regardless of sex, color, or religious preference. Both were hanged for piracy, but not before—on a drunken bet—establishing our college with an endowment which, with wise investments, has sustained our faculty royally and permitted periodic renewal of accreditation through bribery and/or threats. Our name is our outstanding asset; our graduates can claim, whenever asked, "My alma mater? Prinz-Dunne!" Spoken with a practised slur, it opens gates of opportunity.

Unfortunately, our faculty is getting old. I am junior member at seventy-seven. At our monthly meeting, President Samuel Dingle declared, "Other colleges are lowering academic standards to attract the intellectually-deficient offspring of millionaires. Soon we will have no undergraduates whatever."

Faculty members were aghast. "*Caramba!* What do we do?" lamented Pedro Gonzales (Romance Languages).

"Initiate an athletic program," I suggested. "Athletics currently draws students to certain educational institutions."

"But," Dingle objected, "what if we win championships? The media spotlight...our history exposed...utter ruin!"

"Deplorable!" proclaimed Roger Twiddy (Philosophy) so loud he woke up three colleagues.

Then I had a brilliant inspiration. "Appeal to our loyal alumni to scout star high school athletes with low academic achievement. We give each high marks, assuring his eligibility at a major university. Naturally he flunks there and transfers back. *Repeat four times!*"

The vote was unanimous. Only elderly Charlie Potter (Mathematics) abstained, being too arthritic to raise his hand.

HALLOWEEN PERPETUATED

"Drat!" muttered the old woman with the long warty nose and fiery eyes, as she hobbled to the door. "Just when I'm brewing a cauldron of my beauty enhancer. Now I'll probably forget to add eye of newt." She opened the creaking door.

"Halloween's tomorrow night," she cackled to the man and woman standing there. "Besides, ain't you two a bit age-enhanced to be trick-or-treating?"

Ms. Janice Ballantine spoke: "We represent the non-discriminatory gender-balanced Community Improvement Committee. We wish to complain about your defiling air quality with noxious fumes from your unapproved chimney emissions. Unless our detectors show significant abatement, we're calling in the EPA!"

"But, dearie," protested the elderly black-clad homeowner, "I use only natural ingredients in my potions."

"Be that as it may, Ms. Hellchild," declared her other caller, Algernon Twiller, the lawyer, "the major concern of the CIC is your unauthorized display of those six skeletons outside. You are consciously and with malice aforethought perpetuating a distasteful myth with quasi-religious overtones, thereby contaminating the mindset of the youth. Unless you remove those six skeletons, we intend to prosecute!"

"I've had it!" screeched old Hepzibah Hellchild. "Your attitude is completely biased against traditional witchhood!" Extending a bony finger, she uttered magic curses....

On Halloween happy neighborhood children trooped past the *eight* skeletons to the neon sign: TRICK-OR-TREATERS WELCOME! They didn't notice that their generous handouts contained high-cholesterol sodium-rich cookies bearing remarkable resemblances to the missing Ms. Ballantine and Mr. Twiller.

"Nothing like old-fashioned holidays," chuckled the witch.

DEATH OF A BORROWER

The autumn winds gave me away, swirling leaves from my mulch pile and revealing the body of Egbert Hochstetter....

Egbert, who lived between me and Homicide Detective Ryan O'Doole, never returned *anything*. I needed my hammer back and asked Egbert for it.

"Oh, *that!*" he said. "I discarded it last week. Handle broke. Obviously poor quality."

My lawn needed mowing. My mower wasn't in Egbert's cluttered shed. "Okay, Egbert, where is it?" I demanded.

"I donated it to the Salvation Army," he replied. "You wouldn't want it. Blade got dull. You should buy a riding mower. Very comfortable, they say."

No matter what I needed, Egbert had borrowed it—without asking. I started locking my garage, but sometimes forgot. There went my wrench set, screwdriver, and hedge trimmer.

"Egbert!" I exploded. "If you take one more thing from me, I'll throttle you! That's a promise!"

"Not feeling well today?" he asked innocently. "Incidentally, where's your mulcher?"

I bribed Egbert's boss to transfer him elsewhere. Three weeks of uninterrupted bliss ensued! Then one morning my doorbell rang. There stood Egbert.

"Oh, lord," I groaned. "I thought you'd moved."

"Neighbors there were so downright unfriendly, I came back. First, I'll need a chisel to open some crates—"

"That was the last straw, Ryan. I killed him," I confessed.

"Let's not be hasty," advised Detective O'Doole. "Yesterday he 'borrowed' my car and seduced my wife—totaled the car. I'm reporting Egbert Hochstetter was murdered by 'persons unknown.'"

181

MAGOO AND THE PYGMY ELEPHANT

Unexpectedly, Magoo presented me with a pygmy elephant ("Magoo" wasn't exactly his name; the tribe spoke a curious Bantu dialect, and his name began M-g-h-u—which we Europeans never pronounce correctly.)

Young Magoo stood holding this miniature elephant by a vine rope. "This for you, Bwana Mac," he grinned. "He named Yumbo."

I bowed formally, suspecting the tribesmen wanted something in return from me, the District Ranger. Sure enough, after some hesitation, Magoo began, "About Bwana Pierre." (What had the troublesome French trader done *this* time?) "He sell bad cloth, no-good knives," declared Magoo.

"I'll speak to him," I promised.

Pierre Lebeau occupied a shack adjacent to mine. Tying Yumbo to a post, I entered. "Lebeau," I accused, "you're selling shoddy goods to the natives again."

"So what?" he sneered. "If it's red or shiny, they'll buy it." We argued long, neither winning.

That night Yumbo's trumpeting awoke me. "Bwana Mac," yelled Magoo, "your elephant has done awful things! He trample Bwana Pierre's goods, chase him into desert!"

By moonlight I saw Lebeau running desperately, pursued by the elephant with trunk upraised. I overtook them in my Land Rover. The Frenchman's clothes reeked of peanut oil (undoubtedly Magoo's handiwork), explaining why Yumbo chased him.

"Don't come back!" I shouted at Lebeau. Corralling my elephant, I returned.

Protocol demanded a hearing. "This misbehaving elephant," I solemnly pronounced, "I condemn to spend the rest of its life in the jungle—alone and unprotected."

All the tribesmen cheered, especially the unflappable Magoo.

TEMPTATION

In the neighborhood where police ventured only in pairs, Samuel Tillet staggered through the door. Blood dripped from his jacket. Dropping the bags, he gasped, "Viola-Rose, I done it—robbed the (cough) bank. I'm rich! Now...I...can—" He collapsed, dead. Stepping over the body, the young woman left—with the money.

Across town in a posh apartment, Roger Vickers declared, "I did it, Viola-Rose—poisoned my wife. Now we can marry and—"

"What?!" She recoiled, pulling her negligee closer around her curvaceous body. "Surely you don't think I'd marry a *murderer!*"

"But after all we've—"

"Forget it!" she snapped and started dressing.

Mid-town, in political headquarters, Henry Alsop boasted to his charming secretary, "Hah, Viola-Rose, our trumped-up charges, smears, and insinuations paid off. My opponent is finished—kaput. What say we have a few drinks to celebrate?"

"I hope this position pays well, Big Henry," the young woman remarked.

The suave politician looked at her in surprise. "Why?"

"Because I have all the evidence of your skullduggery on tape, Xeroxed forged documents, everything." She reached for her purse. "I'm starting a vacation in Bermuda, but I'll be in touch. Count on it."

In an elegant, dim-lit cocktail bar, the Gentleman in Red checked his list: "Tillet by greed, Vickers by lust, and Alsop by ambition... Yes, we have them all quite securely."

He turned to the young woman beside him. "Congratulations, my lovely. You have done well today, Viola-Rose—or should I call you Jezebel, or Delilah, or..."

HEAVENLY DECISION

You earthbound mortals perpetuate the silly idea that Saint Peter stands at the Pearly Gates, deciding who to let inside. The truth is: heaven has no gates, and Old Peter only comes around as final authority on difficult cases. I should know—I'm George Hawkins and I pull the Wednesday afternoon shift on Admissions.

Jenny Durfee was taking longer than most. "Any problems on earth?" I asked.

"None."

Having reviewed her life-cassette, I knew she was lying. Abused as a child, then abandoned, she'd stolen food for herself and her brother. There were later sins aplenty.

"What about your term in Juvenile Detention?"

"Mistaken identity." She'd faced so many judges below, Jenny knew all the angles.

"I'd like to help," I sighed, "so you can join your brother."

Suddenly her eyes gained the proper light. "Little Joey! How is he?"

"No longer little," I informed her. "Thanks to kind adoptive parents, Joseph became a judge before he was killed in an accident."

"So he made it! I haven't seen Joey since the court separated us years ago. Is he okay now? How about his leg—did it heal?" Her eyes grew misty.

I had to decide quickly. Jenny Durfee was holding up the line. With some reservations, I stamped "Temporary/On Approval" and directed her to Processing to be fitted for gown and wings.

"Good decision," said Saint Peter over my shoulder. "Jenny's already demonstrated compassion. I predict she'll quickly develop the other essential virtues. Anyhow, she has eternity."

THE PERFECT CELL

The political aspirations of Pedro Corrales soared high above the dusty streets of Oxalita and far beyond its adobe hovels. As village constable, he had designed something desired at all governmental levels in Mexico: the perfect jail cell. His Excellency, provincial governor, was himself coming to view it.

Bedsprings overlain by mattresses (scrounged from Mexico City dumps) made the room soundproof. Lights and air circulation were controlled from outside; the cell had one of the few flushing toilets in all Oxalita; food and requests were passed through a clever device; and prisoners could not injure themselves. Further, it was practically escape-proof. Proudly, Pedro spray-painted it pure white.

All it needed for display to His Excellency was a prisoner. The constable stepped outside into the brilliant sunlight and arrested Isabella.

"What for, Señor Peeg?" she asked.

"The usual—soliciting."

Isabella seemed satisfied; she went submissively. To avoid contamination of his grandiose cell, Pedro made her bathe—with soap—putting aside her dirty clothing in favor of a thin dressing gown. Straining, she enclosed her ample body within it. Quickly Pedro shoved her into the cell, locking the door. His Excellency was due any minute.

Federal investigators found his car on a side street, but His Excellency was missing. A week passed. Pedro continued pushing tortillas and frijoles inside to Isabella.

Discouraged, he gave up, opening the cell. There were Isabella *and* His Excellency! He had arrived early, unobserved. Would Pedro get a city position anyhow?

His Excellency was smiling broadly.

THE JOKER NO LONGER JOKES

The moment my taxi turned into Rosemont Avenue and I saw my home still standing, not even scorched anywhere, I realized Harry had played his final joke on me.

I blame myself. Friends cautioned me that Harry was a practical joker who often went too far. But I married him anyhow. Love? Infatuation? Foolishly, I thought he'd settle down.

As soon as we returned from our honeymoon, however, he phoned my sister Kate. "Mrs. Argosi? Your husband Tony just had a *horrible* accident!" Harry hung up, chuckling.

I rushed right over to explain. "Kate, Harry was just joking." Our relationship was never the same.

"Harry," I warned, "you'll regret these vicious pranks!"

We vacationed in Italy, visiting my relatives. In a restaurant, Harry spilled ketchup on his coat. Accidentally? Attempting to clean it back in our hotel, I discovered a letter in the pocket: *Contract fulfilled. The fire burned your house completely, leaving charred female body of proper size. You still owe me fifty big ones.* No signature.

I confronted Harry. "So, you plan to kill me for the insurance!"

He laughed uproariously. "Figured you'd find that fake letter. I really scared you, didn't I?"

I wondered. Could Harry have had our home torched with a convenient body inside, giving him the perfect alibi while murdering me here?

Anyhow, I told my brothers about it. Soon thereafter, Harry's car mysteriously exploded and burned—with him inside.

Harry had *his* warped sense of humor. We Borgias have *ours.*

PRETTY LADY ON A MEAN STREET

When Helene Vickers moved into Wofford Street it was like a kitten falling into a pit full of bulldogs. I watch my step along that wretched street and I'm the champion boxer of the New Orleans Police Department. Frankly, I didn't think the pretty young widow stood a chance.

She proved braver than I'd thought. She never complained. But I learned that while she was out working as bookkeeper for the Great Mississippi Steamboat Company, her laundry was torn off the line and her windows spattered with filth. One evening as I came by she was trying to scrub away the sign somebody'd painted on her door: WHORE.

So it went. Women despised her beauty; men hated her virtue. All were determined to make her life hell.

"Why not give up and move away?" I asked. "A lady like you don't belong on a mean street like Wofford."

"And move where?" she retorted. "This is all I can afford. I'll survive somehow."

Then unexpectedly she announced, "I'm leaving on the boat tomorrow night."

I dropped around to wish her goodbye. All the other residents had taken their families to the free minstrel show down on the levee. Mrs. Vickers, dressed in her finest, stood alone in the street, watching smoke pour from every house.

"Well," she challenged defiantly, "aren't you going to arrest me?"

I shrugged. "Probably spontaneous combustion, ma'am... You'd better hurry now to catch that packet boat."

LA BELLE DAME

No one in New Orleans knew whence she came, but everyone agreed she was the most beautiful woman the city had ever seen. Several duels had been fought upholding her reputation. Madelaine Lemoine was her name and she lived on Perdue Street.

Naturally she had many suitors but, one by one, they mysteriously expired—no marks of violence. Lately the lady was being ardently wooed by François Dupre, heir to the Dupre fortune.

That fateful Sunday morning a dark-skinned lad pounded upon my door. "My mistress—" he panted, "—she say come quick—Jasmine Court!" Hurriedly grabbing my medical satchel, I followed him.

The chatelaine of Jasmine Court greeted me, wailing, "*Mon Dieu*, nothing like this happened in my houses before—"

"What, *madame*?" I interrupted.

She led me to number 6. The door stood ajar and I entered. The naked body of M. Dupre lay sprawled across the silk-sheeted bed. I examined the corpse thoroughly.

Stepping into the street, I encountered Mme. Lemoine, dressed in height of fashion, with bearing of a goddess. "I need not inform you, *mademoiselle*, that he is indeed dead," I declared.

She paled. "Then you know."

"*Oui.*"

"Beauty is a curse!" she exclaimed bitterly. "Men want everything but marriage."

"I would marry you this day—regardless," I said gallantly.

"At last," she breathed. "A *man*—a man of honor and compassion." Removing her huge tulle-bedecked hat, Madelaine Lemoine let the long bloodstained hat pin drop. Then she embraced me passionately.

THE FEUD

The property dispute—call it a feud—between the Garvers and us Wilkins began before Jim and I were born. It involved the boundary between two halves of sixty acres of rich bottom land alongside Cattarugus Creek, about the only good fields on either farm.

Originally it heated into gunfire; Grandpa Wilkins and two Garvers were shot. Things quieted after Sheriff Jones threatened to "take care" of the next one to fire a rifle.

Dad died saying, "Don't never trust a Garver."

Jim was seventeen and I was fifteen, and times were tough in '32. It didn't take a hawk's eye to see that *our* thirty acres somehow got smaller each year, but we boys couldn't retaliate.

One hot August day Jim and I were taking turns plowing corn with our two mules. We could hear the ruckus of young Bill Garver's new tractor. Suddenly the motor idled and Bill screamed. His tractor'd overturned, pinning him.

"One less Garver," said Jim, mopping his forehead.

I couldn't stand it. Unhitching the mules, I used them to pull the tractor off Bill. He was bad hurt. We slung him over one mule's back and rode to the village doc, explaining what happened.

Next morning Old Man Garver drove his Essex into our yard. "Damn!" Jim swore. "We should've left Bill."

Garver strode up to the porch. "Bill told. I now reckon yore Grandpap owned *forty* of them acres. Leastwise, that's where I'm puttin' the fence."

Then he rode off.

THE PANTYHOSE MURDER

A murder! Right in the Vienna Hilton. I was excited at the prospect of assisting Inspector Sfalzi and learning something of his methods.

We sat in Superintendent Neumann's office as he outlined the case. "The murdered man is Roger Haskell, an American banker who frequently visits Vienna. The woman whom he registered as his wife is Frau Helga Ault, from the village of Mödling some fifteen kilometers south of here."

"Who discovered it?" Sfalzi inquired.

"Frau Ault began screaming. The hotel people notified police. They are there now. It has all the earmarks of a lovers' quarrel gone bad."

Inside room 357 of the Hilton, Helga Ault sat red-eyed and incoherent. The patrolman on guard pointed to the body.

Roger Haskell had been strangled with a pair of pantyhose!

To my disappointment, the inspector gave only a cursory glance at the body. Instead, he examined the personal effects of the deceased and Frau Ault.

"We should find Herr Ault," he declared. "The wife is innocent—of murder, that is." He grinned slyly.

The husband's alibi quickly broke down. He had trailed the lovers to the hotel and, while his wife was absent, strangled Roger Haskell.

I still didn't understand. "Sir, how did you know it wasn't Frau Ault? Why did you suspect her husband?"

Inspector Sfalzi seemed puzzled by my questions. Then, shrugging, he smiled. "You are not married, young man. No woman would use up her last pair of pantyhose in that manner. At least, not in Vienna."

THAT EVERLASTING WALNUT TREE

Slippery Jack Snyder pointed from the cab of his pickup. "Walnut tree like that, Johnny," he said to his cutter, "straight bole, knot-free—worth $5000."

"Yeah." (Johnny never said much.)

"Come along, Johnny, watch me skin this yokel." Snyder braked at the mailbox, noting the name painted on it. With his helper trailing behind, he strode up to the door and knocked. An elderly farmer peered out. "Cyrus Jensen?" began Snyder smoothly.

"Yep."

"See you got a walnut tree. Thought you'd want to sell it before it gets phyllodropsicus. Lot of that spreading this way."

"Oh!" The old man's eyes widened.

"I'll give you $300 for it—cash, naturally." Snyder began peeling off the crisp bills.

"To make it leegal-like," said Jensen, "sign this here paper sayin' the tree's your'n and the $300 is mine to keep."

"Gladly!" The timber buyer signed with a flourish. "We'll be back tomorrow to cut it."

"I'll tack a SOLD sign on it. You kin cut soon as you buy the easement."

"Easement?? What easement?" asked Snyder suspiciously.

"Why," drawled the farmer, "the right-of-way to yore tree. You see, the tree is your'n, *but the land leadin' to it is mine.* I calcalate that easement is worth $5000."

Slippery Jack was still swearing as he drove off.

The farmer's wife plodded from the barn, leaning sideways to balance the pail of milk. "Cyrus, you sly old dog," she grinned, "you sold that walnut tree *agin.*"

"Yep."

THE SYMPATHETIC HANGMAN

When the prison guards lodged Jimmy Carson in death row, the hangman recognized him at once, and felt a great pang of sympathy mixed with sorrow. Not that Albert Jones was maudlin or over-emotional; he had pulled the lever on too many scaffolds for that. His mind drifted back nineteen years, to the time when his name had been Henry Carson. He couldn't quite remember why he had quarreled with Charlotte—something about his drinking—but she had left with baby Jimmy. Through the years he had secretly followed the life of his son.

The prison superintendent spoke. "Carson is scheduled tomorrow morning, Albert. I hope this winter storm lets up. Makes it all so damned inconvenient."

"I understand, sir," ventured the hangman, "the kid now claims he confessed only to shield Dan Darrow, who was captured up at Denver last month."

The superintendent snorted. "They all grasp at straws when their time approaches."

"But," protested Jones, "newspapers reported that the sheriff there is investigating. Maybe Darrow's the one did the shooting."

"Makes no difference. Telegraph lines are down and no rider could get through this time of year. Besides, Carson's convicted."

"If only he had a delay—just a few weeks."

"Well, he hasn't. So be ready at dawn."

Next morning they discovered Albert Jones's tracks leading through the deep snow, up to the scaffold. There his body swayed with each frigid gust of wind.

"Damn!" swore the superintendent. "It'll be weeks before we get another hangman."

SHOWDOWN AT CHAPARRAL

When the little train chugged into Chaparral, an unlikely figure descended from the solitary coach. The portly man was middle-aged. His polished shoes had never touched a stirrup, and his holster was carried awkwardly high.

He consulted the gold watch from his vest pocket, glanced up and down the dusty street, and entered the saloon. As he did, a slender man turned quickly away and approached the bartender. "Who's the fastest gun hereabouts?" he asked anxiously.

The bartender motioned. "That's Kid Carter in the corner, the bearded guy in the black sombrero. Fastest *I've* ever seen."

The slender man sidled up to Carter. "I'm John Adams. I'll pay $10,000 to kill the man who just entered."

"Why?" Kid Carter inquired coldly.

"He's Andrew Jameson, president of a New York bank. He's become a bulldog since his son Tom ran away ten years ago. I embezzled—"

"Where's the money?"

"My room upstairs."

The Kid strode to face Jameson. Toward one side he saw Adams with his pistol aimed, ready.

"Draw!" commanded Kid Carter.

As the banker fumbled to get his gun out, Carter fired. Unbelievably, his shot went far wide, killing Adams instantly. Then Jameson finally drew and fired.

As Kid Carter lay bleeding on the barroom floor, he whispered, "Sorry, Dad."

Andrew Jameson bent down, peering closely. "My God!" he cried. "It's Tom!"

The bartender, who'd witnessed many gunfights in his time, came over. "You just creased him, sir. He'll recover. But I'd never have believed it. *You* shot Kid Carter!"

THE NAVAJO WAY

To Soaring Dove
Navajo Reservation
Kayenta, Arizona

Dear Grandmother,

My greetings to the schoolteacher, who will read this letter to you and explain it.

When I left the Reservation for the university you warned me: Beware of belacani *—white men. You were right!*

I won a grant to study ancient Egyptians, people older even than the Anasazi. At a party in Cairo I met Hakkim ben Kaffik, who said, "American student, eh? Got enough money?"

"Twenty thousand dollars," I told him.

"I know of a secret temple, a labyrinth of passageways. Here's a map I made. Interested?"

"Let me study that map overnight, please."

Next morning he drove us to a distant temple in the desert. As we entered I said, "Here's your map. I now know the way in. I'll lead." Deep inside the temple, Hakkim lighted a torch, then said, "Sign over that money if you want to ever leave here! Think about it. Meanwhile I'll fetch more treasure." Laughing, he disappeared with the flashlight. We Navahos never get lost. Quickly leaving the temple, I drove his jeep back to Cairo and reported to police.

The sympathetic captain said, "Someone should have warned you about that scoundrel. He's wanted for stealing antiquities. Don't worry. Temple looters always find their way out."

This time, I knew, Hakkim ben Kaffik would not. I'd spent the previous night making critical changes to his map.

May your life be long, your hogan contented, grandmother!

Little Brown Owl

THE LIN-KUN CONTROVERSY

In A.D. 500,000 Earth officially celebrated WHY—World History Year—the opportunity for scientists to examine legends and lore of the past. One intriguing problem involved the Ancients' open-air temple at a place still called Rush-Mor, with its four gigantic faces of gods carved in stone.

The President of Universal Mankind himself addressed the Assembly: "Progress has been made! Using the newly developed TAR—the Time Audio Retrieval machine—we now know the four gods were named Wah-Shing-Tun, Jeff-Ur-Sun, Roe-Zee-Velt, and Lin-Kun. Our next goal is to discover how the aborigines sculpted their graven images."

Controversy developed. Some postulated the Ancients reached such heights by mounding up earthworks. Geologists objected: no evidence existed of huge piles of rock and soil removed later.

Others contended the builders had lowered themselves by primitive ropes from above. To test their hypothesis, a volunteer descended thus from the top of Lin-Kun's head. "Impossible!" he declared. "It would require fifty thousand sculptors suspended simultaneously and laboring for centuries."

The ASS—the All-knowing Scientific Society—met for weeks. Finally the Chief Scientist announced their conclusion: "Indeed a great advance in our knowledge of history! In only one way could the aborigines have sculpted the image of their great god Lin-Kun. It is indisputable that at that early stage of evolution mankind had already invented what we still regard as a supreme achievement. I refer, of course, to the CHAD—the Controlled Holistic Atom Disintegrator!"

The audience solemnly nodded, grateful for enlightenment, knowing ASS decisions constituted Truth.

THE HAPPY MARRIAGE

My dear sister,

Remember how you advised me against marrying Emile Doddsworth, saying he only wanted my fortune? That he was twenty-five, athletic, and 175 pounds, whereas I was forty-four and, well, slightly over-weight at 195? Furthermore, you said, he was a famous archaeologist, whereas I read only lurid romance novels? Well, you were wrong!

For our honeymoon, Emile took me to a remote ancient temple. "I'll fix you a special breakfast, darling!" he boasted. It looked delicious; but I was trying to diet, so when he stepped outside I traded plates with him. The poor boy was dreadfully sick that morning, but I nursed him back to health.

Later he invited me into that temple, very dark inside despite the torches, with spooky winding corridors. He laughed when I took my walking stick, "No snakes in here, my sweet. Walk straight ahead for your big surprise!"

Luckily I groped with my stick, for there lay a deep pit. I turned back to warn dear Emile of the danger. He was nowhere around. Then it dawned on me—he wanted to make love in that romantic setting! I hurried back to camp, put on that filmy night-ie (the one you laughed at), and returned to the temple bearing a candle.

Seeing me, Emile was quite overcome. He ran outside, screaming across the hot desert, doubtless seeking some precious gift to lay at my feet!

Sunstroke, the doctor decided. Sweet Emile really died of love. His funeral is Tuesday.

Sincerely,
Evelyn

SWEET JENNY UNDER THE WALNUT TREE

Old Sheriff Buck Olson leaned an elbow on the still-cluttered table in the Starlite Cafe. "C'mon over and sit, Elmer," he called out.

Reluctantly, Elmer Fogarty obeyed.

"See you sold a walnut tree," stated the sheriff, watching Fogarty's expression. "When are the cutters comin'?"

"Tomorrow, they say."

"Interestin'," said Olson. "That tree is about of a size to be blown over by a storm. That'd expose the roots, I reckon."

"Yeah," acknowledged Fogarty nervously.

"As I recollect, Elmer, that was one of the walnut trees you planted some twenty years back—just after Jenny disappeared." Fogarty began sweating, and the sheriff went on, "I never understood why a sweet woman like Jenny would just run off and leave you so sudden-like."

"But she did, Buck," insisted the farmer quickly, avoiding the other man's eyes.

"Y'know where I think Jenny is?" Getting no answer, Sheriff Olson continued, "I think she's right under that particular walnut tree you sold. In fact, I'll bet my badge that's where you buried her."

"You got no proof," protested Fogarty.

Olson scowled at the interruption. "Proof? I'll get that soon enough. Why did you kill a good, sweet wife like Jenny? Huh? Well, it don't matter *why*. I'll be keepin' an eye on that tree 'til the buyer cuts it. Then I got this warrant to dig out the stump." The old sheriff tossed the document across the table, arose, and walked away.

Elmer Fogarty just sat there, holding his head in both hands.

SARAH AND JOHN

Sarah Barker rocked, nursing her bruised head. How she longed to be back in her old home in Oregon, where she could wake to the sound of surf breaking at the foot of the cliff.

When Father died, she had to see lawyers in Eugene and stay overnight. In the hotel, John Barker introduced himself and proposed. Sarah realized she was 42 and unattractive. She married John and they moved to Milwaukee. Sarah used the money Father left her to buy the house.

Ever since Vacations Unlimited made the fabulous offer to buy her old home and property, life had been the same.

"But I promised Father I'd never sell," she would plead, shielding herself from the inevitable blow.

"Of course I married you for your money!" John would shout. "Stupid, ugly cow!"

Sarah wondered if all married life was like this.

Her neighbors, Mary Trotter on the west and Betty Dawson on the east, knew differently. "You've got to leave him," they urged.

One day she told them, "I'm going back to Oregon and John is going to Africa." Why had she lied? she asked herself.

Sarah emptied the oversized chest she had brought from home and divided the linens and coverlets between Mary and Betty. Then she scrubbed the floor spotless.

Home at last! Getting the wheelbarrow from the tool shed, Sarah trundled the huge chest to the edge of the cliff—and over.

Maybe John *would* get to Africa. She hoped so. It would cleanse away her lie.

ELLEN IS NO LONGER THERE

Albert Johnson was secretly amused when the fat policeman with the bloodhound face called a second time.

"Come in, Sergeant Vrascu," he said deferentially. "I hope you bring news of Ellen."

"Afraid not," said the homely sergeant. "Mind if I sit? It's my feet."

"Please do," Johnson invited.

"Your neighbors say she threatened to leave you—several times."

"Oh, we had little disagreements, true, but we are actually very devoted."

Sergeant Vrascu fumbled awkwardly to locate his pad and pencil. "If you'll give me a description, we'll issue an APB."

"Anything to help find Ellen." Johnson supplied the information.

"Nice place here in the country," remarked Vrascu as he waddled out. "A little far for me, though—walkin'."

Albert Johnson enjoyed the exercise, hiking carefree to his office. He made it in 23 minutes. His secretary handed him a letter marked "Personal." Absently, he tore it open. The handwritten message: *I know what happened.*

Probably a hoax, thought Johnson, and dismissed it. The next day, however, a second letter arrived: *I know where Ellen is.* No one could know—could they?

The third message really worried him. Like the others, it was locally postmarked. It read: *Ellen is no longer there.*

Unable to stand it longer, Albert Johnson that night took his flashlight and went to the back of his property. The grave was undisturbed! He sighed, relieved.

Sergeant Vrascu was back quite early the following morning. "Thanks for using that flashlight," he said. "Incidentally, Ellen is no longer there."

SAY THAT AGAIN?

Maryanne adjusted her hearing aids once more, anticipating the first sounds of footsteps coming to meet her in the chapel. Would it be the minister? Or Harry himself? Time dragged so slowly.

It began that morning. "Finally tidying up your desk, Harry?" she remarked.

"Yeah. I'm transferring to Philadelphia."

"To fill a *what?*" she asked, not quite understanding.

"PHILADELPHIA!" he practically shouted.

"Oh... I thought—after all we've meant to each other—"

"Almost forgot." Snatching a notepad, he scribbled, "Meet me at St. Bonaventure's chapel after work."

Maryanne was on cloud nine. That afternoon she overheard Harry say to Bill, "Maryanne...real pet...in the church." And Bill responded, "That's cool!" At least that's what she *thought* they said.

As hours passed and the setting sun shone through the chapel's west window, she began to have doubts. Her hearing *had* been getting worse.

Then she figured it out. Harry had been saying, "Maryanne's a real *pest*. I'm leaving her in the *lurch*." And Bill had declared, "That's *cruel!*"

So that was Harry's little joke. Well, two could play that game! Stifling her tears, Maryanne hurried back to the office, skipping supper. Seating herself at Harry's computer, she retrieved his final report and began changing figures, making an outlandish transfer from the company's reserve funds to Harry's private account....

Harry nervously awaited the verdict. The jury foreman announced, "Guilty!"

Maryanne heard *that* quite distinctly.

Roger Hazlett succeeded gloriously in everything he tried. So, he had no actual need to boast. But he invariably did. As his closest competitor, I caught most of his sarcastic taunts and sneering contempt. When he won the university scholarship—"Naturally they gave it to me"; and when he married Cynthia—"Of course she preferred me."

I had closed my repair shop and dropped in at the town's only bar for a beer. I'd almost forgotten Roger. Then unexpectedly, he swaggered through the door and glanced contemptuously around until he spotted me.

"Jimmy Lang!" he announced overly loud. "Still stuck in this one horse town as I expected. I was on my way back to my New York investment office and thought I'd drop in at the bar—where I expected I'd find you."

"Hello, Roger," I responded glumly. "Same old Roger."

"Don't take it so hard, fellow, that I'm better than you at everything. What did you find to do hereabouts?"

Everyone at the bar was listening. "Oh," I answered, "I run a little shop, but I find time to do a bit of climbing. I'd demonstrate, except Devil's Face is almost dark. Anyhow, it's too dangerous for you."

"That's suicide," someone muttered.

Roger overheard the remark. "Not for me it isn't! Come on!" All barroom patrons assembled at the cliff base.

"I'll go first," I volunteered.

"Hell no, Jimmy. From the top, I'll enjoy watching you squirm."

Roger made it over half way. Better than I'd ever done.

A WOMAN WAITS FOR ME

Perfectly formed features, emphasized by deepset almond eyes, and a statuesque figure that even her *djellaba* could not disguise. Her beauty defied description. I was sitting at a little sidewalk cafe in Aleppo, finishing a beer to clear away dust of the Syrian Desert. With fluid grace she approached and chose a nearby table. I *had* to meet her! I went over. "May I join you?" I inquired.

"Please do," she invited in perfect English.

In minutes we were conversing easily. Her name was Faleema. "I'm an archaeologist searching for the fabled Temple of Astarte-Baalshamin," I explained.

"It exists," she stated positively.

"You're jesting."

"No, I was there as a girl. A labyrinth inside. My cousin made a map. But he wants $20,000 American for it."

"That's all I have, Faleema. But it'll be worth it!"

"Bring the money with you tomorrow. Here." She arose, blew me a kiss, and melted into the passing throng.

I was ecstatic. "Tom," I told my partner, "we'll be famous!"

"Be careful," he cautioned. "Two years ago a bewitching female promised the same to Professor Hawley. He's still missing."

"Faleema is different," I insisted.

Next morning she was already at the cafe. "You brought the money?"

"Right here."

"Fine. We'll pay my cousin later."

Faleema snuggled close beside me, giving directions as I drove far across the wasteland. There was the temple!!

Faleema laughed, "Be prepared! It's romantic inside! I'll go ahead and light a torch."

Somewhere in there the perfect woman waits for me. But for what purpose?

OUR GREAT TELEPHONE POLE DISASTER

Trouble in our town started when the phone company installed underground cable, leaving scattered poles. "Just what we need!" declared Oscar. "A telephone pole! We'll chop some off every night, build a cozy fire in our fireplace, invite our girlfriends over, and—"

"We can't carry it that far," objected Ralph.

"We'll load that heavy sucker into this trolley. When old Charlie the motorman comes, we'll offer to unload it *only* at our apartment house. He can't refuse."

"It'll never fit all the way."

"Not necessary, stupid. Just so it doesn't fall off en route. Now, climb inside and pull while I push."

Unfortunately, their manipulations jammed one end of the telephone pole against the controls. The trolley lurched forward, accelerating, with Ralph inside and Oscar clinging desperately to the pole's projecting end.

In passing Mayor Jefford's new Lexus, the pole neatly sheared off the top. The impact hurtled Oscar into Veterans Park, where he collided with nearsighted Homer Hochfeller walking his bloodhound Rumbler.

Released, Rumbler eagerly loped over for a romantic interlude with elderly Hepzibah Pritchard's poodle Fifi. Screeching "Pervert!" Hepzibah belabored Rumbler with her umbrella before becoming entangled in his leash and tumbling headlong into the fountain.

Meanwhile, after demolishing all lampposts along Broadway, the runaway trolley slowed, allowing Ralph to jump to safety. It finally wrecked itself in the middle of Clear Creek Bridge, blocking all traffic.

Out town will never be the same. Ralph and Oscar are in jail. Only the lawyers are happy.

LEPRECHAUNS

"Special occasion?" inquired the bartender, mentally hoping this martini would be the customer's last one that night.

"Very special!" Fred Barker was excitedly voluble. "I just got my business partner committed, leaving me in charge." He leaned forward conspiratorially, "Here's how. I convinced Harry Armentrout that the leprechauns leave money to true believers. I told him, 'Concentrate that they'll leave ten thousand dollars in the glove compartment of your Mercedes.' He rushed out of the office and—sure enough—there was the money, right where I'd put it."

"You *gave* him ten thousand bucks?"

"Invested it, really. Then I anonymously phoned the police and Dr. Aikmann, the psychiatrist, saying that Harry had been acting strangely lately, insisting he talked to leprechauns."

"Did it work?" asked the bartender, curious.

"To perfection! They hauled Harry away for testing. I got control of the corporation for a mere ten thousand! Hush, here he comes with the psychiatrist and a cop."

"Very strange case," pronounced Dr. Aikmann. "Mr. Armentrout claims you, Mr. Barker, believe leprechauns exist. He passed all lie detector tests."

Fred Barker began sweating. "Actually, sir, it was just a joke I played on my partner. Harry, tell about the ten thousand dollars."

"What ten thousand dollars?" asked Harry Armentrout innocently.

"The money the leprechauns left in your car. Please," Fred begged, "explain to these men what happened—how you believed in leprechauns and your wish came true."

"Me believe in *leprechauns?*" Harry shook his head sadly. "You must be out of your mind."

THE CASE OF THE MISSING ROYAL SWANS

My notes record the most outstanding example of deduction the world has ever witnessed. That November evening in 19— had turned bitter when my friend Herlock Soames, III, returned to our rooms at 221-C Bacon Street. In answer to my inquiry, he replied, ""I've been to see the Queen, Watley."

"She' s well, I trust?" I ventured.

"Quite well. It concerned her missing Royal Swans."

"I presume you solved it with your usual ingenuity?"

"Indeed. Two suspects had been apprehended by Inspector Letstrade. The first, an American gentleman, had a swan in his possession; upon interrogation, he swore he was a producer of nature films and had leased the bird to record the mating call of mute swans. The other, a Russian lady, was transporting a swan in the rear seat of her auto; she claimed it was from her native country and necessary for her performance in Swan Lake Ballet."

"Which one was guilty, Soames?" I inquired.

"Neither. Their explanations were logical. I arrested the poulterer on Market Street."

"Whatever for?"

"Elementary, my dear Watley," said the Great Detective. "His arm bore a tattoo—H.M.S. *Colchester*—clearly the abbreviation for 'Her Majesty's Swan.' The fellow insists that an American gentleman and a Russian lady sold him the huge dressed fowls he has on display, telling him they were 'exceptional geese.' Obviously, a fabrication."

"Amazing, Soames!" I exclaimed in admiration.

"My case will be complete, Watley, as soon as I determine which Royal Swan was named 'Colchester.'"

WAKE UP!

"Of course," my wife Marge insisted, "we want the very best." I never understood why she invariably said that whenever we went shopping—linens, underwear, a can opener—it made no difference. All I wanted was a comfortable bed to replace our old one, which collapsed the previous night.

"Ah, you're most fortunate, madam!" proclaimed the suave young clerk. "We just received a shipment of Ejectors, the crowning achievement of the bedstead makers' art!"

"*Ejectors?*" I queried, apprehensive.

"The very best," he assured me. "Specially engineered for those sleepy-heads who experience difficulty getting up—automatically sends them on their way, can be set for any wake-up time. Imagine the joy of resting soundly before an open window without fear of oversleeping! I just sold one to Judge Albright."

That decided Marge. She considered the judge, our next-door bachelor neighbor, to be omnipotent.

The contraption was delivered, installed, and set for 7:00 a.m. Surprisingly, we slept well. I was awakened the next morning by the meshing of gears and an ominous *click!* Moments later Marge and I were flying out our bedroom window onto the lawn.

We picked ourselves up just in time to witness two naked figures hurdled out the window next door. As they recovered, the judge tried unsuccessfully to hide behind a shapely young blonde.

"You know, Marge," I commented, "that bed was worth every penny!"

"Oh, shut up!" she retorted. "Crawl back through that window, unlock the front door, and let me inside. I'm freezing."

FAREWELL DINNER

The meal left much to be desired. Cold gravy splashed indiscriminately over mushy vegetables and underdone gristly meat did little to stimulate appetites. At the foot of the table, the hostess, Ardelle Parker, declared, "We'll certainly miss being here at the branch office of Allied Bolt Company. As assistant manager, my husband James brings home such delightful stories from the office."

She turned to the gentleman on her left, "Is it really true, Mr. Robbins, that you're having an affair with Janet Stabler?"

Fred Robbins, manager of the branch office, paled and sputtered. His wife Ellen glared alternately at him and at the hostess. Janet Stabler choked and turned an alarming red; her husband George, the foreman of the Peoria branch, glowered at her.

From the head of the table James Parker chuckled, "Ardelle, you really must keep such things secret."

"You mean I shouldn't say anything about George and that secretary—Danielle Something-or-other? How his 'business' trips always coincide with her vacation time?"

"Absolutely not, dear!"

The dinner party broke up early. Mumbling lame excuses, the guests departed.

James Parker hugged his wife, laughing, "You were wonderful, darling! Now that I'm being transferred to Omaha, we finally had the chance to tell off those obnoxious people."

She slipped from his grasp and said coldly, "Surprise! I found out about your affair with Ellen Robbins. This afternoon I phoned the company president in Minneapolis and cancelled your transfer. I'm divorcing you, James—and *you're stuck here!* Keep laughing!"

PARANOIA PARANOIA

"Whenever these anxieties come on," advised Dr. Hendrik Schwarz, "just repeat to yourself: 'There's *nobody* inside my bedroom walls!'"

The man arose from the couch and wrung the psychiatrist's hand vigorously. "You've given me hope, doc!"

At least, thought Schwarz, he's improving more than the lady who fancies her first husband has returned as a bat that flutters in the chimney whenever she entertains guests. Some deep-seated neurosis there.

The doctor closed his tiny office for the day and started walking home. Odd, he mused, how otherwise intelligent people develop paranoia. The problem probably stemmed from an over-stimulated imagination. Easy enough, he supposed, to believe that the buildings along his route were about to devour him. That men's store did have a hungry look. And the cafe seemed to be whispering some plot to the antique store next door. About *him*, no doubt. At any moment they could block his way, and then...

Don't be silly, he assured himself. He'd been treating too many paranoid patients lately. But what if he looked back and discovered the bookstore tailing him, ready to consume him, turn him into some Victorian novel? He quickened his step, not daring to turn.

Suddenly he stopped. He wasn't afraid of this paranoia—he could cure that. What disturbed him was that he'd developed it in the first place: *paranoia paranoia!* A new kind of affliction for the *Journal of Psychiatry!*

He hadn't had it yesterday. My God, he was also developing schizophrenia!

THE SECRET CONVERSATION

Although Marcella was now Mrs. Jason Armbruster, wife of the leading banker in our city, and Lucretia had become Mrs. Harley Burton, married to the president of Burton Industries, they were snubbed by leaders of society as "those Scalini sisters." Mostly, of course, it was jealousy and spite that their daughters hadn't married as well.

Lady Penelope Worthington, in particular, relished broadcasting at her exclusive clubs, "Their father Giuseppe, you know, was deported to Sicily—unspeakable crimes, I heard!"

Lately, however, society matrons had shifted the subject to the series of bold nighttime robberies of their mansions. Burglar alarms were bypassed; police found no clues. Only valuable gems were taken.

Both Marcella and Lucretia were strikingly beautiful. They continued to dress exactly alike, as they had from childhood. As they met on the street, both were wearing fashionable dark sheath dresses and outlandish tall, floppy-brimmed hats which concealed their faces.

"Have you heard about that horrible robbery last night?" asked Marcella.

"What!" exclaimed Lucretia. "Still another?"

"Yes, indeed!" replied her sister. "Mrs. Vanderhorst's diamond tiara was taken—her prized family heirloom."

"Gracious! Nothing is safe anymore."

The sisters were quite aware that undercover police might be eavesdropping on every word they said. However, taped to Marcella's forehead was the message: DIAMOND TIARA SAFELY SMUGGLED TO PAPA.

And on Lucretia's forehead appeared: LADY PENELOPE WORTHINGTON'S TONIGHT, TWO O'CLOCK, WHILE OUR HUSBANDS ARE STILL AWAY ON BUSINESS.

The two young women giggled. Passersby wondered what the joke was.

FRIENDS NO LONGER

Everybody in our town came to associate Eileen Pinckney and Josephine Legare. Wherever Eileen went, Josephine went along. They even dressed identically: black wide-brimmed floppy hats and sleek sheath dresses. You could spot the two of them on the street, sharing secrets and giggling. They attended birthdays, church, anniversaries, and reunions together, always inseparable.

It came as rather a shock when I spotted Eileen dining alone in Conover's. "Where's Josephine?" I asked her. "Not ill, I trust?"

"She's no longer my friend," snapped Eileen.

"What happened?" I insisted, curiosity overcoming manners.

"Well," she replied, "suppose you finally discovered that a woman has been playing around with your husband behind your back? Even laughing about it to others? Would you stay friends with her?"

"Gracious no!" I gasped. "'I'm beginning to understand."

"Now," continued Eileen, "suppose you went to lunch with that woman, trying to convince her to reform. In the restaurant she embarrasses the waitress by carping about the food, makes a big display of calling for the check, then slips it to you to pay. Would you retain her friendship?"

"Disgraceful!" I exclaimed.

"And consider that this old bridge partner cheats, dealing off the bottom of the deck when she thinks nobody's looking, puts down the wrong score, and blows smoke in the opponents' eyes. I ask you, would you stay friends with a woman like that?"

"Definitely not!" I declared.

"Well, neither would Josephine."

STRAW HAT WITH BIRDS AND FLOWERS

It was the most outlandish hat imaginable. Absolutely unique. A wide-brimmed straw hat spray-painted gold and decorated with artificial doves, roses, redbirds, daisies, and an impertinent ostrich plume in back. Its shape reminded me of the craze for black floppy straw hats among us girls back home years ago. Somewhere I'd seen that hat before but, try as I might, I couldn't recall where.

The wearer recognized me and approached. "Remember me?"

After an embarrassing pause, I exclaimed, "Madeline Conover!"

"I'm Mrs. Giselle now," she laughed. "I married Jerome Giselle."

"Sorry," I apologized. "I'm rather isolated here, researching my history of Sicily. How about lunch?"

At my favorite little trattoria nearby we passed a pleasant hour chatting about old times. After she left, I reflected that Madeline hadn't once referred to her older sister Eileen.

Months later I encountered Sue Longden, my old college roommate, who was touring Europe. In reminiscing I mentioned seeing Madeline. "Quite a tragedy," Sue declared.

"Tragedy?" I queried. "She seemed happy enough."

"Oh, I suppose you haven't heard. Her sister Eileen had just announced her engagement to Jerome Giselle. Madeline joined them on his yacht. As Madeline and Jerome reported later, a gust of wind blew Eileen's hat overboard and she fell into the choppy sea trying to reach it. She drowned despite their efforts. You recall Eileen's ridiculous straw hat—painted gold, all birds and flowers? Poor Eileen, always the original one."

Suddenly I remembered. And, shuddering, wished I hadn't.

THE VOICE INSIDE THE CANNON

I was having tea at Bainbridge's when Marjorie plopped down beside me. "You're looking glum," she said cheerfully. "I thought you had a date with the handsomest boy in Edinburgh."

"I did," I admitted. "It didn't work out."

"Made a pass at you?" Marjorie's eyes lighted up expectantly.

"Oh, nothing like that," I replied evasively.

"It must have been *something*," she persisted. "Tell me all the details."

"Well, okay. But keep it secret. We took my poodle up to Edinburgh Castle, strolling the battlements. As we passed that giant cannon on South Rampart, I heard a strange little voice from inside it: *'Help me! I can't get out!'*

"Standing on tiptoe, I peered inside. Nothing. I stepped back, perplexed. Then it spoke again: *'It's so crowded in here... Doesn't anybody care? Just a bit of a tug, that's all I ask!'* This time I stuck my head farther into the cannon's mouth, determined to discover who—or what—had spoken.

"'What on earth are you doing, Jessica?' asked my solemn-faced date.

"I tried to explain that I'd heard a plaintive little voice inside the cannon. He laughed—*laughed* at me! That did it!"

Marjorie could stand it no longer. "What *was* in that cannon?"

"Nothing," I told her.

"You mean you're hearing voices? At your age?" She found the prospect intriguing.

"Oh," I answered, "I learned the embarrassing truth later. Just take my advice, dearie. Don't *ever* date a ventriloquist—especially one with a warped sense of humor."

BURYING MY HUSBAND THE CHEF

I felt sorry for the gravediggers, having to chop such a big hole in the frozen earth to accommodate my late husband. Karl was so exceptionally tall I'd had to have his casket hand-made. He always was a problem.

A few neighbors offered condolences.

"We'll miss him skiing on the mountainside, always wearing his tall chef's hat and long white apron."

"Karl was a good chef."

"Always so cheerful..."

"Never expected *him* to commit suicide..."

Hans Jaeger remained silent but I knew that, like me, he rejoiced inwardly.

After the priest closed his Bible, I donned my skis and slogged back to my Edelweiss Inn. No longer would I have to endure Karl making passes at every female guest at the inn nor put up with his daily skiing over to "visit" Marieke Jaeger while her husband was at work.

Hans Jaeger and I had got together, delivering an ultimatum to Marieke: either she leave Inglehof secretly or *else!* She promptly left. Her disappearance caused quite a sensation locally. Karl made inquiries, but nobody knew where she'd gone.

That night of Karl's suicide I served him my finest roast, using all the proper spices. He ate greedily.

"Know what this meat is?" I asked.

"Beef?" he guessed.

"Perhaps I should rephrase that," I declared. "Do you know *whom* you are eating?"

Slowly my insinuation dawned on him. Karl gagged and dashed upstairs. Moments later I heard the expected shot of his pistol.

"I'm Carmella," she announced, gliding provocatively into my office. Spanish dames turn me on. I'm Spike Jammer, P. I.

"What's your problem, doll?" I asked.

"You must help me," she pleaded, kissing me repeatedly. "One of my skeletons is missing."

"Don't worry, beautiful," I consoled her, "Spike Jammer will search every nook and cranny 'til I find your skeleton. What's the deal?"

"I operate a little health spa," she replied. "Just innocent massages, you understand. Every Halloween each of my nine luscious female employees hangs a skeleton outside. This year I count only eight. One is missing!"

We discussed it over cocktails at my favorite gin joint. She leaned forward. Her perfume intoxicated.

"You suspect anyone in particular?" I inquired.

"Well—" she hesitated, "—there's this little Chinese gal."

I headed for Chinatown. A blonde stepped out brandishing a derringer. I instantly disarmed her. "What's your moniker?" I growled.

"I'm Olga Rolandova," she panted, struggling to adjust her strapless gown. Russian dames turn me on.

"You got Carmella's skeleton?"

"Gee, I don't think so," she laughed, hugging me passionately.

In Chinatown I spotted her. Oriental dames turn me on. "Okay, Lotus Blossom," I snarled, "where's the skeleton?"

"Search me," she giggled.

I did. She was clean.

I reported back to Carmella. "I'll locate your skeleton yet, babe. Spike Jammer never quits."

"Oh, Spike darling," she murmured, snuggling closer, "please forgive me. I forgot that the little Mexican number quit last week. So, you see, lover, there is no missing skeleton!"

Case closed.

MY WONDERFUL STRAWBERRY BED

March—"Just imagine!" I said to my wife Margaret. "Our very own fresh strawberries, sweet and luscious! No more buying those green-picked, bruised, tasteless things from the supermarket."

"You know what you're doing, George?" she asked.

"Of course!" I replied enthusiastically. "Just look at the illustration in this catalogue. And they're guaranteed ever-bearing, which means we'll enjoy tasty strawberries all summer and fall."

"Okay, I guess, if that makes you happy." Talk about wifely support! Well, she'll be astounded when my strawberry bed reaches full production.

May—I built an eight-inch wall of treated lumber for my strawberry bed and filled it with black dirt from the garden supply store—cost $68.50. The plants arrived, looking rather pathetic—cost $35.67. I planted and regularly watered and fertilized them. To my amazement, most of them rooted and some even have blossoms!

June—When my berries started ripening (considerably smaller than the catalogue picture), flocks of neighborhood birds had a picnic. So, I installed mesh netting, guaranteed to keep out birds—cost $25.85.

The netting worked for birds, but not for chipmunks, which gnawed right through it. The final crisis came when hawks, attempting to catch chipmunks feasting among my strawberries, became entangled in the netting, tearing gaping holes in it.

July—Having enjoyed strawberry shortcake (made with berries Margaret bought at the supermarket), I settled back to peruse my catalogues. "Look, Margaret," I said, "we can start our very own cherry orchard for only—"

"Over my dead body!" she snapped.

A GOOD CHEF IS EVERYTHING

Mr. Herman J. Potter registered from Chicago, Illinois, signing the card with a flourish. "Back home," he grumbled, "hotels furnish better transportation from airports." That was the first of his complaints. "I trust my expensive skis weren't damaged during that wretched sleigh ride!" ... "Tell that clumsy porter not to damage my bags—they're American-made!" On and on.

Subconsciously, I suppose, I was reacting to the fellow's insolence. Anyhow, I slept fitfully and awoke early. I dressed quietly so as not to disturb my guests. (At my prices, they deserve every consideration.) Chancing to glance out my bedroom window, I was astonished to see my chef, Antoine DeLamoreaux, skiing back to the chalet, still clad in his long white apron and tall chef's hat.

Descending to the kitchen, I inquired, "Where have you been, Antoine?"

"Over to Inglehof!" he snapped.

"Whatever for?"

"That damned American insists on *absolutely fresh* eggs."

Mr. Potter was already waiting impatiently in the dining room, the only guest there. As I served him perfect eggs benedict, he shouted, "Tell your abominable chef I want my eggs sunny-side—like any civilized man!"

I found Antoine in the kitchen brandishing a cleaver. "Don't do anything foolish," I hissed.

"Then I quit!"

"Wait!" I pleaded. "We'll work something out..."

"Unfortunately," I announced to my other guests, "Mr. Potter may be late joining you. He went skiing quite early, ignoring my advice about trying the north slope. Dangerous avalanches there."

Mr. Herman Potter never reappeared. A good chef is *everything.*

THAT DAMNED *CLEMATIS* VINE

On a tour through Scotland, our guide pointed out Castle McDermott, badly in need of repairs but what a view! Just the spot for a hotel. The stubborn owner, Angus McDermott, however, refused to sell. "Cannae part wi' ma heritage," he maintained.

I hired expensive lawyers to investigate. He'd borrowed money on his castle repeatedly. Using all my savings, I bought up all his mortgages. Then, to my surprise, he began paying the interest. I flew to Scotland to find out how.

It was spring. As I approached Castle McDermott, I had to join a long line of avid gardeners waiting to pay admission. "What's the excitement?" I asked a balding gent in tweeds.

"Don't you know?" he responded. "Old Angus's cousin sent him a *Clematis* from Java, probably a new species. Flowers at least a foot across! Absolutely breath-taking!"

So *that* was the source of his income. Well, it wouldn't last. Late that night I sneaked into the castle yard with a hatchet. I chopped that damned vine into a hundred pieces. I left silently and returned to New York. And waited. And waited.

Months later I received a letter from Angus. Eagerly I tore it open. Out fell a check for the full amount of his mortgages! I phoned him immediately.

"Congratulations, sir," I said. "Did you inherit a fortune?"

"Nae," he replied. "Soomebody chopped oop ma *Clematis*. Frae th' twigs, I started new plants. Ye'd nae believe th' prices horticulturists pay!"

THE CODED MESSAGE

Vladimir Conescu remained a man of mystery, having worked in intelligence for his native Rumania, France, Germany, and now the United States. At any particular time, his loyalty lay with whatever country paid most. His treacherous duplicity left behind numerous enemies and no friends. Vladimir Conescu was a marked man.

His current hideout in New York was under surveillance by X, hired to assassinate Conescu. When the housekeeper left, X picked the apartment lock, entered, and shot Conescu—and immediately wished he'd waited, for the victim was writing:

POT
LOOPS
KOOL

Glancing at the message, X muttered, "A simple code. Spelled backward the words read: TOP SPOOL LOOK. Obviously Conescu hid secrets there." After stashing his victim in a closet, X departed to look for a nearby dry goods store.

Soon Y, a counterspy, made his entrance into the apartment. He studied the message, still lying on the desk. "Aha!" he declared. "Simple substitution: 'O' is undoubtedly 'E,' 'L' and 'P' repeated... I have it! NEW TEENS MEET. So that's where the old fox hid secrets!" Y hurried to search for a neighborhood hangout for teen-agers.

An hour later Mrs. O'Hara, the housekeeper, returned from shopping. She spotted the note. "Poor Mister Conescu," she muttered, "don't know much English. Lemme see, now. I can loan him a pot. Begorra that man's got queer taste. I'll have to go back to the store to buy him some more Fruit Loops and Kool-Aid."

THE TORO FROM TEXAS

"Aha! So thees ees the bull you *nordamericanos* breeng to España for the bull fight," said Francesco Morales, the matador, disdainfully. "I keel heem in five minute."

"Maybe two minute," said Pedro Velasquez, the banderillero.

"Don' y'all underestimate our Texas bulls," declared Tex Ralston defensively. "Look at them horns on Black Diablo! Ah bet yore Spanish bulls ain't got horns half thet size."

They were meeting at a practice ring outside Madrid, where Tex hoped to sell his bulls for fighting.

"Eet take more than horns to make a *numero uno toro*," said Francesco.

"*Si*," added Pedro. "*Mucho* more. Eet take heart."

"Your *toro* ees stupid," laughed Francesco. "Already he has hees head through the doorway. Why does not he come out? Ees he afraid?"

"Texas bulls ain't skeered of nobody," declared Tex. "Black Diablo is jest standin' there sharpenin' his horns on thet door frame."

"Bah! That's hard to believe," said Francesco. "Bah!"

"*Si*," agreed Pedro. "Bah and double bah!"

The sleek black bull charged from the barn, catching Francesco on one horn and Pedro on the other. One toss of his powerful neck and both landed on the barn roof. Black Diablo continued across the ring, where he stood snorting and pawing sawdust. "*Caramba!*" said Francesco groggily. "What happen?"

"Ah reckon," drawled Tex, "you fellers hadn' oughta said 'Bah!' Y'see, Black Diablo was raised on mah cattle ranch, and when any man or beast from cattle country hears somethin' like a *sheep* he goes plumb *loco*."

219

EXPLOSIVE SITUATION

Ezra Warfield and Caleb Jones got their start dynamiting stumps to clear farmers' fields. Now the two old fellows were Warfield & Jones, Wreckers. Their expertise could bring down a decrepit thirteen-story hotel without a single brick landing outside the foundation! They prospered and together built a mansion for Ezra on the north side of Katabaka Creek, a duplicate for Caleb on the south side, and an artistic bridge connecting their two estates.

The trouble began when they hired Maisie Fuller as their secretary. Sensuous Maisie dispensed her after-hours' favors eagerly and equitably between her two employers. That satisfied all concerned until Maisie up and married Ezra. Caleb was furious, accusing Ezra of lying about him.

However, old habits are hard to break and, whenever her husband was away, Mrs. Warfield resumed giving quality time to Caleb. Ezra found out and the two men argued violently.

Maisie left town on a week-long visit to relatives. Next morning, while Ezra was off estimating the downfall of an ancient warehouse, Caleb planted remote-controlled explosives in the Warfield basement. That same evening, Ezra installed a pressure landmine under the bridge and phoned Caleb to come over.

Gleefully Caleb punched the detonator button and watched both mansion and Ezra explode sky-high over the Warfield estate. He started to drive over the bridge to inspect the damage...

Maisie returned to find herself both a widow and the new owner of Warfield & Jones. Her mistake was trying to run the operation.

Her funeral is tomorrow.

CRIME IN BENSONVILLE

The paunchy man wearing the tin badge kept his feet atop his desk. "Yeah, I'm Sheriff Frank Benson," he drawled. "You got a problem?"

"Sir," I said, "when I stopped for gas, I happened to look across the street. A man choked his wife to death!"

"Across the street, eh? That'd be my cousin Elmer Benson's place."

"Aren't you going to investigate?" I asked impatiently.

"Oh, all right!" He wasn't pleased.

Elmer Benson admitted us, declaring, "Jenny and me was playin' around and she keeled over dead."

"Sheriff, he was choking her!" I insisted.

"Hold yore tongue, stranger. Elmer wouldn' lie. Jenny had a weak heart, like all them rich Cathcarts. Grandma Benson warned him about marryin' her."

"I'll go to the district attorney," I threatened.

"Ain't one here in Bensonville," said the sheriff. "But if you insist, I'll take you to our Justice of Peace—that's my uncle Ambrose Benson."

The elderly justice fetched his gavel and banged it on his kitchen table. "Court's in session!"

I repeated my story.

"Lemme git this straight, mister," said Justice Benson. "You watched—*through their window*—Elmer and his late wife Jenny frolickin' around?"

"But I saw—"

"We don' cotton to Peepin' Toms hereabouts. Three days in jail!"

Sheriff Frank Benson spoke up, "Parkin' yore car overnight on Bensonville streets is illegal. But fer $50 my nephew Lem will store it in his garage."

"That's nepotism!" I shouted.

"Watch it, stranger! We God-fearin' Bensons don' practice them heathen rituals."

THE DAMNING LETTER

Part of his FBI training, I suppose. Anyhow, Agent Wilkins began with an indirect question: "Why would anyone blackmail the man who befriended his sister?"

"I didn't blackmail Freddie Delaney, I didn't threaten him, and I didn't shoot him," I replied. "So why arrest me?"

Wilkins got to business. "Do you accuse the deceased of kidnapping your sister Clarisse?"

"No, sir. Clarisse is really beautiful, but she'd never been out of the mountains. Passing through, Delaney spotted her, persuading her to leave in his big limo. Swept her off her feet. She dreamed of the rich life. Only he stashed her in a big city apartment and used her."

"So, what's your scenario?"

"Delaney's wife found out about Clarisse, confronting him. He tried to explain everything, admitting Clarisse had a big brother—me. Then she shot him."

"It won't wash. Here's the clincher—in Delaney's pocket we found this unmailed letter addressed to your sister. It reads, in part: 'Your brother threatens to blackmail me unless you return home.' Explain that!"

"It's the clincher, all right," I retorted. "That letter's a fake!"

"Have you any proof?"

"Proof? Not directly, sir."

"I thought not."

"Let me finish. In their three months together, Delaney must have learned a lot about Clarisse, things his wife hadn't time to learn."

"Such as?"

"Clarisse had alexia. You know what that is?"

"Of course, she couldn't read... *She couldn't read!*"

"You're getting the picture, sir."

"Hmm. Seems our investigation isn't complete," he admitted. Reluctantly.

THE PRODIGAL SISTER

"Time to bake more meatballs," remarked Ellie. "I spotted another flock of crows movin' in."

"I wish there were some other way," said Becky. "Besides, killing crows is illegal."

"Scarecrows don't work. Those damned crows eat the eggs of our orioles and bluebirds and scare 'em away," snorted her sister.

"Well," sighed Becky, "I suppose they don't suffer long."

"Of course not, sister. One beakful of the cyanide pills in my meatballs and it's off to crow heaven."

Their kitchen door opened, and the two elderly women turned around apprehensively.

"Well, dear sisters," said the arrival, "aren't you glad to see me?"

"We weren't expecting *you*," declared Ellie.

"Naturally not! You two didn't try to contact me in Australia when Daddy died. You certified I'd died in India, of all places."

"It-it seemed best, Sylvia," said Becky placatingly. "That awful business with the bank, y'know."

"Well, the statute of limitations expired on my embezzlement. Now that I'm back, I'm going to sue you both and sell this farm. I'll contact the sheriff tomorrow. Meanwhile, I need rest."

After Sylvia had gone upstairs, Ellie declared, "I'd like to poison her."

"But we can't, sister," protested Becky. "She's *human*. I'll pray."

"Fat lotta good that'll do," grunted Ellie, joining her sister in bed.

Next morning they found Sylvia dead in the kitchen. She'd got hungry, sneaked downstairs, and eaten some meatballs. "Your prayers worked," observed Ellie.

"Wh-what'll we do?" moaned Becky.

"What we do with all dead pests," snapped Ellie. "Bury her."

A TENDER RELATIONSHIP

Uni-Com Investors transferred me to their Oakwood branch. I moved there, determined to establish myself in the community. I'd met all my neighbors except the resident of the Georgian brick. I inquired about her.

I garnered her basic background, bits at a time. "Joselyn Frankel? An old maid...used to be a judge...moved here after retirement...quite a recluse...."

I called on Miss Frankel. She was thoroughly delightful. As we chatted, the door opened and a handsome young man crossed the room, kissed her tenderly, and said, "Here's a dozen roses for your birthday, mother."

Then he noticed me, and Joselyn introduced him as "Henry, my son."

He and I left together. Outside, I commented, "Your mother is a charming lady."

"Unfortunately, my dear," he confided, "I'm an orphan—Henry Burnett. I was a wild kid once. Judge Frankel talked to me like a mother, set me straight. Years later I returned to thank her. Probably old age, but she thought she *was* my mother. She's such a dear, I'll never set her straight."

Next day I impulsively visited the elderly lady again. "Your son is *very* attractive," I told her.

"Dear Henry," she said softly, "he was basically a good boy when he appeared in my court. I lectured him thoroughly, calling him 'son.' He became a fine lawyer. After his auto accident, however, he really believed he *was* my son. I haven't the heart to correct him."

I've grown to love them both. Still...their facial resemblance is *so* strong, their mannerisms *so* similar, I sometimes wonder....

THE BLACK CURTAIN

Most residents of Truchtelberg—even those of purest Aryan ancestry—were shocked when, one night last week, Neo-Nazis painted swastikas all over Jakob Goldblatt's apartments. They must have used ladders, for Jakob owns the five stories spanning above Heiligen Strasse.

Old Jakob was beside himself. Those of us in the synagogue understood why: both his parents and his two brothers had perished in the Holocaust. From somewhere Jakob obtained meters and meters of black cloth and quickly draped them over the offensive symbols.

Herr Kraus, whose butcher shop was located next door, objected. "You're ruining my business! *Gott im Himmel*, get rid of that thing! It looks like...like...like a death shroud."

Goldblatt was unmoved. "You'd rather everybody see the shame?" he retorted. Then, calming down, "Anyhow, *mein alter Freund*, I promise to take it down when I've cleansed my walls."

Grumbling to himself, Kraus stumped back to his store.

Using a rope, my old friend lowered himself behind the curtain, scrubbing away vigorously. He has become a local attraction. Villagers follow his daily progress by the bulge and the undulations of the black cloth, all the while hoping he will soon finish and remove that unsightly curtain. According to their calculations, freely expressed, his task should be completed Friday.

Actually, Jakob Goldblatt has already scrubbed out the last swastika. Now he faces another problem. I know, because I helped create it. How will we dispose of the five Neo-Nazis we have hung behind that black curtain?

DEATH OF A JOKER

Like other folks in our town, I'd often wondered who shot Jake Roswell—who certainly deserved it. *Now* I know. On his deathbed, Albert Tuttle confided to me, his physician, the full story. It's not pleasant.

Albert was extremely hard of hearing. For years I'd urged him to get hearing aids, but he stubbornly refused.

Jake and Albert were unlikely partners in a clothing store. Jake was a "practical" joker of the meanest kind, while Albert was straitlaced. When they were together in a crowd, Jake would say the most awful things about poor Albert just behind his back, knowing his partner couldn't hear a word. It always got a big laugh.

Jake secretly gambled on the stock market. Not even Albert suspected. Jake started losing, plunged wildly, and lost more. Finally, only complete ownership of the store could save him.

So Jake hired an out-of-town hit man to murder his partner. He even met him in the store. "It's okay," he assured the assassin, "my partner is deaf as a doorknob. Now, he always leaves late by the back alley door, he should be an easy target."

Contrary to his usual habit, Albert left that night by the *front* door. Jake dashed out back to tell his hired hit man the plan had changed.

Jake's bullet-ridden body was found next morning in the alley. Authorities never discovered his killer.

Nobody figured out that Jake was shot the very day Albert finally got his first pair of hearing aids.

OUR APOLOGIES

Dere Cousin Jefferson,

I know how disappointed you and yore wife Victoria musta bin that Fannybelle and me didn't git to the wedding of yore lovely dawter Lucinda. Our apologies, but we didn't even know till our son Jethro read about it in a newspaper down at Kwik-Lube where he works part time. Our dawter Bessy-Lou cut up something awful when she heard. Her dock boss-man gives employees time off from gutting fish to attend family weddings.

Course I ain't certain our old pickup coulda made it all the way down to Charleston anyhow. Jethro claims the carborater's shot. He's hoping somebody will wreck a '67 Ford hereabouts so he kin replace it.

Newspaper sed y'all hed shampain and hired a hole orchester. Shore wish I'd knowed in time, I'da saved you a bundel. Shampain ain't nothing but hard cider and Alka Selzer in icewater, and we coulda served the eats during the Lawrens Welk hour. Reckon y'all hed fancy salt pork with beer gravy? Yum, yum!

You folks jest gotta come see our new home! I already jacked it onto concreet blocks, took the wheels off, and painted it pink. Fannybelle moved our sofa inta the yard. We'll let you and Victoria set on the ends where the springs don't jab yore butts. We'll hev lotsa fun out there evenings watching my new bug-zapper work. It makes real music—zzzt-zzzt-zzzt fer moskitoes and ZAT! fer beetles. I'll even go hole hawg and buy four six packs!

Yore loving cousin,
Ambrose

PROTESTS

"You have a very peaceful town," remarked a visitor to the manager of the Homestead Lodge.

"It wasn't always this way," declared the manager. "We had some very active protest groups. Almost daily we suffered parades down Main Street."

"Suffered?" inquired the gentleman. "I don't understand."

"Oh, aside from political rallies, I recall animal rights groups marching and picketing Mullin's Butcher Shop and Discount Leather Store with placards saying, 'ANIMAL MURDERERS!' and 'STOP KILLING INNOCENT CREATURES!' Then human rights advocates paraded and picketed Solomon Brothers Clothing Store and Archie's Grocery waving signs and banners, 'FAIR WAGES TO ALL WORKERS!' and 'NO SWEATSHOPS ANYWHERE!' One faction even attacked our gas plant bearing huge signs proclaiming, 'STOP POLLUTION!' and 'SAVE THE OZONE!'"

"I presume," said the visitor, "these protests were not always peaceful?"

"Peaceful?" snorted the lodge manager. "Far from it! They got worse. Outside agitators poured into Homestead. Violence, fights, broken storefronts—we businessmen were being forced out of our livelihood. We went before Judge Albritton to object, but he shook his head, saying, 'You cannot interfere with freedom of speech.'"

"So, what did you do, sir?"

"We organized our own march. We closed all businesses for the week. Beating drums, we paraded nightly through residential districts chanting, 'NO MORE PROTEST MARCHES IN HOMESTEAD!'"

"Did it work?"

"It certainly did—as soon as housewives ran out of groceries and their husbands had to take time from work to drive into the city. Yes, protests work."

PROMOTING VITABONE

"I've got a monster idea for publicizing our new dog food!" declared Herbert Watkins, head of Promotion & Advertising.

"This one better be good," growled George Turner, company president. "Already we've invested $450,000 in TV spot commercials, $300,000 in newspaper ads, and another $250,000 in billboards. And our total sales are a measly $155,250. Some campaign you've put on!"

"This one will capture public attention—I guarantee it."

"Okay," sighed Turner, "let's hear it."

"It's low budget—"

"I like it already! Continue."

"We target supermarkets in major cities. I anchor a spring-mounted fireplug on the sidewalk outside to which I tie a cute little dog. I carry a sign saying: 'ALL DOGS LOVE VITABONE—THE STRENGTH BUILDER!'"

"So, what happens, Watkins?"

"Behind the sign I conceal a T-bone steak. Smelling it, the little dog struggles to reach it, thereby tipping the fake fireplug. Crowds gather! TV cameras roll!"

"Okay, try a demo and report back."

Herbert Watkins returned late that afternoon, his suit in tatters.

"Good lord!" exclaimed President Turner. "What happened to you?"

"Slight problem, sir."

"Didn't the little dog want the hidden steak?"

"Oh, it tugged with all its might. Trouble was, two giant dobermans, a German shepherd, and three bull terriers also wanted it. They converged on me, ripping my sign to shreds. Then came the catastrophe."

"What?"

"That little dog uprooted the fake fireplug and headed into the supermarket—straight for a rival dog food display. I have another idea—"

"Don't bother!" roared Turner. "You're fired!"

ROYAL ACCIDENT

"'Tis such a fine spring day," declared King Rudolph, "I think I'll go riding with fair Duchess Imogene. Alfonse, drive the Masserati convertible over to her castle and fetch her. Mind you drive slowly around Grimm Mountain! We wouldn't wish to alarm the sensitive young thing."

"Milord," said the royal butler, "I shall return with her ladyship forthwith."

As King Rudolph anxiously paced his battlements, the Masserati appeared in the distance. It came nearer, and he discerned that it contained only the driver. He hastened down as Alfonse sped across the drawbridge, braked in the courtyard, and gasped, "Bad news, milord! Dutchess Imogene has suffered a fatal accident!"

Recovering from shock, the king demanded tearfully, "Tell me all, Alfonse. Spare no detail."

"Your Highness, I reported to the castle and repeated your desire for a riding companion. Minutes later the lady came forth in riding habit. I held open the door of the convertible, and she seated herself comfortably in back. We started off. 'Faster!' she ordered."

"The accident, dammit! What happened?" growled King Rudolph.

"Sire, as we rounded a sharp turn on Grimm Mountain her hairpiece flew off. 'Stop!' she yelled, leaping from the car to pursue her gorgeous locks. Unfortunately, her dentures and glass eye dislodged. Groping for them, her artificial limb collapsed, tripping her. Her grace fell five hundred meters over the cliff."

"Which eye?" inquired Rudolph.

"The left one, milord."

"You ninny!" roared the king. "That wasn't Duchess Imogene! That was her charming daughter Katarina!"

CHANCE MEETING IN A CHEAP BAR

The old man looks down the beer-stained bar at the old woman and edges closer. Aware of his attention, she advances to meet him.

MAN (*gallantly*): "One hardly expects to see such a pretty lady here." *Somehow the old broad reminds me of Mama—brown eyes, flushed cheeks, gray hair, maybe not as fat. At least she's not as drunk as Mama used to get.*

WOMAN (*blushing*): "You're quite the gentleman, sir." *Same glib tongue as Daddy. Even looks like him—dissipated but handsome.*

MAN: "Let's find a table and get better acquainted." *Real diamond in her ring. I'll hate myself, but I need the dough.*

WOMAN: "That would be nice." *Solid gold Seiko wristwatch. I'll hate myself, but I need the money.*

MAN (*seated, making conversation*): "I grew up in a small town. Upstate New York."

WOMAN: "Funny, so did I. A long time ago."

MAN: "Yeah?" He points. "What's that?" *As she turns he dopes her beer.*

WOMAN: "You mean over there?" *As he looks she spikes his drink.*

MAN (*laughing*): "We're seein' things. Anyhow, my parents were a coupla drunks. Mama ran off and Daddy got caught stealin'. Somebody knifed him in prison."

WOMAN (*suddenly alert*): "My story exactly. Then my brother Sam and me got separated—"

MAN (*excitedly*): "Cindy? Are you Cindy Jenkins?"

WOMAN: "Sam! Oh God, after all these years!"

MAN (*remembering he's doped her beer*): "Let's find somewhere else to talk, Sis."

WOMAN (*relieved*): "Yes, let's! Just leave our drinks and go."

SNAKE

Old Jim Allen thought he was losing his mind. His neighbors thought he'd already lost it, but for a different reason.

Jim had been a widower for fifteen lonely years. Hence, while on a trip to Chattanooga, he met Florette in the lobby of the Ramada Inn, and he didn't hesitate. After all, how many chances does a 69-year-old man have to marry a stunning 25-year-old woman? Their honeymoon began immediately, proving to be all he dreamed about and more. When Jim brought his bride home to Texarkana, neighbors shook their heads. But even the women had to admit she was beautiful—maybe a trifle too much makeup, but nevertheless beautiful.

Then her luggage arrived. One box had screened ends. Gently removing the huge rattlesnake, Florette let it coil around her arm. Jim recoiled. "Kill that slimy thing!" he yelled.

"You're frightening poor Striker," cooed his bride. "He hasn't any fangs. But we'll both leave for $50,000—now or after the divorce, which could cost you more."

Jim pleaded, without success. Then he suddenly realized. "You married me for my money."

"Of course, old man," she said casually.

After sleepless nights, Jim told his friend Ed. At first Ed couldn't believe it, but Florette agreed to show him her pet. Privately, Ed told Jim, "Old pal, you've got *two* snakes. My guess is she's a snake handler from a sideshow."

Jim gave Florette a beautiful funeral. It had taken all his courage to capture a live rattlesnake to substitute for Striker.

PAINTING A RICH FUTURE

"Just read these contracts I ran off at Kopy-Kwik," said Frank proudly.

"I ain't no lawyer," protested Archie, "What's it about?"

"We agree to paint any board fence for $20—"

"We ain't painters," Archie interrupted. "Besides, paint costs more'n that."

"But we don't *actually* paint anything. It's psychology. We ring doorbells in very posh neighborhoods. Rich homeowners love bargains. Then, weeks later, when we haven't started, they sue us—that's how rich folks act."

"Yeah, and the judge gives us thirty days in the slammer."

"No, no, Archie. We hire a lawyer on contingency, who points out that our contract doesn't specify a time limit. We counter-sue for defamation of character. Our clients are very embarrassed and settle out of court for, say, $20,000 each. With all the board fences in Rosedale, we'll be millionaires!"

"It'll never work," predicted Archie.

To his amazement, however, the first lady they contacted, Mrs. Vanderhorst, exclaimed, "Truly a bargain! Return tomorrow morning. My friends will wish to share your wonderful offer."

Twenty ladies were lined up to sign contracts. "Thanks, madams," grinned Frank.

"We've already purchased paint," stated Mrs. Vanderhorst "You can begin immediately."

Suddenly Officer Muldoon appeared from the kitchen. "This better not be no scam!" he warned.

They started painting. "This sun sure is hot," observed Archie. "Gonna be a real scorcher today."

From the upstairs window of her air-conditioned mansion, Mrs. Vanderhorst screeched, "Spread that paint evenly!"

"Awww, shut up!" muttered Frank.

GOOD SMOKED HAMS

I read the letter again: Dere Sir, Yore smoked hams is good but not as good as them of Arley Jenkins. Josiah Rigby, Route 4, Beechburg, West Virginia.

I take exceptional pride in my product. Kinkaid's Smoked Hams are famous. I drove to Beechburg and, after several inquiries, located the farm of Josiah Rigby.

He came to his door, a weather-beaten old man in overalls. Introducing myself, I asked, "Where can I meet Arley Jenkins?"

He gave a cackly laugh, "'Nobody knows. About twenty years ago old Arley sold me his farm here and moved away. Y'see, his wife Ellie disappeared. Neighbors accused Arley of murderin' her. Sheriff dug everywheres—no trace of her."

"So," I ventured, "he smoked his hams on this farm?"

"Yee-ep. Over yonder's the foundation of Arley's smokehouse. Lightnin' burned it some years back."

"I'll be back tomorrow, sir." I promised. This called for action.

Next morning I returned. "Mr. Rigby," I said, "bring your shovel. I think I know where Jenkins buried his wife—in his smokehouse."

"Impossible!" he scoffed "It's only four-by-four."

"Suppose he dug *vertically*—like a posthole! Afterward, he probably burned his charcoal to hide it."

Intrigued, Josiah Rigby started shoveling. Ten inches down he uncovered a skull. He turned pale and declared, "On second thought, mister, yore hams is a mite better'n his ever was."

In an abandoned cemetery twenty miles away, the grave of "Saralee Tuttweiler" now lies empty. Yes, I'd do most anything to keep my customers satisfied.

STREET REPAIR ENTREPRENEUR

"I don't want to tell you how to run your business, Sam," said his wife, "but you shouldn't block the center of the street while making pot-hole repairs."

"Why not, Marcie?" he asked.

"Your work zone doesn't leave enough room for vehicles to pass on either side, especially wide trucks," she pointed out. "They knock down street signs goin' one direction and stop signs goin' the other."

"My contract with the city don't specify *where* I put up my work zone bypass," argued Sam. "Just so I don't block traffic entirely."

"But people are complaining. You may never get another city contract."

"Oh, I'll get more, don't fret. The competition can't afford to match my low bids. Actually, I'm losing money on that Mulberry Street repair job."

"That's stupid, Sam!" Marcie stamped her foot for emphasis. "You mean you'd see us bankrupt just so you can erect your idiotic bypass in the *middle* of the street?"

Sam sighed, "I reckon you don't understand business economics, Marcie."

"What's to understand?" she retorted.

"You're forgetting, dear, this isn't my only city contract," he explained patiently. "I also have exclusive rights for installing new street and stop signs—at $200 each.

"So, some truck driver knocks over the Mulberry/Elm Street sign; I immediately replace it for $200. Another totals the Mulberry/Maple sign—another $200. Somebody wrecks the stop sign—yep, $200. Already this week I've replaced twelve new signs. That's $2,400!"

REVEALING SOUNDS

"Wot'cha doin', mister?" asked the little girl in the pink raincoat and blue boots.

"Uhh—listening," replied Arthur Waverly, superintendent of Metropolitan Drainage Systems, annoyed at the interruption. He spoke to his two assistants, "These new sound detectors should tell us whether water is flowing through the system at this junction."

The three men leaned forward, the rods extending from their earphones firmly pressed against the pavement. "I'm picking up something," said Dave, the younger assistant.

"Same here," agreed Jason, the other assistant.

"My name's Becky," announced the little girl. "My daddy owns the warehouse 'cross the street.'

"That's nice," snapped Superintendent Waverly. "Now, run along, missy, before you get soaked in this rain."

"I don't care," she said blithely. "My mommy don't care neither. She's gone to gramma's house."

"I can't hear when you're talking," chided Waverly.

"That's 'cause you got that thing stuck in your ear," she giggled.

"Odd," said Dave, "I hear thumping noises—like somebody's *digging* down there!"

"Even stranger," declared Jason, "I swear I hear someone *talking!* Impossible, of course."

"Wot's a tunnel?" asked Becky.

"Oh, just a long underground hole," replied Dave.

"Thought so," she said with satisfaction. "There's a tunnel right under us."

"No, no, lass," said the superintendent impatiently. "We know what's down there."

"Bet a popsicle you don't!'" she challenged. "I heard daddy and Uncle Amos talking. They say their tunnel oughta reach the bank over there by Saturday."

VISITOR IN THE DEAD OF NIGHT

I can't help myself. I'm a chronic worrier. Living alone, I worry at bedtime: did I turn off all the burners on the stove? When I go away: did I really lock the front door? When I return from shopping: did I make a memo of all the checks I wrote? All inconsequential little things like that. At one time I consulted a psychiatrist; after ten very expensive visits, he advised me, "Don't worry about it," but I promptly did anyhow.

Recently two bizarre events worried me more than usual. I'm a writer, and one morning a completed short story lay on my desk, unquestionably typed on my portable. The next morning, another. Both were really quite good, about a romance with a native girl in Singapore, describing the local setting in elaborate, exquisite detail.

I took them to the club in my briefcase and showed them to Major Thomasen, whom I knew had lived for some years in the East.

"Yes," he said, after perusing them, "the writer is certainly familiar with the place. I recall it well—"

"But what shall I do?" I interrupted.

"Clever devil, sneaking in at night, you say? Had a similar problem in Hong Kong once. Solved it with an infrared camera and trip wire..." He went on to describe particulars.

I arranged the device. Next morning I eagerly developed the film. Gradually the image appeared and I gasped. It was myself! I was a sleepwalker!

What worries me now? I've never been near Singapore.

AT LAZLO'S CAFE

Lazlo's Cafe served the best food in town, but I ate there mostly out of sympathy for his staff, tipping them generously. Lazlo was a hard man. If a waitress served coffee with some spilled in the saucer, he upbraided her on the spot; and if something in the kitchen didn't meet his approval, you could hear Lazlo back there chewing out the cooks.

Once I asked Thelma, the oldest waitress, "Why do put up with him?"

She tossed her orange-dyed hair and declared proudly, "It's an honor to work for a man with a heart of gold." Talk about loyalty!

I felt especially sorry for Janelle, the new young waitress. Nothing she did seemed to please Lazlo.

Then one morning I was the first customer. I couldn't believe my eyes! Lazlo was cradling a baby against his shoulder, gently patting its backside. "He needs a change," he said gruffly.

Janelle grabbed the infant and disappeared into the kitchen. Thelma came to take my order. "The usual, sir?" she asked cheerfully.

"What's with the baby?" I inquired.

She glanced around to check that Lazlo wasn't watching. "It's Janelle's, born out of wedlock. The poor girl was desperate, no family. I got her a job here. She admitted her problem to Lazlo. 'No husband, eh?' he growled. 'Well, maybe you meet somebody nice here.'"

"Lazlo said *that?*" I gasped.

"We don't know what'll develop," she confided, "but Lazlo pays all her bills and Janelle decided to name her baby Lazlo."

NOT ONE OF HIS BETTER WEEKENDS

His prospect in Albany turned him down flat. Next, the southbound train arrived late in Penn Station. "What else?" muttered Alan Bosworth, The surly Spanish-speaking taxi driver made innumerable wrong turns, then overcharged him.

His wife Louise greeted him with: "The most awful thing happened!"

"What?" he asked wearily.

"Well, I attended Mrs. Calabrese's party Thursday night and her brother—Gino Martinelli, the rumored gangster—got fresh. I'm sure he stole my earring. The left one."

"Okay, sweetheart, I'll buy you another."

"It was my grandmother's. I've got everything planned. Drop him a note, saying, 'Return that earring—or else!'"

"He'd shoot me fulla holes."

"No, no, dear, he'll think I'm some rival mobster's girl-friend and return it through his sister."

"I won't do it! Absolutely not!"

"You don't love me," sobbed Louise.

Midnight found Bosworth nervously sneaking onto Martinelli's porch. Shoving the note through the mail slot, he ran.

"I'm home, Louise!" he announced.

"Oh, dear! I found that earring behind my dresser. You *must* retrieve that note!"

Bosworth drove back to Martinelli's mansion. Trembling, he groped through the mail slot. There, he touched it! His hand was firmly stuck. As the door was yanked open, his wrist snapped. Reaching down, Martinelli jerked Bosworth's hand free and growled, "Whatta ya doin', guy?"

Grimacing with pain, Bosworth explained.

"Y'mean that stupid broad?" chuckled Martinelli. Alan Bosworth lost control. He kicked the mobster.

He awoke in a hospital bed. Louise was saying, "Darling, I lost the *other* earring."

THE CASE OF LOOSE ENDS

Mr. Herlock Shoames and I were breakfasting late when his doorbell rang. Moments later his housekeeper, Mrs. Edsel, bustled up the stairs. "It was that Pilldown man!" she reported breathlessly.

"Ah, yes," said the great detective, "our neighborhood druggist, Wanaday Pilldown. He left a message?"

"That 'e did, sir. 'E said, 'Alert Shoames! Big shipment of X slacks stolen!'"

"I deduce that he's branching out, now handling men's wear. But he doesn't know the brand name of the missing slacks—called them 'X.'"

"Amazing!" I declared.

"I must investigate immediately, Datsun. This looks like a job for my Barker Street Irregulars."

He did not return until late afternoon, looking rather haggard. "Something sinister afoot, Datsun," he proclaimed. "My faithful Barker Street Irregulars each greeted me with 'Hell-*loo* again!' and rushed off. Finally one of them offered me a large piece of chocolate. I have been uneasy since. Mark my word, they know something... Oops! I must be off at once!" He hastily visited the lavatory before leaving once more.

The great detective came back to 221 Barker Street quite late and flopped down in his favorite chair.

"Did you solve the case?" I inquired eagerly.

"I fear, Datsun, the world is not yet ready for the truth," he replied. "For now, I shall file it as the Case of Loose Ends. Please remind Mrs. Edsel to supply additional lavatory paper."

I could only surmise that he had somehow located the stolen trousers, but Shoames seemed disinclined to elucidate.

BY THE RULES

Lieutenant Cadwallander Strathmore opened the Monday morning briefing session for assembled patrolmen. "Men, neighbors report plastic-wrapped furniture on the sidewalk outside Lord Aynswotth's estate. Officers Tuttle and Marley, investigate and report back. Remember Rule 17: *Beware unexplained local phenomena.*"

As they departed, Tuttle growled, "The lieutenant's bin this way since 'e took that correspondence detective course—Rule this, Rule that."

"Yeah," agreed his partner Marley, "but Rule 12: *Strictly obey orders.*"

Tuesday morning Tuttle reported, "Lord Aynsworth sold 'is estate. New owners give 'is Paris address. They claim furniture was accidentally left behind by movers."

"Aha!" exclaimed Lieutenant Strathmore. "Something mysterious there. Rule 9: *Never accept obvious explanations.* Investigate further this alleged 'forgotten' furniture."

Wednesday morning Tuttle again reported, "Sir, them chairs and sofa seem perfectly okay. Marrley sat on one, found it real comfortable."

"Not good enough!" snapped Strathmore. "Is it not suspicious that after three days Lord Aynsworth hasn't made enquiries?"

"Mayhap 'is lordship ain't paid the movers," suggested Marley.

"Ridiculous!" declared the lieutenant. "Something sinister's afoot. Examine that furniture minutely. Rule 25: *Search unexplained objects thoroughly for hidden drugs.*"

Grumbling, the officers returned to the exasperating furniture. Tuttle slit the sofa's upholstery, recoiled, and gasped, "Gorblimey! 'Tis Lady Aynsworth 'erself, deader'n a mackerel. I reckanize 'er from pitchers on the telly. There'll be no livin' with the lieutenant now. Wot'll we do?"

"Simple," replied Marley. "We crate up 'er bloody ladyship and ship 'er to Lord Aynsworth in Paris. Yer forgettin' Rule 29: *Confront suspect with evidence.*"

DOUBLE-CROSSING THE DOUBLE-CROSSER

I was enjoyin' a beer in One-eyed Mike's bar—until Slick Sammy Wentzl sidled up to me. Automatically I checked my wallet. Sammy noticed, sayin', "Relax, friend. I'm reformed. Hendrik Vanderhoeft has hired me to guard his valuable furniture whilst he vacations in Europe."

"Surely not *the* Vanderhoeft with the high iron fence around his big estate?" I inquired.

"The very same," Sammy assured me. "Before departing he had numerous valuable antiques delivered—still unwrapped. He's paying me $500 each to insure they do not leave the premises."

"You're kiddin'! Millionaires trust nobody without investigatin' his background. That eliminates you."

"I'll bet a grand that tomorrow morning I collect at least $500 each for said Vanderhoeft antiques."

"It's a bet!" We shook hands.

I remembered the times Slick Sammy double-crossed me. Now was my chance to get even. Usin' a ladder that night, I got inside the estate, broke into the mansion, and began movin' out antique furniture. It was hard work, liftin' them heavy chairs and stuff over the fence. But by dawn they all resided on the sidewalk outside.

I asked One-eyed Mike, "Where's Slick Sammy?"

"He rented a U-haul and drove a load of stolen furniture upstate to a crooked dealer, who's promised him $1,000 each for Vanderhoeft's antiques."

"Damn!" I groaned. "I just lost a heavy bet with Sammy."

"You, too?" One-eyed Mike sympathized. "He bet me a hundred bucks he'd get some sucker to move the stuff over the fence for free."

BEWARE THE BUGGY MAN

Over a tall beer in the Silver Dollar I remarked, "A long time since we rode on the big cattle drive to Abilene, Buck."

"Three years come summer," he reckoned.

"Never expected to find you the sheriff here in Buffalo Gulch," I said. "Any trouble?"

"Not since the Rattlesnake Kid broke outta prison. Y'know, pardner, folks ain't always what they claim."

I allowed as how thet sometimes happened.

"'Bout a year ago," Buck went on, "a feller rode hell-bent inta town. 'I'm Marshall Ballard!' he called out. 'Did a stranger in a buggy ride through?'

"'Nope,' I replied.

"'Then I'm not too late. The Rattlesnake Kid escaped yestidday, stole a preacher's buggy, and headed this away. State prison posted a $10,000 reward fer his return.'

"'He'll never git past me!' I declared.

"'He's slick,' warned the marshall. 'He'll likely claim he's the preacher.'"

"Did you capture him?" I interrupted.

Buck continued, "When the stranger in the buggy arrived thet afternoon, we town folks overpowered him pronto. Shore enough, he insisted he was jest a travelin', soul-savin' evangelist. We headed toward State prison with our hog-tied captive. Every able-bodied gun toter in town rode along to share the reward."

"Haw-haw!" I laughed. "Imagine thet galoot in the buggy tryin' to impersonate a preacher."

"Oh, turned out he really *was* a preacher. But the hombre wearin' the shiny badge warn't no marshall. While every man in Buffalo Gulch rode off dreamin' about big reward money, he robbed our bank.

"He was the Rattlesnake Kid."

243

THE KING OF ZAMBOGUTO

Dear Chief Inspector Willoughby:

As officially ordered two years ago, I tracked down and arrested Basil Billingsgate, the killer of Lord Chittingham. The devious trail led through Cairo to Gambia to Zaire. There a trader directed me to Zamboguto, a new little central African nation.

Natives intercepted me at spear point, parading me through their capital to the palace. Its walls were whitewashed, its thatched roof overgrown with exotic tropical vines. Their king, on an ivory throne, was—*Basil Billingsgate!*

"You are under arrest!" I declared.

"Not so fast, bucko," he laughed. "Actually it is you who are under arrest for illegally entering my kingdom."

Noting his stalwart bodyguards, I refrained from handcuffing him. "As you will discover during your stay," King Basil continued, "we have a model country. I've introduced weaving, brick-making, and scientific agriculture. Schools are crowded. My Minister of Education plans expansion of our libraries. My people learn rapidly—"

"But what about Lord Chittingham's murder?" I interjected.

"That devil! He was secretly a child molester."

(You may wish to investigate this further.)

In view of circumstances, sir, I herewith tender my resignation. This, my final report, will be mailed from Nairobi by Kala-vu-vu, the cleverest of my four wives (and the only one not pregnant).

Respectfully submitted,
Paul Harwick, Prime Minister of Zamboguto

P.S.: Should you decide to send another detective to arrest King Basil, please provide him with sufficient plants to start a tea plantation. We sorely miss our four o'clock teatime.

THE FINE ART OF DOUBLE-CROSS

For many years Albert Trexler, the art dealer on Sangamon Square, and I were partners. Paintings that I obtained discretely (from absent owners), he sold discretely (to unscrupulous millionaires). We divided the profits.

Then investigators *somehow* traced masterpieces from the Vanderhoeft robbery to Albert's gallery. He testified he'd received them from me in good faith. I got two years; Albert got a fat reward.

After my release, however, I still needed Albert for one last job. Just before his gallery closed, I entered bearing a bulky rectangular package. "Back room," I whispered.

There I unwrapped it. After one glance Albert pronounced, "Trash!"

"Hold on," I protested, "Beneath this ugly veneer lies Lorrain's *Twin-spired Abbey with Swans*, recently stolen from the Metropolitan."

His eyes lit up. "You did it—partner!"

"I've lined up a buyer who'll pay $100,000, telling him you have the painting. We'll split the money. Quick! He's coming in! I'll hide here."

The swarthy dark-clad man leaned forward. "I'm told you have the Metropolitan's *Twin-spired Abbey with Swans* for sale?"

"Right here, sir," declared Albert. "Only $100,000."

"It's really under all this paint?"

"I guarantee it, sir!"

The man counted $100,000 cash from his briefcase, paid Albert, and departed with the re-wrapped painting. Minutes later I left by the rear with my $50,000 share.

The Mafia kingpin who purchased it hired an art expert to remove the superfluous fresh paint.

There was nothing under it.

I'll sell the real *Twin-spired Abbey with Swans* tomorrow—right after Albert's funeral.

"Hey, lookit, Maybelle!" exclaimed Herbie. "Here's a historical place we ain't seen yet. What is it?"

His wife consulted their map of Rome. "Says here it's the mausoleum of Emperor Concertinian."

"Probably dead by now," remarked Herbie. "Musta been real famous in his day, though. Anything in the guidebook about him?"

Maybelle thumbed through it. "Yeah, Herbie, it's all right here: 'Emperor Concertinian was known as the Tyrant of the Tiber because of his extreme cruelty to his subjects.' I reckon that means, like, he became a really bad boss-man."

"Yeah? I know guys like that," declared her husband. "Give 'em a little power and they get mean as hell. Anything else about old Emperor What's-his-name?"

"It goes on to say," replied Maybelle, "'On occasion the emperor suffered delusions. He once while inebriated'—that means drunker'n a skunk—'fancied himself a gladiator and actually entered the arena at the Colosseum. Upon his death, citizens of Rome erected a marble mausoleum, featuring a finely sculpted lion, to his everlasting memory.' That's all that's writ here."

"I get it! There musta been some good in the old boy if them Romans remembered him as a brave lion."

"No, no, you dummy. They wanted to forever honor the lion that ate him!"

SOME DAYS YOU CAN'T WIN

"It's a long story, Your Honor...

"Yesterday IRS auditors impounded my company's assets. I headed home. Seeing the street ahead was clear, I eased my convertible past the barricade. A whistle blasted and a patrolman materialized, notebook in hand, snarling, 'Unauthorized entry—$100 fine.'

"'But,' I protested, 'I live in the next block.'

"'A likely story! Resisting arrest—another $100!'

"I sought an alternate route through unfamiliar one-way streets. Hopelessly lost, I stopped to ask a well-dressed lady for directions. 'Please,' I began, 'I really need—'

"She whirled, flashing a. badge. 'Soliciting! That'll be $100!' I added her citation to my collection and drove off, still lost. Night found me cruising a disreputable neighborhood. I spotted another lady. Desperate, I braked and said, 'Okay, officer, I know the routine. Please, just take me to headquarters.'

"Instead of a badge, *this* lady pulled a pistol, growling, 'Outta that fancy convertible, sucker!' She sped off, leaving me stranded on foot. One block later I was beaten and mugged. I staggered into a bar to phone home. The bartender tried to eject me; 'Your kind ain't welcome here!'

"I'd had enough. I retaliated, creating a scene.

"So you see, sir, my company's shut down, my car and wallet stolen, and since I'm broke my lawyers refuse my case. Adding insult to injury, my wife doesn't believe me—"

"And neither do I," snapped the judge, rapping his gavel. "Imagine! Attacking my *favorite* bartender in his own establishment! $500 and thirty days!"

She was the most beautiful woman Norbert Parkins had ever seen! It was her costume which first attracted his attention: frilly blouse and high-waisted long skirt. Her hair was drawn back in a once-fashionable chignon. But it was her exquisite face and dark eyes that captivated him. He had to meet her!

As he approached, she was fumbling with a portable phone. "May I be of assistance?" he began.

"Oh, thank you, kind sir. They never explained such contrivances when I agreed to try their time machine. Oh, I wish I was back in 1912 again!" She fell into his arms, her eyes filling with tears. "My name is Heloise Sanders and I-I-I've fallen hopelessly in love with you. But they'll snatch me back in time soon. We'll be separated forever!"

"I'm Norbert Parkins and I love you, too. I'll give up my partnership with Armbruster Willoughby, make proper arrangements, and join you back here. Don't leave!"

As soon as Parkins hurried away, Ms. Sanders phoned, "He fell for it, Armbruster darling! He rushed off to resign the partnership. He's probably converting his assets into old coins and dressing in a ridiculous frock coat and celluloid collar. You shouldn't have trouble getting him committed and— *ohmigod!* Somehow he's right beside me in a *telephone booth!*"

"I couldn't wait! I'll return later and settle with Willoughby. Ready, sweet Heloise?" Norbert Parkins asked, pulling her inside. "Pretty clever, disguising my time machine as a telephone booth, don't you agree?"

Whirr-rrr-ooosh!

I DON'T LIKE TO MENTION IT, BUT...

Before she'd even taken off her expensive coat, Miriam said, "I don't like to mention it, Daphne dear, but your living room is atrocious! Of course you don't have an eye for color coordination like mine. It comes from my successful career as an interior decorator. You should start with those horrid drapes."

Miriam hadn't changed. Daphne wondered why she'd invited her old classmate for the weekend. "I do plan some changes," she said weakly. "When I can afford them."

"Oh, didn't Clyde leave you anything? I hesitated to bring it up, but I could have told you he was a loser."

"We were quite happy."

"How? Without the cheerful laughter of little children? My two boys were such a joy. And both have eminently successful careers."

"It was impossible for me to conceive."

"It's not my affair, dear, but you should eat better. Your figure is positively scrawny. My late husband Roland insisted that I have the best on the menu. We dined out often."

Miriam stepped onto the balcony, then declared, "I'd rather not bring it up, Daphne, but you do live in a squalid neighborhood. Why, your apartment house doesn't even have a doorman! One should enjoy life, I always say..."

Daphne told police, "I'd invited Miriam for a weekend, hoping to cheer her up. I should never have let her out onto the balcony alone. I don't like to mention it, but she always had suicidal tendencies...."

POOR COUSIN MARCO

"*Buon giorno!*" my cousin Marco Arveccio hailed me on the Via del Quirinale. "You are looking upon the man about to own our family's ancient mausoleum!"

Poor Cousin Marco. So handsome, so likeable—and so gullible. He supports half the con men of Rome, of which there are many.

"Tell me about it," I sighed, thinking I'd probably have to bail him out of trouble.

"Yesterday I met this fine gentleman. Upon learning I was Marco Arveccio, he said, 'How fortunate we met! You are just in time to save your family mausoleum.' He guided me off the Piazza Navone and there it was! A beautiful little garden, statuary, a mausoleum inscribed 'Giuseppe Arveccio, 1567', and in front: a marble lion, ancient symbol of our family!"

"You paid him money?" I asked, knowing the answer.

"Just a modest 'finder's fee.' I go now to the Capidoglio to prove who I am."

"I'd better go with you."

The clerk was at first dubious, saying, "You have proof you are descended from Giuseppe Arveccio?"

"Of course!" replied Marco confidently. "I brought along all our old family records."

After conferring with other officials, the clerk announced, "As the first claimant since the death of Giuseppe Arveccio, you are indeed owner of the property."

We danced for joy. "It's mine!" shouted Cousin Marco.

"One minor item, Senhor Arveccio," the clerk interrupted apologetically.

"What?" laughed Marco, still celebrating.

"The back taxes, senhor. Compounded since 1567, that amounts to, ah...3,569,674,689,149 lire."

THE ARCHERY ACCIDENT

"Deucedly odd," remarked the Countess. "Yesterday I invited Lady Effington to tea and she insisted in standing the whole while. Is there some reason?"

"Ah, yes," replied the Duchess, "Poor Heloise. Archery was responsible. Embarrassing, really."

"Archery? Did she strain a muscle pulling a longbow on the archery range?"

"Dear me, no. It happened in her patio, and it was young Reginald discharging the arrow."

"Intentionally injuring his mother?"

"Of course not!" sniffed the Duchess. "If you must know, dearie, Lord Effington was hosting a barbecue and as Lady Effington leaned over, young Reggie fired into the air."

"I see. So the descending; missle struck her in the—"

"No, no! The arrow landed in the barbecue pit, scattering hot coals."

"I understand now," said the Countess, "A hot coal burned poor Heloise's derriere."

"It did not! The Duke and I attended and witnessed everything. A tablecloth went up in flames and someone shouted 'FIRE!' The yelling and confusion alarmed Heloise's little Pekinese, which fled, yapping. Naturally concerned for its safety, she straightened up and set off in pursuit."

"Oh. Then she tripped and injured herself?" asked the Countess.

"No. Lord Effington saw his wife fleeing in panic and, assuming she had been burned, ran after her."

"But wasn't she injured in some manner?"

"Indeed she was! Y'see, Lord Effington was still clutching the long-handled turning fork when he overtook her."

"Oh dear! So then—"

"Precisely, my dear. He accidentally buried the tines in her big fat butt."

251

ZEKE'S SECRET BAIT

Along with a half dozen avid fishermen, I got off the bus at Lame Moose Pass and started backpacking up the steep trail to Zeke Little-Fox's Glacial Lodge. As a sports writer, I wanted to check Zeke's report of land-locked coho salmon.

Finally reaching the lodge, we all involuntarily gasped. The porch overlooked a charming little glacial lake. Standing in the frigid water, Zeke was skillfully playing a huge salmon in and out among giant chunks of bluish-tinted ice. It broke the surface—a glorious flash of molten silver—then dived again.

"Wow!" someone yelled. "A trophy!"

At last Zeke landed the salmon, held it up for a moment, then casually dropped it into a live-box of wire netting sunk beside his tiny pier. "A mite small," he drawled.

"What bait you using?" somebody asked.

"Jus' takes know-how," replied Zeke laconically.

Those fishermen cast every daylight hour, using every conceivable lure. No luck whatever. If it weren't for Zeke's wife Sadie fixing such delicious meals, they'd all have gone home before their week ended. The following Friday they did depart, disgruntled. I stayed on.

The next morning I overheard Sadie say to her husband, "Hurry, Zeke, another busload's comin'!" Using a long-handled landing net, she scooped *that same salmon* from the live-box and held it while Zeke tied it securely to his line and let it swim offshore.

"Zeke," Sadie remarked, "maybe it's time we bought another live salmon. 'Old Faithful' ain't showin' much action this mornin'."

CRIME HITS BUCKTHORN COUNTY

Sheriff Danvers, who hero-worships Sherlock Holmes, said to me, "Deppity Scroggins, thar's mischief afoot!"

I had to agree. First, Jarred Wiggin's chickens, includin' his prize rooster, disappeared. Second, Gunther Cosswell's hogs did likewise whilst he attended the Sunday night Baptist prayer meetin'. I personally searched Jarred's henhouse and Gunther's pigsty—both empty as politician's promises. About as smelly, too.

Then Hiram and Jessica Sopworth vanished. Joe Deevers the postman reported he'd had a mailorder package for Jessica and nobody was home. Things was gettin' serious. Not that anybody in Buckthorn County would'a missed Hiram, a shiftless scalawag who sometimes beat up Jessica for the hell of it.

I drove Sheriff Danvers out to Sopworth's place in the county's 1981 Maverick (optimistically knowed as our "patrol car"). Avoidin' discarded stoves and refrigerators in the yard, I parked.

The front door stood open. We eased inside, Sheriff Danvers keepin' one hand on his holster. (He does that whenever investigatin'.) Nobody in the livin' room. Same in the kitchen. Ditto in the bedroom.

There bein' no more rooms to investigate, I suggested, "Sir, maybe we oughta look in Hiram's shed out back."

"Good idea, deppity."

The shed was locked, but assorted grunts, squawks, and cackles sounded inside.

"We gotta bust in!" decided Sheriff Danvers.

We did. Out flapped Jarred Wiggin's chickens! Out scampered Gunther Coswell's hogs! And lastly out stumbled Hiram Sopworth.

"Dang-blasted ungrateful woman!" he swore. "Locked me in and run off—after I'd pervided 'er all this meat fer winter!"

INSPECTOR DUPRE AND
THE FRENCH QUARTER FRACAS

"Sergeant," said Captain Feray, "those two damnable Frenchmen sent here by Paris Securité to learn American methods cause nothing but trouble here in New Orleans. Follow them closely—everywhere! Keep in touch with me by walkie-talkie."

"Yessir." Sergeant Lacroix saluted and departed.

SGT: "They are in sight, sir. French Quarter."

CAPT: "Doing what?"

SGT: "Inspector Dupre strikes up a conversation with an elderly lady. She is accompanied by three strong men. Oh-oh! Dupre is starting an argument. Now he's fighting! The guy knows his karate, captain. He just knocked all three men out!"

CAPT: "Oh, God. Lawsuits. I'll dispatch an ambulance. Promise those unfortunate men we'll pay hospitalization. Where are Dupre and Pierre now?"

SGT: "Inspector Dupre is dragging the woman into the bar, sir."

CAPT: "Worse than I feared. What now?"

SGT: "He's plying the lady with liquor, sir."

CAPT: "I'm sending reinforcements!"

Inspector Dupre, faithful Pierre, and the woman were brought into headquarters by a squadron of blue-clad policemen.

"Mother!" gasped Captain Feray. "Are you all right?"

"I am now," the elderly Mrs. Feray declared.

The captain turned on Inspector Dupre. "Now you've done it!"

"He certainly has," beamed Mrs. Feray, taking Dupre's arm. "François is a brave gentleman, like your late father. Three men tried to kidnap me—right on the street! François rescued me. Where were your police when I needed them?"

To the sputtering captain, Dupre remarked, "Madame and I, tonight we visit the nightclubs, listen to *le jazz americaine.*"

"*Oui!*" confirmed Madame Feray.

INSPECTOR DUPRE AND
THE BOURBON STREET AFFAIR

"Patrolman Eversham," said Captain Feray sternly, "today those Frenchmen will be on your Bourbon Street beat. Be on guard."

"You mean Inspector Dupre and his sidekick Pierre, the two who have—"

"I know what they have done," interrupted Feray. "Just stay alert and keep me informed."

"Beautiful weather, Pierre," observed Inspector Dupre.

"*Oui*, Inspector."

"But observe, please, that gentleman emerging from the *banque*. He handles the shooting-gun very incorrectly. Take notes, Pierre."

"*Oui*, Inspector."

"*Une*, nevair point weapon toward people. *Deux*, do not carry weapon while also carrying the heavy sack. *Trois*, especially while walking backward... But come, we correct the ignorant gentleman." Approaching from behind, Dupre grabbed the shotgun. BAM!

"My toes! My toes!" screamed the man.

Without hesitation, Dupre added, "...and *quatre*, Pierre, *toujours* be careful of the triggeur."

Captain Feray answered his phone.

"Patrolman Eversham reporting, sir. Inspector Dupre just blasted off a fellow's toes. BLAM! Right on Bourbon Street."

"Bring him in!"

Minutes later an agitated man burst into Captain Feray's office. "I'm James Devlin," he introduced himself, "president of Louisiana National Bank. About your inspector—chap named François Dupre—"

Feray raised his hand. "My apologies, Mr. Devlin, for whatever he did."

"Apologies, sir? I don't understand. Bravest man I ever knew! An armed bandit held up my bank. As he retreated, Dupre fearlessly disarmed him, captured him with the bandit's own shotgun! My guards recovered the money and took the bandit into custody... Are you well, sir... Sir?"

THE DESCENDANTS OF ROGER THACKERY

When Albert Thackery moved to Salem, Massachusetts, to set up his law practice, he was astounded at the number of Thackerys in the telephone directory. Whenever he was introduced to one of them, he was invariably asked, "From which original Thackery are you descended?"

When he replied that he did not know, the person said, "Too bad, sir. You might be eligible to join our Society of the Descendants of Roger Thackery."

This society seemed to control most of the important activities in Salem—mayor, aldermen, ministers, and businesses. What a boost to his community standing if he proved his genealogy!

On a visit back to Philadelphia he inquired of his grandfather, Elisha Thackery. The old man eyed him suspiciously. "Do you *really* want to know?" he asked.

"Yes, grandfather, it is important to me."

"Very well. But it's a secret we keep in the immediate family." He opened the old family Bible and there it was—seventeen generations, all the way back to Roger Thackery himself!

Albert was elated. Returning to Salem, he informed members of the Society that he had traced his lineage. They invited him to a meeting that night.

The presiding president, Roger Thackery XIV, inspected the list of ancestors. "Unfortunately, sir," he said solemnly, "you are descended through Roger's son Raphael, who left the colony and returned a heretic. Judge Roger Thackery condemned him *and all his descendants* to death."

The heavy doors of the chamber closed and someone tossed a rope over an exposed beam.

THE OLD FAMILY SECRET

"Someday, son, this here stone house will be yours," declared Joe Harkness, "so I reckon you oughta know its secret. Yore great-great-grandpa Mark built it up here atop this peak as a safeguard against Injuns and outlaws. Then he worried about water.

"What old Mark lacked in foresight, he made up in perseverance. He started diggin' under the floor. The trap door's right under this table. About fifty feet down, he broke through into a cave, a big cave, dry as a bone.

"As you well know, we still have to haul water up from the spring. But that dry well of great-great-grandpa Mark has made the family fortune. Why, I got customers from Chicago, New York, and Detroit repeat customers—and they pay right handsome. So, in the future, the business will all be yours. And if'n you have a family, it'll belong to them."

"But what is this business?" asked his son Dave.

"Hush, boy. Somebody's knockin'. Probably another customer." Joe Harkness opened the door.

"Why, sheriff!'" he exclaimed. "Anything wrong?"

"Mighty wrong," stated Sheriff Albright. "Some kids discovered the entrance to a cave down at the foot of this peak. And, Joe, you wouldn't believe what was inside!"

"What?" asked Harkness.

"Bodies!" answered the sheriff. "Human bodies! The cave is crammed with 'em. Some just skeletons, others purty fresh—but *all with bullet holes.*

"Have you seen any suspicious characters around lately?"

CLIFFSIDE REVISITED

At age ninety-two, Edward Danforth was making a nostalgic pilgrimage back to scenes that had brought him success. He had saved for last the place where he had painted *Cliffside*, the picture that launched his career. Little had changed since 1922. The foreboding cliff still defied the wildly churning waves beating against its base. The picturesque old cottage still perched above. He recalled vividly the figure of a young woman facing the sea, outlined against blue sky.

He had been young, vigorous, and carefree that summer. His mind re-created his model, beautiful Marietta Hanson. One rainy afternoon they had made love in that same deserted cottage. He should never have left her. There had been other women through the years, but none who loved him for himself, wholeheartedly, passionately.

"Joseph," he said to his chauffer, "I'll go alone from here." Apprehensively, the old man approached the cottage and turned the once-familiar knob. The door opened surprisingly easily.

"My God!" he gasped. "It's you, Marietta! B-but you're not any older."

"A little older, Edward," she laughed, stepping aside to reveal a golden-haired child of five. "Let me introduce your daughter. I named her Edwina. Now, don't be shocked—we both died during the flu epidemic of 1928. I've been waiting for you."

"Those wasted years!" he cried bitterly. "Now I'm an old, old man."

"Only during your lifetime," she declared. "Later you become whatever age you wish."

The chauffer watched horrified as his employer, smiling radiantly, disappeared over the cliff edge.

THE BODY IN THE BALE

The debonair man in the silk shirt, twill trousers, and tweed jacket idled the motor of his baler to greet his visitor. "Hello, again, Inspector!" he called out. "We meet often these days. Social visit?"

Chief Inspector McCann picked his way across the stubble. "You know better than that, Nick," he growled. "We've known each other too long. When Iggy Carrozi disappeared yesterday, I said to myself, 'McCann, don't be fooled by that nonsense about Nick Nicosi retiring to become a gentleman farmer.' No sirree, this has gotta be another of your hits—and this one I'll prove."

"You do have a suspicious mind, old boy," declared the unperturbed man still seated on his baler. "And now you've started talking to yourself. Dear me."

The chief inspector ignored the needling. "I'm not as dense as you think, Nick," he retorted. "I knew that sooner or later you'd get careless." He grinned savagely. "Whose feet are stickin' out of that bale?"

"Feet?" echoed Nick weakly. "Oh, dear, I must have forgotten to remove the scarecrow before starting—"

"Scarecrow indeed!" snorted McCann. "We both know what I'll find inside."

Nick Nicosi's shoulders sagged in defeat. Inwardly, however, he was laughing as he contemplated McCann's frustration upon unrolling the huge bale only to discover a store mannequin.

The old inspector would be so disappointed and disgusted he would never think to investigate the *other* bales scattered across the field—one of which contained the mortal remains of Iggy Carrozi.

THE LION'S SHARE

The stolen car sped recklessly along the country road, trailed by a cloud of dust.

"Throw that damned moth-eaten plaything outta the window," growled Gino without relaxing his grip on the steering wheel. "With your share of diamonds from that heist you can buy somethin' *real* nice."

"But Leo's my lucky lion," protested Carmen. "For bringin' us luck he oughta get a share himself."

Gino just snorted.

Suddenly the motor sputtered, and the wail of a siren sounded behind them. Then the engine stalled beside an old orchard.

"Hell of a lot of luck he's bringin' us," declared Gino, reaching for his machinegun on the back seat. "Get out!"

"Leo *is* lucky," insisted the young woman. "See, I'll stuff the diamonds inside that torn slit in his back and toss him up in that old apple tree. That way, we're clean and we can come back for him later."

But Gino wasn't listening. His attention was riveted on the approaching patrol car. He started shooting.

"Don't!" screamed Carmen. Her appeal came too late. Minutes later she and her boyfriend lay dead on the dusty roadside, their bodies riddled with bullets...

So, if you are motoring along a country byway and spot a little tattered lion in an apple tree, you might climb up and search him for diamonds. But my advice is to drive on by—that Leo is one unlucky lion.

LORD CHILCOTT VERSUS
THATAWAY'S CLOSE

Lord Chilcott looked out over his rolling estate of Nockam Downs, frowning at the incessant hammering from the direction of Thataway's Close. Hubert Alston, owner of the Close, was putting up another of those cheap wood-frame houses.

"Whole damn district's going to hell," muttered Chilcott. "Can't have that."

He summoned his old gardener. "Algernon," he asked, "what attracts the peasants to buy homes in Thataway's Close?"

The gardener shuffled his feet, then answered, "'Tis my humble opinion, m'lord, that they like the clear little brook runnin' through it. Gives the place a bit o' cheer."

"And whence comes this brook?" demanded Chilcott.

The question astounded old Algernon. "Why, as y'r lordship undoubtedly knows, 'tis fed by yon spring down by your lily pond."

"Exactly as I thought!" declared Chilcott. "Now, what if we should dynamite that spring? What then? Speak up, Algernon!"

"I—I can't really say," replied the old man. "It might open up and spill out a terrific stream. Or it might dry up completely. I just don't know."

"I see," said the lord of Nockam Downs. "Either we flood the rascals out or we stop their brook entirely. Dynamite it!"

"Dynamite it, sir?"

"You heard me. Do it!"

As the Chief Geologist of the Royal Bureau of Mines explained it, "The entire region is underlain by limestone, characterised by occasional springs and numerous caverns. The explosion undoubtedly caused the collapse of an exceptionally large cavern, into which Lord Chilcott and his ancient manor house disappeared."

261

AN AMERICAN PRIMITIVE SCULPTURE

Butterfly, Nebraska! I'd finally located it. And it did have an old Union Pacific station.

"Lost, mister?" The gravelly voice startled me and I turned to face a very old white-bearded man.

"No," I explained, laughing, "I'm what they call a railroad buff. A spur of the old Union Pacific used to run south from here. Actually, I thought this had become a ghost town."

"I ain't no ghost," the oldster bristled. "Town's gone downhill, though." He pointed upward, "I seen you lookin' at that statchoo thar."

"Yes," I commented, "fascinating piece of American primitive sculpture. Baked clay, it seems, and undoubtedly unique. It's definitely not a gargoyle, no gutter spout, and it's not a caryatid because it doesn't support anything."

"Don't know about them things," my informant said. "Fact is, Henry Simpson made it shortly after this dee-po was built. Town paid him $500 to make a pair of statchoos. But Henry finished jest the one, put it up, and bought a one-way ticket to 'Frisco. Ever'body supposed he took his idiot daughter with him." He hesitated.

"Idiot daughter?" I prompted. This was an interesting sidelight.

"Yep. Killed her maw with an ax jest afore Henry put up that statchoo. Since she warn't right, folks was gonna put her in a asylum."

I peered more closely at Henry Simpson's weird creation and suddenly realized the horrifying truth. I left Butterfly, Nebraska, forever. Some day that baked clay will crack off. I don't want to be there when it happens.

A TANTALIZING OLD PHOTOGRAPH

My grandmother Lizette lay unbelievably pale against the silk pillows. I'd always been her favorite and, now that her other relatives had departed for the Great Beyond, I was sole heir to her millions.

"I'm dying, Florella," she said softly. "Fetch the family album from the library."

With palsied fingers she leafed through it to find a sepia-toned photograph: a couple posing in the height of bygone fashion stood erect in a launch, their boatman at the wheel; they were approaching a yacht.

"That young woman was I," grandmother mused. "I was beautiful then."

"And is that handsome gentleman beside you my grandfather?" I asked.

She didn't answer directly. "That was Gilroy, my first husband. Our money came through him. The boatman was my brother Henry."

"Grandmother!" I exclaimed. "I never knew you married twice."

"Gilroy was an expert yachtsman but somehow never learned to swim. He drowned minutes after this picture was taken."

"Who took the picture?"

"My second husband, Clarence, an attractive young photographer I'd invited along."

"What happened?"

She closed her eyes. "Henry tipped the launch and Gilroy fell overboard. He bobbed up twice but I pushed his head under with my parasol. Not long thereafter, I married Clarence."

I was shocked! Sweet little old Lizette a murderer? I watched her fade from life that afternoon.

Now I gaze at that photograph and wonder: was my grandfather that rich, dashing playboy, or that murderous, conniving photographer?

Perhaps I should have asked grandmother before I smothered her.

A CLOSE-BONDED PAIR

The last of the summer sunbathers had long since abandoned the beach. Now a penetrating chill drifted onshore. The only figures along the lonely esplanade were four men sitting quietly on a bench facing the bay. The two on the ends, wearing black overcoats, were silent. The pair in the middle, clad in tan trench coats, were conversing.

"Salvatore," said one, "I see the police gave up dredging the bay for the bodies of 'Big Joe' Mangano and 'Harry the Knife' Corso."

His companion gave a little laugh, "Yeah, Gino, I noticed. Like I told you, police overlook the obvious."

"At least we merchants won't have to keep on paying 'protection' to Big Joe and Harry the Knife any more."

"True. That's a relief. I was having a hard time feeding the wife and kids."

"I know what you mean, Salvatore. Comes a time when a man has to act."

"Not to change the subject, Gino, but does this super-glue really hold?"

"Don't worry. It's guaranteed to bond anything—permanently and forever."

"That's nice to know... The wind is getting colder. The weatherman's predicting snow tonight."

"Oh? Then maybe we should head back to our families, Salvatore." The two old friends got up and strolled away together.

The bodies of "Big Joe" Mangano and "Harry the Knife" Corso, however, remained sitting bolt upright, permanently glued to the bench.

THE PROBLEM OF THE CAR BODIES

Somewhere en route to the National Investigators' Convention, the sergeant had missed a turn.

"Gee," he apologized to his passenger, "I'm sorry, sir. Nothing ahead but that row of car bodies. I'll turn around."

"Wait, Sylvester!" called out the Great Detective. "Here's an opportunity to sharpen our wits."

"But we'll miss the reception," objected Sergeant Collins.

"Never mind, lad," said his superior. "Note the abandoned vehicles are aligned bumper to bumper. Now, put your mind to work—"

"Beggin' your pardon, sir," insisted the driver, "but I think we oughta get back onto the highway."

But the Great Detective was absorbed in masterful deduction. He continued, "The lead car was undoubtedly driven by a rancher who, having just sold his longhorn herd, was speeding to the bank to deposit his new wealth, when..."

(It occurred to Collins that no bank was likely in those desolate surroundings, but he refrained from comment.)

"...several cars bearing rival bandits pursued him closely. However, this rancher outfoxed them. For such an emergency, he had his armed foreman trailing behind. Thus—"

His discourse was interrupted by a strange gruff voice outside. "Hey, Chopper! Lookit what we got—a brand new Lincoln, and we didn' even have to swipe it."

"Yeah, Stripper," responded the man's partner gleefully, "but it ain't gonna be new long." He thrust an automatic through the window.

"You inside! Get the hell out and start walkin'!"

"Remember, Sylvester," cautioned the Great Detective, "discretion is far better than—"

Whereupon Sergeant Collins muttered an unprintable word.

265

THE HORSE KNOWS

Our little village of Sligvesti had been the most peaceful in all Rumania—until now.

"Constable!" roared Mayor Vlad Czumenji. "That damned gypsy murdered my wife Marike!"

I was shocked. "What happened?" I asked.

"I was away overnight. When I got home—blood every-where! He's probably buried her out at the gypsy camp-ground. Hurry, before he escapes!"

Gypsies came and went from their centuries old campsite bordering our village. As we approached, I saw only one wagon, brightly painted. A large gray draft horse was teth-ered beside it.

"Seems deserted," I remarked, poking the cold campfire ashes.

"The killer's already gone," wailed the mayor. "We're too late." Just then a swarthy black-clad youth approached, and I recognized Mikael Rossov, a boyhood friend.

"Your wagon, Mikael?" I pointed. He nodded.

"The mayor here accuses you of murdering his wife. He thinks you buried her nearby. Where were you last night?"

The gypsy's eyes smoldered. "My wife gave birth to our firstborn. I was at the hospital all night. Ask the doctor." Then he added, "Rosante was here; *she* knows what hap-pened."

"Rosante?"

"My mare." He fetched the horse and squatted down. "Did the mayor kill his wife?" he asked it.

The horse actually nodded! "And did he bury her here?" The horse nodded vigorously.

At that, Mayor Czumenji screamed, "Witchcraft!" and fled. I would catch him later. "Truthfully, Mikael," I asked, "did you hypnotize that horse?"

He smiled mysteriously. "How could I, constable? I was busy reading the mayor's mind."

THE SACRED RAVEN TOTEM

Great-great-grandfather pulled his dugout ashore near the salmon cannery where I worked. He was wearing his ceremonial cape and carrying his ancient knobbed war club, symbol of his position as shaman of our Raven clan. His name was Nak-at-se—"fox" in our Tlingit language. His age was ninety-five.

"Ho!" he called out, pointing to a raven strutting along the embankment wall. "Good sign! Go visit ancestors."

I knew he wanted me to paddle him over to Ka-hai-ku, our Sacred Island. Old Nak-at-se had himself carved many of the now-weathered totems there recording our history.

"Okay, great-great-grandfather," I agreed. "Soon as I finish here."

"Uhhh," he grunted.

We set out in a typical British Columbia fog, but the old man unerringly guided us to the island. *Rasp...rasp...rasp...* We followed the sound. A stranger was sawing off the Raven figure from atop one of the totems.

"Stop!" I yelled.

He climbed down. "I'm Henry Witherspoon, a great admirer of poets," he explained. "I was just getting a Poe symbol—"

"Not po' symbol!" rumbled Nak-at-se. "Very *good* symbol."

I started explaining about the famous poem. But the old man had already swung his war club...

I helped great-great-grandfather erect a new totem pole. It's a shame few people will ever see his masterpiece: the carvings are remarkably lifelike, from the triumphant Raven at the top to the lowermost figure, which bears a striking resemblance to the late Mr. Witherspoon, who will nevermore despoil a sacred Raven totem.

THE NEWS FROM CALVIN'S COVE

All that week, business in the city kept me from joining my wife Ethel at our cottage on Calvin's Cove. She'd be mad, as usual. Along the way I bought her some expensive perfume, her favorite.

Old Silas, the local handyman, was the only one there to meet me. "What's the news?" I inquired.

"Bad news, sir," he replied laconically. "Yore boat drifted yesta-day. It's over yonder across the stream."

"How did it get loose?"

"Yore wife used it to git to Mr. Argyle's yacht."

"Oh, she'll get back somehow," I predicted confidently.

"'Fraid not, sir. She took 'er suitcase."

Suddenly I became apprehensive. "What happened then?"

"I heered she got pritty high on dope out that on the water with 'im."

"That's dreadful!"

"Ee-yep. She hit him over the head with a champagne bottle. Broke it. He's suing you."

"Anything else?" I asked, fearing the worst.

"Wal-ll," Silas drawled, "he docked down at Marty's Marina an' called the sheriff—"

"So now she's in jail?"

"Nope. The hospital, sir. Seems yore wife tried runnin' from the sheriff. Stumbled an' knocked 'erself out."

"Badly hurt?" I asked anxiously.

"Reckon so. She's in intensive care. Still unconscious. The doc says she'll need lotsa expensive treatment."

"Good lord, Silas," I groaned, "haven't you any *good* news?"

"Wal-ll," he answered thoughtfully, "yore boat ain't damaged. You kin wade over the stream an' git it—an' they say fishin' has been real good lately out in the bay."

PARKER FOLLOWS INSTRUCTION

Sylvester Carrington spoke to his butler. "You've been with the family some time, Parker."

"I had the great pleasure to serve your grandfather, sire. An admirable gentleman."

"Yes. Well, rather delicate situation. For the weekend I've invited, among others, Jacqueline Rochenbleau and Reggie Tillsworthy. She's the most beautiful young lady, raven-black hair, sparkling eyes, superb every way. The problem, Parker, she also rather fancies Reggie. Jacqueline's rather inquisitive. She'll probably seek your opinion. You will look after my best interest?"

"To the best of my humble ability, sir."

After the guests had departed, Sylvester inquired eagerly, "Well, Parker, did she ask you?"

"She did indeed, sir."

"And what did you say?"

"I told her Reginald Tillsworthy was one in a million."

"What! Now she'll probably marry him."

"That seems most likely, sir."

"But, dash it all, I had hopes."

"If I may speak, sir. Your instruction, as I recall, was to consider your best interest. We servants have our sources. The young woman is the daughter of a Dublin fishmonger. Her name was Kitty O'Dell."

"*Was*, you say?"

"Yes, sir. I made discreet inquiries. Her fourth husband, Archibald Carver, assembled his wealth in oil. According to his maid, he considered divorce a bargain, even at two million pounds. Incidentally, the maid reports the woman's hair is naturally red."

"So you told her Reggie was 'one in a million'?"

"Perhaps I underestimated the number of gullible young men, sir."

"Parker, you're indispensable!"

"Er—will that be all, sir?"

AT NOAH'S COVE MARINA

The water of the crowded marina was mirror-smooth. The yachts rested motionless. Their slender varnished masts, a rich man's forest, stretched skyward to catch the first red rays of sunrise.

Old Caleb Lange had lived all his seventy-nine years right there in Noah's Cove, but the sight of such flaunted wealth still rankled.

"Poor old Caleb," his neighbors said. "Been bitter ever since he had that fight with his only son Barnaby and the boy left home. No word of him all these years."

Caleb accosted a man in city garb ascending the steel stairway from the pier. "Must be nice to be rich," he began.

The stranger was startled. "Yes," he said guardedly, "I suppose it is."

The old man spat disdainfully. "Them with plenty never thinks of nobody but theirselves."

"That's not always true," said the man defensively.

"True enough most cases, mister. Now, if I had the money some of 'em has," he waved a hand toward the marina, "I'd set up a hospital fer the natives 'round here. Maybe start a good home fer the elderly, and especially fer the poor orphan kids."

"Odd," said the man. "Another person had the same idea. Unfortunately, that's impossible."

"Humph," grunted Caleb. "Stock market down a couple points? Interest rate drop?"

"No, he died yesterday. I was his personal physician, and I'm headed ashore to arrange for his burial. Too bad. He was hoping to see his father again. Perhaps you know him—a fellow named Caleb Lange?"

THE LAST BASTION OF THE OLD SOUTH

The old Legare Plantation was a 500-acre anachronism, a relic of vanished grandeur surrounded by steel-girdered progress. It invoked appreciable ridicule from cynical newcomers who had never known true opulence. Its fields, rented to cotton farmers, were but half tended. Pillars of the mansion flaked more white paint with passing years.

The only two occupants of the decaying mansion, both now elderly and white-haired, were the white owner, Gabriel Guilford, and his black servant-cook-handyman, Simmons. Both were contented with their positions in life.

"They's a gem'mun to see you, suh," announced the servant.

"Well, show him in, Simmons."

The man entered the shabby living room, adjusting his eyes to the dim interior. "I'm Thomas Hellman, owner of the adjacent properties," the man said. "I'm here to offer you $500,000 for this rundown plantation."

"Whut's yo'ah opinion, Simmons?" asked Gabriel,

"They's talk goin' 'round 'bout big shoppin' malls and condeemineums, suh."

"Gracious! Mah deah old granddaddy would nevah rest easy. Show Mistah Hellman out, Simmons."

Some days after Hellman's unsuccessful bid, he pushed his way past Simmons, "Mr. Guilford," he sputtered, "this s-s-sabotage must stop! *Immediately!*"

"Sabotage?"

"Yes! My new $550,000 home—burned! My Cadillac—scratched and dented! I'm putting the case in the hands of Sheriff Lemoine!"

"Lemoine? Fine young man," commented Gabriel easily. "Married mah great-granddaughtah Jessamine, Ah recall. Oh, he'll do whut's right."

As the entrepreneur stormed out of the ancient mansion, old Gabriel Guilford chuckled, "Simmons, you been a bad boy?"

"Yassuh."

THE CONVERSION OF
GENTLEMAN JIM SCHULTZ

Deadman Junction ain't the end of the world, but it's close enough. Spiritually, I'd class it three-quarters hell-bent. It delighted the Reverend Forrester, providin' enough assorted sins to combat for the rest of his life. I'm just an ordinary guy, makin' a living and not overly blessed with omnipotence. I didn't mind the Reverend comin' into my bar to fish for lost souls. It gave my place some class, y'know; besides, his salvations generally didn't last more'n a couple weeks.

I wondered how long it'd take him to convert Gentleman Jim Schultz, just released after a term for safecracking. I didn't have to wait long. The next night the Reverend barged in shoutin' "Repent!"

"Look," said Schultz, "with all due respect to your Reverence, I served my time and now desire only long-delayed refreshment."

The Reverend turned to me, "May we use your back room? This sinner and I need privacy while praying for his eternal salvation."

"Okay," I told him. I left the door ajar, curious how it'd end. I heard only snatches.

"Thou shalt not steal..."

"But sinners concealing their ill-gotten gains in safes must be taught to share with fellow men..."

"...the way of the Lord hath everlasting rewards..."

"Money accomplishes good works, Reverend..."

"Yes, I suppose..."

"Imagine, Rev! With sufficient money we can...worldwide missions!...cathedrals!.."

An hour later I looked in. And lucky I did!

The Reverend was kneeling before my safe while Gentleman Jim gave instructions, "Ver-r-ry gently now, listen for a faint click...."

EXORCISING THE HAUNTED
MOBILE HOME

The bizarre tale originated when an ambitious young reporter, hoping for a scoop, accompanied Patrolman O'Donnel on his downtown beat.

"The nerve o' some people," declared the patrolman, "parkin' that vehicle in Lincoln Square! Watch me ticket 'im." Approaching the aluminum mobile home, he knocked. No response. He opened the door.

From inside an ominous voice threatened, *"One step inside and the whole city disappears!"*

"Holy Christopher!" exclaimed the patrolman. "The bloody thing's haunted!"

"What'll you do now?" asked the reporter.

"Call headquarters."

Captain Feldman answered the phone. "Abandoned, you say? And threatening to make the city *disappear*? Sounds like another anarchist. I'll send the bomb squad. Keep everyone away!"

The bomb squad arrived and debated how to deactivate an entire mobile home. Someone suggested X-raying it. But how? Meanwhile, they cordoned off the area.

The reporter's story made tabloid headlines: HAUNTED MOBILE HOME BAFFLES AUTHORITIES! Curious crowds gathered, gaping in fascinated awe from the barricades.

Michael Czyk, the unemployed engineer trying to market his patented protection device, returned. The unexpected publicity thrilled him. Still, he needed to get back inside his mobile home to rewind the tape recorder.

Near midnight he succeeded. He imbibed rather freely, undressed, and fell asleep. Something awakened him. He was moving! Outside, Patrolman O'Donnel was shouting, "Anither ten feet, boys, and inta the river she goes!"

Wasting no time, Czyk leaped out, naked, running pell-mell. "See?" yelled O'Donnel triumphantly. "There goes the thing what's haunted it! Me auld mother always said ghosts hate water."

BALANCING NATURE
IN LAKE WANKATONKA

Chauncey Hollingsworth took his position in State Fish & Wildlife Service seriously. He interviewed old Alec Bodecker, local fishing guide at Lake Wankatonka.

"How's business?" he inquired.

"Great!" replied the old man. "Plenty of clients, all catchin' limits of nice ten-inch bluegills."

"We of SF&WS will make it even better. We'll immediately introduce 50,000 more bluegills."

Two years later Hollingsworth returned. "How's business?"

"Not good. Nobody's catchin' anything but scrawny four-inch bluegills."

"Aha! Clear case of overpopulation. We'll stock 20,000 perch to control those bluegills." Hollingsworth drove away happy.

When he came again two years later, old Alec complained, "Hardly any bluegills left. Nothin' but undersized perch."

"Your SF&WS will solve that promptly," declared Hollingsworth. "Obviously the situation calls for bass to keep perch numbers in check. I'll arrange to introduce 10,000 bass into Lake Wankatonka tomorrow. Glad to be of service."

Two years passed. Chauncey Hollingsworth was back. "Everything fine?" he asked.

"No clients," grumbled old Alec. "Bluegills mostly gone, danged few perch, and hardly any bass. Bass are eatin' theirselves."

"This demands a minor adjustment in the food chain. I'll have 5,000 pike out here promptly. They'll control the bass and perch populations, permitting bluegills to flourish."

On Hollingsworth's next scheduled visit, pike had wiped out all other species. "No problem," he said. "SF&WS will bring in thousands of turtles to eat the young pike."

"Oh, don't bother," said old Alec Bodecker. "I hate turtle soup. Besides, I'm movin' to Lake Tallamonga."

QUICK EDDIE RETURNS THE LOOT

Yesterday I'm enjoyin' a beer with Dan the Dealer Holman in the little corner saloon with the big sign advertisin' bock beer—you know, the place regular customers call the "Bloated Goat." Anyhow, Dan says to me, "Too bad about Quick Eddie Jackson."

I become instantly curious. "What happened to Eddie?"

"He held up Gunther's Print Shop and got $50,000."

"Did the cops nail him red-handed?"

"Nope. Eddie showed me the money."

"Then did Gunther recognize Eddie and finger him?"

"Nope."

"So, what's so awful?" I inquire.

Dan leans forward and whispers confidential, "Quick Eddie then says outright, 'I gotta be honest; I'm returnin' this money.'"

"Not Quick Eddie!" I exclaim. "He'd be crazy to do that."

"Absolutely," confirms Dan the Dealer sadly. "Quick Eddie has lost all marbles."

"That *is* bad news," I agree. "And him the best stick-up artist in circulation."

I'm still reflectin' on this terrible disaster that befalls Quick Eddie when today I encounter him in person. "Can it be true?" I ask. "Did you really *return* $50,000?"

"It was the decent thing to do."

"Didn't Gunther get mad and call the cops?"

"Naw," answers Quick Eddie. "He's actual very grateful and we have gone into partnership."

"But, Eddie," I protest, "you don't know nothin' about printin'."

"True," he admits, "but that ain't necessary. Gunther prints; I handle distribution."

"Exactly what distribution is bein' discussed?" I inquire.

Eddie looks surprised. "Why, them counterfeit twenties Gunther's makin'."

275

THE GENIE IN THE MING VASE

"Just like Aladdin's lamp!" my brother Tom exclaimed excitedly as I returned tired from a buying trip for our antiques business.

"What on earth are you talking about?" I asked.

"That giant vase grandfather brought back from China years ago—you know, tall, decorated with blue flowers and red dragons? Well, it was getting dusty, so I thought I'd polish it up. As I started rubbing it, I swear a voice inside said, 'Your wish, master?'"

"You're certain you weren't imagining it?" I asked. Tom was usually dead serious about everything.

"No! It was real!"

"Okay," I sighed, "what did you wish for?"

"A customer for that ugly Queen Anne suite we've tried to sell for ages. Five minutes later, a gentleman walks in and plunks down the cash!"

That was the beginning. Every time I was away, Tom reported some "magical" sale as a result of his hidden genie inside the Ming vase. Finally I had him committed. The psychiatrist confided, "Such fixations take time to cure."

Two lonely years passed, running business by myself. Thinking of my brother, I absently rubbed the vase.

From somewhere inside, a hollow voice said, "Your wish, master?" Recovering from astonishment, I said, "I wish Tom was home!"

I rushed to the sanitarium. "You were right, Tom!" I shouted. "There really *is* a genie."

"There never was," declared Tom dully.

The psychiatrist stepped forward. "Your brother is cured—but you, sir, have a deep-seated problem."

He beckoned his white-jacketed assistants.

276

BLUEBIRD WITH A BROKEN WING

The mailman handling the rural route brought the message, "Ellie Pardee wants to see you, sheriff. Says it's kinda urgent." Maybe this time somebody'd swear out a complaint against the old devil. I recalled Abner's first wife Delia. She got her face stitched up by Doc Randall—no charges filed, she just left town.

As I pulled into the driveway, Ellie limped forward on her homemade crutch, her arm in a heavy plaster cast.

"What happened?" I asked.

"It was that poor little bluebird, sheriff. Musta flew inta a wire. Broke its wing." Tears trickled down her cheeks.

This was getting nowhere. "Start at the beginning," I suggested.

"I didn' know what I was gettin' into, sheriff. All I seen was a strong man and 200 acres. That first week, Abner says, 'My coffee's too hot,' and poured the potful over my—my front. Blisters didn' heal for weeks. Last week he broke this arm. Set it hisself. Made the heavy cast, not wantin' folks to know.

"Anyhow, I found this bluebird and hid it in the barn, tryin' to fix its wing. Abner discovered it. 'C'mere,' he ordered, 'and watch!' I went kinda slow—he busted my leg, y'know.

"When he wrung its neck, I-I clobbered him with my cast. Hurt somethin' awful. He's lyin' over yonder."

Abner was dead. Lugging his body up to the hayloft, I dropped it headfirst. Then I car-phoned the coroner.

"Abner Pardee had a fatal fall this morning. Bring Doc Randall along."

JACK-OF-ALL-TRADES AND HIS JILL

"Will you be home for supper?" Jill Brandon asked her husband Jack.

"Remember, darling," he laughed, "you married a Jack-of-All-Trades. Today, Marjorie Jones needs a hand with wallpapering; Widow Symington, a man's foot spading her garden; and Daphne French, legwork moving furniture. Then Katie Cuthbert needs a head to figure installing wiring; Rosie Danforth, two strong arms repairing siding; and Eleanor Tillman, a hand cleaning. Oh, I'll be busy."

Jack left their cottage whistling.

Soon, Jill secretly followed his route. Perhaps she could learn to become a Jill-of-all-trades.

She observed how her husband's caressing hand helped Marjorie, his sure feet led Widow Symington into her secluded garden, and his head figured bizarre things for Katie. Jack was indefatigable.

That afternoon, Jill spied how Jack's athletic legwork assisted Daphne, and his strong arms moved Rosie. Jill could hardly believe her man could do so much in one day!

By sundown, having learned enough, Jill slipped away home, leaving Jack still giving the benefit of his free hand to Eleanor Tillman. Jack was completely dumfounded when Jill, cleaver in hand, announced she would become an undertaker.

Jack's left hand she ceremoniously buried near Marjorie's gate, his right one beside Eleanor's mailbox, and his arms in Rosie's shrubbery, Then she interred Jack's feet in Widow Symington's garden, his legs alongside Daphne's walk, and his handsome head beside Katie's. Jack's torso remained. Jill cremated it in the furnace that night, rejoicing to have finally discovered a profession of her very own.

SLIPPERY SAM GIVES A LESSON

Slippery Sam was instructing a new pupil. "Use psychology at all times, especially when sizing up your prospect. Now, how would you describe those two over by the park bandstand?"

"Well," replied Marco, "the young guy acts kinda dumb, just watchin' the pigeons. And the old dame clutches her purse like she's scared somebody'll snatch it."

"Which would you pick?"

"The stupid young guy, I reckon."

"Wrong! Anything goes haywire, dull-witted guys his size beat hell outta you. Now, the old broad clutching her handbag values money foremost. Observe my technique."

Slippery Sam approached her. "Excuse me, madam. You appear to be an intellectual lady interested in getting the most from every dollar." She smoothed her gray hair self-consciously and smiled coyly. "How do I do that, sir?"

"Glad you asked, madam. This little card, costing only $50, entitles you to 50% discount on all household appliances and personal items everywhere."

"My, that *is* a bargain!" She fumbled in her purse, then groaned, "Oh, dear. All I have is a $100 bill."

"Quite all right, madam. I just happen to have change."

As she hastened happily away, Slippery Sam declared, "See, Marco? All a matter of psychology."

The young man lounging nearby approached Sam, flashing his police identification. "You're under arrest!"

"There must be some mistake, officer—"

"No mistake. We've been shadowing 'Funny-money' Annie for days, trying to nab all her passers. I'll take that counterfeit $100 bill she just gave you for evidence. You have the right..."

NOSTALGIC RETURN

On a chill, overcast afternoon, Joe Horton and Bill Duvall flew back into Curtisville, landing at the fairgrounds. Nobody saw them—not that anybody could.

"Sure seems neglected now," observed Bill. "The old roller coaster is rusting away, and the ticket office is weather-beaten. Neither has seen paint in ages."

"Somehow I still can't believe my sister Alice would do such a thing," said Joe sadly. "We'd always seemed so close."

"Well, she did it—and here we are," stated Bill. "She heard your Uncle Avery'd made a new will in your favor."

"My case I can understand. Greed overwhelmed her. But why did she include *you?*"

"I brought it on myself, old buddy, telling her that after we were married I'd still have to support my invalid mother. Alice couldn't bear sharing with anybody."

"She had us both fooled, Bill. Last time I looked in on her, Alice had grown fat—still unmarried, with no friends. I'll never forget that night. 'Oh, c'mon,' she pleaded, in her sweet irresistible way. 'One last ride, boys!' We'd reached the peak of Devil's Loop yonder. Suddenly she unlatched our safety bars! A few terrifying seconds and—it was all over!"

"Yeah, Joe," chuckled Bill wryly. "If only we'd had these wings *then!* Imagine Alice's expression if we'd flapped off and circled the fairgrounds!"

"Enough nostalgic reminiscing," declared Joe firmly. "Time to fly back up home, before our wings get damp and dirty. Hey, man, Gabriel's serving ambrosia again tonight!"

DUEL AT DAWN

Two handsome young blades confronted each other at the Natchez Cotillion. Brady Traylor declared, "You have dishonored the fair name of Cynthiana Carstairs, you contemptible Yankee interloper!"

"I have only honorable intentions toward that young woman," responded Daniel Moore.

"You're a worthless, lying hypocrite!" shouted Traylor.

Moore reddened. "If it's fight you seek, so be it."

"I accept your challenge. Pistols, ten paces. Dueling ground at dawn. I'll supply weapons. Last man standing wins!"

Miss Carstairs intervened. "Act civilized, both of you!"

"I'll defend your honor to my death," stated Traylor. He stalked away. The crowd was stunned, silent.

Brady Traylor *had* to eliminate his rival for Cynthiana's hand. Only the Carstairs fortune could pay off his gambling debts. But he'd win! He'd tested the pistols; both shot to the left.

Dawn. The dueling ground still wet with dew. The referee intoned, "Gentlemen! Ten paces, turn and fire at will!"

Ten! Traylor turned and raised his pistol confidently. The next instant—*bang!*—a bullet struck his shoulder and he slumped down.

A buckboard approached wildly. Cynthiana Carstairs leaped down. "Brady Traylor! You cowardly, cheating, despicable dog!" she exploded. "You knew about those pistols. Well, so did I. Your grandfather told my grandfather he didn't want young hotheads getting themselves killed dueling, so he had those pistols specially made to shoot three feet to the left at twenty paces.

"Yes, I told Daniel about them so it would be a fair duel. And the better man won!"

"Hello, Idella." The man nonchalantly sat down at her table.

"Henry, you rat," she hissed, hoping other diners in the restaurant didn't hear. "What do you want?"

"To apologize, my dear. I should never have said those things, never have walked out on you. Let's start over."

She forced a smile for the benefit of the couple at the adjacent table and said, "So, you somehow learned I made a fortune in business and now, after six years, you come crawling back. God, another year and I could have had you declared legally dead."

"Honest, Idella, I've reformed."

"Yeah, and elephants fly. Well, come on home and we'll discuss the situation."

"You won't regret it. I promise."

Idella drove her new Mercedes. Already she was planning. Her seaside estate was secluded and Treachery Rock, a mile offshore, was exposed only at low tide. And Henry couldn't swim!

"Let's picnic over on Treachery Rock," she suggested. "We'll take my yacht."

"Great!"

On the tiny island she served the wine laced with sleeping pills. Henry never suspected. Soon he lapsed into unconsciousness.

From her mansion, Idella watched the tide finally cover Treachery Island. Success!

The next morning her doorbell chimed. There stood Sheriff Anson. "This may be unpleasant, ma'am."

She feigned distress. "I warned Henry about strong undertow at high tide. He must have fallen asleep on the beach. Did he drown?"

"No, ma'am. My unpleasant news is that two years ago in Tahiti Henry finally did learn to swim..."

CHRISTMAS WITH CLAUS

A blizzard swept across the Midwest, dumping unexpectedly deep snow and freezing rain and closing all airports. So, on Christmas Day, my plane made an unscheduled landing at the emergency field at Buzzards Bluff.

"Ain't no flights north of here fer two days," the morose ticket agent announced.

Lacking something to do meanwhile, I thumbed through the local phone directory on the odd chance I had distant relatives nearby.

Not many people surnamed Kringleheimer. But what to my wondering eyes should appear but the name Claus Kringleheimer. Renting a car, I drove to the address.

Claus came from his cabin to greet me, his long-barreled rifle over one arm, his white beard blowing in the wind. Warming beside his little round-bellied stove, we established that we were indeed distant cousins. Claus asked, "Don't smoke, do ye, young feller?" I assured him I didn't.

"Then you still got good lungs," he pronounced.

"Excuse me," I said, "but what do you do for a living?"

"I got connections with a certain little hospital," he replied.

"Oh, you're a retired doctor?"

"Not exactly. Very few relatives visit me. Take Uncle Avery—outstanding kidneys. And my first cousin Harrison, who never drank liquor—his liver was like new. My late wife Ellie—now, she had perfect organs. What? You ain't leavin'?"

I dashed for the car. "On, Volvo!" I shouted.

And I heard him exclaim ere I drove out of sight, "Yeah, I sell human body parts!"

COINCIDENCES?

"As City Traffic Controller, Mr. Eggleston," I told him, "I must insist that you make necessary changes in this tunnel, straightening out those sharp turns."

"Why?" he challenged. "I posted traffic signs before all angles. Just look."

"Frankly, sir," I said, "I don't know how the City Engineer approved it."

"You been listenin' to rumors started by my competitors," he accused. "It was pure coincidence that my brother Mike is City Engineer." He handed some papers from his briefcase. "See? All the contract calls for is a tunnel thirty-two feet wide under the Passiquac River connectin' Monroe Street on the east with Linden Boulevard on the west. I fulfilled that contract."

"There's also talk that you never studied engineering."

"What's to study?" he retorted. "Anyhow, it's only coincidence that my Uncle Avery certifies engineers in this state. Any other problems?"

I pointed upward. "Some of the ceiling up there is already cracked,"

"The contractor who installed it says that's to be expected."

"I suppose," I asked sarcastically, "he's also a relative of yours, Mr. Eggleston?"

"Okay, he's my brother-in-law. So what?"

"You *must* remedy this situation promptly," I said sternly. "There have been fifteen accidents in your tunnel to date."

"I know what you're thinkin'," he snapped. "But my ownin' two auto repair shops nearby is—"

"I know," I interrupted. "Just another coincidence."

IN TEATRO DIABLO

Talk about desperate! While bumming around Europe that summer I got mugged in Naples. Money, passport, everything! To top it off, the American Embassy was closed for the weekend.

On a little side street I spotted the Teatro Diablo. Below its marquee was a sign crudely lettered in several languages: *Comedy Acts Wanted.* I was hungry. Besides, what did I have to lose?

I wandered inside. In a back room I met Vittorio Gallio, a fat little man in a rumpled checkered suit. "I need a job," I confessed. He shifted his cigar and asked, "English-speaking comedian?"

"I suppose so," I said doubtfully.

"We need a new comedian tonight. There's a dressing room next door with costumes and makeup. But I oughta warn you—'Mitragliatrice' Scarlotti, the local Mafia capo, attends every performance."

Funny name, I thought. Nevertheless, I made myself up like a clown in time for the performance. While waiting in the wings, I spoke to Gallio, "Those painted flames obviously call attention to the name of this theater. But what are those horizontal rows of perforations across the backdrop?"

"Oh," he answered, "I guess you don't understand Italiano. 'Mitragliatrice' translates as 'machinegun.' You see, when Machinegun Scarlotti don't like the act, he eliminates the comedian."

"Good God! You mean he—"

"Yeah, mows 'em down right there on the stage. Rat-a-tat-tat-tat! We lose a lotta comedians that way."

My knees were rubbery as he shoved me onstage with a guttural, "You better be good tonight, kid!"

CASE OF THE CLONE PRINCE

Agent Larry Garrison burst through the front door of the isolated cabin, his pistol drawn. "FBI!" he announced loudly. "The game's up, Yussef Haddam—otherwise known as the Clone Prince of evil genetic scientists infiltrating these United States!"

"You have no right to invade my private laboratory, Yankee pig," objected the swarthy white-coated scientist. "Of what am I accused?"

"You know very well!" retorted Garrison. "Your dastardly plot to clone millions of sheep, thereby overgrazing our nation and turning it into wasteland. It won't succeed! My assignment is to destroy your insidious laboratory and arrest you."

"How did you find me?" inquired Haddam.

"Simple. Our aerial surveys show flock after flock originating here, clogging roads in all directions. So, you'd best come quietly."

The door to an inner office opened and an exact duplicate of the scientist said, "I am the real Yussef Haddam. You've been talking to my cloned double."

"Actually," insisted a third Yussef Haddam, appearing behind the second, "I am the original. Furthermore, I have seven more of myself in the next room. You can't arrest us all!"

"Wrong!" declared Garrison. "Yours isn't the only country performing cloning. I have this place surrounded—*myself!* Just look outside!"

From the window, they looked out upon a horde of grim-faced Larry Garrisons, each with an identical weapon raised.

The ten Yussef Haddams simultaneously raised their hands in surrender and, in unison, began cursing in their native language.

THE QUEEN AND THE GARDENPERSON

Once upon a time, not so long ago and not so far away—by jet, that is—there lived in a little kingdom by the sea good King Athelbert and beautiful Queen Roxanne. At least that's what the tabloids proclaimed, for any editor publishing otherwise unwillingly found himself a nonpaying resident of the Royal Dungeon.

Now, Queen Roxanne had certain egocentrically-inspired feminine yearnings. The King and male persons of available royalty disappointed her. Hence, despite her discriminatory, classconscious background, the queen began an affair with an unenlightened and undereducated gardenperson named Elmo.

They secretly met back-to-back in the Royal Garden—among tulips, as it were—their conversation rendered clarity-deficient by their facing opposite directions. "Keep thine eye peering through thy Minolta," warned Roxanne. "The gossip-hungry court would love learning about us." (Actually, they'd known for some time.)

"Your Highness," whispered Elmo, "the King is in distance-enhanced provinces collecting illearned taxes from impoverished peasants."

"I know that, you braindeprived idiot," snapped Roxanne. "Now the coast is clear. Get with it!"

She turned brighteyed, eagerness-filled—but Elmo's work-hardened hands throttled her.

At the inquest, held in the Royal Dungeon with the Royal Executioner in prominent attendance, the coroner astutely pronounced, "Heart failure!" and promptly withdrew.

Whereupon King Athelbert delivered unto his gardenperson a goodly quantity of gold, saying, "Excellent work, Elmo. She was becoming a damned embarrassment."

"About burial, sire?" inquired Elmo respectfully. "Another tulip bed—as customary for thy queens?"

"Good thought! A wise monarch always demonstrates ecologyawareness."

WAITING FOR THE 09:15

I'll never become entirely comfortable in my job. Probably that's one of the unwritten prerequisites for an IRS auditor. You encounter the worst and best of humanity, devious to pathetic. Like that case assigned to me in Fowlerville: it turned out to be an arthritic 94-year-old surviving on Social Security. He didn't owe the government a dime.

I'd checked out of the village's only hotel and stood waiting for the 09:15 train to take me back to the city. I couldn't help noticing the frail little old gray-haired lady anxiously waiting its arrival. "Visiting the city?" I inquired.

"Oh, no, sir," she answered. "Just waiting for my boy. Johnny always comes home on the 09:15."

I strolled to the far end of the platform. The baggage loader whispered, "Her Johnny ain't never comin' back."

"Why not?" I inquired.

"You've heard of Johnny Deveaux?"

The name seemed familiar but I couldn't place it. "What about him?" I asked the man.

"The kid left Fowlerville claimin' it was just a hick crossroads. Planned to make it big. Anyhow, Johnny got mixed up in the drug-dealin' crowd. T-men closed in and gunned him as he was runnin' for the train.

"His old ma won't believe it. Thinks there was some mistake. She meets the 09:15 every mornin', rain or shine—hopin', just hopin'."

The train arrived and I boarded it. As it pulled away I glanced back at the saddest disappointment ever registered on a human face.

MUTTON CHOPS

"Kinda expected this," muttered old Sheriff Olson, parking the Jeep on the shoulder of the country road behind the wrecked Jaguar. Everybody in Pecos County knew that sleek black convertible, but he checked the registration anyway. Yep, it belonged to Jesse Ainsworth, President of the Cattlemen's Association. Blood spattered the dented fenders, and carcasses of several sheep lay in the nearby ditch. "Looks like young Ainsworth plowed inta a flock of sheep," observed Deputy Jimmy Mason.

"Obviously," snorted Olson. "Common knowledge he hated sheep. He wouldn' slow down for 'em, even with thet SOFT SHOULDERS sign. I wonder whar he went."

"Probably hikin' back to his big ranch," chuckled Mason, "cussin' every step."

"Walll, since we're here," said Olson, "we might as well inform the herder. I see his covered bunkwagon on yonder hill."

The two trudged uphill. The sheriff called out, "Anybody home?" A familiar Mexican emerged, wiping his bloody hands on a much soiled apron. "*Señor* Olson! Somebody drive very fast into my sheeps. Keel many!"

"Yeah, Rodrigo, we know. You see the accident?"

"No accident, *señor*," the sheepherder scowled. Then he brightened, "Now eet ees noon. You hungry? I make veree special mutton chops—weeth biscuits."

"Doan' mind if we do, *amigo*," replied Olson, inhaling the fragrant aroma issuing from the skillet on the brushwood fire.

They topped the hearty meal with Rodrigo's strong coffee. "Delicious!" declared the sheriff. "*Gracias!* Gotta git yore recipe sometime. Why, them chops didn' taste anything at all like mutton."

WHAT'S FOR LUNCH, DEAR?

Herbie said, "Dear, once again, I fear,
  "The company's sending me far from your side.
"But the fridge is replete with left-over meat."
  (To which he had added much cyanide.)
His wife's spreading hips and thick puffy lips
  For him had lost all their erotic appeal.
Herbie's roving glance had sparked new romance
  His life had become exciting and real!
Mabel said, "Honey bunch, I've packed you a lunch.
  "Your tummy won't tolerate airplane-type food.
"So be on your way without further delay."
  (That tainted crab should fix him but good.)
'Twas not chance that he met sweet luscious Florette.
  They boarded the plane and giggled with glee.
She softly nuzzled, "That loot you embezzled
  "I've electronically transferred, my lover—tax free."
From the airport bazaar they sped off in a car
  'Til Florette exclaimed, "Stop, please, my dove!
Atop yon cliff so high let's make love—don't be shy."
  (All it took to be rich was just one tiny shove.)
Florette looked far down at Herbie's smashed crown
  And wickedly laughed, "Now the money's all mine!
"And there's nobody who'll really miss the old fool."
  Then suddenly hungry she sat down to dine.
Oh, Florette did munch on the picnic lunch
  That Mabel had doctored for Herbie with spite;
And Mabel did eat of the poisonous meat—
  But Herbie'd completely lost all appetite.

MY UN-COOL BET

My uncontrollable temper cost me a cool ten grand. It was early morning. As I arrived at the public links and started to get my clubs from the trunk, Herbie Wilcox rushed over. "How about a friendly bet—one hole?" he asked.

"How much?" I asked suspiciously, knowing Herbie's tricky reputation.

"Ten thousand," he replied.

I felt confident I could beat him. "You're on!" I said. We teed off on the par four hole.

As we holed out, Herbie said, "Pay me! I won—five to your six."

"Like hell you won!" I retorted. "Your drive landed in the pond and you made a drop—that's one penalty stroke."

"Okay, okay, so we're even. We'll play another hole."

"You're forgetting you kicked your ball out of the sand trap. That's another penalty stroke. I won—six to your seven. Why are you trying to cheat?"

"I-I need the money," he confessed. "I owe the casino $50,000. If I don't pay something soon I'm in deep trouble. Besides, I was only kidding about our bet."

I was boiling mad. We strode back to our cars in silence. Two scowling men were waiting. "Okay," said the larger, "which one of you is Herbie Wilcox?"

"H-h-herbie *who*?" asked Wilcox, turning pale. His eyes pleaded with me not to give him away.

"You mean Herbie Wilcox the cheating weasel? The welsher? That's him!" I declared, pointing.

Now, all because of my hot temper, I'll probably *never* collect from Herbie Wilcox.

RETURN TO BIXBURG

Waiting on the doorstep, Charles Timmons nervously ran his fingers through his thinning white hair. Finally the doorbell was answered by a man near his age. "What's this about, Mr. Belleveau?" he demanded. "I thought your blackmailing me ended years ago. Now you write about some emergency."

"Come in, Charles," welcomed Belleveau. "Not really an emergency. I just wanted you to know I used your money to finish medical school. So it did considerable good."

"Hummph!" snorted Timmons. "It cost me plenty."

"You were a handsome devil when you were young, Charles," the host reminisced. "You breezed into Bixburg here and swept my sister Clarisse off her feet. But it was a horrible thing you did, driving her to suicide."

"Anything else?"

"Let's have a drink together and call things even. What'll it be?"

"Er—gin and tonic, Gene."

Belleveau mixed their drinks at his small bar. "Here's to memories."

As Timmons tossed off his drink, he declared, half-seriously, "That better not be poison. I took the precaution of advising the local sheriff to investigate if I died here in Bixburg."

"That would be Sheriff Tom Charville. Poor Tom never quite recovered from Clarisse's death. They were engaged—or didn't you know? I say, Charles, you're not looking well!"

Timmons was gasping. "You won't...get away with this...I asked...sheriff...to demand...autopsy."

"Ah yes, Tom phoned me that you'd done that. But no matter, Charles. You see, I am now the coroner."

GRANDFATHER'S MEMORY

After grandfather completed his annual check-up, I conferred with his physician. "I'm worried about him," I confessed. "He's becoming forgetful. He even forgot his eightieth birthday. When the matron at the retirement home wheeled in the big candle-lit cake, he asked, 'What's the occasion?' And he hasn't remembered to phone on my wedding anniversary or birthday this year, which he always did before."

"Has he shown other symptoms—lack of concentration, for example?"

"Definitely not, doctor," I assured him. "Last night when I visited him, he beat me three games out of four at cribbage."

"Then it's probably not Alzheimer's. I'll give him a prescription that should improve his memory. One tablet each day at bedtime."

It apparently helped. Grandfather phoned weekly to inquire about his grandchildren. Then his phone calls stopped. One month later I went to see him.

"Are you still taking your pills?" I asked.

"Pills? What pills?"

"The pills to restore your memory. Those Dr. Creighton prescribed."

"Don't recall any Dr. Creighton," grandfather declared.

"You must concentrate, grandfather. You wouldn't want to lose your memory entirely, would you? Of course not."

"Oh, speaking of memory, do you recall I beat you three games out of four last time you visited?"

"That's right!" I said, amazed.

"Okay, how about a couple games of cribbage—dollar a point? Oh, don't worry, I can afford it. I've been busy selling Doc Creighton's memory pills to the other residents."

IT HAPPENED LIKE THIS....

"...and, furthermore," continued the little old gentleman with pale eyes, "the murderer informed me that on the mantelpiece in Mrs. Winslow's parlor stands a china dog with one ear chipped."

This fact had not been publicized. Detective Moran became alert. "The case is still under investigation, Mr. Jones. Medics prove that Elvira Winslow died of a heart attack. Yet you seem certain she was murdered. Why would her killer confide in you?"

"Bragging? Or perhaps he wanted to exonerate young Philip Tornquist, her bodyguard, who stands accused? Anyhow, he showed me how he did it. Could we visit the murder scene?"

The two approached the cottage on Chestnut Street. Moran led the way past yellow tape, unlocked the door, and stepped aside for Jones to enter. "Now, sir," he said, "the deceased was discovered dead in that chair, no marks of violence. *How* was she murdered?"

"With your cooperation, I'll demonstrate. Please turn around." Curious, Detective Moran obeyed.

"Her killer readily overpowered frail little Elvira," declared Jones. "Using elastic bandage, he bound her hands behind her—like this. Then her ankles—like this."

"Obviously leaving no marks later. Then?"

"He gagged her—like this." Jones stuffed a handkerchief into the detective's mouth, then continued, "After young Tornquist went home that night, someone knocked.

"'Who's there?' asked Elvira.

"'Philip!' answered the voice. 'An emergency!'

"She opened the door.

"Only it wasn't Tornquist, sir; it was me, her ex-husband. I frightened her to death, found her money, and left—like this."

THE MIRACULOUS REAPPEARANCE
OF DUCKS

"I had so hoped to present dressed ducks to the poor of my parish," lamented the Reverend Dickinson. "Now only two remain in my pond."

"I see," said Sergeant Tilford. "'Thieves by night will destroy til they have enough.' Jeremiah forty-nine, verse nine."

"You do know your Bible," declared Dickinson, amazed. "But the latest incident didn't occur at night. At breakfast I heard a commotion at the pond and rushed out immediately. Nobody around, yet even with my failing eyesight I could see that two more ducks had vanished. Confidentially, sir, I suspect my neighbor, David Blankenship. Poor old fellow is living on Social Security."

"Still, we mustn't act hastily," advised the sergeant. "Remember, 'Neither shalt thou bear false witness against thy neighbor.' Deuteronomy five, verse twenty."

"Indeed not!" agreed the minister. "That would be quite sinful."

"Well, for the present, 'I give my heart to seek and search out all things by wisdom.' Ecclesiastes one, verse thirteen." With that, Sergeant Tilford departed.

Next morning he returned, saying, "Watch your pond closely, Reverend." Moments later a form surfaced, gasping. The two remaining ducks also reappeared, ruffling their feathers.

"My word!" exclaimed Dickinson. "A miracle!"

"Not really," said Tilford. "Inquiring around the neighborhood I learned young Abner Carstairs was a swimmer. Discovering his hidden snorkel, I simply plugged the tube. 'When all air shall cease, then shall the sinner emerge.'"

"I don't recognize that passage," said the Reverend Dickinson, clearly perplexed. "Is that in Scripture?"

"Heavens no," grinned Sergeant Tilford. "I just made that up."

TORTURED TRYST BY THE TULIPS

To the eagle-eyed woman secretly watching, the man and woman with their backs to each other were innocently photographing tulips in the otherwise deserted remote section of City Park. "Just let 'em turn around *once*," she muttered to herself, "and I'll have 'em both back in jail." She might have been surprised to know that neither camera held any film. But again, she might not.

Manfred Carruthers whispered to his wife Jeanette, "This probation is pure torture, darling."

"Keep looking through your Minolta, sweetheart. How do you think I feel, spending lonely nights in my icy cold bed—"

"Hush, sugar-doll, you're making it harder for me. But you know what the court-appointed psychiatrist said: when face to face, we each inspire the other to criminal acts."

"What nonsense! And that silly Judge Atherton believed it. Simply because we enjoy breaking-and-entering, occasional muggings, and some minor shoplifting together—"

"Jeanette!" Manfred suddenly shouted. "I can't stand it any longer!"

Both whirled, instantly in each other's arms, tearfully kissing. Glancing over her shoulder, he said, "Oh-oh, here comes your probation officer."

Their eyes met. "You know what to do, lover."

"Certainly," he growled. "We'll bury her under these tulips."

"That might not be such a good idea," said Jeanette thoughtfully.

"Why not?" he inquired.

"Don't you remember, honey pie? That's where we buried your Uncle Fred and my cousin Mabel and that pizza delivery guy and—"

"Now I recall! But there's space for another chrysanthemum bed." Laughing, together they throttled the probation lady.

RACING TO AN EXCITING WEEKEND

Twilight dimmed the athletic field. Three men waiting at the starting line shifted nervously. Eddie spoke. "You guys think this Madame Beauchamp's Dating Service is on the up-and-up?"

"We'll soon find out," replied George. "Remember, you told her you were the fabulously rich Rajah of Kalinoor, Joe here claimed to be a playboy owner of a huge yacht, and I impersonated the Duke of Colchester."

"I sure hope these rented outfits don't get damaged," muttered Joe. "These top hats alone must cost a fortune."

"I'm just worried my wife Lola will find out," said Eddie. "We're supposed to be at our bowling tournament."

"Yeah, my wife Becky would kill me," declared George.

"Likewise with my wife Ruby," added Joe. "But it's worth the risk. Madame Beauchamp arranged everything. Winner of the race gets his pick of three beauty queens waiting at the far end of this track—for a whole exciting weekend! Losers get the other two ... Look! Three gorgeous dames are taking their places there now!"

At the far end of the track, Ruby was saying, "Seems downright sinful somehow, arranging this exciting weekend while our husbands are away at their silly bowling tournament. If Joe ever found out—"

"Relax!" laughed Lola. "Madame Beauchamp guaranteed absolute confidentiality after we convinced her we were beauty queens."

"It'll serve George right," added Becky, "desertin' me this way."

Back at the starting line, Madame Beauchamp's assistant raised his pistol and called out, "On your marks, gentlemen!....Ready!...Set!..."

THE DUDE

When Annabelle Perkins went east to a university, everybody here in Turkey Junction figured she'd come back and marry some local farmer to manage the thousand acres her daddy left her. Instead, she came back Mrs. Theodore Wentworth. One look at Theodore's fancy clothes showed he'd never chased hogs outta a mudhole. All he did was ride the train inta the state capital and back every weekday.

"Where'd ya git that dude?" Jeb Elkins asked her.

Annabelle got downright furious. "Theodore's got a Ph.D. from Yale, and studied postdoctoral at Oxford," she snapped.

"Yeah?" snickered Jeb. "We know what *thet* means!"

Jeb made a perfession of ridin' Wentworth. "Hey, Dude, I jest sold my hogs fer $4,576.90!" he yelled. "What'd ya git fer yours?"

Another time, "My hay crop netted $5,632.75, Dude! How'd ya make out on yore big acreage?"

Jeb never let up. Every time he showed a profit, he'd rub in how well he'd done. We reckoned Mr. Wentworth lacked backbone, 'cause he never answered. Jest walked away.

Then one Saturday late April, a bunch of us was loafin' at the depot when Wentworth stepped off the train. "May I speak to you, Mr. Elkins?" he asked.

"Shore, Dude, if'n yew kin talk plain English," retorted Jeb.

"Very well, my name is Theodore Wentworth. I'm with Internal Revenue Service—here are my credentials. Your return shows numerous omissions, including $4,576.90 from sale of swine and $5,632.75 from sale of hay... All told, sir, you owe $27,342.89—*plus penalties.*"

LITTLE JOE CELEBRATES CHRISTMAS

"C'mon, big man," commanded Little Joe. "It's Christmas and I need you!"

Despite their extreme size difference, Rico obeyed. Little Joe wasn't somebody who took *no* for an answer—as some in the slum neighborhood had learned to their dismay. Little Joe carried a sharp switchblade and wielded it proficiently.

"What's up, Little Joe?" asked Rico apprehensively. "You gonna do somebody?"

"Shut up and tag along. And be ready to do what I say. Okay?"

They entered Ziggy's pawnshop. "Ziggy," said Little Joe, "that widow down the block—the one with seven kids—oughta have somethin' special fer Christmas dinner. I'm collectin'—"

"It's robbery!" moaned Ziggy.

"You want maybe Rico should re-arrange your shop and you, too?"

"Okay, okay, I'll pay. How much?"

"Fifty would be appreciated."

As they walked out, Rico asked, "Where to?"

"I reckon Sam's Used Clothing is about ripe." They went there.

"Sam," began Little Joe, "kids 'round here ain't got no toys. It's Christmas. You'd like to contribute, maybe, fifty bucks? Or should I turn Rico loose?"

Grumbling, Sam paid.

On went Little Joe and Rico, hitting merchants for "contributions" for "lil' kids' shoes" and "blankets fer the street bums."

"That all?" asked Rico.

"Nah. We gotta buy them groceries fer the widow...an' clothes, an' toys—"

"But," ventured Rico, "I thought, y'know, we'd split the take—sorta personal Christmas presents."

Little Joe turned, threatening. "Rico," he growled, "do I gotta do somethin' drastic to get the Christmas spirit inside your thick skull?"

299

THE DAUGHTER WHO DIDN'T EXIST

Working in Emergency in Philadelphia General, death didn't usually bother me. Still, the girl seemed so young. She'd been brought in too spaced out to give vital information. We couldn't pinpoint the drug before she expired.

Her bracelet said "Rebecca Heffelfinger." Vital Statistics disclosed she'd been born 23 June 1975 in nearby Lancaster County, daughter of Henrik and Joanna Heffelfinger.

At the end of my shift, I asked Dr. Malvers if I could break the news to her parents.

"You sure you want to?" he asked. When I nodded, he added, "They're probably Pennsylvania Dutch. Better change from your scrub suit. And don't be disappointed."

I rushed home and donned the longest skirt I could still wear, being seven months pregnant. Leaving a note for my husband George explaining why I'd be late, I drove off. After several inquiries, I located the Heffelfinger farm.

The impassive bearded man who answered my knock queried, *"Ja?"*

"I bring sad news," I said. "It's about your daughter Rebecca."

"Ve haf no daughter."

"Aren't you Henrik Heffelfinger?"

"Ja. But ve haf no daughter since she left the Way." His wife came to stand behind him.

"Well, I just came to say I tried to save her life."

"Ach, so did ve try." Neither parent shed a tear.

"That's all," I said dejectedly.

"Thou hast journeyed far." He turned to his wife, "Joanna, haf ve no gift for our visitor?"

She hurried to fetch a tiny lace bonnet, murmuring, *"Gluck."*

Guess who cried!

UPWARD ALONG A DUSTY ROAD

The day was hot, the man was tired, and the dusty road endless. Heat waves created shimmering, taunting images ahead. Suddenly he became aware of the urchin striding along beside him.

He said, "You startled me, lad. I'd no idea anyone ever traveled this road. I'm Harold Wasser."

"I've bin along it a-fore, guv'nor."

"Somehow it's always uphill."

"That it be," agreed the lad with a wink. "Allus upward."

"Where does it lead?"

"To wherever yer like."

They walked along in silence for some distance. Harold Wasser spoke again, bitterly, "No road can do that—now. If only..." his voice trailed off.

"Yer got sumfin' ter say?" prompted the boy.

"A sorry tale, I must confess. I lost my job through drink. My wife Sarah lay ill and I had no money left for doctors and medicine. She's buried back in Carleyville. I begged some sleeping tablets from an old friend and took several."

"They helped?"

"Yes. When I woke up I felt like starting a new life. This time, I promised myself, it would be different. After covering poor Sarah's grave with wildflowers, I left Carleyville. Perhaps eventually I'll succeed."

"Yer will, guv'nor."

"Come now, how can you be so certain?" inquired Wasser. "You seem to have a lot of faith in my future."

"I do! Yer no bad'un, Mr. Wasser—jus' took too many o' them sleepy pills. Bye-th'-bye, I'm Michael, yer guardian angel. Didn' yer guess? They buried yer yesterday back in Carleyville."

301

DEATH OF A CLOWN

At the peak of his career, Eddie Jack was the world's funniest clown, the star attraction of Hannagan's Circus. That was before his pretty wife Roseann left him and moved in with the circus owner, Alexander Hannagan.

Then Eddie started drinking. Soon he was no funnier than any other drunk. One night he passed out and woke up to find the circus had moved to another town. Thereafter, his life skidded downhill.

Eddie tried playing the county fair circuit. The verdict of the farmers and their wives: "Mebbe he was funny once; he ain't now." Fame had indeed been fleeting.

After twenty-five years of drifting, odd jobs and cheap booze, Eddie finally approached Hannagan. "Why should I hire you?" challenged the latter.

"Please, Alex, I'm hungry. A job just for eats?"

The owner relented. "But stay away from Roseann," he warned.

"She'll never know I'm here." Eddie had spotted Roseann. She'd grown older, much older, and flabby.

Alexander Hannagan was his own ringmaster—whip, pistol, black boots, and all. Eddie in his clown outfit strutted up to him, shouting, "TAKE MY WIFE!" The audience tittered, anticipating.

"Get away, damn you," hissed Hannagan.

Eddie brazenly persisted, "BUT SHOOT ME FIRST!"

Goaded beyond endurance, unthinkingly Hannagan fired his pistol at Eddie, unaware that the latter had substituted real bullets for the blanks.

The whole audience witnessed it.

Eddie Jack had his revenge. Behind his grease-painted smile, he lay peacefully dying...young Roseann...the fanfare of trumpets...the smell of sawdust...beautiful Roseann....

THE SEARCH

The pain is still intense. I lose track of time, I keep passing out so often. Probably I'll end up dying here, my foot clamped in this bear trap. It was set in the middle of the trail, ever so well camouflaged. I have cursed the scoundrel who set it a thousand times. When Randy Taylor's daughter Lilith disappeared, half the county volunteered to help in the search. Randy had been a good neighbor to everyone, doing chores when the man of the house was ill, taking an extra ham to old folks at Christmas, that sort of thing.

It wasn't just folks' sympathy for Randy in his time of grief. Lilith was the most beautiful young woman in the whole region. Most everybody loved her. People said she was growing into the very image of her late mother.

I myself volunteered to search in this, the most rugged section of the area.

Now I can't move. The chain holding the trap is stapled too deep into the log. I tried to chip it free. My knife blade broke. I fire the last round from my rifle, hoping someone will hear it...hoping, praying. *Anyone.*

Someone did! I see him coming!

"Randy!" I call out hoarsely. "Over here!"

Why is Randy stopping? He smiles grimly. My God, he's turning away, carrying his rifle cradled over his arm just as he did back when we hunted together. He vanishes around the bend.

Suddenly it becomes clear to me.

Randy must *know* the awful thing I did to Lilith.

BEST IN THE PROFESSION

Normally when a man becomes the best in his profession, everyone knows him. But Alfred Baker appeared on no television shows, his picture was never in magazines, and only a select few could recognize him. Baker was a contract man. Bombs were his specialty. His lucrative hits included politicians, underworld bosses, judges, and corporation executives.

Now Mr. Baker wanted to disappear—permanently—not easy for one with his much-desired talents. Then he spotted the man at the corner table. He glanced at his own reflection in the barroom mirror. A perfect likeness!

After the stranger departed, Baker inquired about him. Tim the bartender replied, "Him? Comes every night. Seems kinda lonesome." Next evening, Baker struck up an acquaintance. The man's name was Freddie Jones. Quickly they became friendly. "Freddie," confided Baker, "I have a problem. An old girl friend I'd like to avoid—hasn't seen me in years. Since we look alike, would you entertain her later in my apartment?"

Jones eagerly agreed. They took a taxi to the apartment. Baker excused himself and set the timer. One final act remained: knock Freddie unconscious and switch billfolds. The explosion would leave mangled remains to be identified as Alfred Baker. Free, forever!

Freddie Jones had never chanced on such a beautiful setup. This man had money. Freddie was waiting behind the door when Baker returned to the living room.

Freddie blackjacked him almost tenderly, then tied him up. He'd have all night, he thought, smiling, to ransack the apartment.

THE INEPT PUZZLE SOLVER

On one of his business trips, Herbert Addams took a country road. Fate, he reflected, guided him to the deserted mountain cabin, the solution to ridding himself of his stupid, very plain wife Mary. She had become a liability. At parties to entertain clients, she persisted in wearing her hair in that unattractive knot in back and her dresses never quite fit.

How different was the alluring Samantha Nordstrom, who had recently joined his firm. Always vivacious, knowledgeable about world affairs, Samantha could make any party a success. Their affair had seemed a natural progression.

No one would know where they had gone, and the isolated cabin was seldom (if ever) visited. With little persuasion, Mary packed picnic provisions for the weekend.

Soon after arriving, Mary unpacked their suitcases and settled down with her crossword puzzles. Herbert read his *Wall Street Journal* and, as usual, Mary asked his assistance.

"'Lodging place', five letters?"

"H-O-T-E-L," he spelled out absently.

"'Lovers' meeting', five letters, middle letter 'Y'?"

"Tryst. T-R-Y-S-T."

"'Illicit lover', eight letters starting with 'P'?"

"P-A-R-A-M-O-U-R," Herbert answered.

"'Become cozy in bed', beginning with 'S'?"

"Samantha Nord—" He caught himself too late.

"I suspected as much."

Mary had discovered the pistol while unpacking his luggage. Now she raised it from her lap and shot Herbert three times, which was quite enough.

She'd also realized that no one knew where they had gone, and the isolated cabin was seldom visited. As she started the motor, she murmured, "The word was S-N-U-G-G-L-E."

THE PHRYGIAN COUNTERFEITER

One might anticipate that the first to discover a new profession would be forever famous. Yet the name of Nem-bul-asor is forgotten and his grave, somewhere in the desert of Asia Minor, lies unmarked.

It happened three millennia ago. King Ash-bar, Lord of All Phrygia, exasperated by his nobles appropriating from the peasantry, assembled them before his throne.

"No more thievery!" he thundered. "I give you each fifty pieces of silver stamped with my Royal image. One shall be worth thirty sheep, or ten cattle, or one horse. Use them as you desire, but *death to any thief!* Go!"

Nem-bul-asor, an aging silversmith, learned about the king's silver pieces. More than anything in this world, he desired the maiden Yah-sa-bel to comfort his old years. However, her father demanded thirty sheep for payment.

Nem-bul-asor labored weeks perfecting a likeness of King Ash-bar in silver. With it, he purchased the sheep. He was on his way to claim his bride when the Royal Guards hauled him into Court.

King Ash-bar glowered ominously as he held out Nem-bul-asor's silver coin. "Know thee, lowly one, only I can have tokens made," he rumbled.

The silversmith quaked. The Queen leaned over, whispering into the royal ear.

"I also wish to be remembered as the Merciful," declared Ash-bar, subdued. "Return the sheep to their master. Tomorrow, before me, the maiden Yah-sa-bel *shall* marry you."

Thus ends the tale of the first counterfeiter—who in the end received his heart's desire.

DEATH OF A PHILANDERER

Suave, debonair George Allyn had a certain irresistible appeal to women. He usually evaded matrimony by glib ruses; if these didn't succeed, he had enough money to placate his rejects. His name and picture appeared in tabloids frequently, linked with an actress, a debutante, an heiress—Allyn had cosmopolitan tastes.

His death generated wide speculation. Police concluded it was a bizarre murder.

Becky Trittner unexpectedly encountered Helen Sanders in Roseanne's Tea Room. Both their husbands were police detectives; they knew each other quite well. Roseanne herself waited on them.

After commiserating about the long hours their husbands spent away from home, conversation turned to the murder. "Too bad about George Allyn," declared Becky. "Such a nice man. My husband Tom says he was poisoned by arsenic in ginger cookies. You make such good ginger cookies."

Helen's eyes narrowed. "Naturally, that's a coincidence. My Jim says Allyn's stomach also contained strychnine in Capolito wine, the brand you always serve guests."

"A lot of people buy Spanish wine," Becky informed her coolly.

The two women parted with forced smiles, each suspecting the other had set her up.

Roseanne also smiled. She knew all about Helen's ginger cookies and Becky's Capolito wine. She also knew the two women were the reasons George dropped her as his favorite. Using *two* poisons had been a stroke of genius.

Then a disturbing thought quickly erased her smile. How many other times, in how many other bedrooms, had George Allyn talked in his sleep?

EBENEZER'S FOLLY

That particular Saturday took on a carnival air in Berryville, West Virginia. Television crews elbowed their way through the throng of local citizens to see the ancient trolley car bob and careen its way along the rusty tracks. Old Ebenezer Watkins stood proudly at the controls, his white hair flowing in the breeze, exultant in his final success.

"How long has he been restoring this antique?" a newsman asked the pompous little mayor.

"Years and years," the latter replied. "We call it 'Ebenezer's Folly.' Around 1915 that trolley ran just down Main Street. But ever since, the old fool's been laying more track, weather permitting, 'til now it goes all the way around our fair city. Eb was a persistent old codger. He was so sure it'd run, he's advertised it far and wide." The trolley flashed by again, "BERRYVILLE ELECTRIC TRANSIT CORPORATION" freshly painted on its side.

"But what's the point of it?" persisted the reporter.

"I think I can answer that," declared the governor of West Virginia, stepping forward. "Ebenezer Watkins has officially registered the Berryville Electric Transit Corporation at the State Transportation Authority with himself as sole owner. An old 1884 statute, still valid, grants any electric transit company title to as much land as it can travel around in one day, so—"

The mayor visibly paled. "Y-y-you don't mean—"

"I'm afraid so," stated the governor. "Ebenezer Watkins now owns all of Berryville."

REAL MANNEQUINS DON'T SNEEZE

The manager of the huge Customers' Merchandise complex was pacing his office floor.

"Calm down, Mr. Ferguson," I said. "What happened?"

"Okay, officer," he sighed. "Just at closing time, department heads brought me their cash receipts for the day. In strolled a masked man with a gun. Keeping us covered, he stuffed the money into his satchel, backed out, and ran."

"Notice anything about him?"

"He wore a green jumpsuit and had long dark hair sticking out below his stocking mask."

"What did you do?"

"Punched the alarm, locked all exits. Our store detectives checked everyone leaving. Then we inspected all dressing rooms, looked under all racks and counters. It's hopeless."

"Then he's still here," I reasoned.

We searched the sales area. No luck. Finally we came to a storage room crammed with undressed mannequins, a sea of bald heads.

"No long-haired robber here," snorted Ferguson.

"Maybe he was bald and shucked his wig and jumpsuit. Please fetch a can of pepper from your grocery department."

He seemed puzzled, but brought it anyhow. Turning on the ceiling fan, I tossed a handful of pepper into the air.

Moments later "K-k-kerchoo! Kerchoo!" sounded from the midst of the mannequins and a teary-eyed figure stumbled out.

Was I wrong! It wasn't a guy at all! Just a naked teenage girl in a flesh-colored swim cap!

"Oh my God!" gasped Ferguson. "It's you, Sylvia!"

"Yeah, dad," she snapped. "You wouldn't increase my allowance. 'Use your ingenuity!' you said. Well, I tried."

"DEATH ON THE HIGH SEAS"

My late husband had some admirable qualities: he was deadly with a silenced pistol at thirty paces, he was money-hungry, and he was absolutely heartless. Unfortunately, "Killer" Canelli was also stupid to accept the contract on the Big Boss. Which explains why I'm carrying on our "business" alone.

Anyhow, I'm taking a Caribbean cruise 'til the heat cools from my latest hit. On the dock, two gentlemen nod toward a well-stacked dame. I overhear snatches of their conversation.

One is saying, "...worth a fortune to us...death on the high seas."

"Yes indeed," the other agrees. "One hit is all we need."

I sidle up and say confidentially, "I'll kill her for one million bucks—cash."

They look startled as I edge away. Later, I see them escorting the dame up the gangplank.

When I figure we're far enough offshore, I take the switchblade from my luggage. The target stands at the railing, letting the sea breeze cool her face. I ease forward, blade ready...

Suddenly powerful hands spin me around! I'm facing Captain Larcom of the NYPD! My switchblade drops.

"Well, if it ain't Nellie the Knife," he chuckles. "I expected it'd be you."

He turns to the two gentlemen. "Why did you contact me?"

"That woman proposed to kill Lizette Mancellini, the rising young soprano, for $1,000,000," replies one. "We're Lizette's agents. One hit and she'll be a rich and famous opera star."

"Yes," adds his partner. "Miss Mancellini is really death on those high C's."

UFO

Two years ago Amyl Zik moved into the little community of Cactus Bloom. He was almost instantly admired and trusted. His crown of white hair, handsome face, and perfect manners appealed to the ladies, especially older widows. Men liked Amyl for his endless fund of stories and generous rounds of drinks at the local bar. Amyl Zik was *perfect.*

Little wonder that young Edith Louderback married him. It was a grand wedding. One week later the new Mrs. Zik disappeared.

"Tell me that again," demanded Sheriff Ralph Snyder.

Amyl spoke clearly. "We were hiking out by Twin Boulders. I stopped to rest, but Edith went on ahead, down the trail to Lonesome Peak. A UFO descended, aliens snatched her, and they vanished."

"That's the most cockeyed alibi I ever heard!" snorted Snyder. "Admit it. You killed her somewhere out in the desert."

"It's true, sheriff. Anyone going down that trail will end up like Edith."

"Nonsense. But my deputy and I will go out there with you to find what we can."

Deputy Ted Kilmer parked the squad car below Twin Boulders.

"Okay, Ted," said Sheriff Snyder, "climb up there with Amyl and keep an eye on him. I'm goin' down that trail."

As Ted Kilmer gazed down, observing his boss's progress, Amyl Zik spoke into his wristwatch: "Sergeant Zik calling captain of Xyla spaceship 723-99-Y-21. Male of hominoid species, mid-life, excellent specimen. Potential mate for perfect female delivered yesterday. Creature should reach critical coordinates about—now!"

DID I KILL MR. GODWIN?

"Did I kill Arthur Godwin? Honest, lieutenant, I just don't know."

Lieutenant Foster scowls at me. "Jesus, you *must* know. You were there."

"Yeah," I admit, "I was there when he died."

"Okay, okay. Start at the beginning."

So I do...

I run the Flow-with-Joe Shop, installin' bathtubs, sinks, disposals—anything that connects with water pipes and sewers.

My phone rings. The guy says he's Arthur Godwin and he's read my ad. "Is it true you'll install a lavatory, complete, for $500?"

"Yessir," I reply. "Ready to turn on the faucet."

He gives the address and I go to install it. The old house sits in the middle of ten acres near the edge of town. I hand him a contract and ask, "Where's the main pipe?"

Godwin snickers, "Out at the northwest corner of my property."

"Holy cow!" I protest. "Runnin' pipe all the way to the house? I'll lose a bundle doin' that."

"I have your signed contract," he grins. "$500!" So, I install the lavatory and go to collect.

"What?!" yells Mr. Godwin. "I don't want that damned lavatory out here in the middle of nowhere!"

"If you'll read that contract you're wavin' around," I inform him, "it don't mention *where* I gotta install that lavatory on your property."

He puts on his glasses...

"That's when," I tell the lieutenant, "I notice his face turnin' red, then sorta purple, and the old geezer keels over. So, maybe I *did* kill Arthur Godwin."

NU UPSILON TAU

The Twilight Limited pulled out of Union Station and I settled back for the jolting ride.... Stops at Niles...Kalamazoo...Battle Creek...

An elderly white-haired gentleman stumbled, flopping down beside me. We introduced ourselves.

"I'm Elmore Throckmorton," he said. "UM Class of '13"

"Stopping in Ann Arbor?" I inquired.

"Yes, a journey of nostalgia and duty—final reunion of Nu Upsilon Tau."

"I haven't heard of that fraternity," I ventured.

"Not surprising, young man. I'm the last living member. It went downhill after the initiation of '13. That murder, you know."

"Murder?" I asked, suddenly interested.

"We ordered two pledges to spend the night inside that haunted house out Dexter way. Returning at dawn, we heard a curious thump-thumping and entered cautiously. One student was dead, horribly mutilated. The other, completely mad, was pounding the severed head upon the upstairs floor.

"Every reunion thereafter," he continued, "one member of Nu Upsilon Tau has gone into that same house, trying to unravel the macabre mystery of that dreadful night. Each of them became stark raving mad within the hour."

I shivered involuntarily. "Are *you* going in, sir?"

"Necessary, my boy. I *must* know the truth,"

Time had passed so quickly I hadn't realized how far we'd traveled.

"Ann Arbor! Ann Arbor!" announced the conductor.

As we alighted, two men seized my acquaintance. "What's going on here?" I demanded.

"Oh," replied one, "Elmore escapes from the asylum now and then. Crazy old coot always heads back to Ann Arbor—where he killed that student."

A HAPPY ENDING

Never suppose that murder cannot have a happy ending. (Names are here changed to protect the innocent, if any.)

Midnight. Windows suddenly opened and shouts of "Quiet down!" rang through the neighborhood. Those Allens and Browns again.

Alvin Allen shouted at wife Alice, "You been unfaithful again, you (censored) slut!"

Bessy Brown yelled at husband Bert, "Get a job, you lazy, rutty goat!"

Next morning the two women met for coffee as usual. "Did your $750,000 insurance on Alvin go through?" asked Bessy.

"Yeah," answered Alice. "Then last night he beats me for infidelity."

"With my husband Bert?"

"You know?" Alice gasped.

"Of course, dear. But you're welcome to the bum. I wish he'd get a job like your husband. I gotta make all the livin'."

"Whatcha doin' today, darling?" inquired Alice.

"Pullin' another stickup."

"I came home from visitin' Bessy next door," sobbed Alice. "There hung Alvin from my best chandelier."

The detective took notes. "All morning?"

"Oh, yes. Ask her."

He inquired next door, "Where were you this morning?"

"Right here," Bessy replied. "Ask Alice."

Eventually Alvin's death was ruled suicide, although the lump atop his head was never explained.

Alice shared the insurance money with Bessy, who divorced Bert. Bert married Alice and moved away. Bessy retired to Florida.

So, society is rid of a wife-beater; two lovers live in marriage instead of sin; a woman gives up a life of crime; and the neighborhood enjoys peace at last.

Most everything ended happily.

314

AGATHA'S ADVICE

Dear Agatha: I write to your newspaper column in desperation. My husband Gus (not his real name) is indifferent and drinks too much. Lately he has become abusive.
—Disillusioned in Cincinnati

Dear Disillusioned: Yours is a common complaint among young wives who fail to appreciate their husbands. Put on your best dress and prepare a candlelight dinner he will never forget. He will respond.

Dear Agatha: I followed your advice. Gus came home late and drunk. When he saw the preparations—they took hours—he accused me of entertaining a boyfriend behind his back. He made a terrible scene, slapping me and cursing until neighbors intervened.
—Disillusioned

Dear Disillusioned: You must make allowances for your husband's little outbursts. They are quite normal in the American male. I have myself recently met a man who is resentful that his wife contributes nothing to their marriage, sitting at home and immersing herself in undeserved pity. Discuss your problems openly.

Dear Agatha: Nothing seems to work. I started discussion at supper. Gus went absolutely berserk, showing me an expensive present addressed to his paramour.
—Disillusioned

Dear Disillusioned: Let's call your husband by his right name—Herbert. I find him a charming gentleman. Overwrought from work, he needs a long vacation.

Dear Agatha: Acting on your advice, I shot Herbert last Tuesday, sending him on a long, no-return vacation. I kept that expensive present, substituted a bomb, and forwarded it to his new love. Hoping to hear from you soon.
—Disillusioned

KLEPTOMANIA CAN BE FATAL

"Mr. Danvers?"

I not only recognized the voice, I knew what had happened. Johnathan Vandruck—familiar to police as Johnny the Dip—had been arrested for shoplifting again. He'd inherited the Vandruck fortune and could afford anything he wanted. But Johnathan was an incurable kleptomaniac. Irrational, compulsive. In a drugstore, he'd lift another toothbrush even though he'd already filched enough to last the whole town a lifetime.

"Mr. Danvers," he went on, "I need your services badly, very badly. Second precinct."

I promised to be there soon. This time he sounded really worried. Maybe some owner resented his shoplifting and beat the hell out of Johnathan. If so, perhaps it would cure him.

To the desk sergeant, I said, "Vandruck again. Case of shoplifting."

"Oh, hi, Danvers," he said. "Only this time it's murder."

Johnathan sat dejected on the cell cot.

"What happened?" I asked. "Start at the beginning. Everything."

"Byram's Hardware was having a knife sale. A whole open table of knives. Irresistible. I chose one and left by the rear door. In the alley I saw one man stab another. The killer dashed back into the hardware store, dropping his knife among those for sale.

"It was better than the one I'd taken so I exchanged—"

"But you're in the clear. It had the killer's fingerprints."

"Unfortunately, sir, I was wiping it clean when they arrested me."

"For God's sake, *why*, Johnathan?"

He seemed surprised. "I didn't want blood on the nice lingerie I'd stolen next door."

As last resort, we'll plead insanity.

A TALE TOLD BY AN OLD HOUSE

"Okay," agreed the chief of the wrecking company. "I'll hold up for twenty-four hours." Actually, I think he was as intrigued as I: why had tenants refused to occupy the old apartment house? Ghosts, they claimed. Nightly moans. "Thanks, Mike," I said.

As head of an exterminating organization, I suspected termites. Mice. Maybe roaches.

The whole interior had been stripped of furnishings. In apartment 5E, the lighter area of the floor where the carpet had lain still bore peculiar dark reddish stains. Looked like long-dried blood. Strange, I thought.

Working my way lower, I tore into the old mail chute leading down to where the clerk's desk had been. No sign of termites anywhere, but I did spot an envelope, now yellowed with age, stuck in a joint of the chute. It was addressed in delicate handwriting to "Mr. Johnathan McCollom, Apartment 2C." No harm in opening it now. I did so and read the brief note, which still retained a faint violet fragrance:

Dearest Johnny
Don't come up tonight! My suspicious husband is staying home from his watchman's job. Hurriedly, but with all my love,
Joanne

Somehow 5E had seemed smaller than the other apartments. I returned there and suddenly realized why. One closet had been sealed off, its entrance seemingly a continuation of the wall.

Curious, I smashed through the thin plaster. Then I knew the fate of Joanne and her lover Johnathan.

Staggering to a window, I shouted down, "For the love of God, Mike, come quick!"

IMPOSTOR

Self-consciously I adjusted my new uniform. I didn't want to appear sloppy on this job. A handsome young man stood loitering nearby, clearly a plainclothes operator. I approached and pirouetted.

"How do I look?" I asked smiling.

"Like a million bucks," he responded enthusiastically. "I'm Mike. New here at Customs?"

"My first day," I admitted. "I hear Ellen Bosworth, the millionaire's wife, is due on the next flight and may be smuggling gems for a lark."

"We'll find out," he said.

Amid the confusion, we spotted her, standing in line. Mike picked up her luggage and I said, "Step this way, Mrs. Bosworth." She started to protest, but realized the embarrassment any outburst would engender. She went meekly into a little side room. "Mike," I said, "check her luggage. And, Mrs. Bosworth, I'll have to ask you to strip behind that screen."

"Outrageous!" she declared, but obeyed.

I folded her expensive clothes, laid them aside, and emptied her purse. $2,875 in cash and a diamond necklace.

The woman was shivering. "Aren't you through?" she pleaded.

"I'll have to check the number on that wristwatch." She quickly handed it over.

Just then I heard the door open and a man's voice demanded, "What the hell are you doing here? Stealing luggage?"

Suddenly it was clear: Mike was no Customs agent!

I waited until the authorities had dragged Mike away, then grabbed money, necklace, watch, and clothes and stepped outside, leaving a perplexed and naked Mrs. Bosworth.

I'm no Customs agent either.

THE LAST DINOSAUR

Persistent rumors of a living dinosaur filtered out of central Africa. Ansel Eversham, the intrepid explorer, decided to investigate, to settle the matter once and for all.

He outfitted a safari with native bearers. For weeks they hacked their way into the jungle, sidestepping treacherous quicksand, killing deadly mambas.

Then one of his scouts dashed back into camp, his eyes bulging. "Bwana, bwana," he gasped, "me see um! Beeg, be-e-eg—"

Nerves tingling, Eversham demanded, "Show me, M'Gumba."

Cautiously they advanced. Suddenly, M'Gumba pointed and fled in terror. To Eversham's amazement, some hundred yards away stood a living brontosaurus! Its giant head swayed atop its forty-foot neck. Quickly, he snapped photograph after photograph.

If only he could bring it back, the world would have to believe him. He raised his elephant gun, excitement racing through his veins.

The moment the head stopped swaying, he aimed at the cervical vertebra and fired. The colossal creature uttered a soft cry—*wh-o-o-o-sh*—and the great neck slowly settled earthward. Overjoyed, Ansel Eversham started forward.

Instantly he was surrounded by fierce black warriors, their spears pointing at his chest. They prodded him forward, down a long avenue lined with skulls. Their chief sat on an ivory throne, scowling down.

Trembling, Eversham tried to explain slowly: "Oh Exalted Highness! Me sorry. Not know big-big creature belong you—"

But the chief directed his anger onto his witch doctor. "Me tell you once, me tell you twice: *No rent brontosaur balloon for tribal Thanks-givum-day parade!* Now somebody gotta pay."

NASTY LITTLE TOWN

It did not take long for Harry Villers to size up Annville: typical midwestern town, neither so small that strangers were conspicuous nor so large he would encounter competition. Annville boasted a large department store and that is where Harry headed. Within the hour he spotted one—a well-dressed redhead slyly slipping expensive gloves into her purse. He followed her outside and confronted her.

"Lady," he said, "you have something that isn't yours."

She paled. "Please, I didn't mean..."

"They never do," Harry chuckled. "I'd hate to see a nice lady like you arrested. Perhaps we can make a deal."

"H-how much?" she quavered.

"I think perhaps twenty would be appropriate."

She opened her purse. Seeing its contents, Harry wished he'd demanded more. However, he accepted the bills, adding them to the 2,150 tax-free dollars in his wallet.

The woman screamed, "Bill!" and from around the corner a burly cop appeared.

"Another one, Mary?" he asked.

She nodded and winked. "He took twenty in marked bills."

"Okay, mister," growled the cop, "let's have your wallet." Nervously Harry handed it over and the man deftly stripped it clean.

"Hey," protested Harry, "that's all I got. How about a trial?"

"If you like," shrugged the cop. "But Mary's Uncle Jim, the judge, is pretty hard on strangers who attack and rob her. And her husband Elmo, who runs our jail, wouldn't like you..."

"Okay, okay, you two win," declared Harry bitterly. "I'll leave your nasty little town."

He'd been had.

THE BORDER OBSTACLE COURSE

Even the United States Marines, bless 'em, never had an obstacle course as tough as this. As I rounded the old barn for the fourth time, I noticed my opponent was still twenty strides ahead of me.

Then off to the north we headed, leaping an arroyo, dodging in and out among the sharp-needled cacti, sliding down a rocky slope, and starting to crawl through a rusty culvert.

I was nearly winded but determined to finish it. Thankfully my partner, Bill McCloskey, ended the chase. As I emerged from the culvert, he was holding the squirming immigrant in a firm grasp. My uniform was dirty and snagged in a dozen places.

"Gave you quite a chase this time," Bill remarked.

I caught my breath and looked at our captive. As I'd suspected, it was Manuelo Ortiz.

"Dammit, Manuelo," I panted, "why the hell do you persist? This is the third time this week. We both know how it will end: we'll send you right back to Mexico."

As usual, the wiry little Mexican shrugged and said, "*No hablo ingles.*"

"I know you don't understand English," I retorted. "To you this is just a game."

"*No hablo ingles,*" he repeated.

"This has got to stop!" I said sternly. I turned to Bill, "I'd give twenty bucks if this guy would just call it off for a week."

It was then that Manuelo said something we hadn't expected. He grinned and said, "Hey, man, it's a deal. What about *next* week?"

TRAGEDIES AT GIANT'S DROP

We always suspected that Barbara Hastings pushed her husband Alfred off the cliff at Giant's Drop. It seemed incredible that the little guy's body could land so far out, even taking the tricky wind currents into account. Barbara was hefty enough to have done it. But when my partner Larry and I arrived to investigate, Alfred was already dead, so we couldn't prove anything. Barbara collected his insurance.

I suppose we should have warned Brian Wilcox before he married the widow Hastings two months later. He was such a nice fellow, easy going. But, after all, we had no proof.

Now another tragedy at Giant's Drop, only this time the victim was Barbara. Poor Brian was still in shock as my partner Larry guided him to a chair in our interrogation room.

"My fault," muttered Brian, wincing.

"Explain that, please."

He fiddled with his hearing aid. "What?"

I repeated my request.

"Oh," he said. "Well, Barbara insisted we go up there. We sat on the brink a while, looking out over the valley, and I got up to leave.

"She held out her hand and I grasped it. I thought she said, 'Let go!' So I did. She must have said, *'Let's* go!'"

"It was an accident, then," I said. "You're free to leave now."

As he was going out the door, I whispered to Larry, "It must be hell, going through life with a hearing problem like that."

Brian Wilcox turned, smiling strangely, "It sure is, sir."

THE PATIENT HUSBAND

Nobody quite understood the patience of Andrew Gordon. It was downright unnatural. Regardless of what his overweight, overbearing wife Sadie said or did, old Andrew never lost his temper.

Right in public she derided his best efforts. "I told Andy to fix that gate. But with his usual stupidity, it fell off the hinges next day. Finally I did it myself—and right, too."

She was an embarrassment to the whole neighborhood, the way she henpecked her poor little husband.

Everyone knew the Gordons' roof leaked that day. Sadie's strident voice yelled, "I told you to fix it! But, no, you didn't, just like you never do anything a man oughta. Hold that ladder! Steady, I tell you!"

Sadie climbed up with shingles, hammer, and nails. Minutes later she screamed and fell, landing heavily. She was dead.

"I can't understand it," the old man told police. "I was holding the ladder steady, just like Sadie told me. But I must not have been doing it quite right."

The Chief of Police consoled him, "No one's blaming you, Andy. Just one of those things, the rain and all."

Out local undertaker found a coffin to accommodate Sadie Gordon, but didn't have much success erasing her perpetual scowl.

Just after the funeral, I saw old Andy up there repairing that roof himself. He did a very creditable job.

The neighborhood is quiet now. I didn't say anything. Nevertheless, I sometimes wonder how Sadie could have missed that ladder by over six feet.

THE DEER HUNT

Our Happy Valley Hunt Club was never the same after the Harleys moved into town and joined. Not that we expected all men to be big and burly and all women to be petite and meek, but when the husband-wife roles are reversed—well, it seemed downright unnatural.

Mabel Harley weighed around 200 pounds, brawny, voice like a drill sergeant. Her husband Bertie weighed maybe 140, his retiring manner no doubt induced by his domineering wife.

That first deer season she showed up with him at the cabin, camouflage-suited, her rifle ready.

Jake Tolliver made bold to suggest, "We're not exactly prepared for women—"

Mabel dug a hefty elbow into Jake's ribs, laughing, "Boy, you won't see nothin' you ain't seen before. Besides, somebody's gotta get our deer. Bertie can't hit the outhouse from inside it."

Determined to be "one of the boys," Mabel insisted on joining our nightly poker game. (She won most of the pots.) Bertie quietly read a book in one corner.

Next morning she bellowed, "Come along, Bertie, you can at least drive one past me!"

We never saw Mabel alive again.

Sobbing, Bertie led us to the spot. Mabel had been drilled squarely between the eyes. From 200 yards away, Bertie had fired at some movement. It was Mabel.

That was seven years ago. Every year since, Bertie has bagged his deer cleanly. We all notice that his marksmanship has miraculously improved. Maybe the absence of Mabel's nagging had something to do with it.

BORIS

Apart from a sneer and some sarcastic remarks, Big Gino Balucci raised no objections when Sergeant Lindgren of homicide arrested him on suspicion. He climbed peaceably into the patrol car.

"We both know this is futile," he said confidently. "I got a perfect alibi for the Carbone hit. And my lawyer will have me walking inside the hour."

Lindgren shrugged. "We just want to ask a few questions." Over the police radio came the report of a hit-and-run on Elm and the sergeant detoured to the scene. Two patrol cars were already there and the sheet-covered victim was being loaded into the ambulance.

"Well," remarked Lindgren, "it looks like Boris did his job as usual."

Balucci considered this for a minute. "You mean you *expected* this?"

"The guy's own fault," growled the driver. "He wouldn't talk, so we turned him loose and gave his name to Boris."

"Hey, I thought it was illegal for police to do anything like that."

"Oh, we don't. But no reason we can't hire Boris."

No more was said until they were seated in an office at headquarters. Sergeant Lindgren passed over some gruesome enlargements of past murders. "Boris does good work," he commented. "You can go as soon as I phone Boris your description."

"Wait!" interrupted Balucci. "I didn't gun Carbone, but I know who did..."

Later Captain Allen, who had listened in, asked, "Who in hell is this 'Boris'?"

Lindgren smiled. "Frankly, I doubt he exists."

THE EROTIC MANUSCRIPT

Mary Turner arrived back on an early flight from tending her sick mother in Philadelphia. Her husband Jim was at work, would be all day. She inspected the house, wondering how he had fared during her absence.

In his study she found a thick pile of manuscript beside his typewriter. Curious, she began reading: *George pressed Audrey's luscious body still closer to his own heaving chest...* As she delved further into the explicit erotic tale, Mary's face grew redder from both embarrassment and anger. Intimate filth!

Her husband had even used the names Herbert and Audrey Meaders for the unsuspecting husband and the unfaithful wife. Their next-door neighbors!

It was painfully clear. Her Jim and Audrey were having a tawdry affair. The only thing changed was the name of the sex-hungry interloper—*George* instead of *Jim*. Nevertheless, all her friends would recognize the obvious if ever this were published.

Mary got Jim's pistol. She was prepared when at last he came home. "You filthy beast!" she raged. "I'm not away two weeks before you start cheating behind my back!" Before he could respond, she pulled the trigger.

Emotionally exhausted, she rolled the sheet from Jim's typewriter and read:

Dear George:

I'm returning your manuscript. The writing is okay but, really, old boy, that's a cruel way to flaunt your affair with Audrey Meaders. At least change the names.

Perhaps Mary and I can help salvage your marriage to Joanne. We have always been able to work things out.

MR. CRAWFORD'S SOLUTION

Quentin Crawford enjoyed wielding power. He was, after all, Head Librarian at the Public Library of Maplehurst. Quentin ran a tight little ship. Carla Hayworth and Amy Stoller, two elderly spinsters, were properly cowed by his weekly dictums. Not so Mrs. Phyllis Bates, who had been widowed early by her husband's death in an auto crash. She actually *laughed!* Mr. Crawford wanted to fire her; however, when he hinted at the possibility, she snapped, "Just try it! Without just cause, you'll be in deep, deep trouble!"

Yes, Mrs. Bates was the ultimate thorn in Crawford's sensitive side—until Benjamin Glover came to do research on Maplehurst's history. Glover, a confirmed bachelor of fifty, owned everything worth owning in the town and chaired every conceivable committee—including the Library Committee.

"I'll require a suitable desk—and fetch me these volumes," ordered Glover, handing him a lengthy list.

"Perhaps one of the girls—" suggested Crawford.

"I prefer *you* do it."

That was the beginning. Every day Glover's demands multiplied. Finally Quentin Crawford hit upon a solution to one of his problems, perhaps both: Glover would either dismiss Phyllis or abandon the library himself in fear.

"Mr. Glover," he confided, "beware of Mrs. Bates. Knifed her husband, y'know—recently released from the mental ward. Keep this secret."

The next day Phyllis said to Crawford, "Over cocktails last evening, Benjy and I discussed your novel version of my past. We agree that your job is proving too much..."

HARRY'S WIFE

Harry was nursing his bourbon. He wasn't drunk, though I suppose he had every right to be, his wife bein' notoriously unfaithful. Another customer entered my bar. As expected, Harry sidled over to him. "I'm Harry Tabbs," he introduced himself. "Your face seems familiar. You are—?"

"Eugene Cathcart," the man replied nervously.

"Have a drink on me, sir," invited Harry. "What'll you have?"

"Oh, just a draft beer. And thanks very much."

I drew a cold one and slid it over the bar. I was familiar with Harry's routine.

"Married?" asked Harry.

"Er—not at present."

"Better that way. Take my advice; stay single, my friend. Now, take my wife Maxine. Never should have married her." Harry leaned forward confidentially, "She runs around."

"Sorry to hear that," declared Cathcart, but without conviction.

"Yeah, I'm sure of it, sir. But once I catch her at you-know-what I'm gonna chop her and her bedfellow into little pieces. With an ax!"

The other man's face paled.

"Yeah, I'm goin' home now," declared Harry. "Gonna check on Maxine. A husband's gotta keep an eye on a wife at all times." He stomped out.

Eugene Cathcart was sweating. "Good lord!" he exclaimed. "That man's dangerous!"

"Don't worry, Mr. Cathcart," I told him. "Maxine is seein' half a dozen other guys regularly besides yourself. And Harry's just spoutin' off. He don't really have an ax."

"You're certain?" he asked anxiously.

"Absolutely!" I assured him. "She told me so herself last night."

MY ENCOUNTER WITH THE OLD VOYEUR

"I can't believe my luck," I told Loretta Talmadge. "Being hired as an exercise leader at Gorby's Gym!"

"Don't get your hopes too high, honey," she warned. "I do the hiring and Old Man Gorby does the firing. He'll return soon from that phys-ed conference. But with your gorgeous red hair and shape, he might even let you do his TV commercials."

With that encouragement, I came back to work out that night. As I was showering afterward, an oily masculine voice said, "You gotta lovely body, even through that glass. Redheads turn me on."

"Get out!" I screamed.

"Okay, okay. Just lookin'."

I heard the door close and dressed hurriedly.

I told Loretta about it. "Oh, that was old Frank, our janitor," she laughed. "You learn to lock the shower room door."

I was seething mad. The next night I heard fumbling outside the shower before undressing. I peeked out. There stood an old geezer in coveralls with a mop. I yanked him inside and worked him over.

"Okay, mister!" I yelled. "Strip! Let's see how *you* like being seen nude!"

He was too scared to refuse. I grabbed his clothes and tossed them into the alley.

When I started to tell Loretta later, she cut me off. "Steer clear of Old Man Gorby today. He's in a foul mood."

"Why?" I asked.

"He fired old Frank and decided to clean the gym himself. Some nutty red-haired gal forced him to strip stark naked, then stole all his clothes!"

VICTIM OF A DASTARDLY SCAM

"Gertie," said Mitch Fairfield to his wife after breakfast, "you're lookin' tired. Why not take a day off from work?"

"You're so thoughtful, darling," she said, kissing him. "Bye-bye. Have a nice day."

Half an hour after he left, the doorbell rang. A handsome young man stood there nervously. "Good day, madam," he greeted Gertie. "May I please step inside to offer you a lifetime opportunity?"

"I suppose so," she replied warily.

"I'm Drake Chadwick, representing the Oberwich Company, makers of the world's finest vacuum cleaner. As part of our promotion, you have been selected to receive one absolutely free!"

"There's some catch?"

"Not really, madam. We require only $25 shipping and handling."

"I'd better phone my husband."

"Of course. We want everyone satisfied."

Gertie retired to the kitchen to phone Mitch. She returned saying, "He thinks it's okay if I really like it. Suppose you go over the brochure."

Mr. Chadwick spent an hour answering her questions.

Suddenly the front door swung open and Mitch Fairfield entered with pistol drawn.

"Wh-wh-what's going on?" stammered Chadwick.

"You oughta know, mister," rasped Mitch, "forcin' your advances on my wife. I oughta phone the police."

"No, don't!" the man pleaded.

"Well, a man oughta be compensated when a stranger propositions his wife."

"Please, all I have is $65."

"Leave it and get out!"

When he had gone, Mitch said, "The nerve of these amateurs, hornin' in on our racket."

THE AFFAIR OF THE GORILLA OUTFIT

The president of Argetsinger Industries entered his office shaking the rain from his umbrella. His secretary Sylvia rushed forward to relieve him of his dripping trench coat.

"Well," he asked cheerfully, "what did you think of the company ball?"

"Oh, you were the life of the party in your gorilla outfit, Mr. Argetsinger. Shall I return it to the rental agency?"

"Later, my dear. Did my employees enjoy it?"

"I'm afraid, sir, Mr. Fitzroy in shipping imbibed too freely. He said some uncomplimentary things—"

"Like what?"

"Well, he said the role fitted you—words to that effect."

"Did he report this morning?"

"Yes, he staggered in rather hung-over, I would say."

"It's time Fitzroy was taught a lesson! Contact advertising and have a sandwich board made quickly: 'Argetsinger Industries Doesn't Monkey Around.' I'll order him to put on the gorilla rig and carry it all over town. That'll sober up the fool."

"In this rain—isn't that rather severe?"

"No! I won't tolerate insolence."

Grumbling, Fitzroy complied and left.

Later that morning Argetsinger was summoned to police headquarters. "Are you this man's employer?" asked the captain.

"I am."

"And did you order him to wear that gorilla get-up in this cold rain?"

"Yes, yes," answered Argetsinger impatiently. "I'll pay whatever fine he has incurred."

"Afraid it's not that simple, sir. His union has filed charges of inhuman treatment, and I must agree with them. I'll have to detain you until the case is resolved."

TRIBULATIONS OF AN EDITOR-IN-CHIEF

Oh, the tribulations besetting the life of an editor-in-chief, sighed Gerald Sinclair, will they never cease? He dreaded the morning. Some antiquated fuddy-duddy, who evidently wasn't capable of using e-mail, had actually sent a *handwritten* letter—his secretary had laughingly showed it to him!—requesting a personal appointment. With resignation he pressed the intercom. "You may show Miss Fellows in now, Madeline."

Abigail Fellows was what he'd expected: elderly, white hair drawn into a chignon, long taffeta dress, and an angry glint in her eye. He arose gallantly—this type of subscriber expected it. "Won't you please be seated, madam?" he invited.

"Sir," she began, "I am a charter member of your Choice Books for Thoughtful Readers. I have read every monthly volume, cover to cover, and I must say the quality has recently seriously declined."

"That opinion, I presume, is somewhat subjective?" he countered.

"Subjective?" she snorted. "Of course it's subjective! Do you think your readership is incapable of forming an opinion?"

"What precisely led you to this conclusion?"

"I was so disgusted with *Interlude Between Enemies* that I actually visited the author. Do you realize he didn't really write it? The entire book was generated by a *computer!* How could you consider it 'outstanding work'?"

"Rest assured, madam, CBFTR's selections are now made with ultimate objectivity. The tape of every submission is run through our computer, whose program examines it thoroughly for originality, consistency, and quality of expression."

"But who designed this program?"

"That, Miss Fellows, was generated quite impartially by another computer."

AN UN-ROMANTIC TALE
OF THE SOUTH SEAS

"So, you want to write about the South Seas, eh?" said my well-traveled friend. "No better way to see it than from a tramp steamer!"

Obviously he'd never traveled aboard the *Samoa Maid*. The ship was rusty, the captain surly, the Malay crew lackadaisical, and the cook unfamiliar with soap. The ports at which we called invoked nothing romantic, all much alike, a cluster of native huts isolated from civilization.

Lapura was no different. The *Samoa Maid* laid up there for repairs. As our longboat came ashore, it was met by the Resident, a balding man in tattered dungarees. He introduced himself as Henry Longstreet and wrung my hand at length.

"You'll stay with me?" he asked anxiously, as though I had a choice.

I thanked him politely and followed to his thatched home, where his half-caste wife Meelina and numerous children awaited.

After supper we sat smoking on his lanai. Suddenly Longstreet said, "Last visitor was a fellow named Arthur Simpson. Scrawny chap."

"What became of him?" I asked.

"One night the scoundrel stole all my money. Taking Leila, my wife's sister along, he headed into the interior. Wild place, the interior. Anyhow, natives took 'em prisoner. Leila escaped and got back. She told me about it. Very strange."

"Perhaps not so strange," I ventured. "She being a woman, they probably didn't guard her as closely."

"I was thinkin' of Simpson," my host said. "Natives ate him. Strange. Of the two, I'd have thought they'd eat her first."

THE NEW HIGHWAY

Lightning and thunder flashed and boomed above the tumulus. Cold rain pelted down. Professor Leland Bannister tucked his notebook under his anorak and sprinted to the Land Rover. Thankful the motor started, he turned and drove back to the highway. He braked in the nearby village of Quimby-on-the-Downs and dashed into the Goat-and-Eels, "Quick!" he said. "Can I use your phone, bartender?"

Old Dan Rumford distrusted impatient strangers. "Lemme see your phone card, feller." He inspected it slowly. "Hmmm. Perfessor of the Royal Archaeological Society, eh? Seems okay. Go ahead."

The professor dialed. The drinkers all listened attentively as he said, "Royal Engineers? Bannister here. I've just confirmed that the tumulus, marked by a half-sunken stone stele, is authentic Stone Age ... Yes, a national treasure! ... More later."

The men closed around Bannister. Suddenly his head exploded. He awoke tightly bound.

"Sorry I hit you so hard," apologized the bartender. "But we couldn' have the new highway held up fer Gawd knows how long whilst you piddled around with your bloody Stone Age whatever. Well, it's all over. We dynamited the damned stone and bulldozed the hill away."

"But *why?*"

"We villagers need the money the new highway'll bring to Quimby-on-the-Downs."

Professor Bannister alternately wept and laughed.

"What's so blasted funny, perfessor?"

"That new highway was planned solely for access to a museum on the Stone Age site. It would have brought tourists by busloads. Now, of course, the whole project is off..."

But old Dan Rumford had ceased listening.

THE HIDDEN LOOT

A chill drizzle with patches of fog settled over the landscape. Moe Janowicz, steering the souped-up Cadillac cautiously along the rutted country lane, spoke to the man beside him, "Think we can trust Zeke?"

"Sure," replied Art Stroop. "Besides, he's the only guy who knows this Gawd-forsaken backwoods. Keep lookin'. He said he'd meet us somewhere around here after he hid the First National loot."

Moments later a figure materialized, waving frantically. It was Zeke.

Moe braked. "Okay, where'd you hide it?"

The bewhiskered old man grinned. "Whar nobody'd ever find it! Now I gotta borry the car to git grub an' stuff. Meanwhiles, yew two hide out in yonder swamp."

"In *there?*" asked Art dubiously.

Zeke pointed, "Keep goin' thataway to a lil' rise with a tall pine. Wait thar. I'll be back shortly." He sped off.

The two robbers gingerly groped forward, at last reaching the tall pine. Hours passed. "I'm f-f-freezin'," complained Art. "There's a big hollow log we could burn. Gotta match?"

"Yeah." After several attempts they set the damp log afire. Finally warming himself, Moe said. "Geez, Zeke oughta be back by now. I'm gonna go wait for him." He stumbled back to the road.

An hour later the Cadillac reappeared. Zeke got out bearing groceries.

"I vote we split the loot and scram," declared Moe. "Where is it?"

"Yew fellers musta bin sittin' on it," chuckled Zeke. "It"s inside thet holler log."

I KNEW IT WAS WRONG

Most any other eleven-year old boy would have known it was wrong. I did. But I did it anyhow, so I've just got to live with my conscience. Now that it's over, Mr. James is dead, Mrs. James is in prison, little Anna-Marie has gone to her grandparents, and somebody else lives next door.

It began when the James family moved in last summer. Everybody in the block knew Mrs. James's voice long before they met her. It was s-h-r-i-l-l.

"Henry! Dammit, do something!" she yelled at her husband. It wasn't easy for him doing anything from his wheel chair. I found out later he'd been shot in Viet Nam.

"Anna-Marie, you little brat!" her mama would screech. "I told you what I'd do!" This was always followed by screams from the girl. She was four.

Mrs. James—her name was Sally—wasn't popular.

I got acquainted with Henry when he rolled himself into the back yard. We played chess. One day shy little Anna-Marie showed me the bruises and welts. "Ain't you gonna do *anything* about that?" I asked her daddy.

His face showed pain. "It's the liquor, boy...but Sally promises she'll quit."

She didn't and things got worse.

Then Anna-Marie ran to me crying. I followed her home. Sally lay drunk, passed out. Henry was dead. He'd shot himself and left a note: *I can't take it any longer.*

What did I do? Before dialing 911, I pressed the pistol into Sally's hand and burned the note.

THE SMART MARITIME LAWYER

"Briefly, the problem facing Carruthers Shipping," Alfred Carruthers told the dapper little lawyer, "is this: During a storm, my cruise ship, the *Talakeena*, struck rocks off Sitka. Captain Olaf Angstrom swears she was still seaworthy when Captain Fitzsimmons of Fitzsimmons Salvage steered his tugboat alongside and shoved the *Talakeena* free, claiming her as salvage."

"My fee is $100,000," said Sylvester Eggleston confidently. "I've never lost a case involving maritime law."

A grizzled old sea captain stomped into the office. "Ye'll lose this one! I'm Captain Timothy Fitzsimmons and I'll bet me tugboat, the *Elliemarie*, agin y'r $1,000,000!"

Eggleston smiled slyly. "I'll draw up a binding agreement."

"Good! We'll both sign!"

Before the Maritime Commission, Eggleston called upon Captain Angstrom to testify. "In your opinion—under oath—was the *Talakeena* seaworthy at the time?"

"Absolutely not, sir!" responded Angstrom. "Another hour and she'd have sunk."

The Commission decided quickly; The *Talakeena* belonged to Fitzsimmons Salvage. "I can't believe this!" declared Eggleston, stunned.

"Oh, win some, lose some," said Carruthers blithely. "Here's your fee -$100,000."

Captain Fitzsimmons approached. "Avast thar, lubber! Where's me million bucks?"

"It—it will take time to raise that amount—"

"Phone yer accountant and write the check now!" ordered the tugboat captain. "Y'see, Alfie and me know exactly how much ye're worth."

"Alfie?! ... Mr. Carruthers...and *you*! You set me up!"

"Yep. That extra $900,000 oughta cover repairin' the *Talakeena*. A really smart maritime lawyer shoulda known—Fitzsimmons Salvage is a subsidiary of Carruthers Shipping."

THE DANGEROUS LAND
OF MAKE-BELIEVE

Jason Melville was a superb actor, but not on stage or screen. In his imagination he participated in make-believe adventures and, it must be admitted, he could be convincing. Tonight he was Robin Hood, dread nemesis of the selfish rich, generous savior of the downtrodden poor.

He sauntered into the dimly lit cocktail lounge of the Hilton. And there she was! Beautiful Maid Marion, shoulder-length dark hair, revealing gown. He eased over to her table. "How canst a lovely maiden like you lack companionship?" he began.

She smiled, waving him to a chair. "I'm Georgina," she said, "but friends call me Gigi."

"May I count myself among your fortunate friends, Gigi? I'm Robin."

"What do you do, Robin?" she inquired sweetly.

"I take from the wealthy and give to the needy."

"Hmmm, like this afternoon's holdup of Federal Savings?" Gigi suggested.

"Just one of my little escapades," Jason boasted. "That one I masterminded."

"Do you really have all that money, Robin?"

"Safely tucked away for later distribution to deserving unfortunates."

"It had earmarks of a hit by Nick Malvasi's gang," Gigi declared.

Jason played his role whole-heartedly. "Oh, Nick is my lieutenant." Gigi fumbled in her purse and drew out her badge. "Detective Watkins," she identified herself. "You're under arrest."

Jason became alarmed. "Hey, I was only kidding," he protested.

"We picked up Malvasi already. He's boiling mad. His gang double-crossed him and took the loot. You can share a cell with him."

THE IRS SCAM

Miss Tillett checked the small ad she'd clipped from the *Tribune*. "SIMPSON & SIMPSON, TAX CONSULTANTS AND ADJUSTORS." The location was in a rundown neighborhood, but that figured if she was right. She climbed the dirty wooden stairs and knocked.

A balding little man opened the door, saying, "No problem Simpson and Simpson can't handle, madam. Come right in! Have a seat! Now, the details."

"Wel-ll..." she hesitated, "my name is Helen Idella Tillett and I came into some money illegally—"

"And you want to get right with the government without going to prison," he surmised. "I handle numerous cases like yours. Contrary to popular belief, we tax consultants have considerable influence with the Internal Revenue Service. What's the amount?"

"Fifty thousand dollars."

Simpson's beady eyes lit up. "I'll just have you sign this check payable to 'I.R.S' for $50,000, and another to me—Ira Russell Simpson—for $10,000. Simple!" He looked up.

Miss Tillett was holding a silenced pistol. "You pulled this same scam on Manny Scalisi last week. After the 'I.R.S.' you added the rest of *your* name, Mr. Simpson."

He began sweating. "Okay, lady, I'll refund his dough."

She laughed scornfully. "You should have investigated. Manny is head of the local Mafia. Didn't you wonder about my own initials? Helen Idella Tillett—H.I.T.? I'm the Mafia's hitperson."

She pulled the trigger, stuffed the incriminating checks into her handbag, and walked out, closing the door softly on Simpson & Simpson.

MY HUSBAND GEORGE

"How is he, doctor?" I asked in a hushed voice.

"We'll need to run additional tests first, Mrs. Hopkins," he replied cheerfully, "but unless something unexpected shows up, I'd say your husband could return to his office within a week. This appears to be stress-related and his heart is none too good. He'll have to exercise more and learn to relax."

I entered the hospital room. George lay still, pasty white. I almost felt sorry for him, then remembered our seven years of marriage. I'd tried to be the perfect housewife, but George thought only of himself. He invariably complained the meat was either underdone ("absolutely raw!") or overdone ("practically cremated!"). And when we went out on rare occasions, I was either overdressed ("I don't want to give the office people the impression we spend money lavishly!") or underdressed ("I can't have my wife appearing like we can't afford better than that!").

"How are you feeling, George?" I asked.

"If I live," he whined, "this won't look good on my company record."

"Anything I can do?"

"If the worst happens, give Maxine D'Arcy my contingency fund from my safety deposit box."

"Why should I give your secretary anything?"

"We had a—a relationship."

I was shocked, but managed to inquire, "How much is this 'contingency fund'?"

"Fifty."

"Fifty dollars?"

"Fifty thousand."

Fortunately, no nurses were about and the door was closed. For a man anticipating death, George struggled quite a bit before I smothered him.

SYMPATHETIC WOMEN

Becky Garrels anticipated that moving into the village of Thorburgh would be absolutely dull. She'd agreed only to please Carl, who insisted they retire away from the hurly-burly of the city. How delightful, then, to make friends like Janice Wallingford, Angela French, Flora Ingles, and Genevieve Lambert. All were widows her age; Becky felt a little proud to still have her husband Carl, even though he still chased after his former secretary Paula. Meanwhile, Becky joined the ladies' bridge group and shared their excursions to the city theater.

"I'm flying into the city," announced Carl. "Janice checked out my plane."

"To see Paula again?" Becky challenged.

"Perhaps."

At their afternoon tea, only Janice was absent. Becky confided her problem to the other women. "Furthermore, I even suspect he's starting an affair with Janice."

"Don't fret, sweetie," said Angela. "Janice learned plenty while serving as an airplane mechanic during the war. She's one of us. My late unfaithful husband Dan retired as an electrician. Yet while Janice was helping him he got electrocuted."

Genevieve spoke, "My late mate Phil was like that. After Janice helped him overhaul his BMW he suffered a fatal auto accident."

"And," added Flora, "my philandering husband Henry had a heart attack in our hot tub, although Janice never *fully* explained that."

"Dearie," said Angela gently, "we learned all about your late husband and Paula."

"Late? But Carl's still alive," protested Becky.

"No, I'm afraid he'll have had a fatal crash on takeoff."

THE SECRET OF B-AND-B COTTAGE

The three Maggione brothers met as arranged in the Keswick Hotel. "I finally traced old Uncle Luigi to a secluded little place nearby," reported Giuseppe. "He's changed his name to 'Algernon Treacher' and calls his home 'B-and-B Cottage.' Significantly, he doesn't take guests."

"So, he fled here to England with the family fortune," muttered Leonardo.

"*Si*," added Tomas. "*Our* fortune!"

B-and-B Cottage was small, with sturdy stone walls and darkened oak beams across the ceilings of its three rooms. Terrified by the appearance of his nephews, elderly Luigi collapsed and died. Giuseppe dragged the body outside. "Okay," he directed, "Leonardo, take the bedroom; Tomas, the kitchen. I'll search the living room. Look for secret panels. Our Maggione family fortune's here somewhere!"

An hour later the priceless antique furniture was reduced to splinters. No sign of gold or gems. "Tear up the floor!" ordered Giuseppe. The beautiful parquetry floor became rubble. Still no fortune.

"It's got to be in the walls!" declared Leonardo. At day's end, only traces of foundation marked where B-and-B Cottage had stood.

As the three Maggione brothers were packed to leave Keswick, an elderly gentleman approached. "Do you know where I might find Algernon Treacher?" he inquired. "I'm to meet him today. Like myself, he greatly admired English authors. He spent over 1,000,000 pounds authentically restoring the cottage where Elizabeth Barrett and Robert Browning spent their honeymoon, humorously naming it 'B-and-B Cottage.' I'm offering him ten times his investment..."

FOUR DEAD SALESMEN

Sheriff Jim Mercer dismounted from his dappled mare and addressed the old sheepherder squatting by the campfire. "I'll git right to the point, Oswald. Bodies of four travelin' salesmen hev bin found hereabouts. Did you murder 'em?"

"'Twarn't exactly murder, sheriff," objected Oswald Hinkley. "Y'see, the first one called hisself Arnold Finch. Claimed my sheep smelled bad. Afore I could stop him, he sprayed blue April Hyacinth deodorant all over 'em. The whole flock panicked."

"So you killed him?"

"Not exactly. I sprayed *him* good with the stuff. He keeled over, blue and dead."

"What about Bertie Gaskins?"

"He come around advertisin' Ever-So-White detergent. Said it'd remove the blue stains. It did—along with big patches of wool. I tried it on *him*. Bleached him a mite, but he died."

"What about Claude Jones, the third victim?"

"He showed up sellin' Magic-Gro-All. Swore it'd make wool grow back on my sheep. Instead, it give 'em a rash. Didn' grow any wool on him neither when I tried it. He died."

"I see. So, them three salesmen died of natch'ral causes connected with their products. But what about Darrell Kemp, the last salesman?"

"Poor devil," sighed Hinkley sadly. "He was promotin' Nu-Vigor testosterone concentrate. Claimed it'd double my flock in no time."

"I presume you tried it on him?"

"Never tetched him," declared the old sheepherder. "He was attacked by a sex-crazed old ram named Samson, who'd sampled his concentrate." He shuddered. "Horrible way to die, sheriff—simply horrible!"

APPOINTMENT IN ALBANY

At the alarm clock's first buzz, Fred Hansen bounded from bed and began dressing. To his wife Stephanie, still half-drowsy, he said, "This is my big chance! My boss Geoffrey Hutchins is sending me up to Albany to negotiate the Parson account. I'll be back late tonight."

"Whoopee," she grunted. "Maybe we can move outta this dump." Before driving off, Fred checked the revolver in his glove compartment. He suspected Stephanie was two-timing him. After stopping for coffee, he returned home.

Silently he let himself inside. From the bedroom came Stephanie's giggles. Fred flung open the door. There lay his wife and his boss. At sight of his raised revolver, Stephanie pleaded, "Oh, God, Fred, don't shoot!"

Hutchins groped for his trousers, "Wh-wh-what happens now?" he asked fearfully.

"First," declared Fred, "you sign this paper giving me ownership of Hutchins Enterprises."

The man signed, protesting, "It's robbery!"

"Oh, you'll have a chance to get it back. We'll play Russian roulette. I'll be a good sport and go first."

Click!

"Your turn, Geoffrey."

Stephanie screamed, "This is insane!"

Hutchins snatched the revolver, shouting, "Now you're a dead man, Hansen!" He pulled the trigger: *Click... Click... Click-click-click!*

In disgust he dropped the weapon.

"No bullets—this time," Fred laughed. With his gloved hand he retrieved the revolver and slowly, carefully loaded it. "I needed your fingerprints, boss, to make it appear a suicide pact," he said.

He calmly shot Geoffrey, then Stephanie, closed the apartment, and headed for his Albany appointment.

MY CONFESSION

"Officer, I wish to report a murder," I declared.

The captain looked up from his desk, instantly alert. "Did you witness it?"

"I not only witnessed it, I committed it."

"Sit down, please. I must warn you that anything you say—"

"Yes, yes," I interrupted impatiently, "I know the Miranda perfectly. My name is Arthur Paul Keeler. I'm an investigator for United Indemnity Insurance."

"Just who did you kill, Mr. Keeler?" he inquired.

"His name is—was—Charles Manulik."

"And what was the provocation?"

"To begin, Manulik was a computer expert. A genius, actually. He could manipulate and erase personal data for anyone—birth certificate, social security and employment information, bank account, tax records, everything needed for survival. He was a blackmailer. When the victim became desperate, his assets transferred to Manulik, his employer notified of his resignation—all electronically—Manulik demanded that he work for him personally."

"Doing what, sir?"

"Theft of national security documents, murder, you name it."

"How did you discover all this?"

"He did it to me. My access to insurance records made me a prime prospect. He summoned me to his high-rise office suite. To make it brief, I heaved him out the window."

"We know about his death. It was suicide—*officially*."

"But," I protested, "I just confessed!"

"Frankly, Mr. Keeler, you're not alone. Manulik had half our police force under his domination. Our computer experts are now working to restore the records he destroyed. Go home! Forget it! ...And thanks."

RESPECTS TO THE DEPARTED

I'll never understand why folks say us Auffenschlupps are peculiar. We simply believe in honoring the dead. Like Cousin Mervin: everybody swats flies; but Mervin puts 'em in little matchboxes and conducts services over 'em. Or Sister Bunny: she cries louder than anybody at funerals, even if she doesn't know the deceased; well, *somebody's* gotta fill in for relatives who couldn't attend. Right?

I suppose we inherit it from Grandpa Wrolf, operator of Auffenschlupp's Funeral Emporium. It's rumored that some of his customers weren't fully deceased when entering his establishment. However, as Grandpa explains, "Everybody's gotta die sooner or later. Jest happened their time come when business was slow."

Not everyone agrees on paying respects to the departed. Like my, boss Mr. Gaddis, who owns the warehouse where I operate the forklift. When I asked for time off to attend my grandmother's funeral, he just laughed, "Boy, I already gave you days off to attend funerals of *two* grandmothers."

I started to explain that grandpa married three times, when *somehow* that forklift lurched forward and pinned Mr. Gaddis against the wall. I went home and phoned 911, but the ambulance arrived too late. Sheriff Carson said, "Not your fault, Boy. Old tightwad Gaddis shoulda replaced his wore-out equipment long ago."

The whole Auffenschlupp family happily attended the final rites. Grandpa Wrolf even molded a smile on Mr. Gaddis's face, the first anybody recollected. Sister Bunny wailed especially loud. Afterwards we voted it Best-Funeral-of-the-Year—unanimously.

A NIGHT VISIT OF LOVE

Late that night Arthur Asbury impulsively returned to his office high in the Chrysler building. He was retiring as head of Asbury Financial Consultants. He was only forty-seven, but the incentive was gone—had been gone for a week, ever since the tragic death of his adopted daughter Jennifer. Most of his personal possessions had already been removed; only her picture still graced his desk.

He recalled clearly: Jennifer had excitedly announced she had finally located her birth father. "I'll phone you after I visit him, daddy," she said as she breezed out the door, blowing back a kiss.

A phone call came from police. Jennifer had been instantly killed in a traffic collision. After the heartbreaking death of his wife Edith, only Jennifer had kept him going. Now she also was...no more.

Nothing was the same. Tonight Arthur had even missed Joe Marston, the friendly night watchman usually on duty at the building entrance. Arthur turned out the light and leaned back in his deeply upholstered chair...reminiscing...brooding.

His reverie was interrupted by a figure in the hallway outside, indistinct through the frosted glass. A key turned. The figure entered; its flashlight beam alighted on Jennifer's photograph.

Arthur Asbury switched on the light. There stood Joe Marston. "She," said Arthur, "was my daughter."

"And once," said Joe, "she was mine."

Noticing tears streaming down the night watchman's face, Arthur *knew*. Moments later the two men were in each other's arms. Neither spoke. Words would have been superfluous.

THE CONTRACT

"Now, listen carefully, boy!" The older man leaned forward on his desk. "All you do is phone 805-255-2716 and say, 'The contract is for Roy Jameson, employed by Eberhard Construction. Detroit, Michigan. If agreed, phone Max Eberhard at 313-357-8000. Full payment upon satisfactory completion.' Then hang up. Now, repeat the message." Phil Talbot, junior clerk, did so. Max Eberhard, president of his corporation, nodded approval and waved a hand in dismissal.

Roy Jameson in Finance & Accounting had uncovered every shady deal Eberhard ever made and was blackmailing him dry. Jameson had to be eliminated. After many discrete inquiries, Eberhard learned the phone number of a reliable hit man. Talbot, who placed the call, would be the patsy—if needed.

All next day Eberhard anxiously waited. No phone call. Five o'clock. The rest of the staff departed; only Talbot remained. Eberhard demanded, "Did you make that phone call, boy?"

"Relax, boss. Everything's taken care of."

"What do you mean?"

"Well...knowing Mr. Jameson handles all payments, I checked with him, repeating your message exactly."

Max Eberhard turned pale. "Quick! What did he say?"

"Funny thing, boss. He just chuckled, 'So, he's contacting my old friend Bruno in California, is he? I'll handle the whole matter."

"Ohmigod!"

"Don't worry, boss. Your contract will get done. Mr. Bruno arrived by plane this afternoon. Matter of fact, he's in the waiting room now. I'll show him in and go home. Will that be all, boss? Boss?"

THE BET

I've hated Count Dmitri Romanov ever since he embarrassed me at Monte Carlo. Exasperated at losing to him at baccarat, I questioned his title.

"Oh, it's genuine," he declared suavely. "Is it worth one million francs to you to see the proof?"

Other gamblers stopped to stare. My bluff had been called. I departed in confusion and anger.

My revenge could wait. Finally the opportunity came. One night Romanov lost heavily at roulette. "That wipes me out completely," he said cheerfully, tossing his last chips to the croupier. He strode nonchalantly from the casino amid little expressions of sympathy from the veteran players.

He would return the following night, I was certain. Count Dmitri Romanov couldn't stay away. I was right! He stood watching the table wistfully.

"Aren't you playing tonight, Count?" I asked him. "Surely your royal friends will stake you."

"Friend," he said, "how about a private bet, just you and I? Cut the cards, high card wins five million francs."

"B-but you haven't got five million francs!" I blurted.

"Would you repeat that, please?"

I retorted loudly, "You haven't got five million francs and neither have I!"

All eyes turned on us. "That's where you're wrong, sir," said Count Dmitri Romanov coolly. "You see, I bet each of these ten players five hundred thousand you'd approach me and say *those exact words*... Shall we cut the cards?"

I was defeated—again. What could I do but slink away in disgrace?

FINAL JUSTICE

The train made an unscheduled stop in Cactus Junction, and a dapper gent carrying an alligator suitcase alighted into the glaring sunlight. As the train chugged toward the distant pass, he squinted over the thirty-odd squarish adobe buildings.

Not what I'm accustomed to, thought Giorgio Scalini, but they'll never find me here. He started up the dusty street, then stopped to ask an odd-looking dwarf with oversize head, "Any hotel here, boy?"

In answer the dwarf responded in a falsetto voice, "I'm Billy and I seen you somewheres." Pointing a stubby finger he shouted, "You're guilty! Guilty! Guilty!"

"Quiet, kid," hissed the professional assassin, and walked away. The dwarf pursued him on stubby legs, still yelping, "Guilty! Guilty!"

Exasperated, Scalini drew the silenced pistol from his shoulder holster and fired. Then his head exploded.

He regained consciousness securely bound in a dirt-floored room. A stern-faced man dressed in red sat behind a cast-iron bench, fingering a three-pronged pitchfork. Six scowling men stood alongside one wall.

"I'm Judge Oldnick," announced the red-clad man. "We've been waiting for you a long time. You made quite a record, Giorgio, before that lawman shot you."

"I want my lawyer!" protested the prisoner.

"This court appoints Billy as your lawyer."

Had the dwarf survived? Scalini was losing his touch. Billy pointed, "Guilty! Guilty!"

"Guilty!" chorused the six standing men. Odd. Scalini hadn't noticed before: the six were among his previous victims! They and the dwarf vanished.

Suddenly the room became unbearably hot.

THE CHIPMUNK PROBLEM

My garden was inundated by chipmunks that summer. The little devils dug up everything I planted, sampled whatever they liked, and strewed the rest around the yard.

I complained to my wife, Alice, "I'm tempted to shoot the varmints."

She was horrified. "Shoot such cute little creatures? You wouldn't! Besides, discharging firearms in the city is illegal."

"Can't you see the damage?" I argued. "Our rock wall riddled with their burrows! All my flower bulbs uprooted and nibbled—"

"Calm yourself," she said. "They migrate in from Veterans Park next door. I've read about them in the library. Chipmunks can't swim."

"Good! I'll drown the whole lot!"

"Just listen! We can live-trap them, take them across Bass River, and release them in the new Bloomhill subdivision. They will soon adjust to their new home, poor little things."

"Okay, Alice," I said. "I'll do it your way."

I invested a fortune in live traps. Twice daily I drove a carload of captives over to Bloomhill subdivision and set them free. Still, my chipmunk population seemed unaffected.

Chancing to meet my cousin Ed downtown I mentioned, "Chipmunks are sure a problem this summer."

"They must be all over town," he said. "They're playing hell with my place in the Bloomhill subdivision. I heard they can't swim, so I've been live-trapping the pests, taking 'em across Bass River, and releasing 'em in Veterans Park. Doesn't seem to help, though. You got any suggestions?"

"No, Ed," I said quickly. "Somehow I can't think of anything."

CONFESSIONS BEFORE A DEATH

The pale invalid huddled in his wheel chair. Now and then, pain wracked his features. The bright plaid shawl around his shoulders was like a garish shroud.

"A little more soup, *liebchen*?" asked his young wife, lifting a spoon to his lips.

"It's no use, dear," he declared. "I'm dying."

"Perhaps not yet, Alfred," she said softly.

"But I *know* it," the man insisted, stirring slightly. "The agony grows worse each day."

"More soup?" she asked again.

"I have something on my mind," he said weakly.

"*Ja?*"

"Yes. Although we've been married only a year, you've been a good wife, Frederika."

"*Ja?*"

"I suppose," he continued philosophically, "I've always been partial to German *fräuleins*." He paused, grimacing and drawing the shawl tighter around his hunched shoulders. "Now that my time is almost up, I need to confess to someone.... I poisoned my first wife, Hildegarde Bauer...thought she was unfaithful...later learned I was mistaken...by then too late.... Now you know."

For a long time his wife was silent. Then, "*Ach*, you say it is the time for secrets? I too poisoned a mate. So nice he was before we married, so cruel afterward. My family learned what I'd done, never spoke my name again. To save them further embarrassment, I changed my name.

"I was born Frederika Bauer—*ja*, Hildegarde was my older sister. She wrote me her suspicions before she died. *That's* why I married you. Have you never wondered why you suffer, Alfred? Have you any idea what was in your soup tonight?"

FELICITY'S SHOES

Leaning on his crutch, Jason Hazlett watched his wife Marietta and his daughter Felicity. Maybe he should leave now, before they spotted him. They seemed happy, sitting there polishing an array of shoes. Shoes! Shoes started it all. He recalled...

The sergeant yelled, "Letter for Corporal Hazlett!" He snatched it and hastily read the brief message: "Darling—Felicity needs new shoes. Please send your next paycheck. Love, Marietta." He stuffed it into a pocket of his camouflage fatigues, picked up his rifle, and left on nighttime reconnaissance.

Orange flashes lit the jungle darkness! Shrapnel burst ever closer! He regained consciousness in a Red Cross ambulance. A medic leaned over. "Lie quiet, corporal. We're getting you to a hospital quickly as possible." Day followed days, operation followed operation. All very hazy.

Finally his mail caught up. One letter: "Jason—Maybe you don't care enough to buy shoes for our daughter, but *I* do! M."

Jason asked for pen and paper. "Dearest—Wounded. Will forward money soon. Love, J." His letter was returned: ADDRESS UNKNOWN.

Back in the U.S.A., getting adjusted to his artificial leg, Jason started tracing his wife and daughter. One place, then another. At last he located them. Marietta was operating a boarding house, polishing shoes of her boarders.

Little Felicity—older now—said, "Mommy, tell me about Daddy."

"He was a soldier, honey. The government wrote he'd been injured. But someday he'll find us."

Fighting back tears, Jason limped forward. The past was forgotten, the future beginning.

DELUSION?

"It's so bizarre, doctor, I *must* have imagined it," I declared. "Maybe I'm losing my grip on reality."

The psychiatrist, Doctor Stefan Mylenko, sat patiently jotting in his notebook. Finally he spoke: "Repeat your story. From the beginning."

"Well, as I said, I'm a park ranger at Mount Rushmore. The recent earthquake caused small cracks in Lincoln's beard—"

"Referring to the giant sculpted likeness?"

"Of course," I replied impatiently. "To plan repairs it had to be inspected closely. So, I phoned Mikael Tschendo, who had done climbing for us previously. Mikael laughed, 'I'm returning home to Transylvania. But I'll send someone as good as I—Vladimir Cziske.'"

"And this replacement showed up?"

"Yes. I swear he could have been Mikael's brother—the same long, sharp canine teeth, even the same two welts on his neck."

"Continue, please."

"Last night we went together to the top of Mount Rushmore. Vladimir descended by rope to Lincoln's nose. Then it happened!"

"Exactly what?"

"The rope went slack. I looked. Vladimir Cziske had turned into a huge bat! He flew down, examined the cracks, then swooped back up and resumed his human form on the rope!"

"There was a full moon, I believe?"

"Yes, doctor. I saw him clearly."

"A common delusion, sir, experienced when looking downward from great heights. Don't mention it to anyone. That is all."

As I arose from the couch, Doctor Mylenko smiled. For the first time I noticed that he *himself* had long, sharp canine teeth.

354

TIGER HUNT

Tam-bu, the mahout, urged the huge elephant forward, all the while jabbering. The howdah swayed and bounced, continually jarring the two passengers.

Viola Turner spoke. "I'll never understand why you have to kill such lovely animals," she complained.

Her husband Rick glared at her. "A hell of a lot you'll never understand. I should have married a *woman* instead of a whimpering bleeding-heart."

"Why did you have to bring me along?" she asked.

"Don't you really know, darling?" he leered maliciously. "I'm going to leave you here for the tigers."

Viola paled. "You wouldn't! You can't, Tam-bu would tell."

"A few rupees will shut his mouth."

The elephant suddenly balked, and its little mahout kicked it behind both ears. Ahead an especially tall clump of grass projected above the savannah.

"The elephant smells tiger!" announced Rick eagerly.

"Oh, please don't shoot it," Viola pleaded.

"Shut up!" he snarled, standing for a better view.

"THERE!" she shrieked. "Behind you!"

"Where?" Rick whirled, his double-barreled rifle ready.

At that moment Viola lunged with all her strength. Over the low railing toppled her husband.

The tiger, a sleek nine-foot female, was hungry. It pounced, white fangs gnashing. Rick screamed only once.

Back home in Chicago, the memorial service was attended by Viola's numerous friends. All tried to conceal their true feelings about the deceased behind sugary condolences.

"It needn't have happened," explained the widow, "but you knew Rick—always impatient and excitable. He fell off the elephant and a lovely tiger ate him."

Call it accepting challenges, or call it time-wasting obsession.

The fact is that Roscoe Dermott couldn't resist a contest. He ate unpalatable cereals just to get the required boxtops. His postage far exceeded his winnings.

He read the newspaper notice again: "Mayor Albright offers $10,000 reward for information leading to whereabouts of City Building Inspector Howard Ballou..."

No mention of how many entries one might submit. Sitting down at his typewriter, Dermott turned his imagination loose: Ballou was absconding with undisclosed city funds...hiding out after uncovering massive fraud in city-sponsored projects...kidnapped by disgruntled contractors whose projects he'd turned down...working undercover for the FBI...at the bottom of nearby Lake Wallagamo, shot by mobsters for double-crossing them... On and on.

Roscoe Dermott stamped a stack of envelopes and mailed his numerous suggestions to Mayor Albright.

To Dermott's surprise, two days later the mayor phoned. Would Dermott come to his office? Secretly? Of course! He had won the $10,000! In the mayor's office a dark-suited stranger closed the door and produced a gun. Dermott nearly fainted.

"Please, mayor, what's all this?"

"You seem to know all about my connections, Dermott. Even where we sank Ballou's body in Lake Wallagamo. In fact, you know too much—"

The mayor was interrupted by a bullhorn: THIS IS THE FBI. YOU ARE SURROUNDED...

Still trembling, Dermott asked an FBI agent, "Where's my reward?

"Reward?! Hell, we've been investigating this shady administration for months. Run along, Dimrott."

"That's *Dermott*, sir." Nevertheless, he left.

AFTERMATH OF A PRISON DEATH

During the aborted prison break, Franz Karzola died in a mysterious fire. Immediately, newsmen, anxious to create another angel from the scum of society, dredged up his brutal child killings five years ago, implying his trial was unfair. Because of a technicality, his sentence was only twenty years.

As I testified, Karzola was in my office when the explosion occurred. He pushed me to safety, then dashed back into the inferno. The child molester and killer became an instant public hero.

Frankly, I was surprised when, a week later, the head of Corrections Facilities barged in unannounced. Sylvia Symons was a hard-nosed old woman with a jutting jaw.

"Go over it again," she demanded.

"I already explained everything to your investigating team," I protested.

"Nuts, warden. They see only facts—how hot was the fire, how many involved in the riot, how soon you restored order. I go for motive."

"Oh?" I questioned cautiously.

"Yeah. How did you arrange it?" Her eyes were steel.

"Look, ma'am, that's a pretty heavy accusation."

"Be honest. Franz Karzola didn't rescue you. You clobbered him and set the fire. You see, I learned his last victim was your grandson."

I began sweating. "You'll try to prove that?" I probed.

"No."

"No?!" I was astounded.

"You have no idea the trouble it took me getting that slimeball transferred to your prison. I figured you'd get him."

"But—what made you do that?"

"You don't know? One of his victims was my granddaughter."

357

RIGHT ON THE NOSE

Jakey dared not look down. Even the slightest night breeze threatened his perilous position. Maybe he was gettin' too old for such cloak-and-dagger treason stuff, he told himself. Gawd, what he'd do for ten thousand bucks. Here he was, danglin' at the end of two hundred feet of rope, a thousand feet above the rocks below.

His flashlight showed no sign of any inscription, and he was already nearing the end of Lincoln's nose. Something was wrong! He reviewed the day's events, dead sure he'd followed instructions. The letter had said: "Be at the foot of Mount Rushmore selling tourist trinkets. Your contact will wear red suspenders."

Sure enough, the last man off the tour bus wore red suspenders.

He sauntered over to Jakey's souvenir stand, glancing cautiously around. Nobody nearby except a Native American, dozing in his colorful blanket. The stranger whispered, "The message is on Lincoln's nose," and passed Jakey a five-dollar bill.

"Gotcha," Jakey whispered back, pocketing the money.

Now it was almost daybreak and still no damned message. Suddenly Jakey was being hauled upward!

"Careful!" yelled a voice. "Don't lose the sucker!"

The trip to the top seemed to take forever. A park ranger waited. Beside him that same native, now wearing a marshall's badge, declared, "Jacob Coswell, you're under arrest for espionage. Empty your pockets!" Jakey did so.

The marshall snatched up the five-dollar bill. Inspecting it through a magnifying lens, he exclaimed, "Very ingenious! A microfilm dot—right on Lincoln's nose!"

Jakey groaned. Uncontrollably.

Upon entering the Red Bull Bar, I observe Harry the Cat Ballou looking very sad at his usual table. Sitting down beside him I ask, "What's wrong, Harry?"

"Close call," he replies. "Just lucky I had a alibi for midnight last night."

"What happened?"

"Things have not been going well professionally lately. Every heist I plan, Quick Jimmy Lomanski beats me to it. I spend days casing a prospect, figure how to bypass the alarms, and when I arrive Quick Jimmie has already done it—*exactly like I planned.* It gets weird, like he's inside my mind."

"What could you do?"

"I consult Eddie the Brain, who reads lotsa books, explainin' this terrible calamity befallin' me. 'Friend,' says Eddie, 'you are broadcasting thoughts on Quick Jimmie's wavelength. It's called mental telepathy. You must concentrate on a caper that will land Quick Jimmie in the slammer, thereby eliminating this unfair competition. That'll be fifty bucks.' I pay, thinkin' it's a bargain."

"Just how do you frame Quick Jimmie?" I inquire.

"I write out on paper: 'At midnight I will throw a brick through Paulson's Pool Parlor window and leave a note saying, *I, Quick Jimmie Lomanski, threw this brick!* All day I keep readin' it over and over, thinkin' hard as I'm able."

"Seems foolproof," I comment. "Does he throw said brick and leave behind the note?"

"He does. And police arrest him. But they have to let him go."

"Why?"

"The note is in *my* handwritin'!"

THE STOLEN TIRES

Deputy Jake Brownell greeted the sheriff's arrival at the office with the announcement, "Just got a call from Bill Zarvus. Somebody jacked up his car durin' the night. Took off with all four tires. That's the sixth case out in that neighborhood."

"Tell you what, Jake," said old Sheriff Arley Jenkins, "you run out there and investigate. Report back what you find."

"Seems almighty strange. The night *after* Halloween a thief stripped tires from Joe Wilson's car and truck. The next night he hit Peter Haller. Then Hy Overbeck, Cal Norton, and David Lytle. What do you suppose the thief's gonna do with all them tires?"

"Hard to say, Jake. But I've never had a case yet I couldn't solve. So get movin'! It's a far piece out to that section of the county. Keep track of your mileage; I'll squeeze 20 cents a mile outta our budget."

Actually, Sheriff Jenkins knew exactly where the stolen tires were—they were neatly stacked in his garage, each tagged with the owner's name. Next week he would "discover" them in some remote woods. Maybe get his picture in the *Hickory Corners Gazette* again. Publicity never hurt a body none.

Deputy Brownell was ideal for his position—scrupulously honest and too dumb to figure out that all the tires were stolen from Republican voters so they couldn't reach the polls on Tuesday. This was the only way old Arly Jenkins could get re-elected this year.

OVERHEARD CONSPIRACY

Upon being transferred to Augusta, my boss Arnold Becker made me welcome. His wife Vivian promptly invited me to a "cozy little party," as she termed it.

"Yes, Edmund," added Mr. Becker, "all the staff will be there. Chance to get acquainted."

It was a gala affair. I met so many husbands and wives I could scarcely remember names.

Then as I wandered down a hall, I overheard low women's voices coming from a bedroom.

"No problem," declared the first lady. "You can hold 'em up with this."

I peeked in, but their faces were obscured in the dim light. "Thanks," said the second lady. "I'll not forget this. I'll return it later."

"Oh, no need, my dear," said the first. "I keep another in reserve. Need any help?"

"I can handle it from here," replied the other. She laughed, "Have to keep up a good front, you know."

That conversation troubled me. Finally, unable to hold my anxiety back, I sought out my hostess. "Vivian," I whispered, "ordinarily I'm no eavesdropper, and I wouldn't want to alarm you unnecessarily. How ever, I feel I should warn you that one of your guests plans to rob others present." I proceeded to relate exactly what I'd overheard. "Of course," I added, "I've no idea who the conspirators were."

She blushed crimson. "Well," she declared stiffly, "if you really must know, sir, Ethel Norcross was loaning me a safety pin. A strap broke on my bra."

THE MIDNIGHT INTRUDER

The gentleman and attractive young woman crept stealthily up the fire stairs for a midnight tryst in the Bal-Tex office.

"Careful, Cynthia my dear," he whispered. "Don't disturb the night watchman. I'll carry your heavy bag."

"Whatever you say, Reggie," she whispered back.

Opening the fire door, they cautiously stepped into the upper hallway. Reggie extended a restraining hand. "Dearie," he hissed, "there's a light in yon office. Methinks we have unwelcome company."

"Let's leave, Reggie."

"First we'll see who this intruder is."

A man was hunched over examining the safe with his flashlight. Reggie boldly stepped into the room, switched on the overhead light, and demanded, "What are you doing here?"

Startled, the man turned his beefy face. "I didn' mean no harm," he whined.

Reggie noted the man's rough tweed coat and baggy trousers. "I'm tempted to phone police."

"Please don't," pleaded Cynthia. "Let the poor fellow go quietly."

"Thankee, ma'am!" The man dashed out, clattering down the stairs.

Reggie laughed, "Neatly done!"

His charming accomplice donned rubber gloves and spread the tools from her heavy bag. "I'll have to drill this one in a hurry."

"Forget it!" boomed a deep voice from the hallway. The old man was back, a score of policemen behind him.

"My lucky night!" chuckled Detective Shaunessy. "There I was, checkin' safes, when you two wanted yeggs walk right in. I hadda stall 'til I could summon backup.

"Y'know, Reg and Cindy, you oughta take up actin'—on the stage."

EDDIE MCGINITY'S FATEFUL END

The man at the station, quite formally dressed,
Was really an odd and devious bloke.
    Shoes highly polished, striped trousers pressed,
    Briefcase, umbrella, and all the rest,
Were Eddie McGinity' s private joke.

To his neighbors he couldn't be blanker,
For Eddie McGinity spoke not a word.
    Yet to know about him they did hanker
    And many concluded he was a banker,
But that guess proved to be absurd.

Yes, rumors around McGinity roiled,
But he was not what they thought at all.
    His secret that had the villagers foiled:
    In a *distillery* Eddie toiled
And his briefcase contained—his *coverall!*

For Eddie's job was to sweep the floor,
And he wasn't honest, alas too true.
    His employer was rich and he was poor,
    So when he left each day at four,
The bottles he took he considered his due.

With Eddie playing that dual role,
He'd be contented, one might think.
    But all that liquor that he stole
    Started weighing on Eddie's soul
And, sad to say, he took to drink.

That fateful morn Eddie dressed up again,
Drank two fifths of whiskey ere leaving his flat
    Arrived at the station feeling no pain,
    Teetered and fell 'neath the oncoming train
The only thing saved was his bowler hat.

HYPNOTIC DEATH

"Perhaps it was a freak accident," I suggested to my old friend Charley Taggert, the NYPD detective. "Time after time, along with hundreds of other spectators, I've watched Ralph Simmons and his vice-president get publicity for their construction company by dining on an I-beam suspended high above the street, served by two waiters in tuxedos. Maybe they tempted fate once too often."

"It was murder," Charley insisted. "Two men who've done that stupid routine daily wouldn't jump overboard simultaneously. Uh-uh. I'm certain who did it and how, but there's no way to get a conviction—absolutely no way." He sounded frustrated.

"I often wondered how they got up nerve for that," I remarked.

"Aha! There you have the key. I discovered that before every performance they had themselves hypnotized."

"So *that* was their secret. But how were they murdered? And by whom?"

"As to who did it, it was Simmons's wife. He shouldn't have married that chorus girl, Florabelle Latour. Obviously, she married him for his wealth. And now beautiful but heartless Florabelle owns the whole corporation."

"But," I argued, "she's already proved she was nowhere near the scene. And hundreds of witnesses neither saw nor heard anything unusual. How were they killed?"

"Posthypnotic suggestion. Florabelle found out about her husband's dependence upon his hypnotist to perform his crazy stunt. So, she made sure Ralph Simmons and his vice-president were pre-programmed to jump to their deaths. Don't you see? She simply hired a hypnotist to hypnotize *their* hypnotist!"

ELIJAH EVERMORE

Upon arrival, his housekeeper discovered Elijah Evermore slumped over his desk, dead. Beneath his body was the following curious message, handwritten and unsigned:

To young men everywhere:

I hasten to set down this account so that, knowing, you may escape the dread fate awaiting me. I am truly James Turner, age twenty-two, a senior at Walcott College.

Yesterday as I jogged in Memorial Park an elderly man invited me to share his bench. His face was deeply lined, his hair snow white. He introduced himself as Elijah Evermore and we fell into conversation.

He had an unbelievable store of knowledge, and we spent a pleasant, stimulating half hour.

Then he produced a silver flask. "My Elixir of Youth," he explained. "Keeps me young."

"Methusaleh should have had some," I joked.

"He undoubtedly did," the old fellow declared seriously. "Care for a swallow?"

It was the most delicious liquid imaginable, pure nectar. Somehow I fell asleep. When I awoke my whole body felt peculiar. It was evening. My unusual acquaintance was gone. Confused, I stumbled along streets only faintly familiar. Entering an apartment, I collapsed upon the bed. Sunlight awakened me. This was not my apartment. Locating the bathroom, I stared into the mirror and recoiled.

I had become Elijah Evermore! Growing old, he had exchanged his body for mine!

How many other young men has he thus inveigled down through the centur....

Here the writing trailed off. Elijah Evermore was a very old man, without known relatives.

SPECIAL DIET

"I'm skiing out for things I need," announced Armand, my new chef. I raised no objection, although I'd just checked and my kitchen was stocked with sugar, flour, milk, eggs, spices—everything. I watched until Armand's tall chef's hat and long white apron disappeared against the snow of Mont Blanc. Then I involuntarily shuddered, recalling what happened recently in my Edelweiss Resort...

The Hogarths registered two weeks ago. The father—Hermann—was obnoxious from the start. He ate voraciously, but remained scrawny and gaunt. Although his wife Katarina tried to resist seconds and desserts, she continued to grow even more corpulent. All during each meal, Hermann Hogarth berated his wife, "Stop being so piggish! Lord knows you're fat enough now!"

He turned on his unattractive young daughter Margaretha, "See!" he snarled, "someday you'll look like *that!*" To make matters worse, the child was clubfooted.

"A most detestable man," I declared to Armand.

"Ah, yes," he responded, "they need my 'special diet.'"

Each day thereafter Herr Hogarth became more bloated, his wife more slender and attractive, and little Margaretha more active. By the end of two weeks Hermann Hogarth was an obese, toadlike monstrosity; Katarina had become a svelte young goddess; and beautiful little Margaretha skipped happily down the hallways!

I never ask Armand about his "special diet." I only know it turns people into what they *deserve to be.*

As for me, I now watch very carefully everything I say and everything I do.

RACE TO ETERNITY

Scene: Anywhere. Time: Anytime. Three men in top hats prepare to start a race. Two passersby watch: Youth—carefree, energetic, and History—old, tired, and scarred.

YOUTH: Who are those racers in formal attire?
    And who is the starter about to fire?
HISTORY: I've seen them many times before.
    They have existed since days of yore.
    The first is known quite simply as *Fame.*
    ('Though some suggest "Luck" is his actual name.)
    The second, with evil, leering face,
    Despised by all, he's called *Disgrace.*
    Death, the last, isn't always the winner,
    But he'll finish the course for saint or sinner.
    And the starter gives each an equal chance.
    His name, you see, is *Circumstance.*
YOUTH: Why do they run? For a silver bowl?
HISTORY: Nay, lad, for some poor fellow's soul,
    His memory that I'll record
    After he goes to his last reward.
YOUTH: For me those three create no fears.
    I'm sure to live for many years.
HISTORY: Beware, my boy, of what you say!
    Mayhap they race for *you* today.

HOW THESE STORIES CAME
TO BE PUBLISHED

It was, I suppose, the chill draft coming up the stairwell that awakened me. Since making final revisions of my short-short stories I hadn't slept well. Donning my bathrobe and awkwardly slipping feet into moccasins, I crept down. A light burned in my study. A trifle fearfully, I peered in.

There sat my old high school English teacher! She was nearly through my pile of typescript.

"Miss Engleby!" I gasped. "But surely you must be—"

"Dead?" she snapped. "Naturally I'm dead. Otherwise I'd be a hundred twenty-seven years old, practically senile. Which I'm not! Your punctuation needs improvement: too many choppy sentences, dashes where commas would suffice."

Hesitantly I objected, "But, Miss Engleby, that's modern writing—"

"Nonsense! Didn't I teach you to revise, revise, revise until each noun, verb, adjective, and adverb conveys *precise* significance?"

"Yes, ma'am," I murmured.

"Your characters lack individuality," she added, reducing my self-esteem still further. "Absolutely lifeless!" Relentlessly she continued, "Be creative! You have borrowed from Poe, O. Henry, G. K. Chesterton, de Maupassant—*somehow* you overlooked Feodor Dostoevsky."

"Never read him," I apologized weakly.

"Obviously," she snorted.

"Wh-what should I do?" I asked in desperation.

"Publish! Perhaps some *real* author will be moved to re-write your stories."

At that moment my wife yelled down from our bedroom, *"Aren't you EVER coming to bed?"*

Miss Engleby began slowly dissolving until she was just a voice hissing, "I'll see you later!"

I always hated it when she said that.

(I can't resist including this one, composed by one of my granddaughters at age twelve.)

WITCHCRAFT IN TRYX-ON-THE-SLYE
BY LAURA MCPHEE

Witchcraft is probably the only reason our little village of Tryx-on-the-Slye appears on the map of England. Old men and women recall the infamous witch trials, and even today many residents believe witches live among us. They are right.

Early Thursday morning as I was tending my garden, a gray mare clip-clopped out my kitchen door. Its face seemed familiar and it wore my wife's corset around its middle. I suspected what had happened.

"Hester," I asked, "did old Mrs. Thiggleby do this to you?" The horse nodded vigorously.

"Don't worry, Hester," I said. "I know what to do."

At midnight I cut two branches from the white oak in the graveyard and bound them with gut of salamander, forming a cross. Intoning a secret incantation, I buried the cross in Mrs. Thiggleby's yard.

Within minutes, the old hag flew from her house, scratching frantically at her plump body.

"Oh, lordy-lordy," she wailed, "this white oak itch is drivin' me mad!"

"Let's make a deal," I offered. "You remove the curse on my wife, I dig out the cross. Otherwise—well, white oak itch is a horrible death."

She quickly agreed.

Hester was immediately restored to her old self—horse-faced, overweight, and cantankerous. "You took y'r sweet time!" she railed. "And while I was gallopin' helpless 'round the village, where were you? Drinkin' at the pub, no doubt..." On and on and on...

So now I'm wondering—how much would Mrs. Thiggleby charge to teach me that curse?

Printed in the United States
1415400003B/289-321